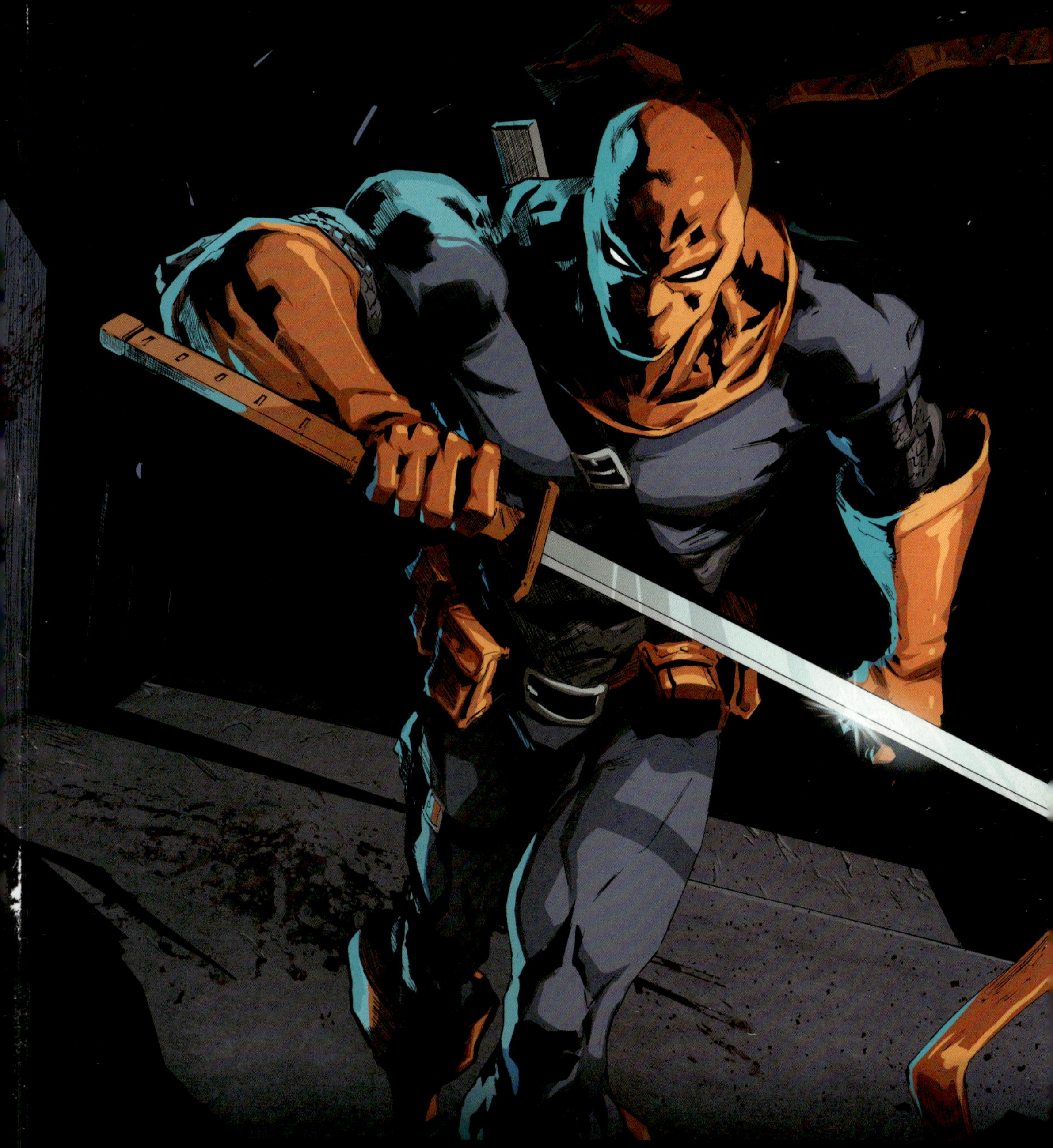

DEATHSTROKE INC.

VOL. 2
YEAR ONE

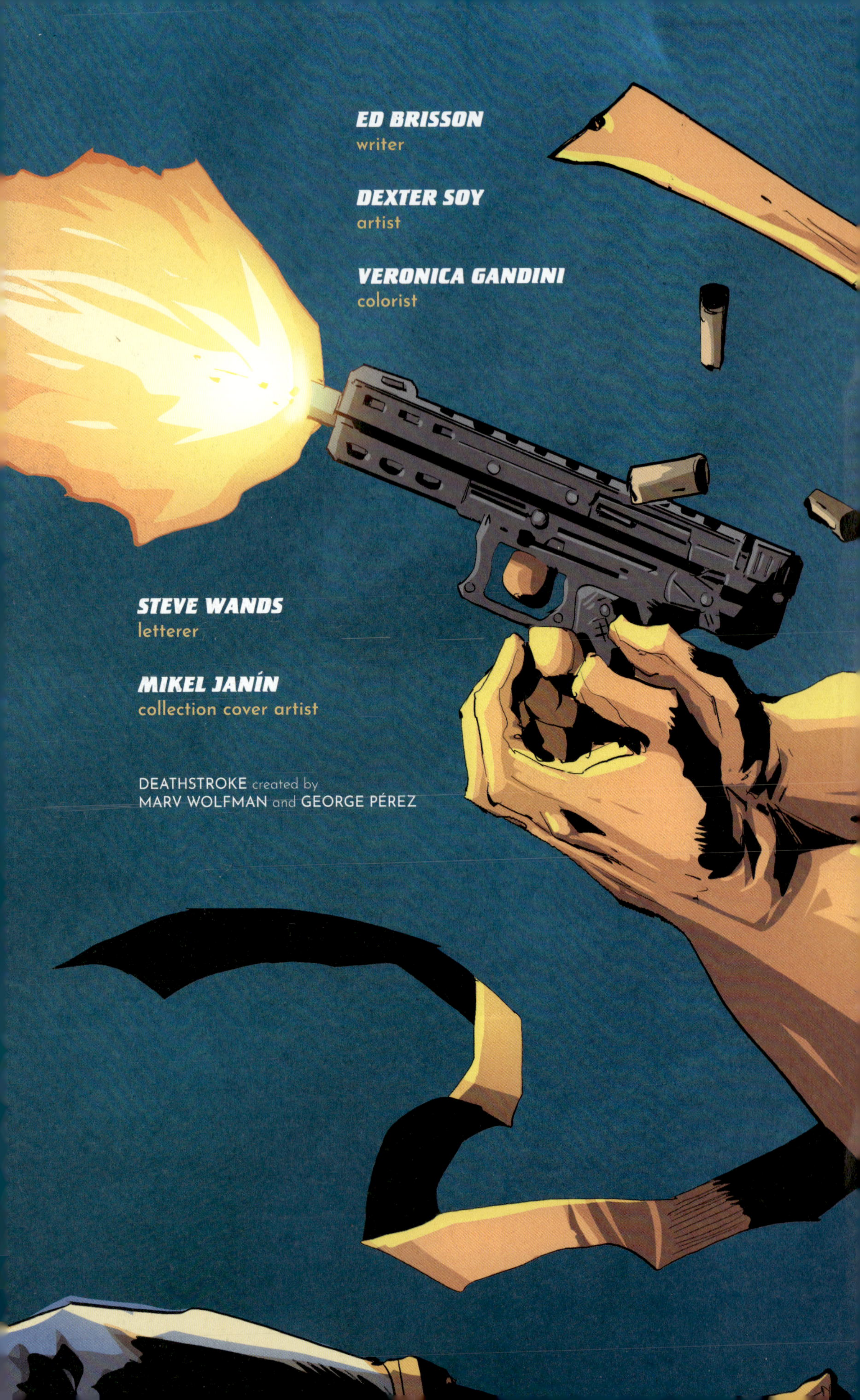

ED BRISSON
writer

DEXTER SOY
artist

VERONICA GANDINI
colorist

STEVE WANDS
letterer

MIKEL JANÍN
collection cover artist

DEATHSTROKE created by
MARV WOLFMAN and GEORGE PÉREZ

DEATHSTROKE INC.

VOL. 2
YEAR ONE

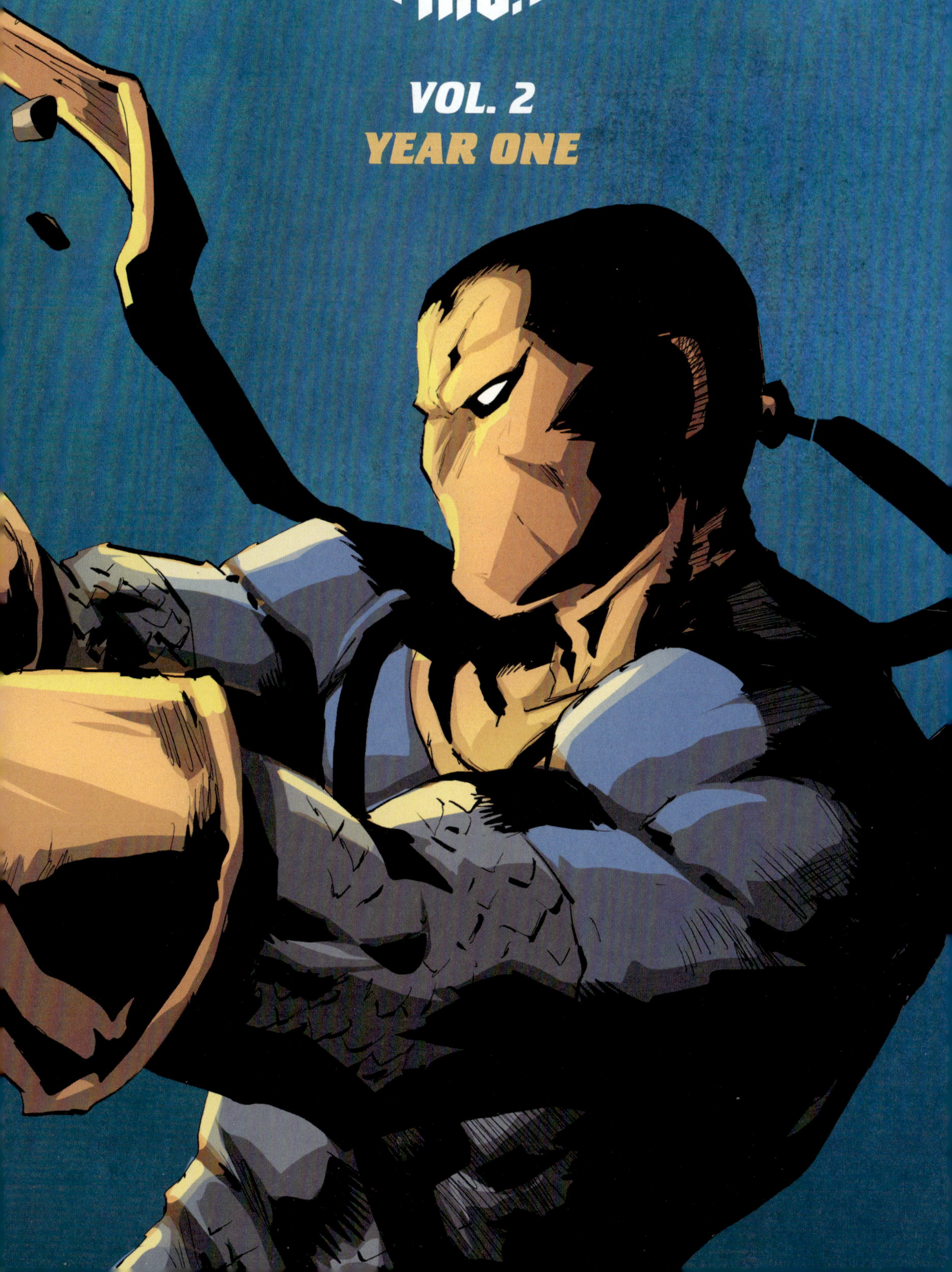

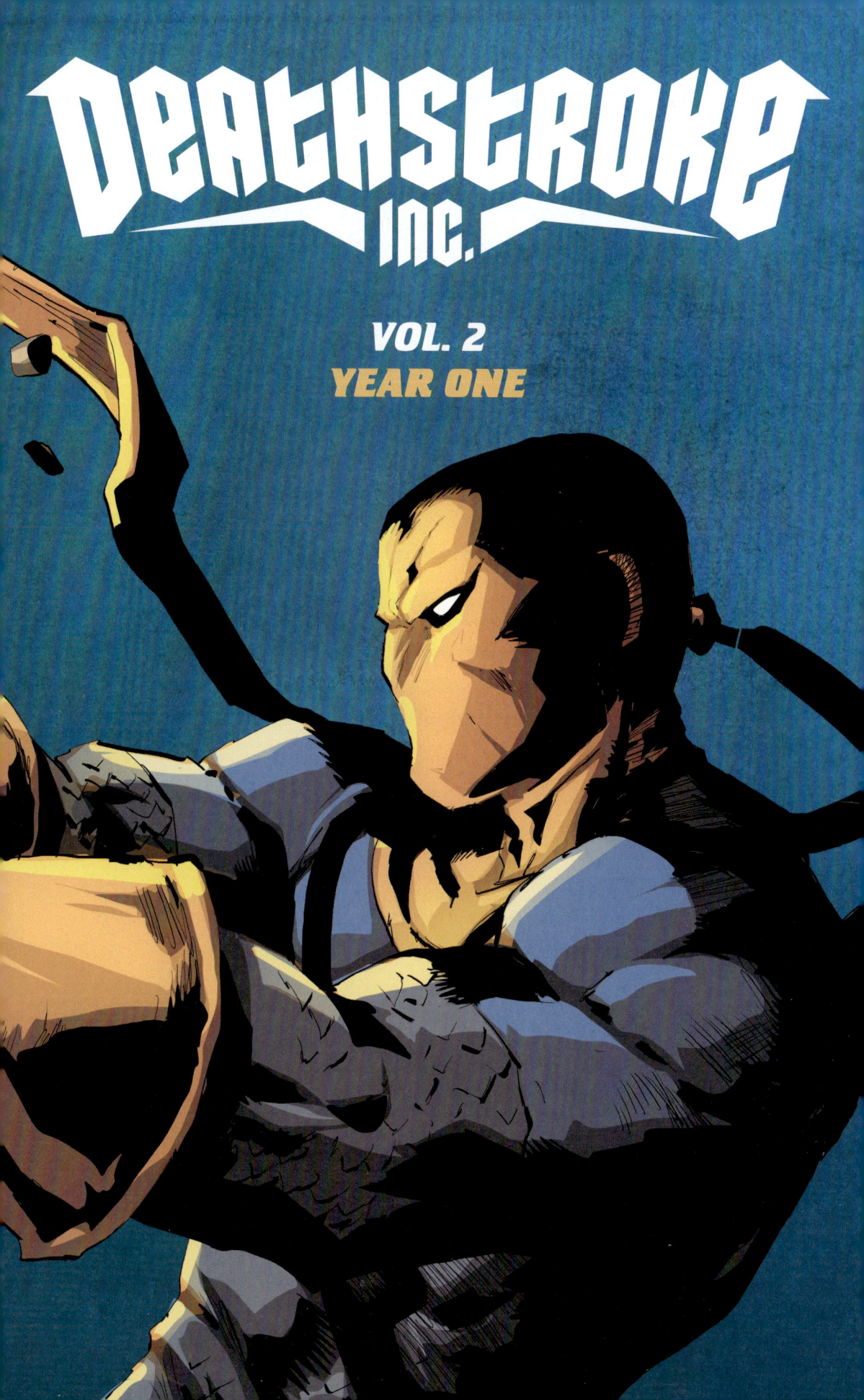

BEN ABERNATHY Editor - Original Series & Collected Edition
STEVE COOK Design Director - Books
MEGEN BELLERSEN Publication Design
RYANE LYNN HILL Production Editor

MARIE JAVINS Editor-in-Chief, DC Comics

ANNE DePIES Senior VP - General Manager
JIM LEE Publisher & Chief Creative Officer
DON FALLETTI VP - Manufacturing Operations & Workflow Management
LAWRENCE GANEM - Talent Services
ALISON GILL Senior VP - Manufacturing & Operations
JEFFREY KAUFMAN VP - Editorial Strategy & Programming
NICK J. NAPOLITANO VP - Manufacturing Administration & Design
NANCY SPEARS VP - Revenue

DEATHSTROKE INC. VOL. 2: YEAR ONE

Published by DC Comics. Compilation and all new material Copyright © 2023 DC Comics. All Rights Reserved. Originally published in single magazine form in *Deathstroke Inc.* 10-15. Copyright © 2022 DC Comics. All Rights Reserved. All characters, their distinctive likenesses, and related elements featured in this publication are trademarks of DC Comics. The stories, characters, and incidents featured in this publication are entirely fictional. DC Comics does not read or accept unsolicited submissions of ideas, stories, or artwork.

DC Comics, 4000 Warner Blvd., Bldg. 700, 2nd Floor, Burbank, CA 91522
Printed by Solisco Printers, Scott, QC, Canada.
1/27/23. First Printing.
ISBN: 978-1-77951-982-5

Library of Congress Cataloging-in-Publication Data is available.

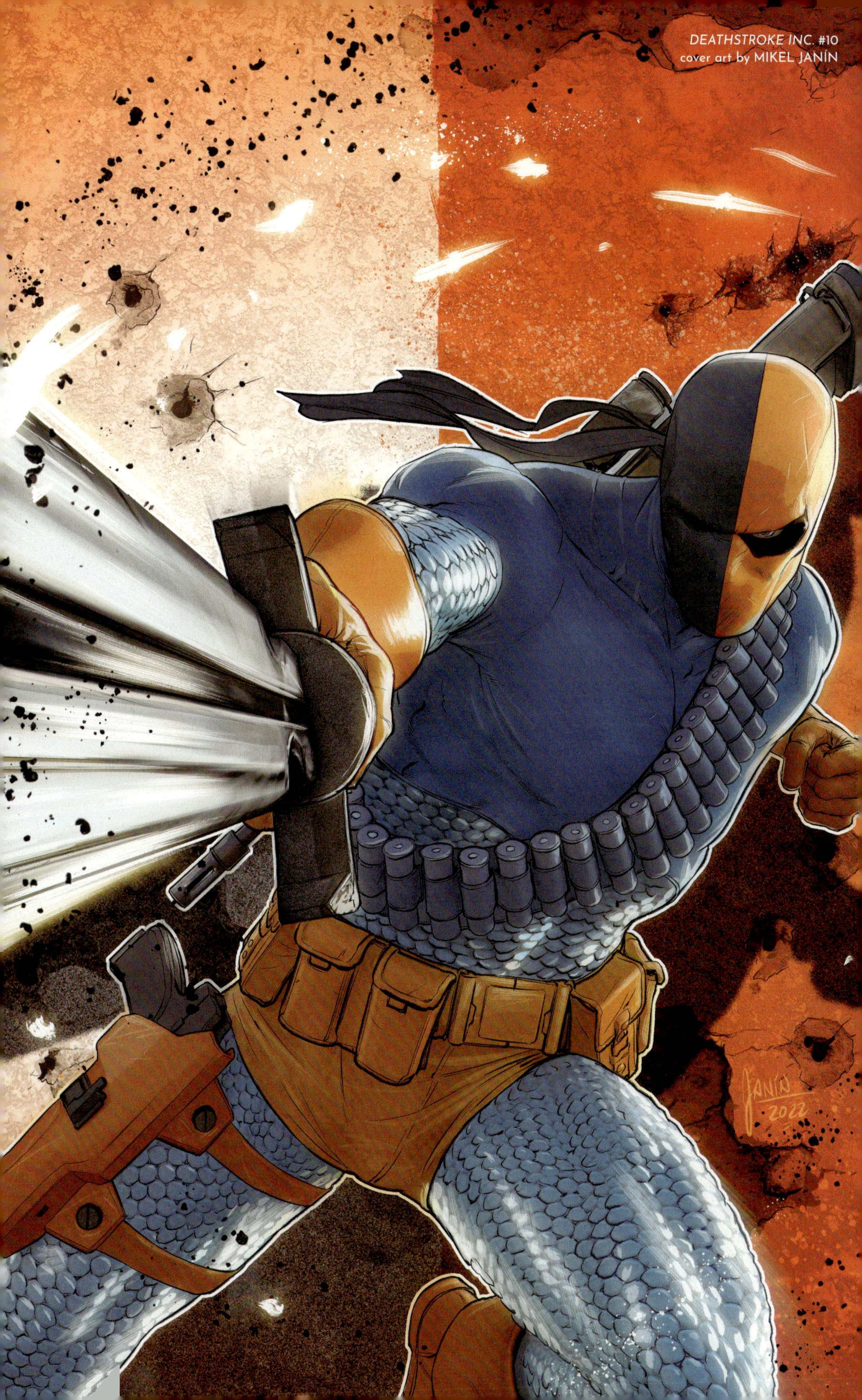
JANÍN
2022

DEATHSTROKE INC. #10
cover art by MIKEL JANÍN

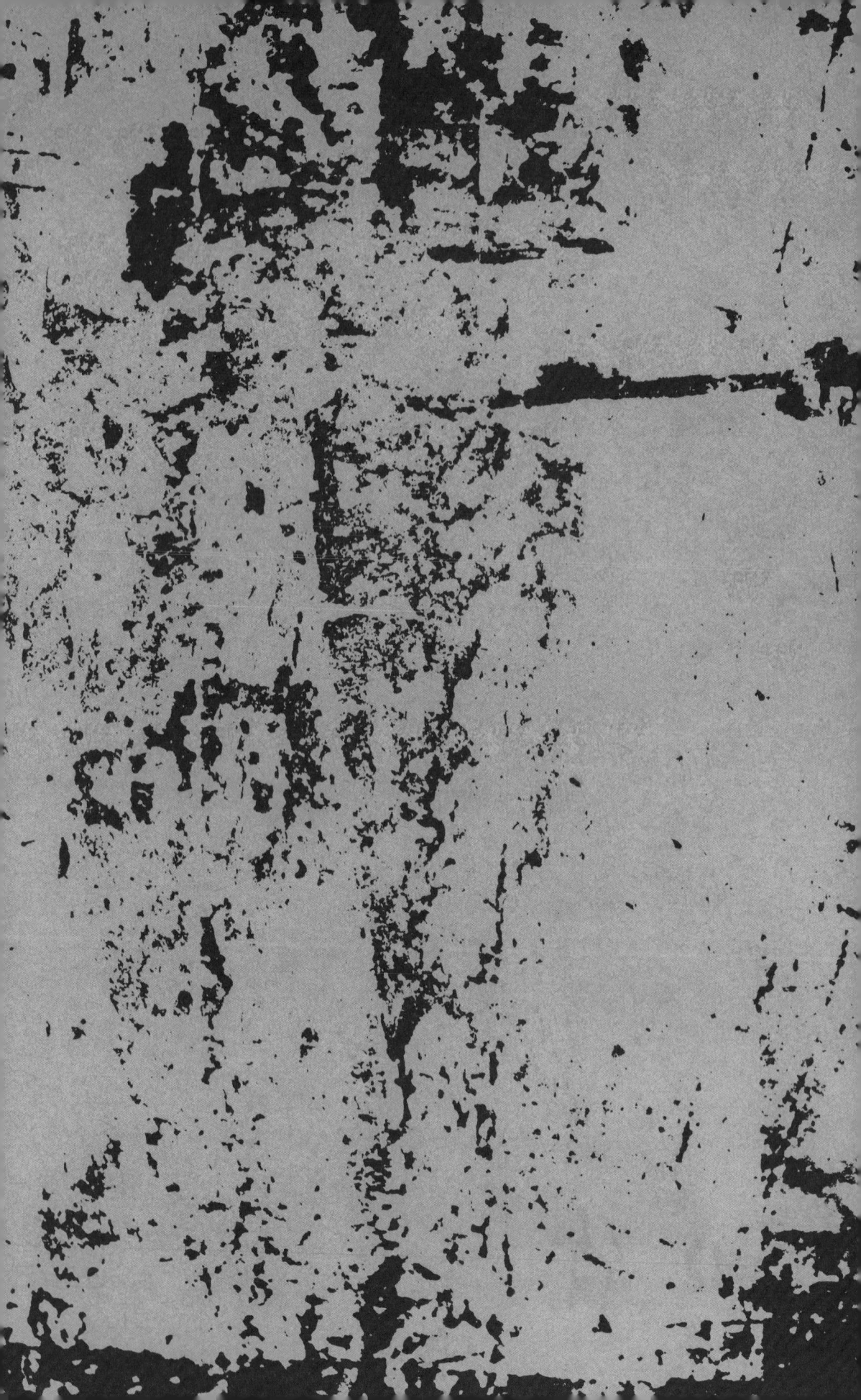

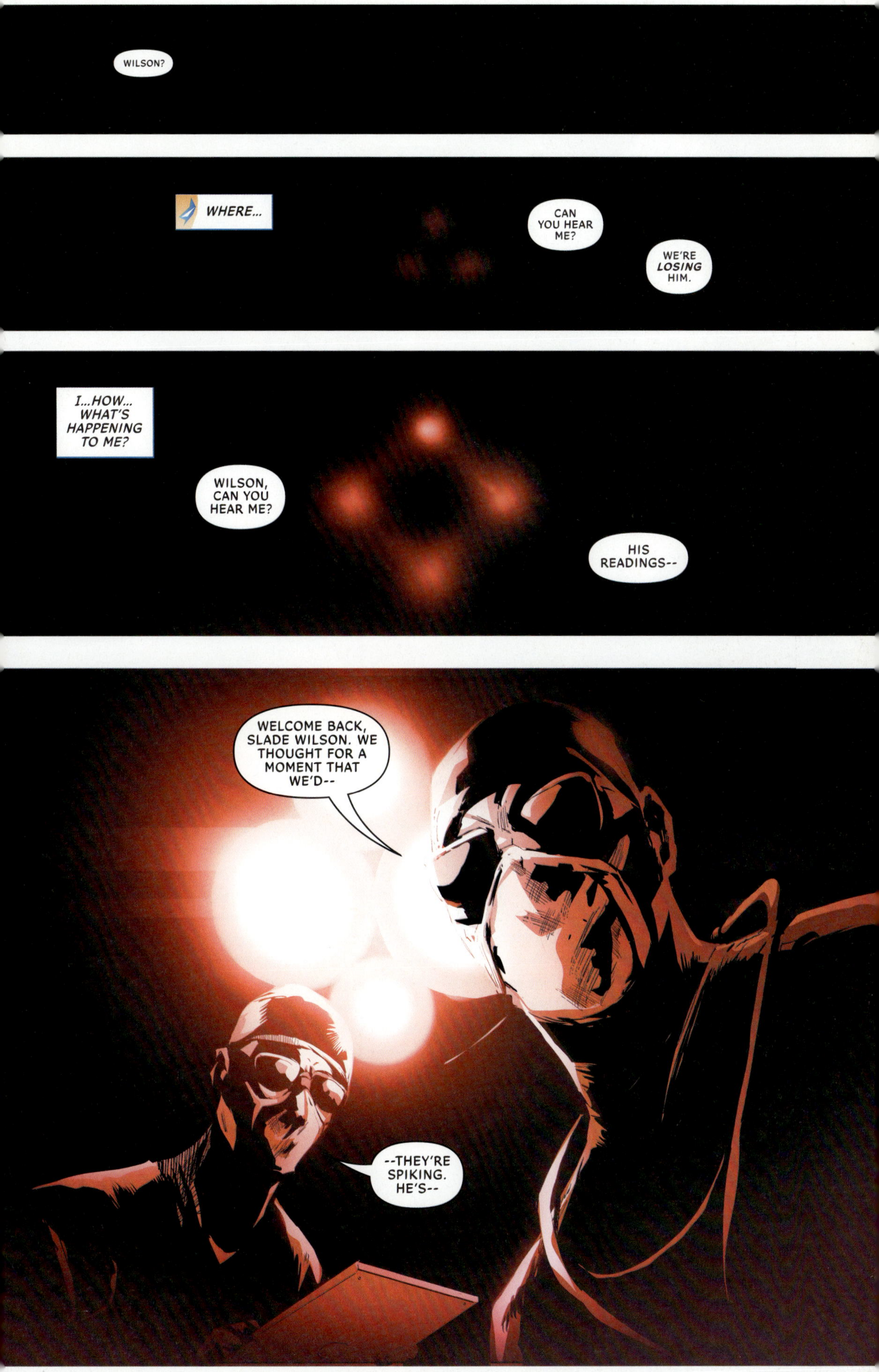
WILSON?
WHERE...
CAN YOU HEAR ME?
WE'RE *LOSING* HIM.
I...HOW... WHAT'S HAPPENING TO ME?
WILSON, CAN YOU HEAR ME?
HIS READINGS--
WELCOME BACK, SLADE WILSON. WE THOUGHT FOR A MOMENT THAT WE'D--
--THEY'RE SPIKING. HE'S--

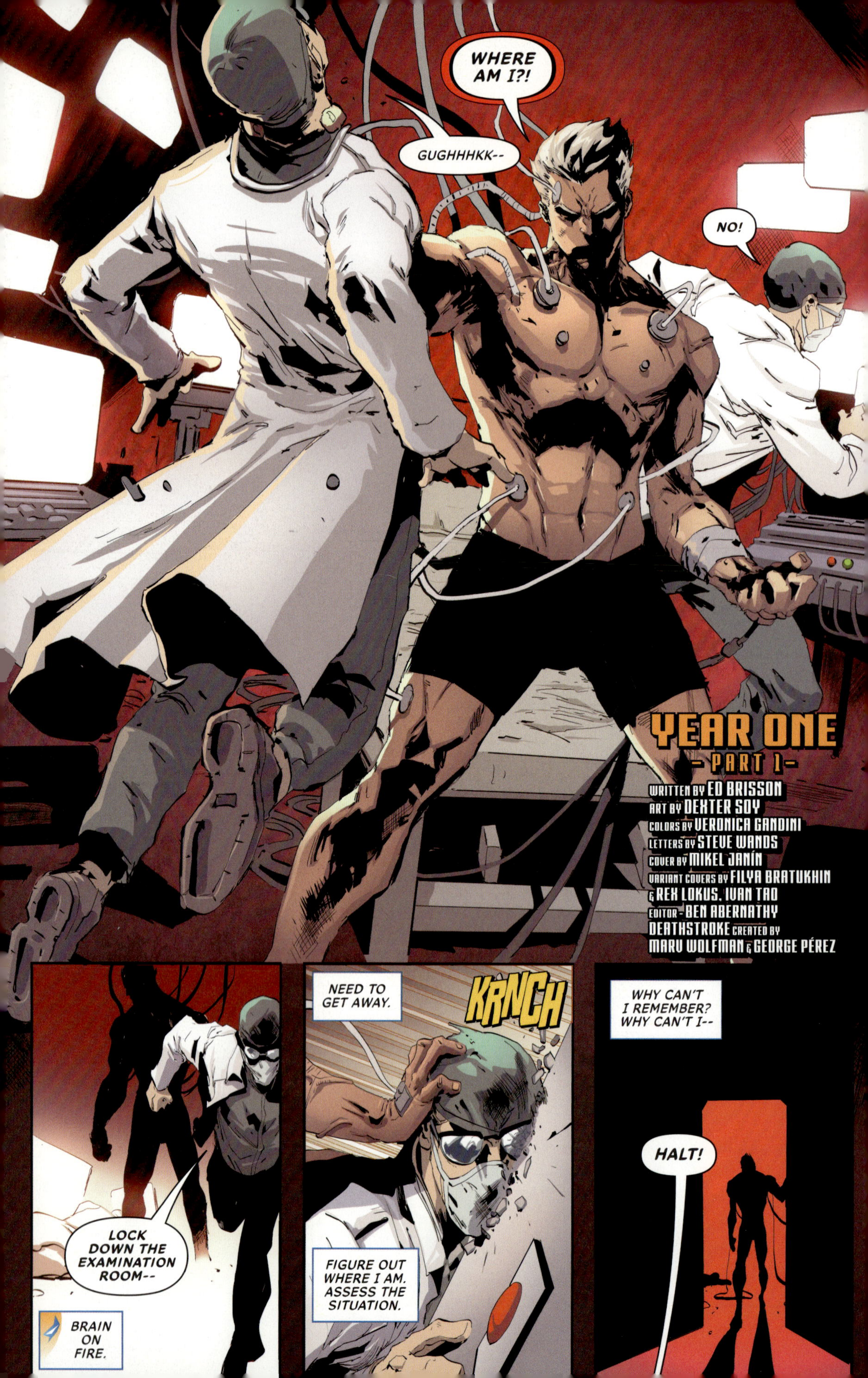
WHERE AM I?!
GUGHHHKK--
NO!
YEAR ONE
- PART 1 -
WRITTEN BY ED BRISSON
ART BY DEXTER SOY
COLORS BY VERONICA GANDINI
LETTERS BY STEVE WANDS
COVER BY MIKEL JANÍN
VARIANT COVERS BY FILYA BRATUKHIN
& REX LOKUS, IVAN TAO
EDITOR - BEN ABERNATHY
DEATHSTROKE CREATED BY
MARV WOLFMAN & GEORGE PÉREZ
LOCK DOWN THE EXAMINATION ROOM--
BRAIN ON FIRE.
NEED TO GET AWAY.
KRNCH
FIGURE OUT WHERE I AM. ASSESS THE SITUATION.
WHY CAN'T I REMEMBER? WHY CAN'T I--
HALT!

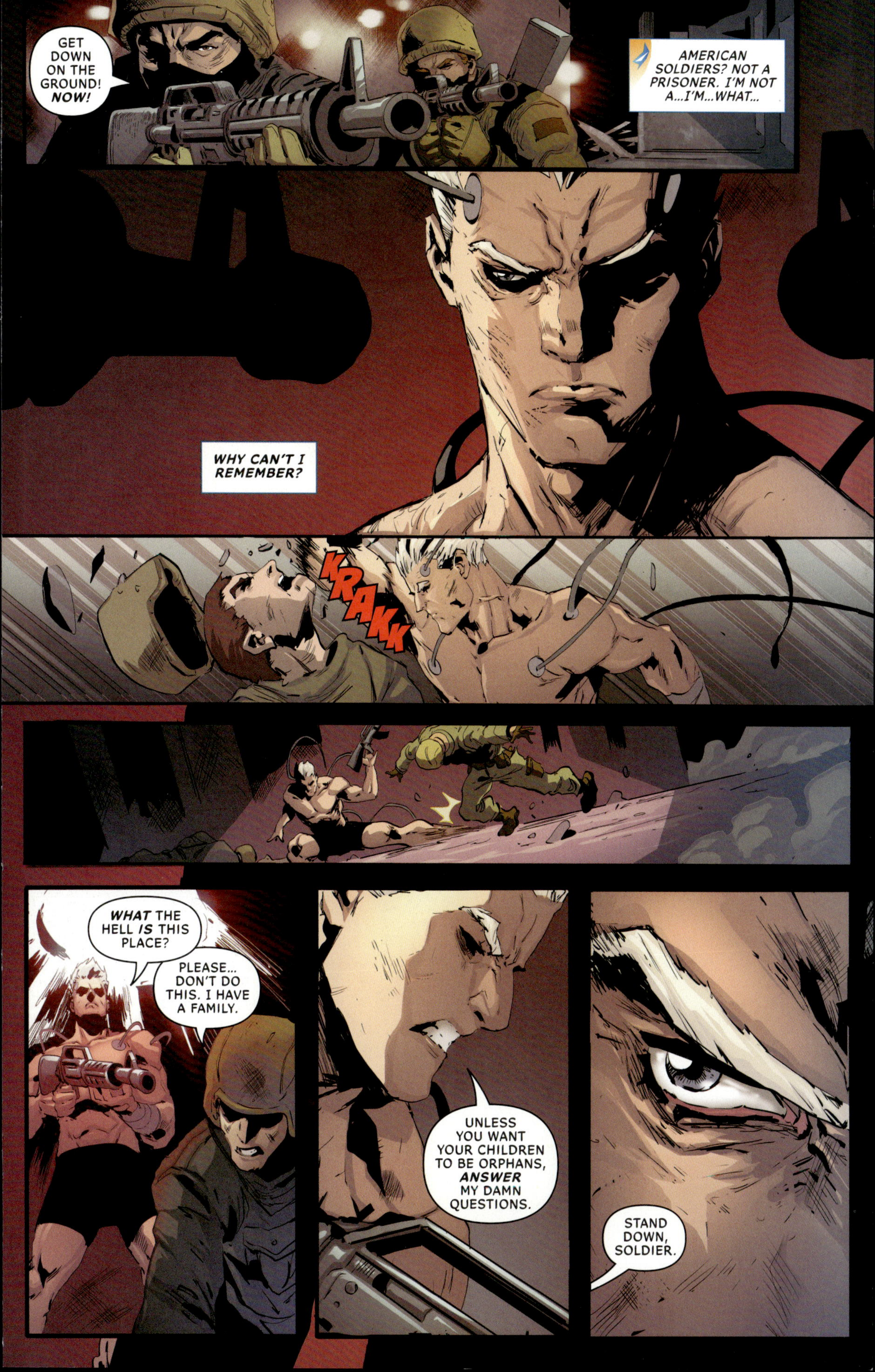
GET DOWN ON THE GROUND! NOW!
AMERICAN SOLDIERS? NOT A PRISONER. I'M NOT A...I'M...WHAT...
WHY CAN'T I REMEMBER?
KRAKK
WHAT THE HELL IS THIS PLACE?
PLEASE... DON'T DO THIS. I HAVE A FAMILY.
UNLESS YOU WANT YOUR CHILDREN TO BE ORPHANS, ANSWER MY DAMN QUESTIONS.
STAND DOWN, SOLDIER.

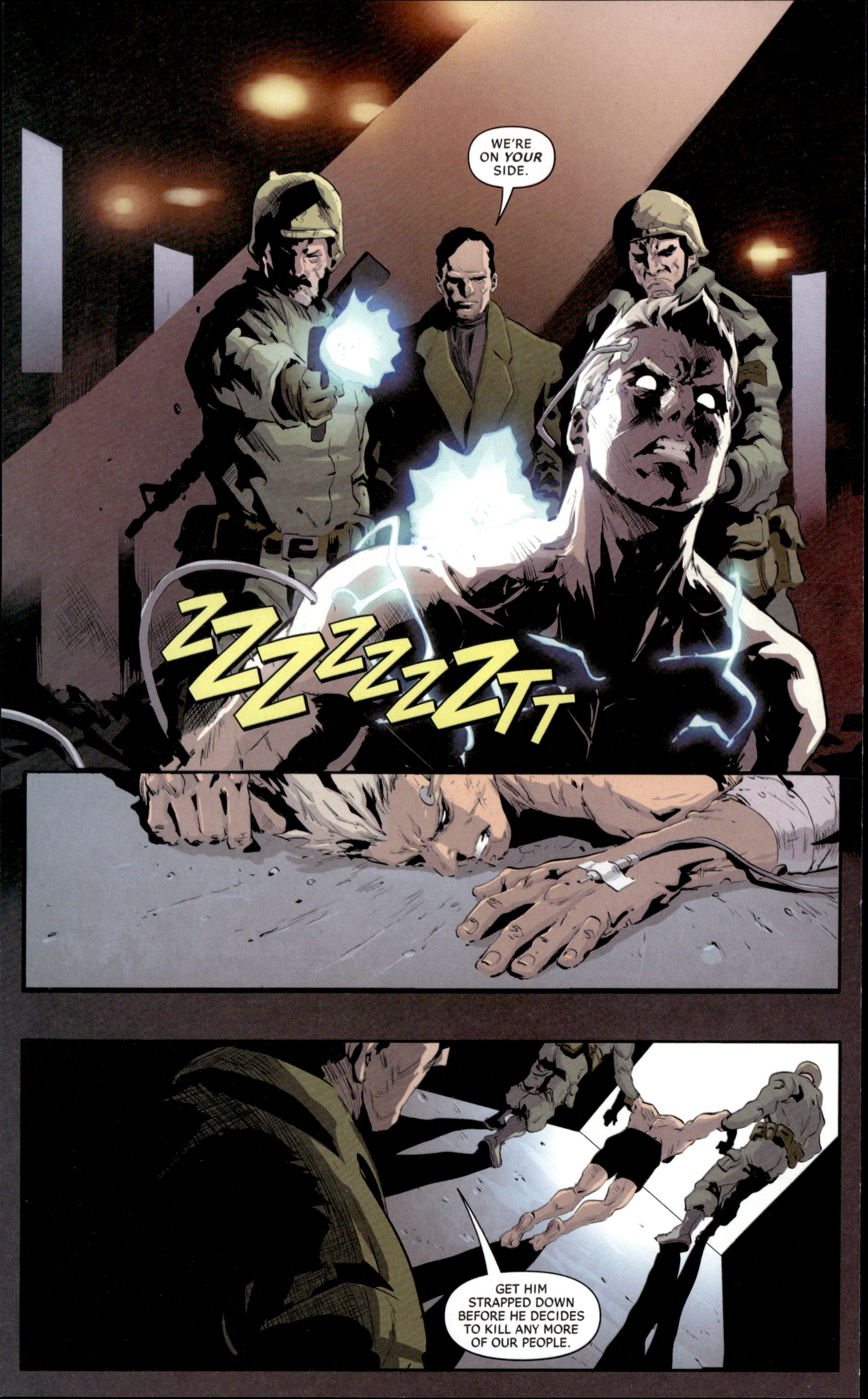
WE'RE ON *YOUR* SIDE.
ZZZZZZZTTT
GET HIM STRAPPED DOWN BEFORE HE DECIDES TO KILL ANY MORE OF OUR PEOPLE.

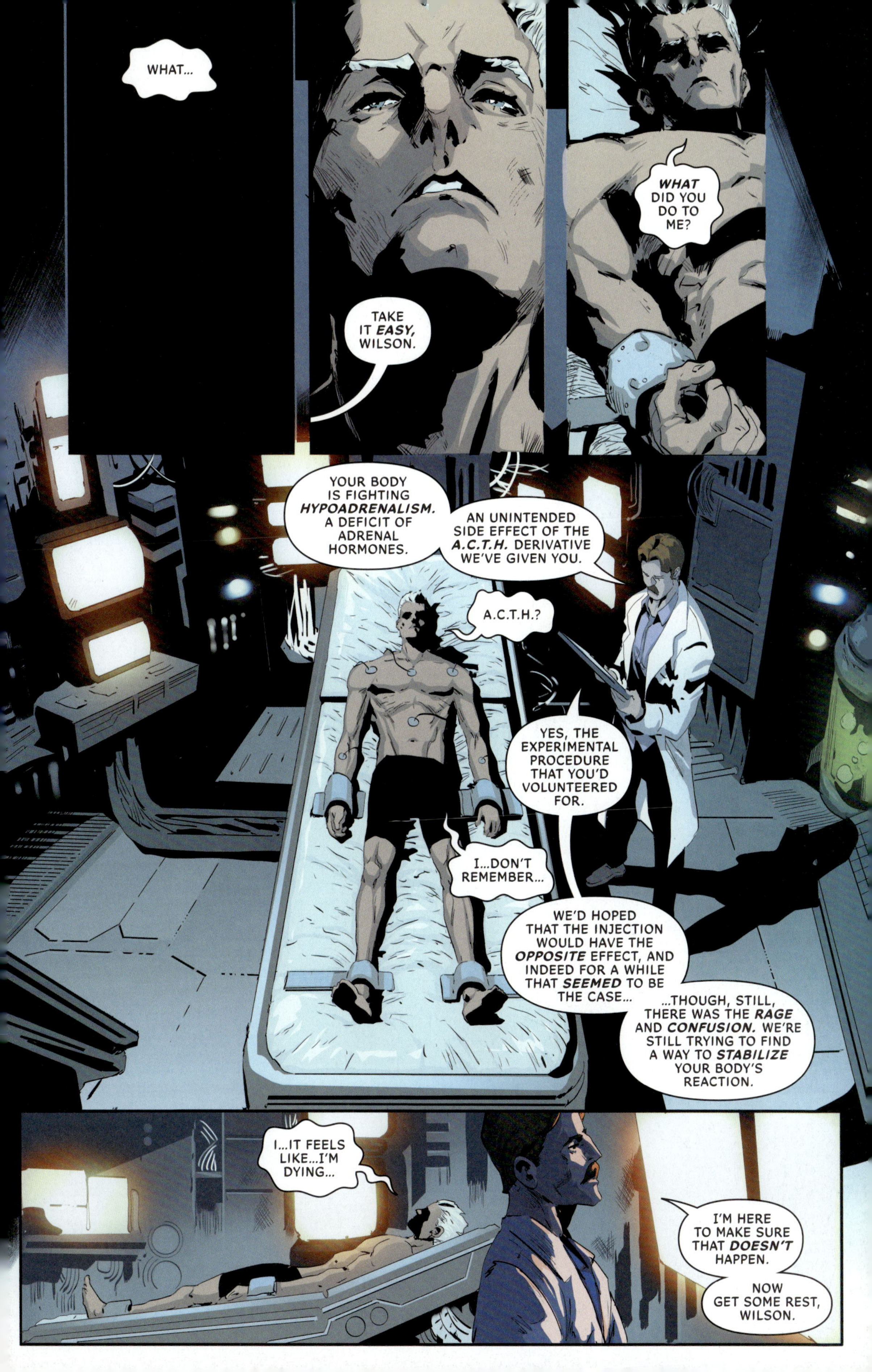
WHAT...
TAKE IT *EASY,* WILSON.
WHAT DID YOU DO TO ME?
YOUR BODY IS FIGHTING *HYPOADRENALISM.* A DEFICIT OF ADRENAL HORMONES.
AN UNINTENDED SIDE EFFECT OF THE *A.C.T.H.* DERIVATIVE WE'VE GIVEN YOU.
A.C.T.H.?
YES, THE EXPERIMENTAL PROCEDURE THAT YOU'D VOLUNTEERED FOR.
I...DON'T REMEMBER...
WE'D HOPED THAT THE INJECTION WOULD HAVE THE *OPPOSITE* EFFECT, AND INDEED FOR A WHILE THAT *SEEMED* TO BE THE CASE...
...THOUGH, STILL, THERE WAS THE *RAGE* AND *CONFUSION.* WE'RE STILL TRYING TO FIND A WAY TO *STABILIZE* YOUR BODY'S REACTION.
I...IT FEELS LIKE...I'M DYING...
I'M HERE TO MAKE SURE THAT *DOESN'T* HAPPEN.
NOW GET SOME REST, WILSON.

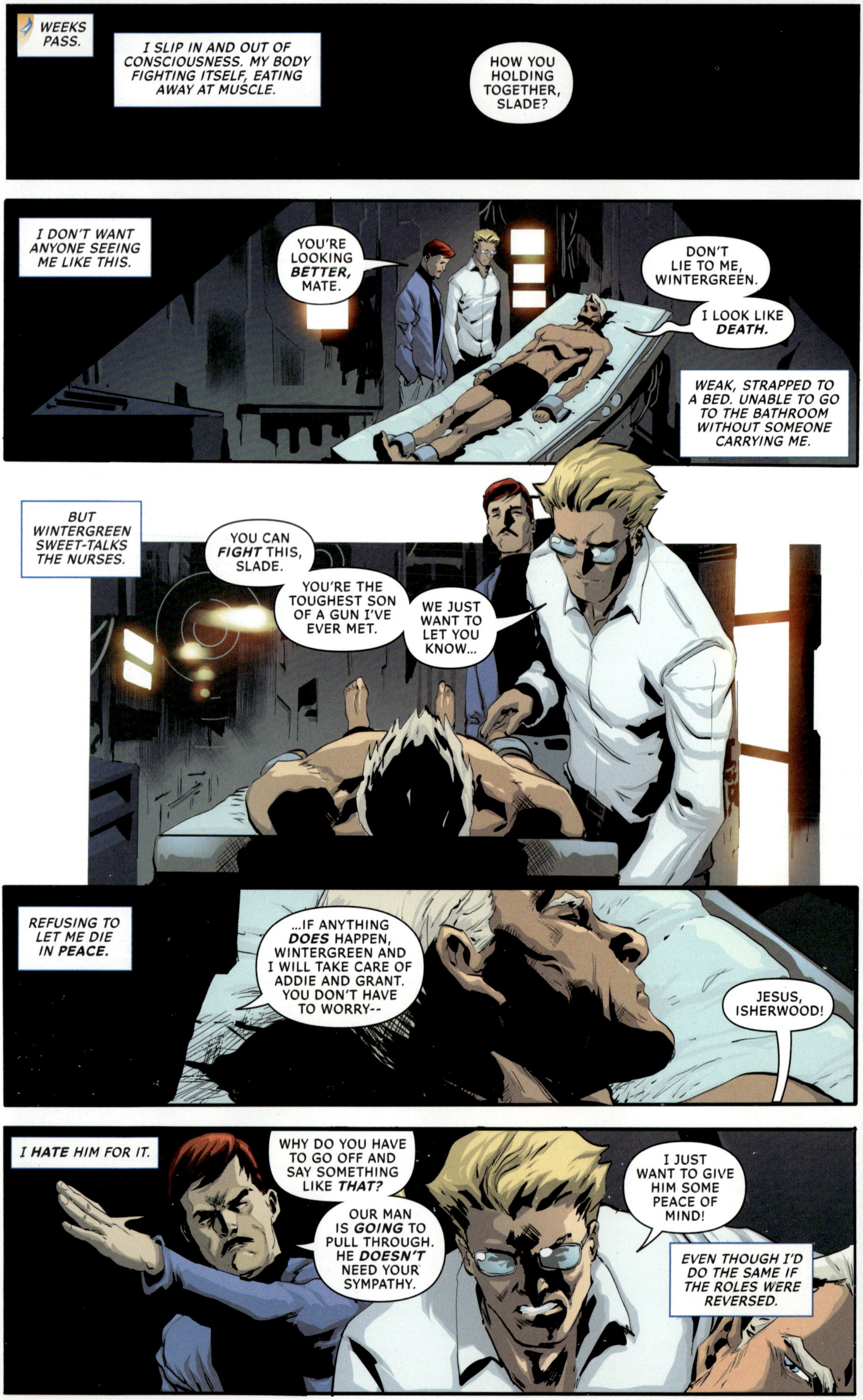
WEEKS PASS.
I SLIP IN AND OUT OF CONSCIOUSNESS. MY BODY FIGHTING ITSELF, EATING AWAY AT MUSCLE.
HOW YOU HOLDING TOGETHER, SLADE?
I DON'T WANT ANYONE SEEING ME LIKE THIS.
YOU'RE LOOKING *BETTER,* MATE.
DON'T LIE TO ME, WINTERGREEN.
I LOOK LIKE *DEATH.*
WEAK, STRAPPED TO A BED. UNABLE TO GO TO THE BATHROOM WITHOUT SOMEONE CARRYING ME.
BUT WINTERGREEN SWEET-TALKS THE NURSES.
YOU CAN *FIGHT* THIS, SLADE.
YOU'RE THE TOUGHEST SON OF A GUN I'VE EVER MET.
WE JUST WANT TO LET YOU KNOW...
REFUSING TO LET ME DIE IN *PEACE.*
...IF ANYTHING *DOES* HAPPEN, WINTERGREEN AND I WILL TAKE CARE OF ADDIE AND GRANT. YOU DON'T HAVE TO WORRY--
JESUS, ISHERWOOD!
I *HATE* HIM FOR IT.
WHY DO YOU HAVE TO GO OFF AND SAY SOMETHING LIKE *THAT?*
OUR MAN IS *GOING* TO PULL THROUGH. HE *DOESN'T* NEED YOUR SYMPATHY.
I JUST WANT TO GIVE HIM SOME PEACE OF MIND!
EVEN THOUGH I'D DO THE SAME IF THE ROLES WERE REVERSED.

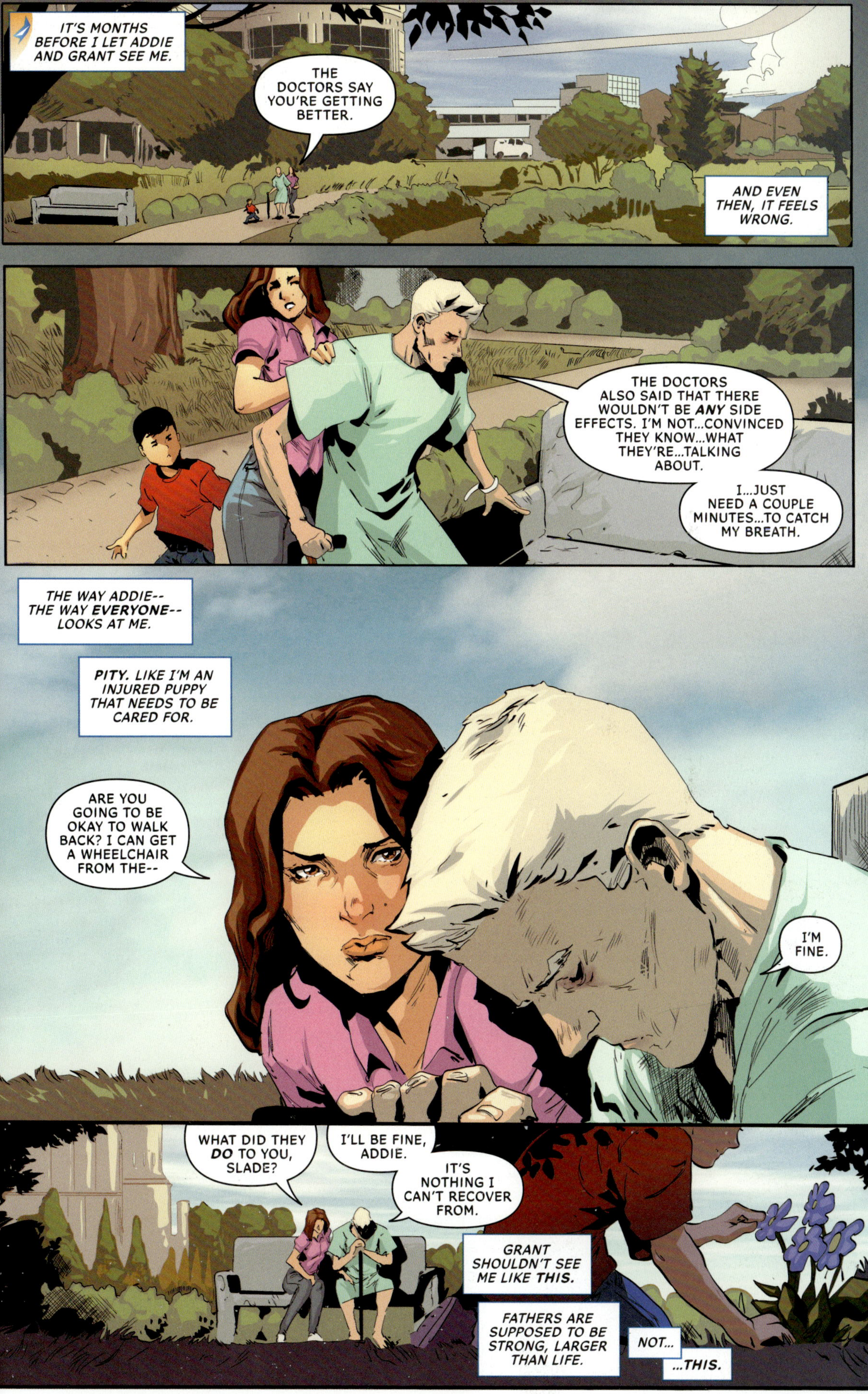
IT'S MONTHS BEFORE I LET ADDIE AND GRANT SEE ME.
THE DOCTORS SAY YOU'RE GETTING BETTER.
AND EVEN THEN, IT FEELS WRONG.
THE DOCTORS ALSO SAID THAT THERE WOULDN'T BE **ANY** SIDE EFFECTS. I'M NOT...CONVINCED THEY KNOW...WHAT THEY'RE...TALKING ABOUT.
I...JUST NEED A COUPLE MINUTES...TO CATCH MY BREATH.
*THE WAY ADDIE-- THE WAY **EVERYONE**-- LOOKS AT ME.*
***PITY.** LIKE I'M AN INJURED PUPPY THAT NEEDS TO BE CARED FOR.*
ARE YOU GOING TO BE OKAY TO WALK BACK? I CAN GET A WHEELCHAIR FROM THE--
I'M FINE.
WHAT DID THEY **DO** TO YOU, SLADE?
I'LL BE FINE, ADDIE.
IT'S NOTHING I CAN'T RECOVER FROM.
*GRANT SHOULDN'T SEE ME LIKE **THIS.***
FATHERS ARE SUPPOSED TO BE STRONG, LARGER THAN LIFE.
NOT...
*...**THIS.***

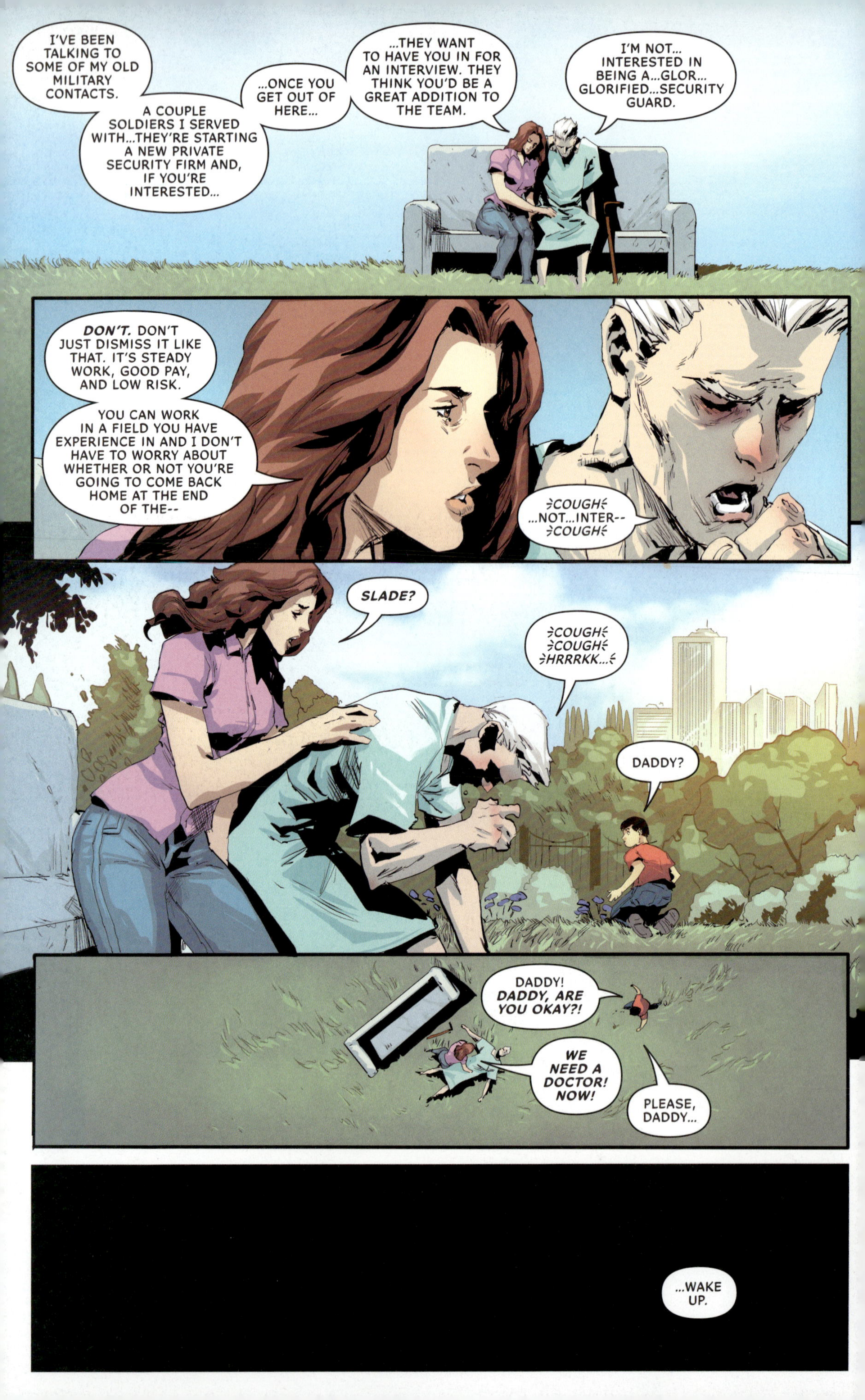
I'VE BEEN TALKING TO SOME OF MY OLD MILITARY CONTACTS.
A COUPLE SOLDIERS I SERVED WITH...THEY'RE STARTING A NEW PRIVATE SECURITY FIRM AND, IF YOU'RE INTERESTED...
...ONCE YOU GET OUT OF HERE...
...THEY WANT TO HAVE YOU IN FOR AN INTERVIEW. THEY THINK YOU'D BE A GREAT ADDITION TO THE TEAM.
I'M NOT... INTERESTED IN BEING A...GLOR... GLORIFIED...SECURITY GUARD.
DON'T. DON'T JUST DISMISS IT LIKE THAT. IT'S STEADY WORK, GOOD PAY, AND LOW RISK.
YOU CAN WORK IN A FIELD YOU HAVE EXPERIENCE IN AND I DON'T HAVE TO WORRY ABOUT WHETHER OR NOT YOU'RE GOING TO COME BACK HOME AT THE END OF THE--
COUGH ...NOT...INTER-- *COUGH*
SLADE?
COUGH *COUGH* *HRRRKK...*
DADDY?
DADDY! ***DADDY, ARE YOU OKAY?!***
WE NEED A DOCTOR! NOW!
PLEASE, DADDY...
...WAKE UP.

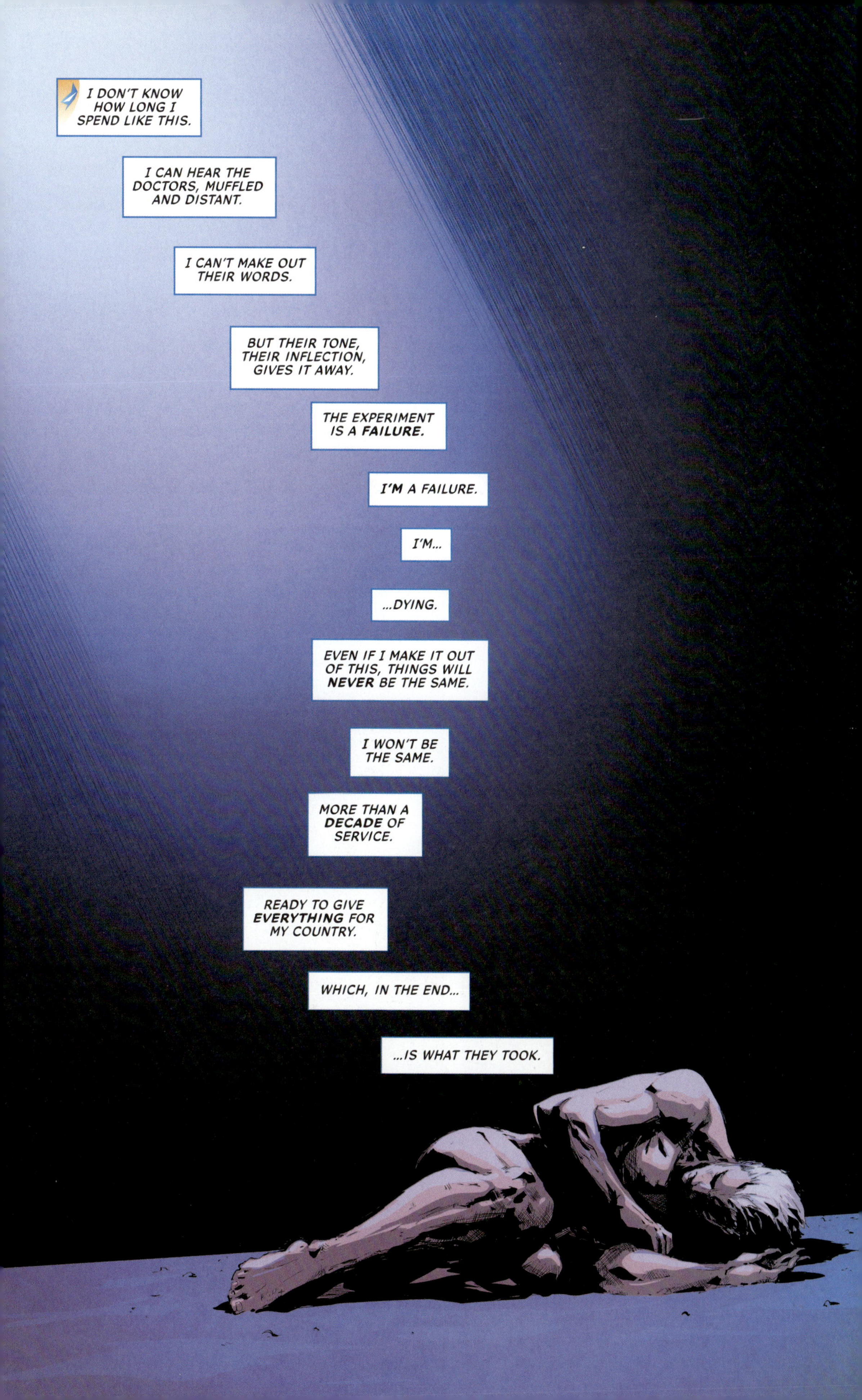
I DON'T KNOW HOW LONG I SPEND LIKE THIS.
I CAN HEAR THE DOCTORS, MUFFLED AND DISTANT.
I CAN'T MAKE OUT THEIR WORDS.
BUT THEIR TONE, THEIR INFLECTION, GIVES IT AWAY.
THE EXPERIMENT IS A **FAILURE.**
I'M A FAILURE.
I'M...
...DYING.
EVEN IF I MAKE IT OUT OF THIS, THINGS WILL **NEVER** BE THE SAME.
I WON'T BE THE SAME.
MORE THAN A **DECADE** OF SERVICE.
READY TO GIVE **EVERYTHING** FOR MY COUNTRY.
WHICH, IN THE END...
...IS WHAT THEY TOOK.

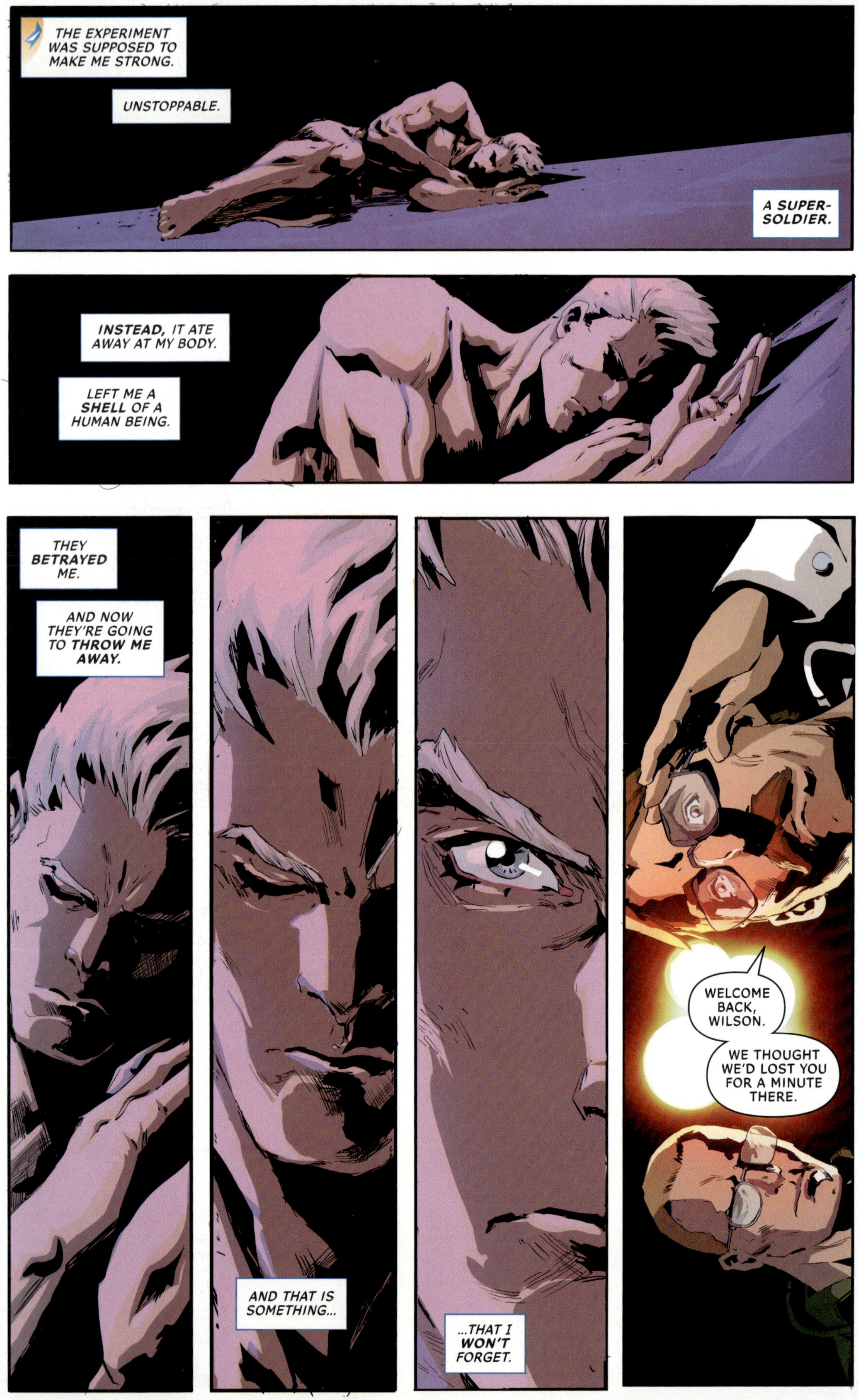
THE EXPERIMENT WAS SUPPOSED TO MAKE ME STRONG.
UNSTOPPABLE.
A SUPER-SOLDIER.
INSTEAD, IT ATE AWAY AT MY BODY.
LEFT ME A SHELL OF A HUMAN BEING.
THEY BETRAYED ME.
AND NOW THEY'RE GOING TO THROW ME AWAY.
AND THAT IS SOMETHING...
...THAT I WON'T FORGET.
WELCOME BACK, WILSON.
WE THOUGHT WE'D LOST YOU FOR A MINUTE THERE.

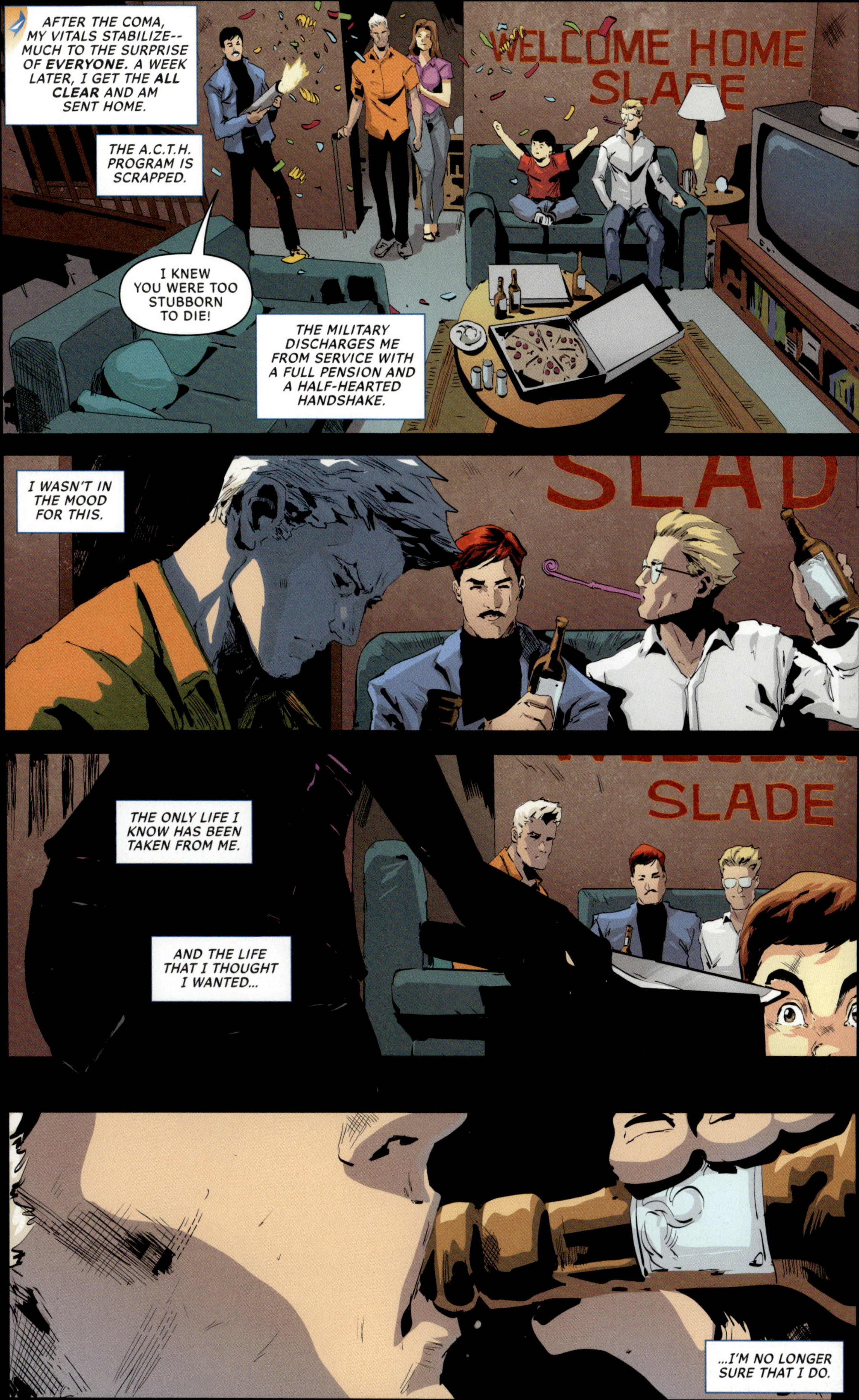
AFTER THE COMA, MY VITALS STABILIZE-- MUCH TO THE SURPRISE OF **EVERYONE.** A WEEK LATER, I GET THE **ALL CLEAR** AND AM SENT HOME.
WELCOME HOME SLADE
THE A.C.T.H. PROGRAM IS SCRAPPED.
I KNEW YOU WERE TOO STUBBORN TO DIE!
THE MILITARY DISCHARGES ME FROM SERVICE WITH A FULL PENSION AND A HALF-HEARTED HANDSHAKE.
I WASN'T IN THE MOOD FOR THIS.
SLAD
SLADE
THE ONLY LIFE I KNOW HAS BEEN TAKEN FROM ME.
AND THE LIFE THAT I THOUGHT I WANTED...
...I'M NO LONGER SURE THAT I DO.

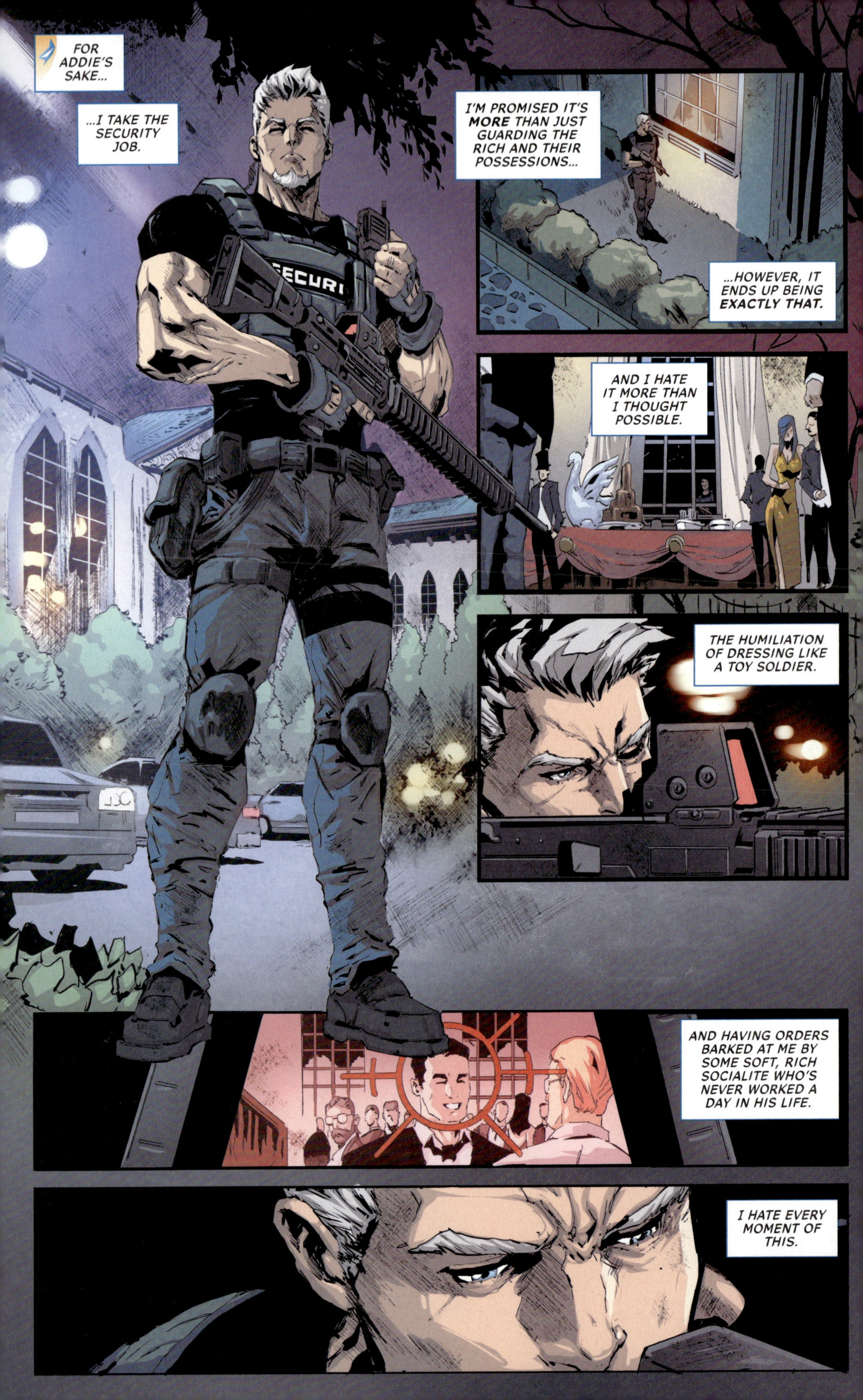
FOR ADDIE'S SAKE...
...I TAKE THE SECURITY JOB.
SECURI
I'M PROMISED IT'S MORE THAN JUST GUARDING THE RICH AND THEIR POSSESSIONS...
...HOWEVER, IT ENDS UP BEING EXACTLY THAT.
AND I HATE IT MORE THAN I THOUGHT POSSIBLE.
THE HUMILIATION OF DRESSING LIKE A TOY SOLDIER.
AND HAVING ORDERS BARKED AT ME BY SOME SOFT, RICH SOCIALITE WHO'S NEVER WORKED A DAY IN HIS LIFE.
I HATE EVERY MOMENT OF THIS.

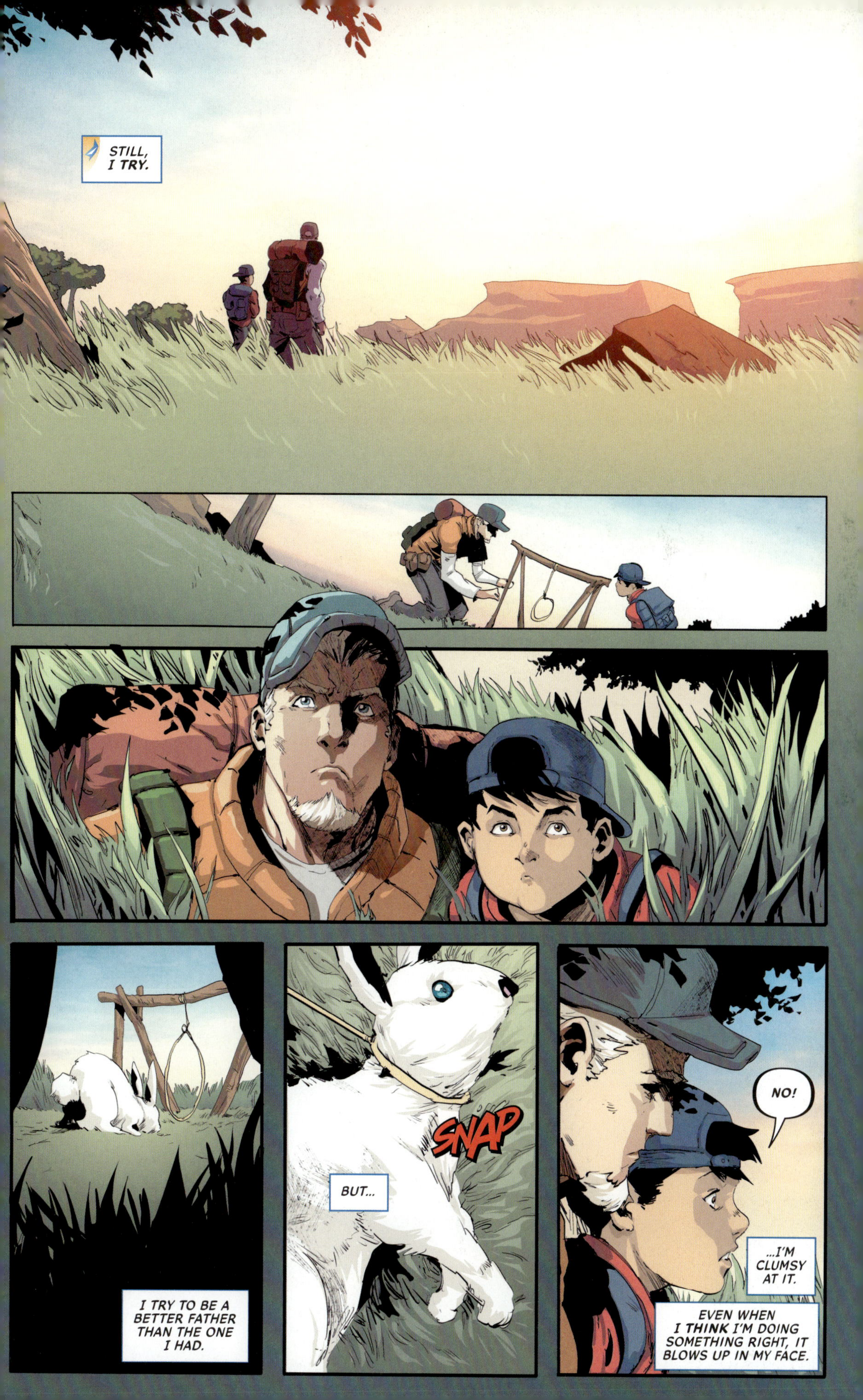
STILL, I TRY.
I TRY TO BE A BETTER FATHER THAN THE ONE I HAD.
SNAP
BUT...
NO!
...I'M CLUMSY AT IT.
EVEN WHEN I THINK I'M DOING SOMETHING RIGHT, IT BLOWS UP IN MY FACE.

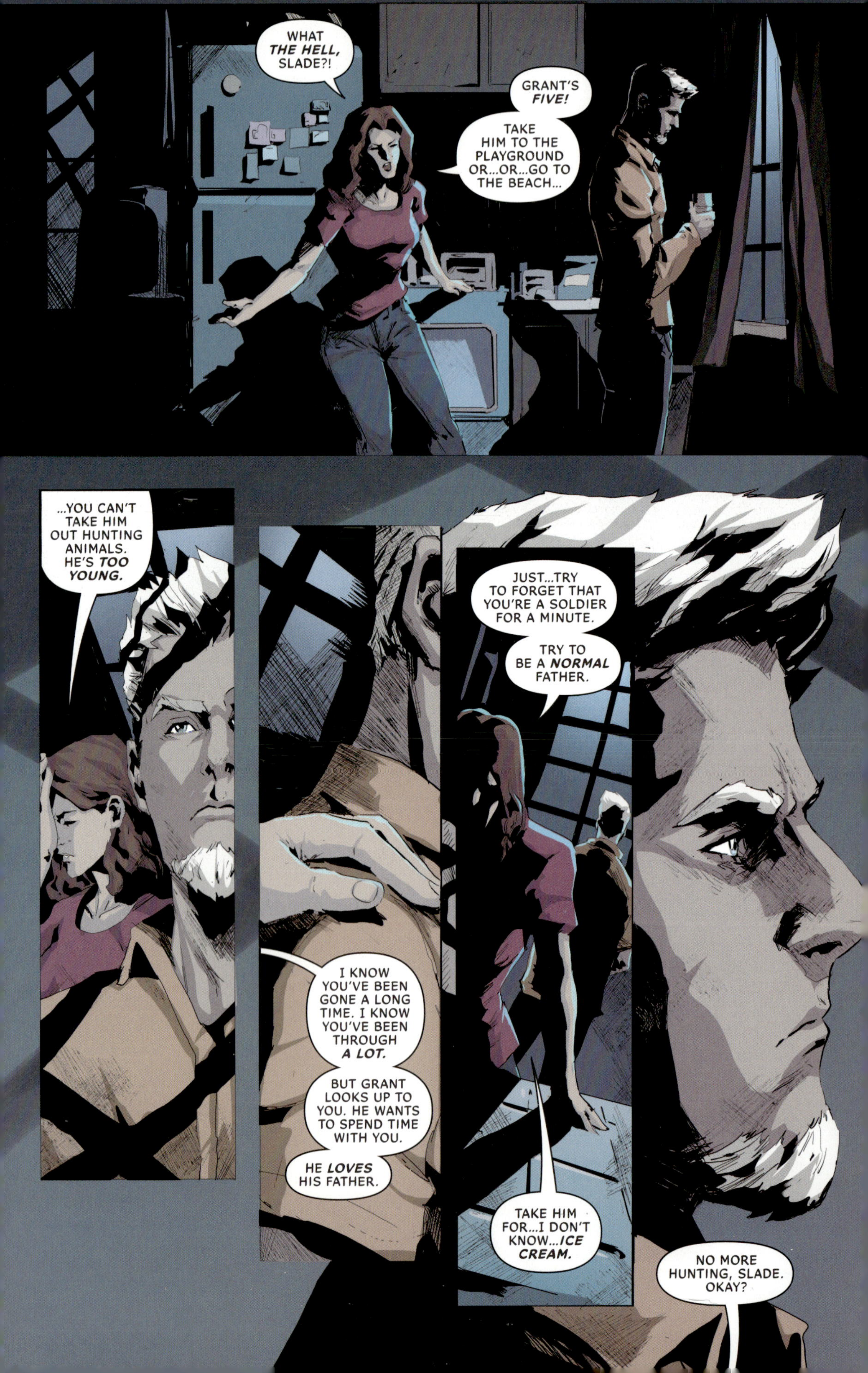
WHAT THE HELL, SLADE?!
GRANT'S FIVE!
TAKE HIM TO THE PLAYGROUND OR...OR...GO TO THE BEACH...
...YOU CAN'T TAKE HIM OUT HUNTING ANIMALS. HE'S TOO YOUNG.
I KNOW YOU'VE BEEN GONE A LONG TIME. I KNOW YOU'VE BEEN THROUGH A LOT.
BUT GRANT LOOKS UP TO YOU. HE WANTS TO SPEND TIME WITH YOU.
HE LOVES HIS FATHER.
JUST...TRY TO FORGET THAT YOU'RE A SOLDIER FOR A MINUTE.
TRY TO BE A NORMAL FATHER.
TAKE HIM FOR...I DON'T KNOW...ICE CREAM.
NO MORE HUNTING, SLADE. OKAY?

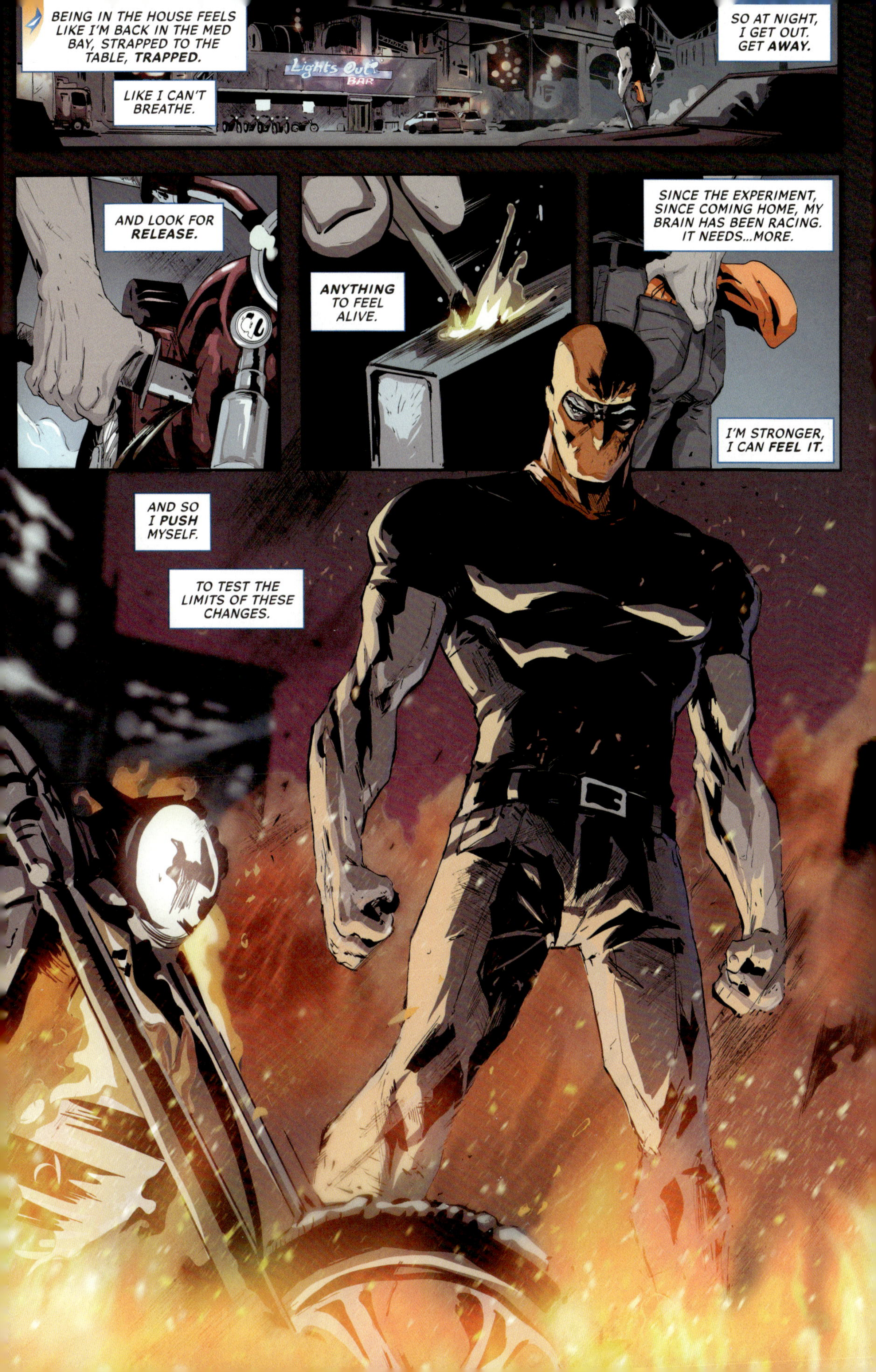
BEING IN THE HOUSE FEELS LIKE I'M BACK IN THE MED BAY, STRAPPED TO THE TABLE, **TRAPPED.**
LIKE I CAN'T BREATHE.
Lights Out BAR
SO AT NIGHT, I GET OUT. GET **AWAY.**
AND LOOK FOR **RELEASE.**
ANYTHING TO FEEL ALIVE.
SINCE THE EXPERIMENT, SINCE COMING HOME, MY BRAIN HAS BEEN RACING. IT NEEDS...MORE.
I'M STRONGER, I CAN **FEEL IT.**
AND SO I **PUSH** MYSELF.
TO TEST THE LIMITS OF THESE CHANGES.

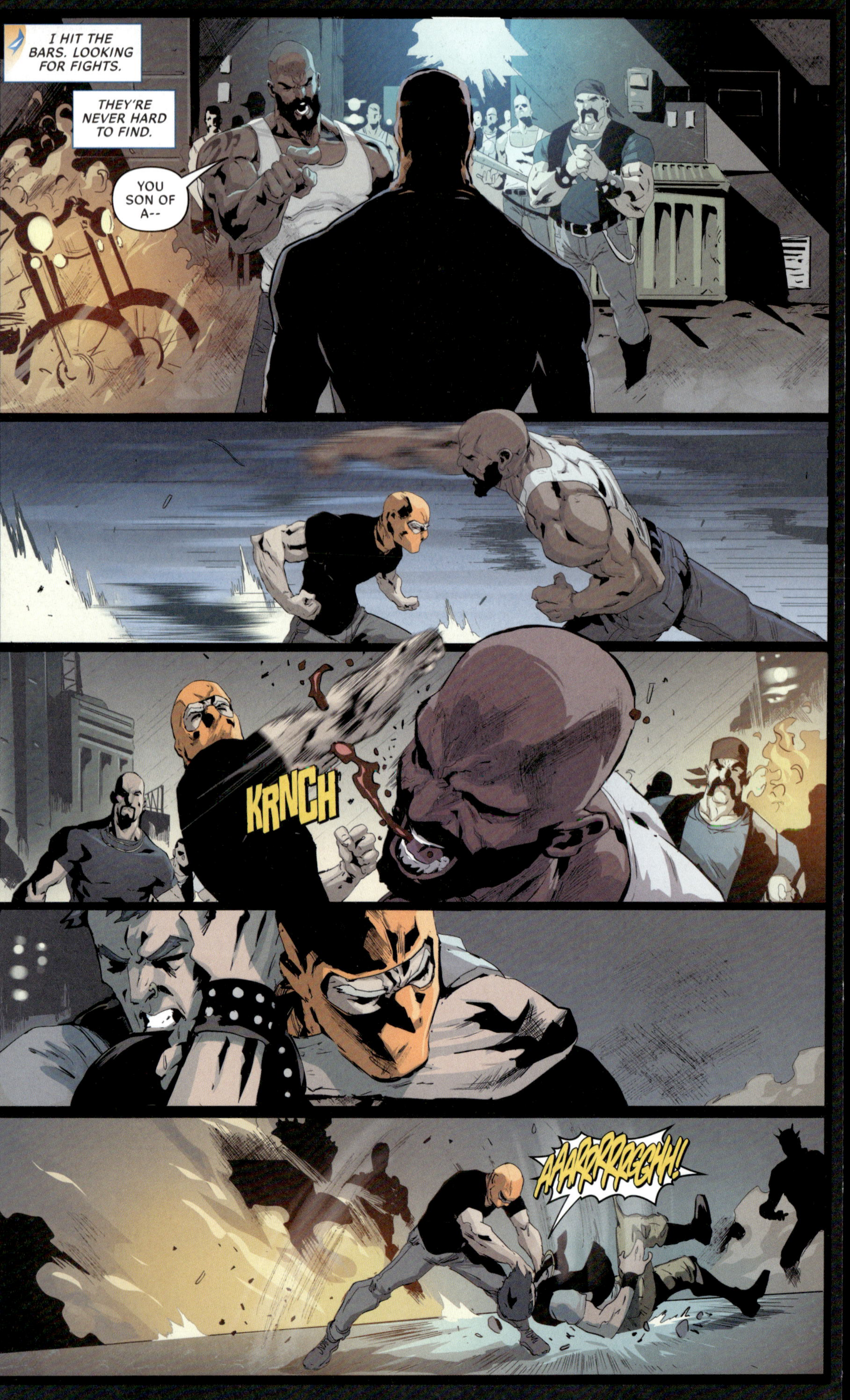
I HIT THE BARS. LOOKING FOR FIGHTS.
THEY'RE NEVER HARD TO FIND.
YOU SON OF A--
KRNCH
AAARRRRGGHH!

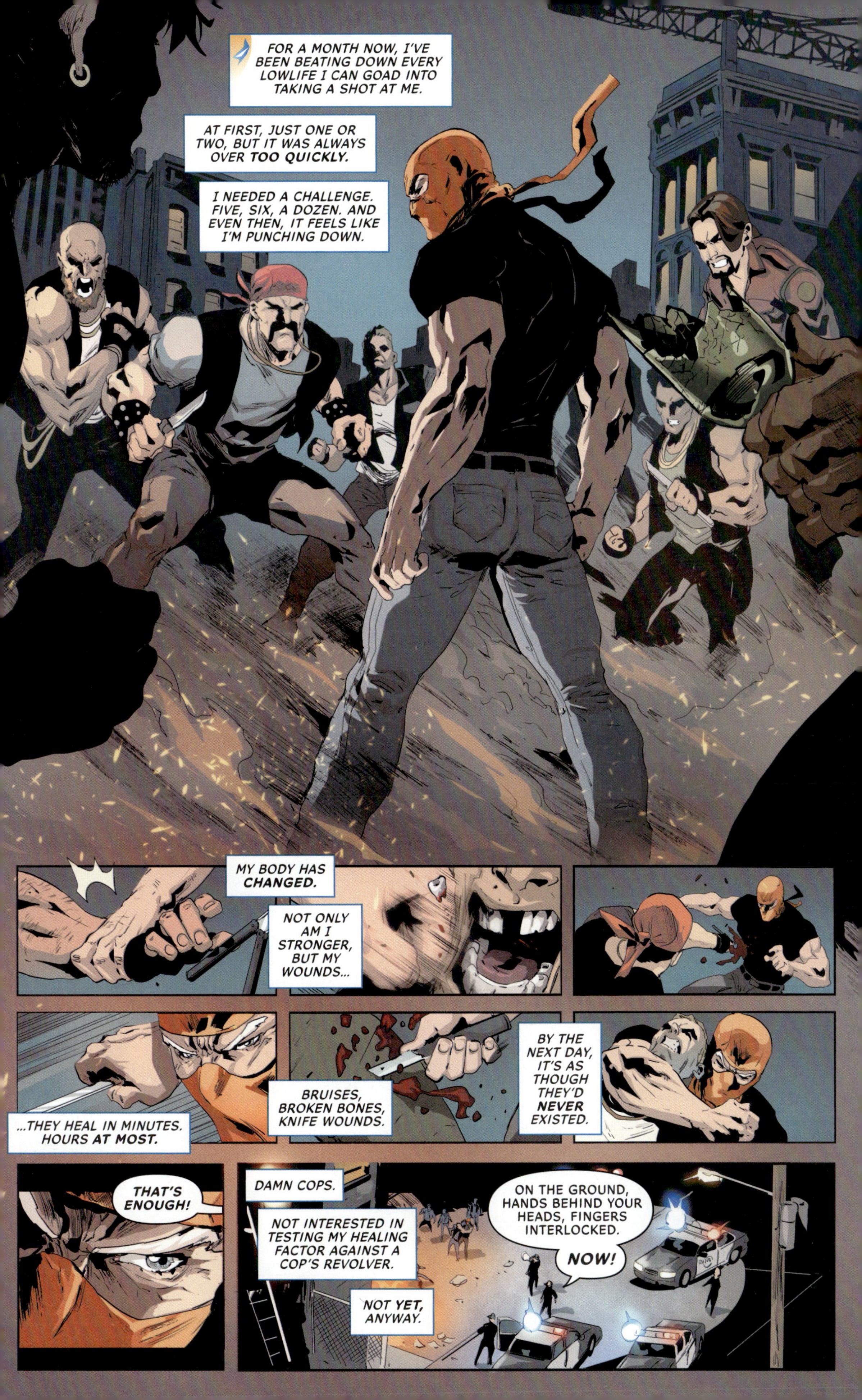
FOR A MONTH NOW, I'VE BEEN BEATING DOWN EVERY LOWLIFE I CAN GOAD INTO TAKING A SHOT AT ME.
AT FIRST, JUST ONE OR TWO, BUT IT WAS ALWAYS OVER **TOO QUICKLY.**
I NEEDED A CHALLENGE. FIVE, SIX, A DOZEN. AND EVEN THEN, IT FEELS LIKE I'M PUNCHING DOWN.
MY BODY HAS **CHANGED.**
NOT ONLY AM I STRONGER, BUT MY WOUNDS...
...THEY HEAL IN MINUTES. HOURS **AT MOST.**
BRUISES, BROKEN BONES, KNIFE WOUNDS.
BY THE NEXT DAY, IT'S AS THOUGH THEY'D **NEVER** EXISTED.
THAT'S ENOUGH!
DAMN COPS.
NOT INTERESTED IN TESTING MY HEALING FACTOR AGAINST A COP'S REVOLVER.
NOT **YET,** ANYWAY.
ON THE GROUND, HANDS BEHIND YOUR HEADS, FINGERS INTERLOCKED.
NOW!

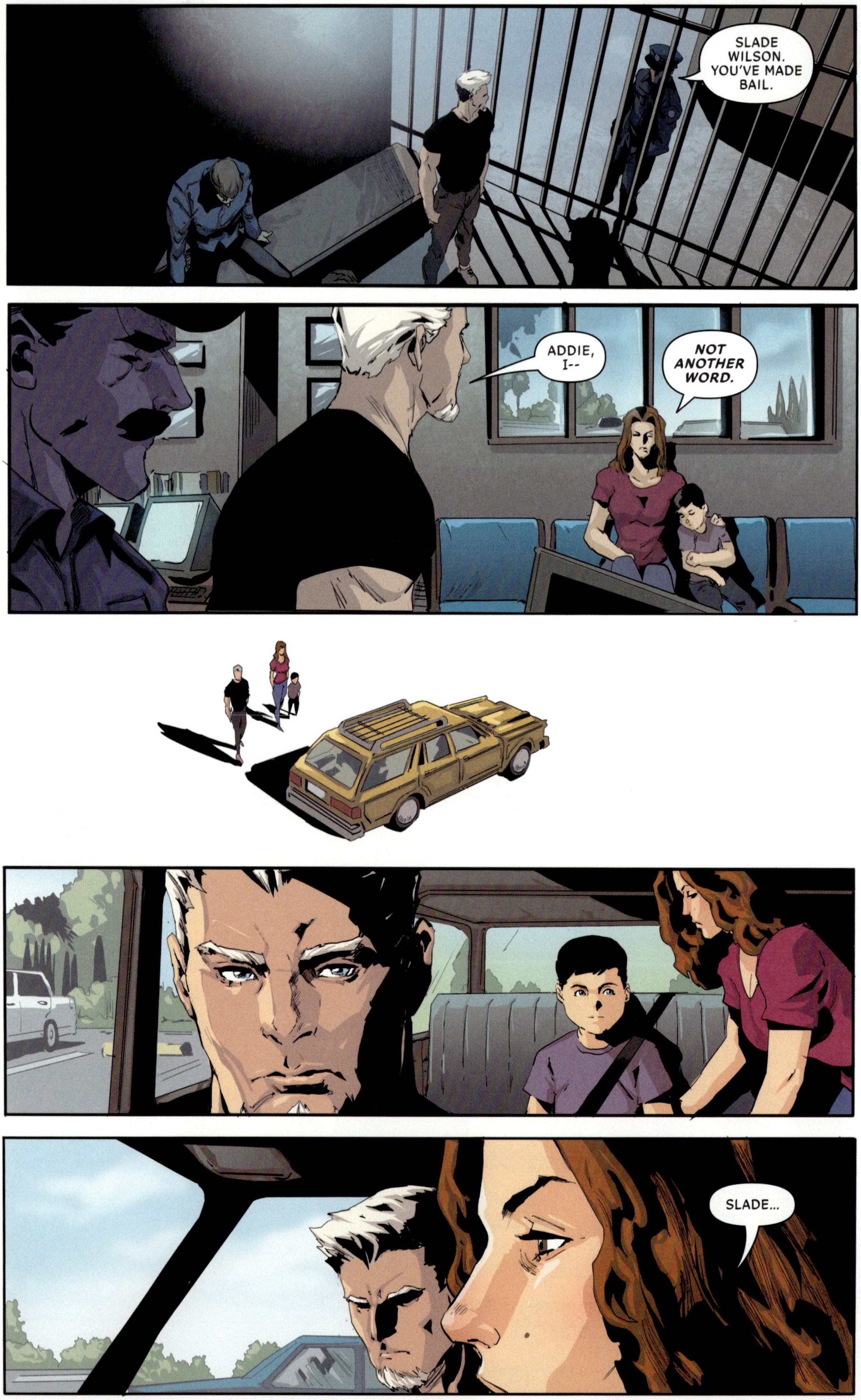
SLADE WILSON. YOU'VE MADE BAIL.
ADDIE, I--
NOT ANOTHER WORD.
SLADE...

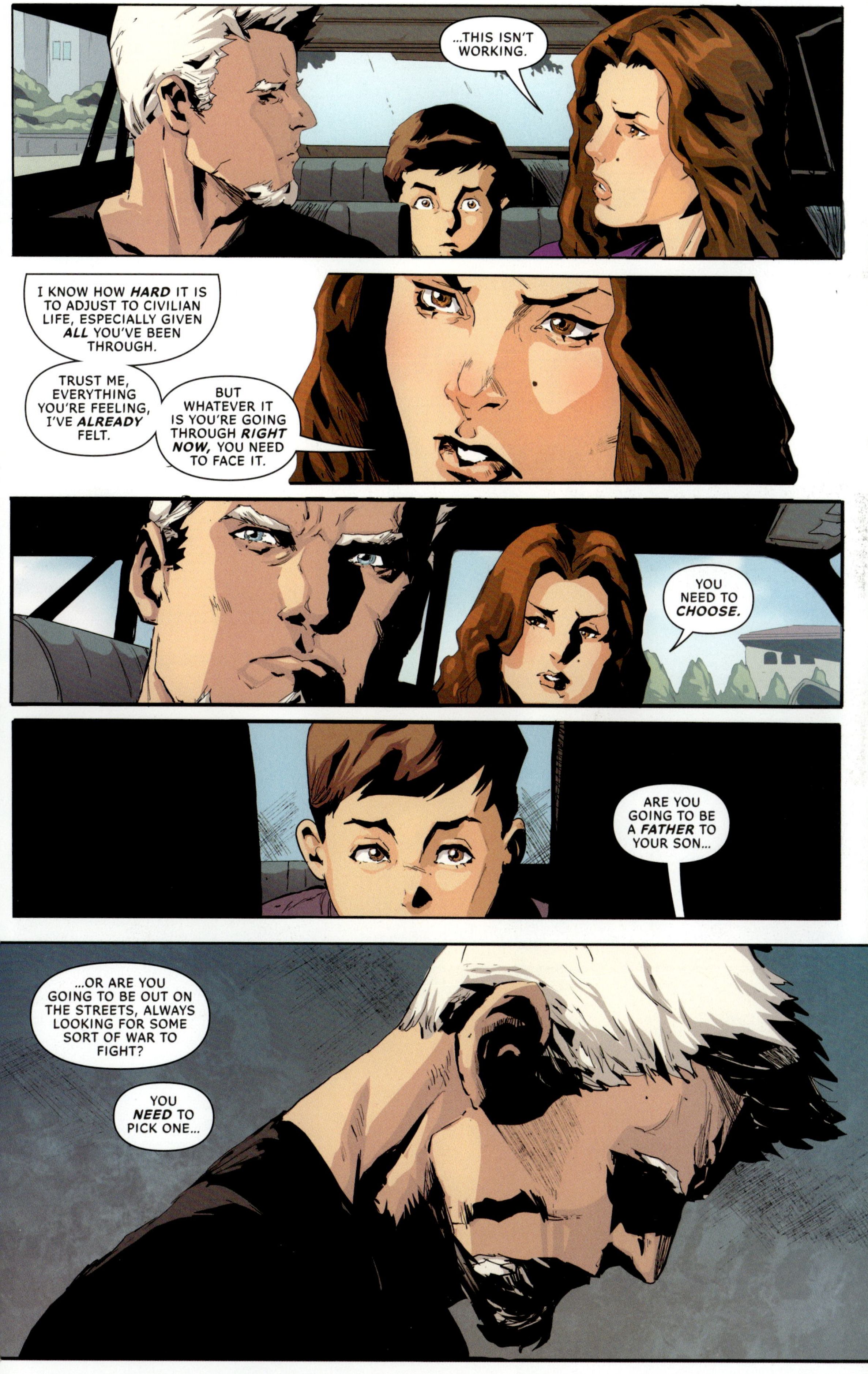
...THIS ISN'T WORKING.
I KNOW HOW **HARD** IT IS TO ADJUST TO CIVILIAN LIFE, ESPECIALLY GIVEN **ALL** YOU'VE BEEN THROUGH.
TRUST ME, EVERYTHING YOU'RE FEELING, I'VE **ALREADY** FELT.
BUT WHATEVER IT IS YOU'RE GOING THROUGH **RIGHT NOW,** YOU NEED TO FACE IT.
YOU NEED TO **CHOOSE.**
ARE YOU GOING TO BE A **FATHER** TO YOUR SON...
...OR ARE YOU GOING TO BE OUT ON THE STREETS, ALWAYS LOOKING FOR SOME SORT OF WAR TO FIGHT?
YOU **NEED** TO PICK ONE...

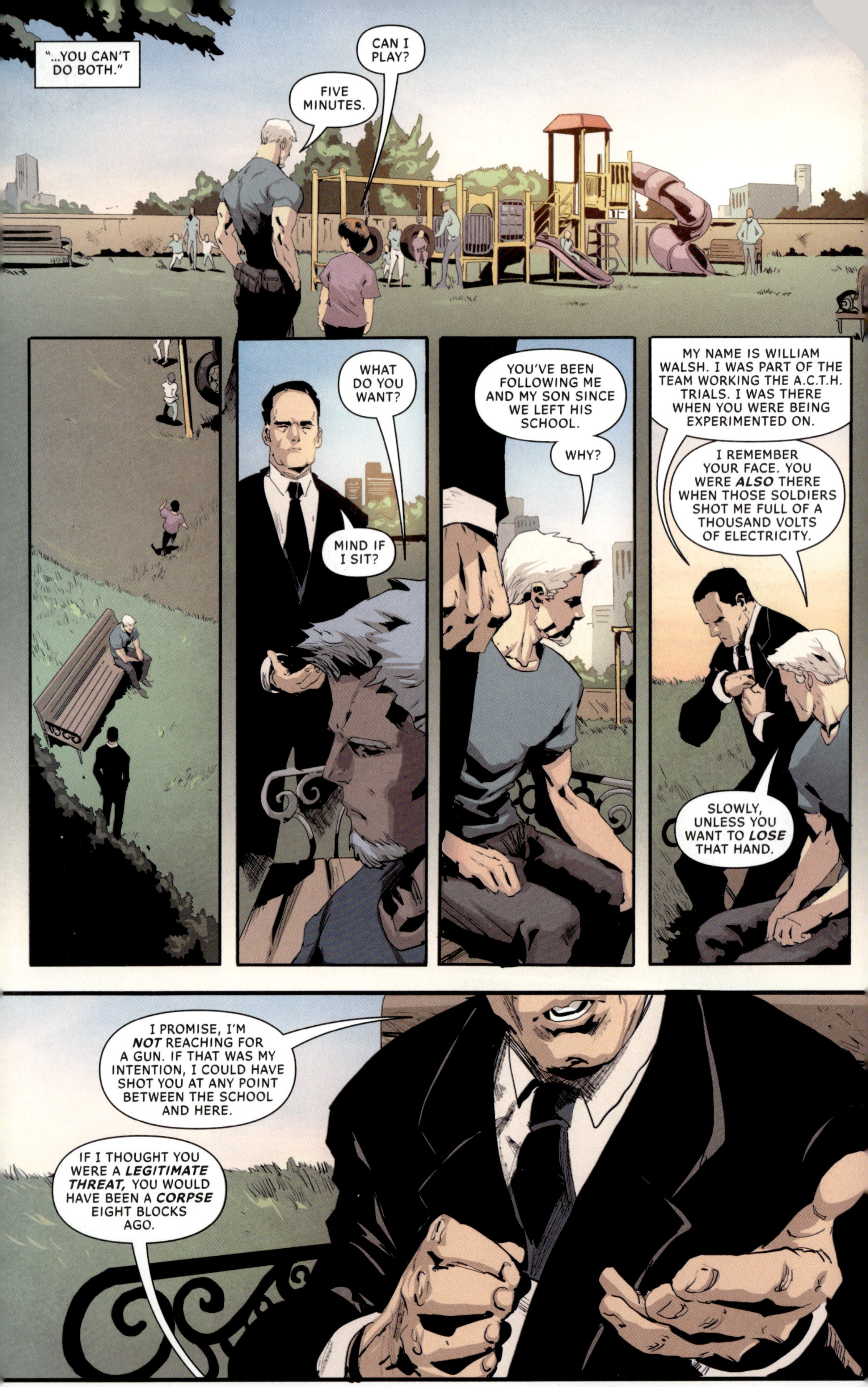
"...YOU CAN'T DO BOTH."
CAN I PLAY?
FIVE MINUTES.
WHAT DO YOU WANT?
MIND IF I SIT?
YOU'VE BEEN FOLLOWING ME AND MY SON SINCE WE LEFT HIS SCHOOL.
WHY?
MY NAME IS WILLIAM WALSH. I WAS PART OF THE TEAM WORKING THE A.C.T.H. TRIALS. I WAS THERE WHEN YOU WERE BEING EXPERIMENTED ON.
I REMEMBER YOUR FACE. YOU WERE *ALSO* THERE WHEN THOSE SOLDIERS SHOT ME FULL OF A THOUSAND VOLTS OF ELECTRICITY.
SLOWLY, UNLESS YOU WANT TO *LOSE* THAT HAND.
I PROMISE, I'M *NOT* REACHING FOR A GUN. IF THAT WAS MY INTENTION, I COULD HAVE SHOT YOU AT ANY POINT BETWEEN THE SCHOOL AND HERE.
IF I THOUGHT YOU WERE A *LEGITIMATE THREAT,* YOU WOULD HAVE BEEN A *CORPSE* EIGHT BLOCKS AGO.

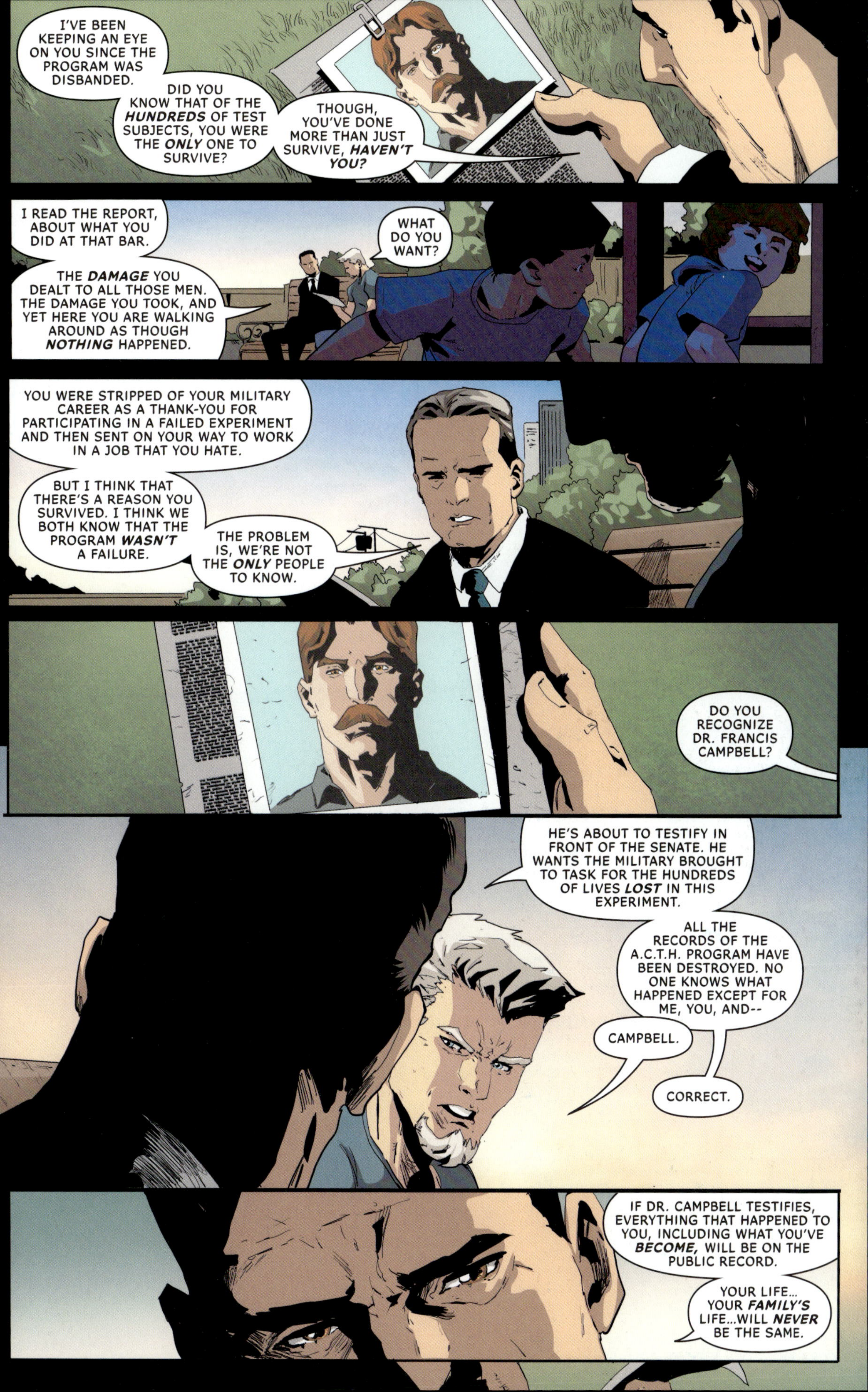

I'VE BEEN KEEPING AN EYE ON YOU SINCE THE PROGRAM WAS DISBANDED.
DID YOU KNOW THAT OF THE HUNDREDS OF TEST SUBJECTS, YOU WERE THE ONLY ONE TO SURVIVE?
THOUGH, YOU'VE DONE MORE THAN JUST SURVIVE, HAVEN'T YOU?
I READ THE REPORT, ABOUT WHAT YOU DID AT THAT BAR.
WHAT DO YOU WANT?
THE DAMAGE YOU DEALT TO ALL THOSE MEN. THE DAMAGE YOU TOOK, AND YET HERE YOU ARE WALKING AROUND AS THOUGH NOTHING HAPPENED.
YOU WERE STRIPPED OF YOUR MILITARY CAREER AS A THANK-YOU FOR PARTICIPATING IN A FAILED EXPERIMENT AND THEN SENT ON YOUR WAY TO WORK IN A JOB THAT YOU HATE.
BUT I THINK THAT THERE'S A REASON YOU SURVIVED. I THINK WE BOTH KNOW THAT THE PROGRAM WASN'T A FAILURE.
THE PROBLEM IS, WE'RE NOT THE ONLY PEOPLE TO KNOW.
DO YOU RECOGNIZE DR. FRANCIS CAMPBELL?
HE'S ABOUT TO TESTIFY IN FRONT OF THE SENATE. HE WANTS THE MILITARY BROUGHT TO TASK FOR THE HUNDREDS OF LIVES LOST IN THIS EXPERIMENT.
ALL THE RECORDS OF THE A.C.T.H. PROGRAM HAVE BEEN DESTROYED. NO ONE KNOWS WHAT HAPPENED EXCEPT FOR ME, YOU, AND--
CAMPBELL.
CORRECT.
IF DR. CAMPBELL TESTIFIES, EVERYTHING THAT HAPPENED TO YOU, INCLUDING WHAT YOU'VE BECOME, WILL BE ON THE PUBLIC RECORD.
YOUR LIFE... YOUR FAMILY'S LIFE...WILL NEVER BE THE SAME.

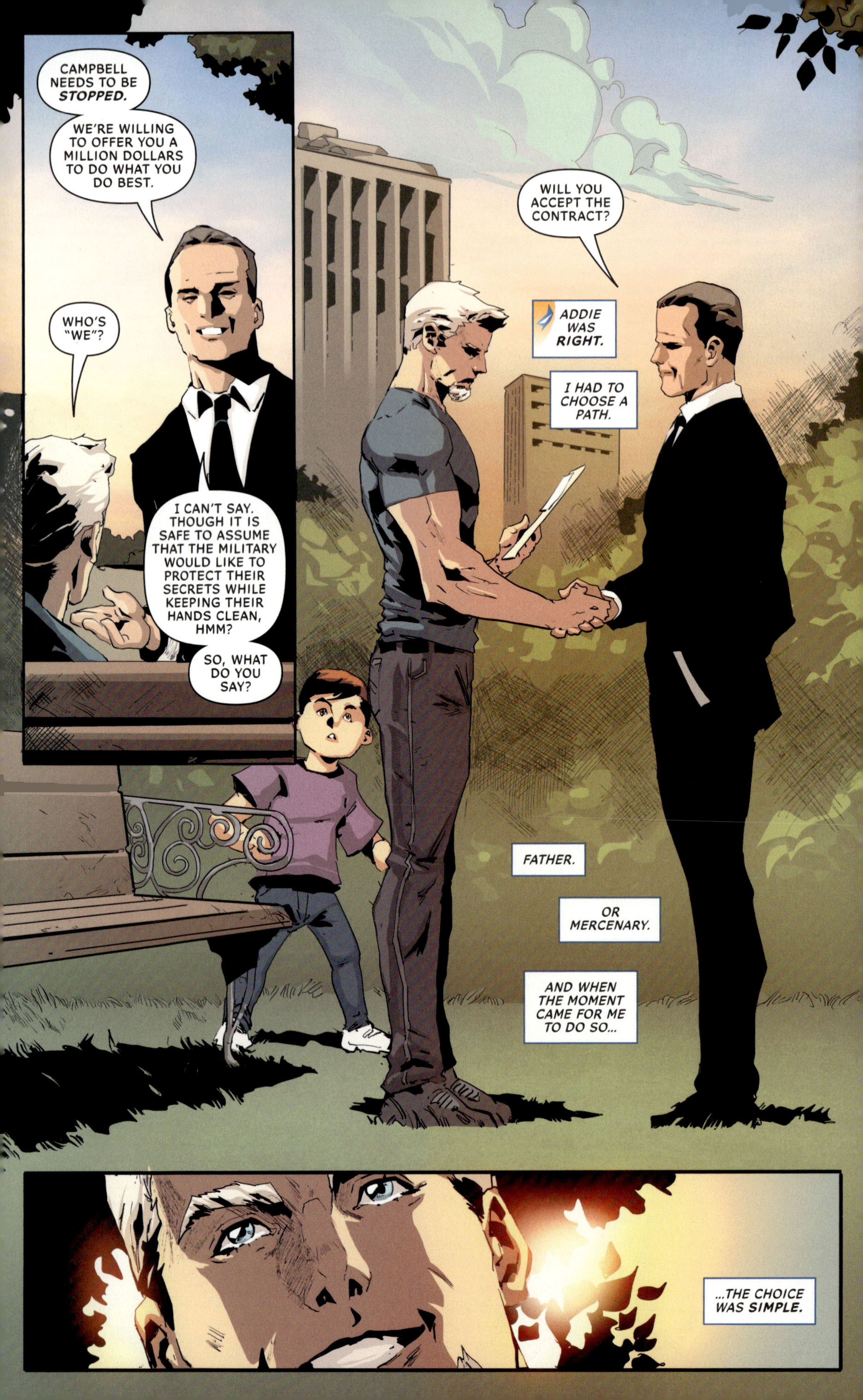

CAMPBELL NEEDS TO BE STOPPED.
WE'RE WILLING TO OFFER YOU A MILLION DOLLARS TO DO WHAT YOU DO BEST.
WHO'S "WE"?
I CAN'T SAY. THOUGH IT IS SAFE TO ASSUME THAT THE MILITARY WOULD LIKE TO PROTECT THEIR SECRETS WHILE KEEPING THEIR HANDS CLEAN, HMM?
SO, WHAT DO YOU SAY?
WILL YOU ACCEPT THE CONTRACT?
ADDIE WAS RIGHT.
I HAD TO CHOOSE A PATH.
FATHER.
OR MERCENARY.
AND WHEN THE MOMENT CAME FOR ME TO DO SO...
...THE CHOICE WAS SIMPLE.

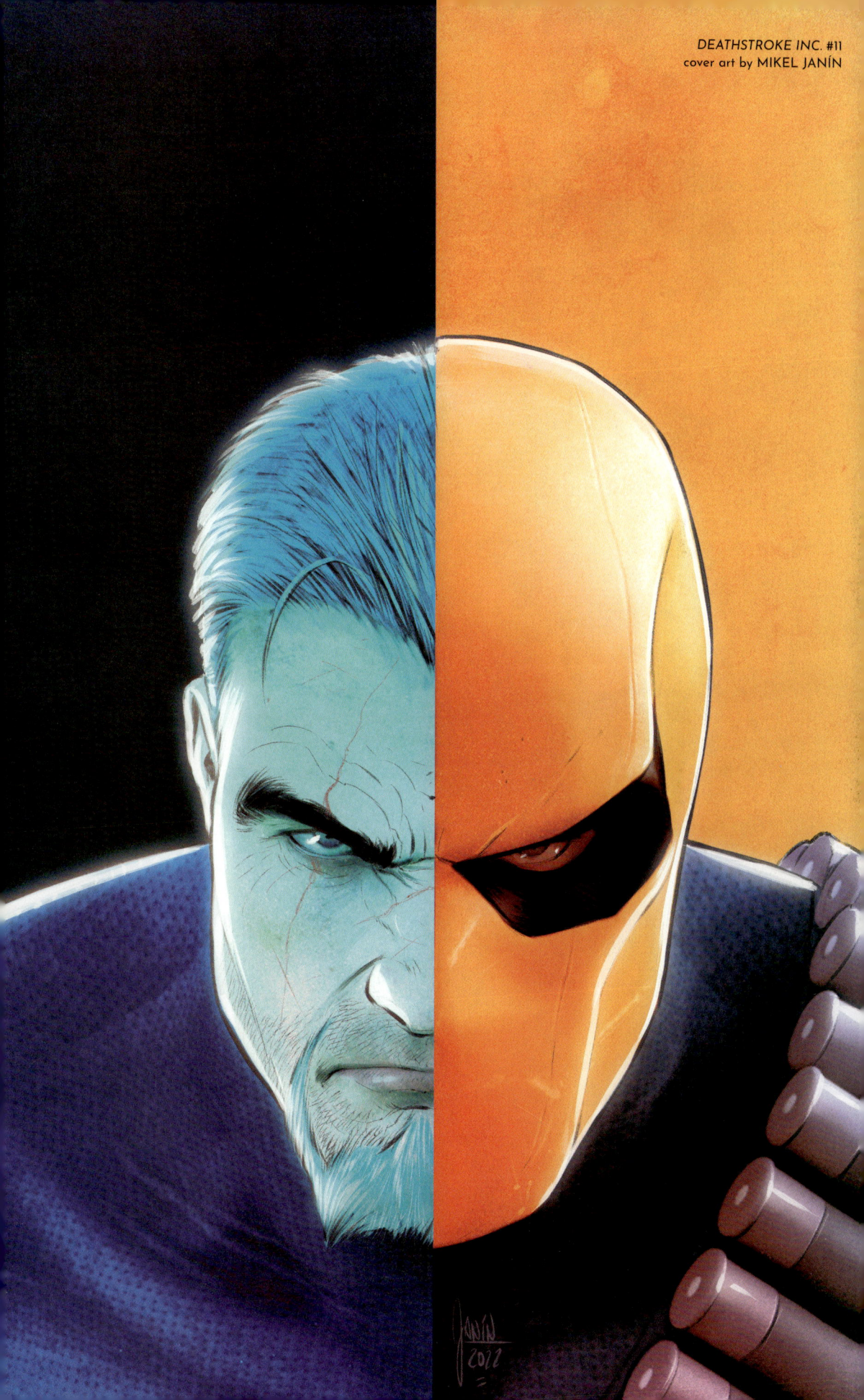

DEATHSTROKE INC. #11
cover art by MIKEL JANÍN

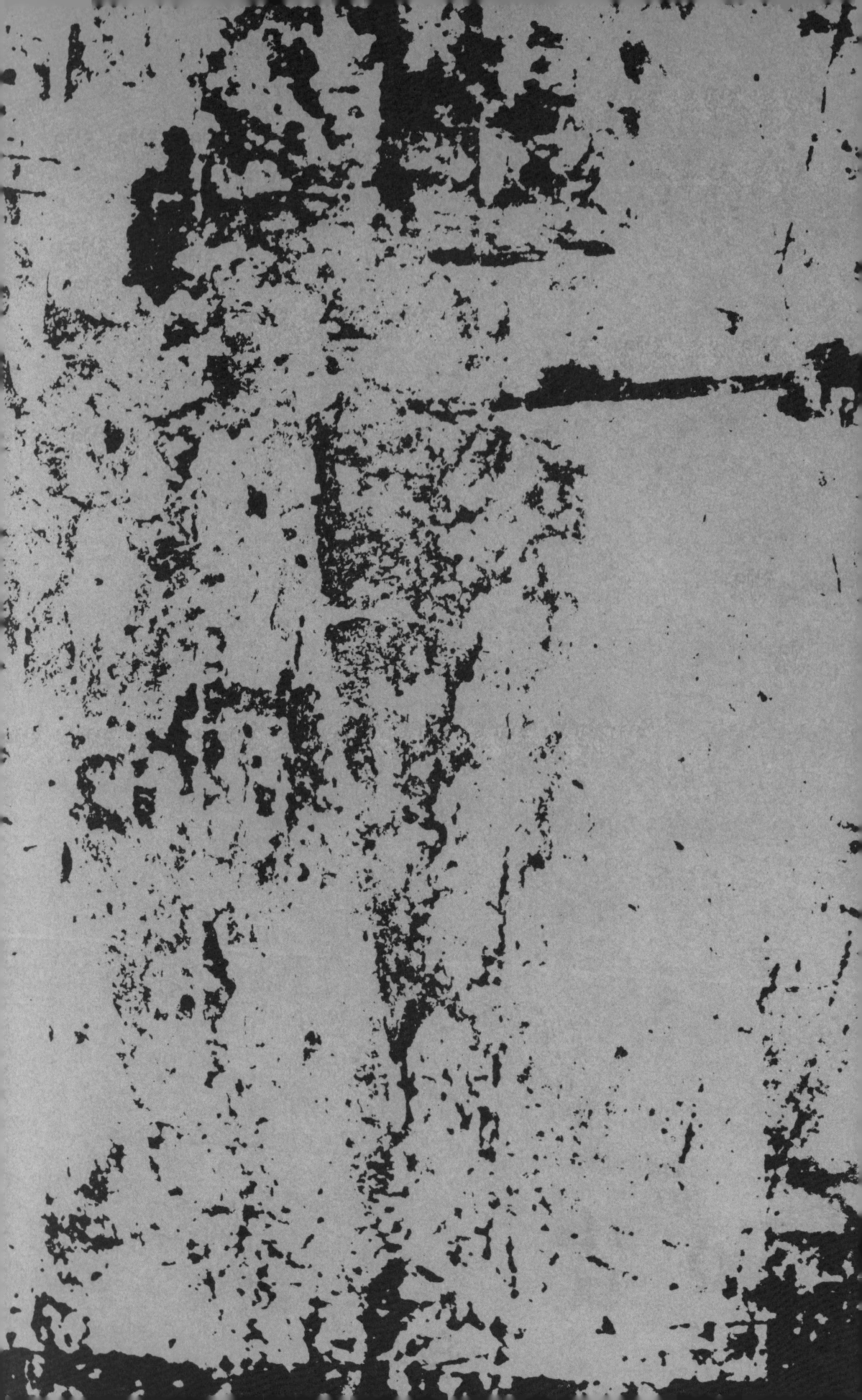

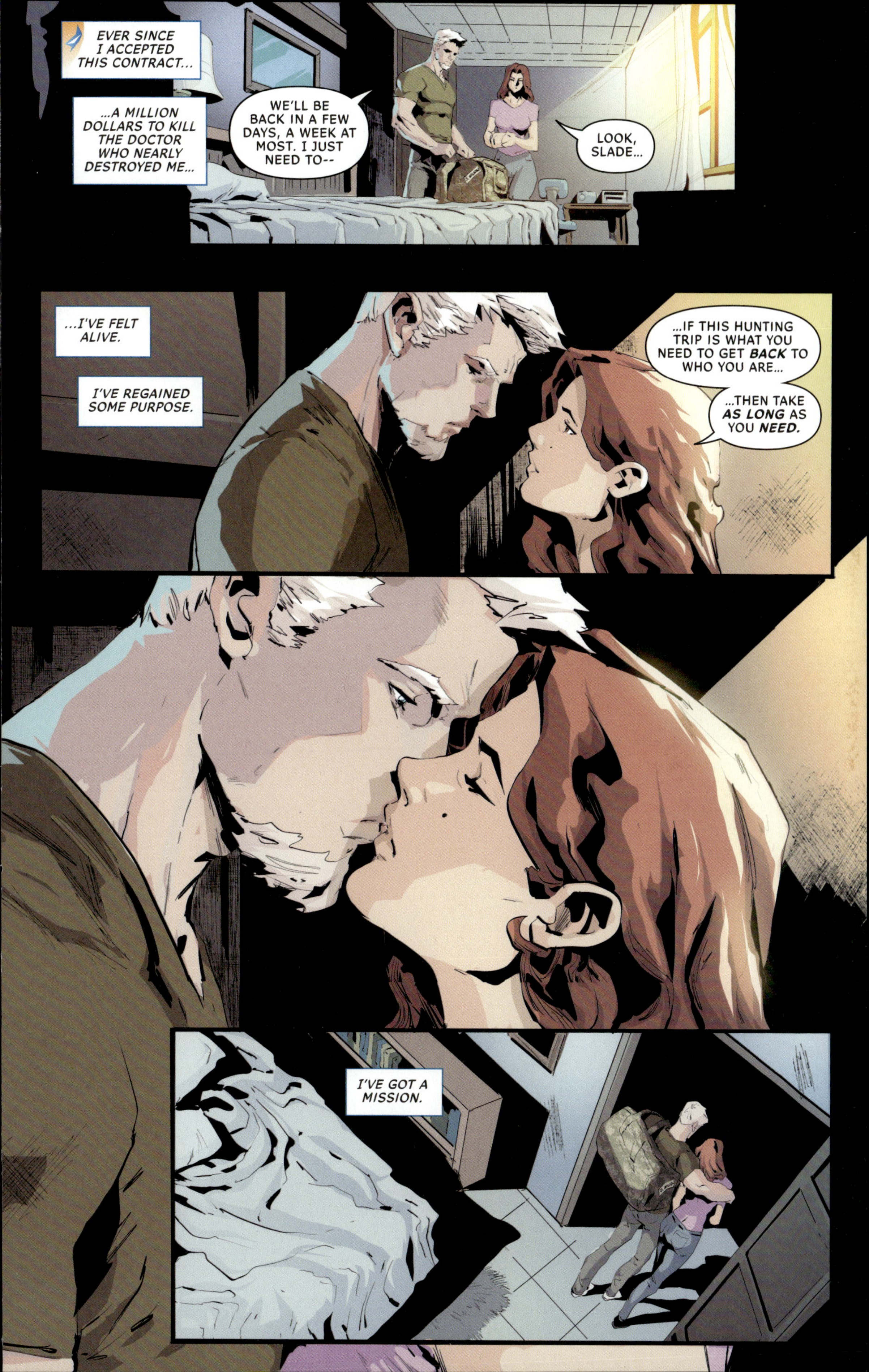
EVER SINCE I ACCEPTED THIS CONTRACT...
...A MILLION DOLLARS TO KILL THE DOCTOR WHO NEARLY DESTROYED ME...
WE'LL BE BACK IN A FEW DAYS, A WEEK AT MOST. I JUST NEED TO--
LOOK, SLADE...
...I'VE FELT ALIVE.
I'VE REGAINED SOME PURPOSE.
...IF THIS HUNTING TRIP IS WHAT YOU NEED TO GET BACK TO WHO YOU ARE...
...THEN TAKE AS LONG AS YOU NEED.
I'VE GOT A MISSION.

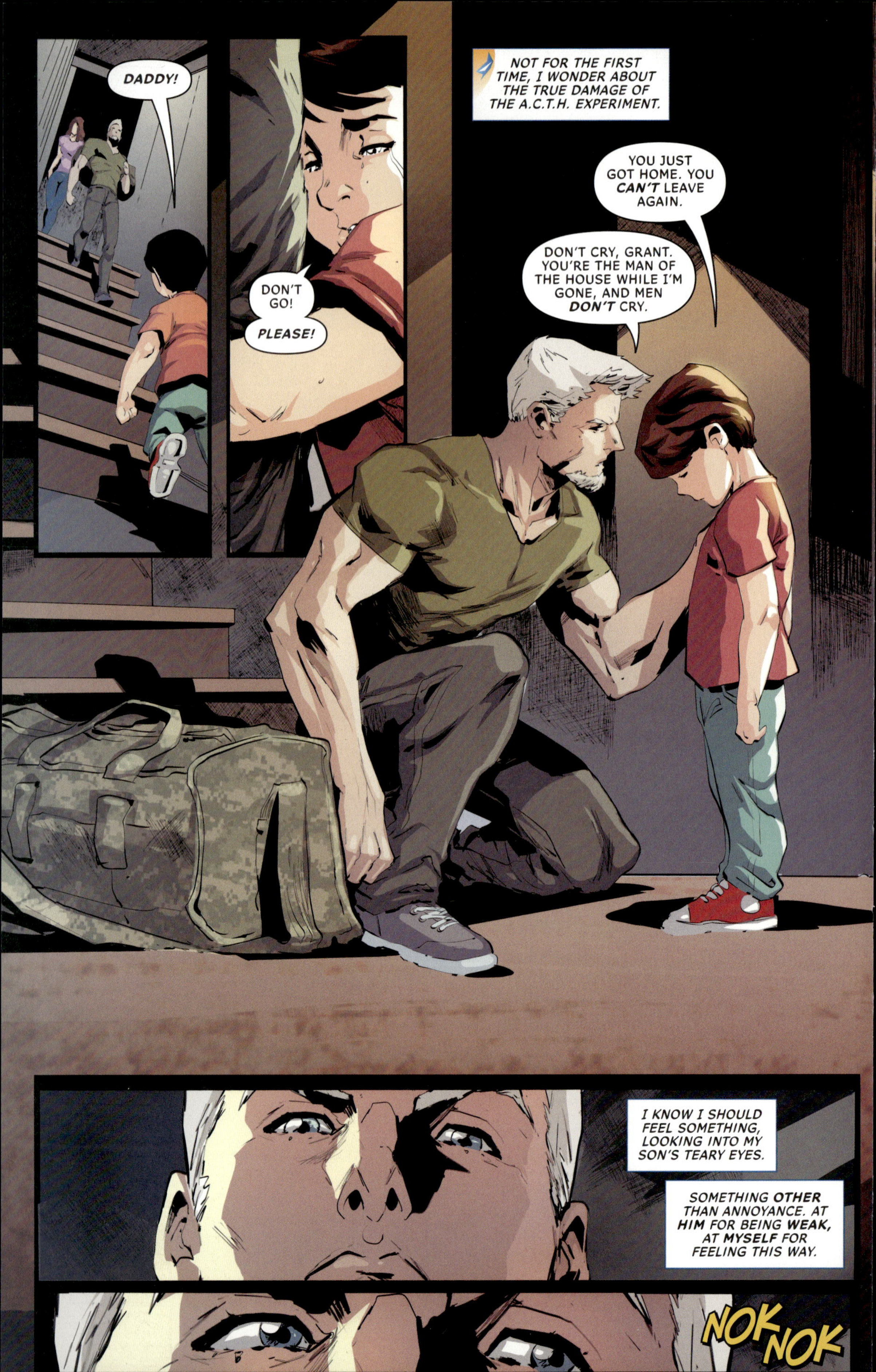
DADDY!
DON'T GO!
PLEASE!
NOT FOR THE FIRST TIME, I WONDER ABOUT THE TRUE DAMAGE OF THE A.C.T.H. EXPERIMENT.
YOU JUST GOT HOME. YOU CAN'T LEAVE AGAIN.
DON'T CRY, GRANT. YOU'RE THE MAN OF THE HOUSE WHILE I'M GONE, AND MEN DON'T CRY.
I KNOW I SHOULD FEEL SOMETHING, LOOKING INTO MY SON'S TEARY EYES.
SOMETHING OTHER THAN ANNOYANCE. AT HIM FOR BEING WEAK, AT MYSELF FOR FEELING THIS WAY.
NOK NOK

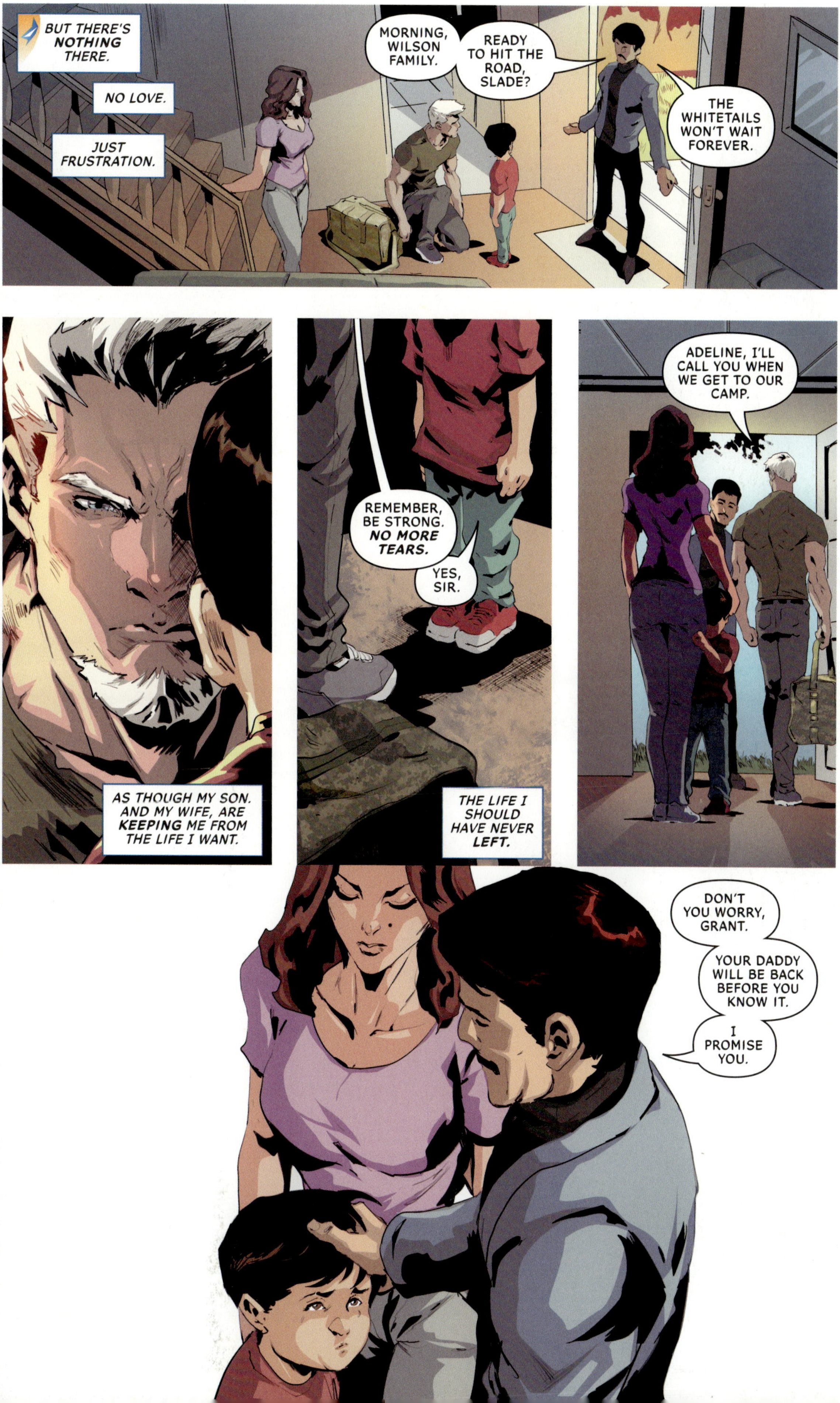
BUT THERE'S NOTHING THERE.
NO LOVE.
JUST FRUSTRATION.
MORNING, WILSON FAMILY.
READY TO HIT THE ROAD, SLADE?
THE WHITETAILS WON'T WAIT FOREVER.
AS THOUGH MY SON. AND MY WIFE, ARE KEEPING ME FROM THE LIFE I WANT.
REMEMBER, BE STRONG. NO MORE TEARS.
YES, SIR.
THE LIFE I SHOULD HAVE NEVER LEFT.
ADELINE, I'LL CALL YOU WHEN WE GET TO OUR CAMP.
DON'T YOU WORRY, GRANT.
YOUR DADDY WILL BE BACK BEFORE YOU KNOW IT.
I PROMISE YOU.

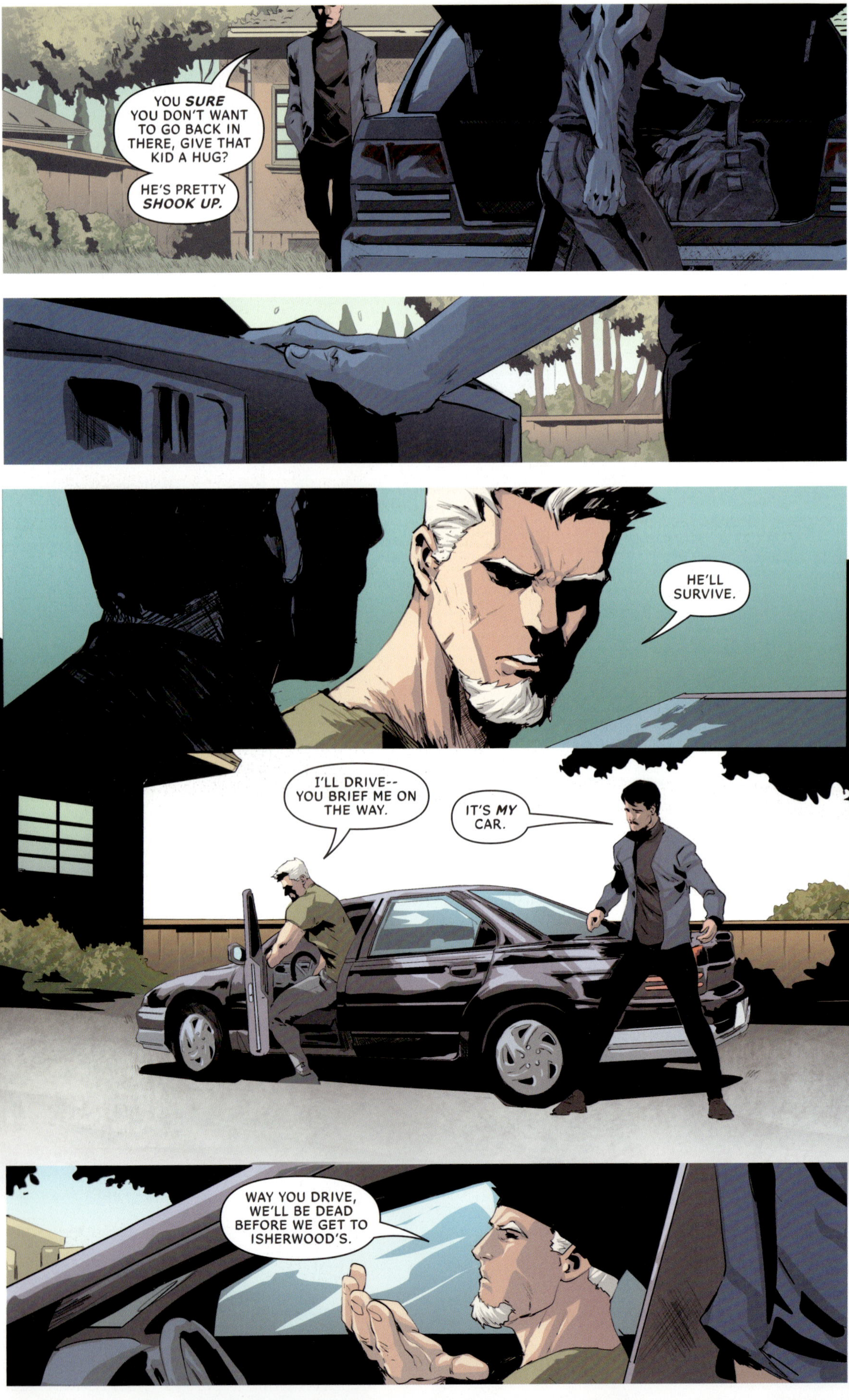
YOU SURE YOU DON'T WANT TO GO BACK IN THERE, GIVE THAT KID A HUG?
HE'S PRETTY SHOOK UP.
HE'LL SURVIVE.
I'LL DRIVE-- YOU BRIEF ME ON THE WAY.
IT'S MY CAR.
WAY YOU DRIVE, WE'LL BE DEAD BEFORE WE GET TO ISHERWOOD'S.

YOUR MAN WILLIAM WALSH WAS TELLING THE TRUTH ABOUT OLD DOC FRANCIS CAMPBELL.
CAMPBELL WAS THE LEAD ON THE TEAM THAT CONDUCTED THE A.C.T.H. EXPERIMENTS ON YOU AND ABOUT...
...47 OTHER SOLDIERS.
ALL OF THEM, LIKE YOU, REENLISTED OR PREVIOUSLY INJURED IN THE LINE OF DUTY.
ALL OF THEM LOOKING FOR A SECOND SHOT AT GLORY.
UNLIKE YOU, ALL OF THE OTHER SOLDIERS ***DIED*** DURING THE EXPERIMENT.
EVERY DEATH, COVERED UP. ***MILLIONS*** PAID OUT TO FAMILIES, WIDOWS, AND WHOEVER ELSE MIGHT ASK ***QUESTIONS.***
PROPER MILITARY BURIALS. CAUSE OF DEATH LISTED AS EITHER AN ACCIDENT OR COMBAT RELATED.
THIS IS A HELL OF A COVER-UP.

NOT THE FIRST TIME THAT THE GOVERNMENT HAS PAID PEOPLE OFF TO COVER UP THEIR MISTAKES.
TRUE.
BUT STILL.
CLASSIFIED
MORE THAN A DOZEN DOCTORS INVOLVED IN THE EXPERIMENTS. TWICE AS MANY GUARDS AND ADMIN WORKERS...
...ALL DEAD.
CAR ACCIDENTS, SLIPS IN THE SHOWER, CARBON MONOXIDE POISONING, HOUSE FIRES, THE LIST GOES ON AND ON.
THAT'S A HELL OF A BAD LUCK STREAK.
DR. CAMPBELL'S THE LAST ONE STANDING. IT APPEARS HE'S GOT A HORSESHOE LODGED DEEP WHERE THE SUN CAN'T REACH.
THE MAN'S SURVIVED A CAR BOMB AND A GAS LEAK.
HE KNEW THE FIX WAS IN. TURNED HIMSELF IN TO THE FBI, LOOKING TO TURN STATE'S EVIDENCE ABOUT A CONSPIRACY WITHIN THE MILITARY.
HE'S HOLED UP IN SEATTLE, NEGOTIATING THE TERMS OF HIS DEAL.
WHY WOULD THE MILITARY SPEND MILLIONS TO SILENCE THE VICTIMS' FAMILIES, BUT JUST KILL OFF THE SCIENTISTS?
BECAUSE THE DOCTORS AND EVERYONE ELSE THERE KNEW WHAT WAS REALLY HAPPENING.
AND DEAD MEN DON'T TALK.

BAYERS DRUG MART
WHY DON'T YOU GO GET YOURSELF A TREAT, GRANT?
BUT YOU HAVE TO SAVE IT UNTIL AFTER DINNER, OKAY?
OKAY, MOMMY.
FAMILY PLANNING
MOMMY...
Clear
Pregnancy Test
...I PICKED MY CANDY BAR! I PICKED ONE FOR YOU TOO.
YOU'RE SO THOUGHTFUL.
C'MON, LET'S GET HOME AND WATCH A MOVIE IN OUR PJs.

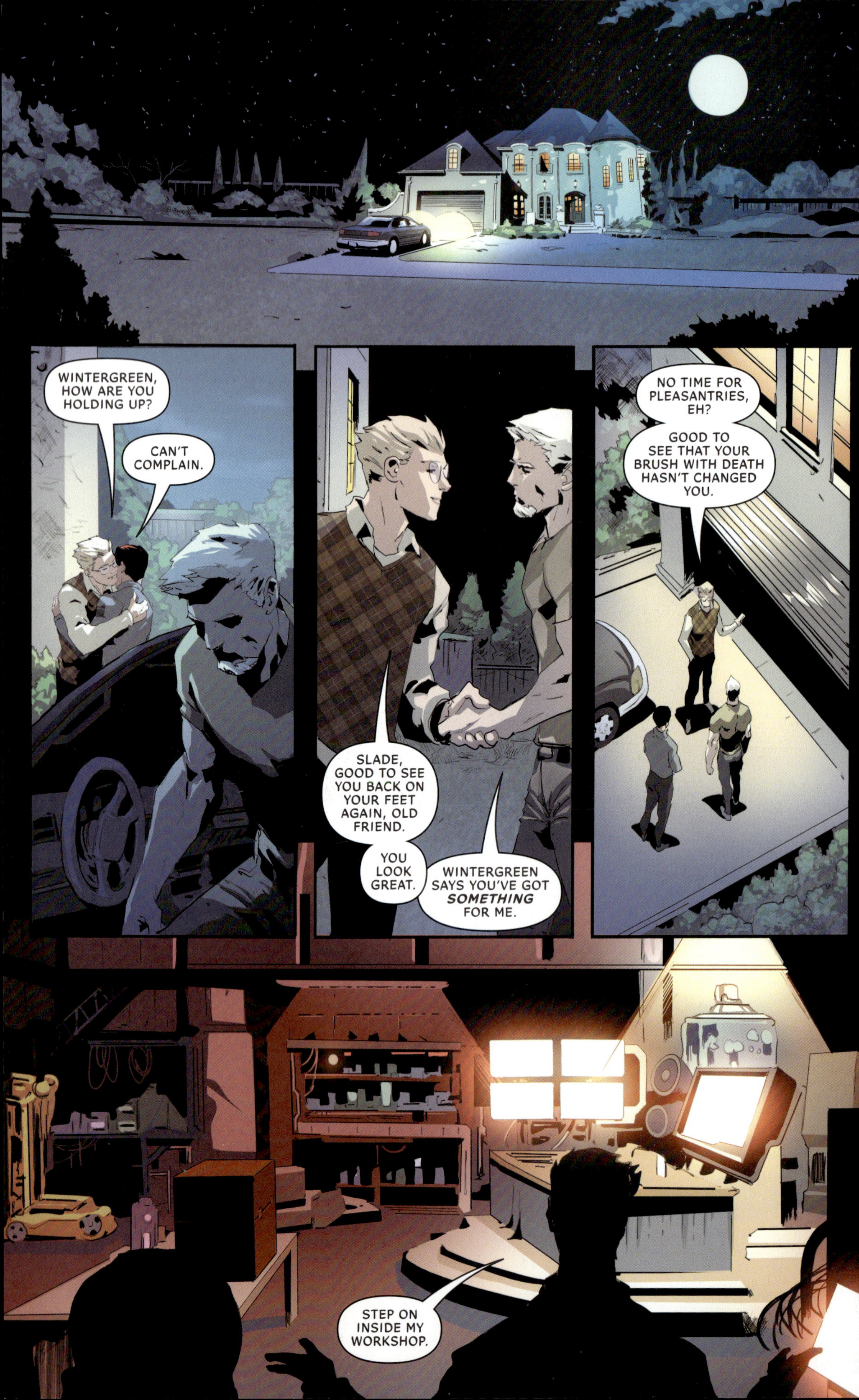
WINTERGREEN, HOW ARE YOU HOLDING UP?
CAN'T COMPLAIN.
SLADE, GOOD TO SEE YOU BACK ON YOUR FEET AGAIN, OLD FRIEND.
YOU LOOK GREAT.
WINTERGREEN SAYS YOU'VE GOT *SOMETHING* FOR ME.
NO TIME FOR PLEASANTRIES, EH?
GOOD TO SEE THAT YOUR BRUSH WITH DEATH HASN'T CHANGED YOU.
STEP ON INSIDE MY WORKSHOP.

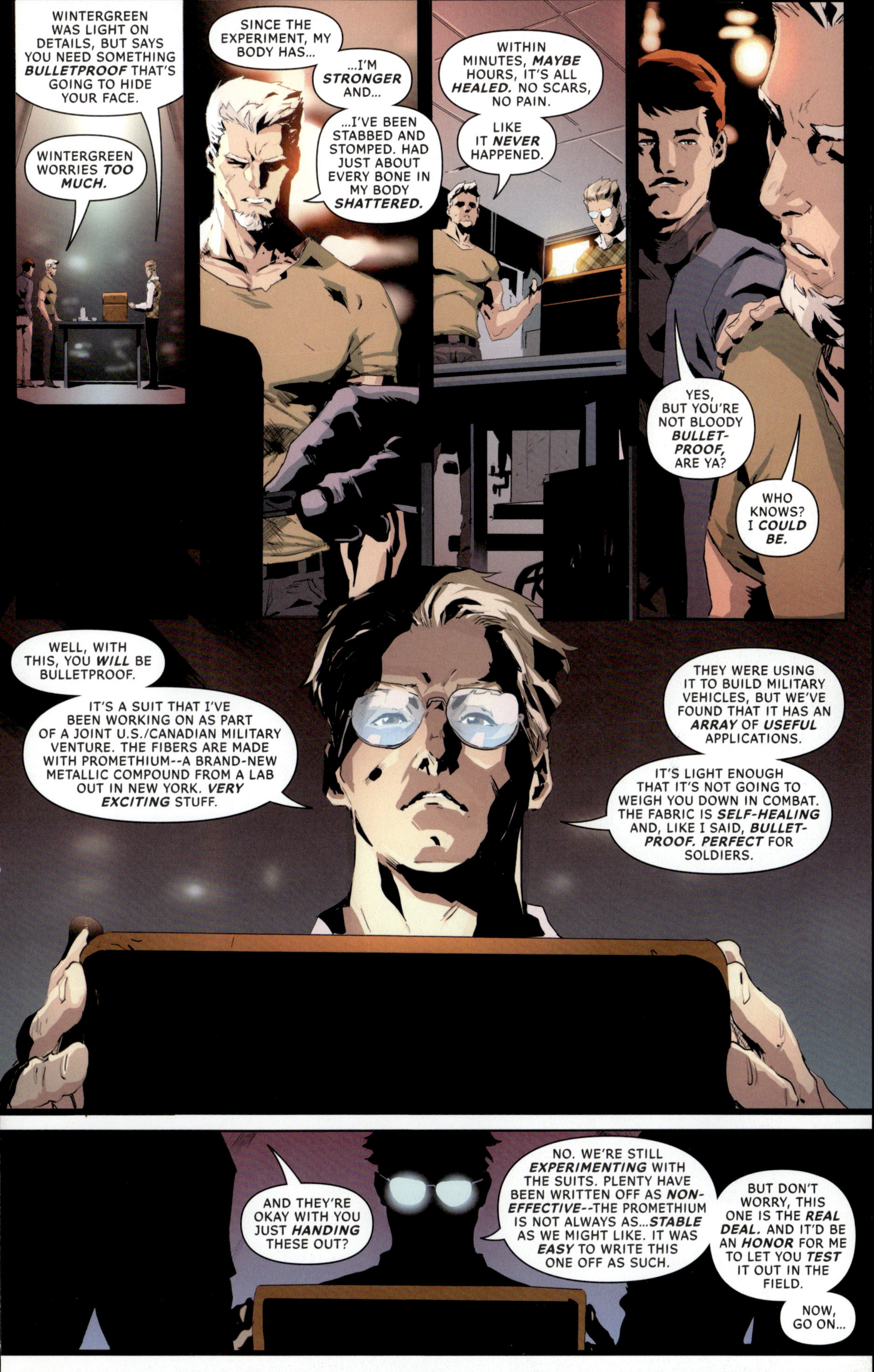
WINTERGREEN WAS LIGHT ON DETAILS, BUT SAYS YOU NEED SOMETHING BULLETPROOF THAT'S GOING TO HIDE YOUR FACE.
WINTERGREEN WORRIES TOO MUCH.
SINCE THE EXPERIMENT, MY BODY HAS...
...I'M STRONGER AND...
...I'VE BEEN STABBED AND STOMPED. HAD JUST ABOUT EVERY BONE IN MY BODY SHATTERED.
WITHIN MINUTES, MAYBE HOURS, IT'S ALL HEALED. NO SCARS, NO PAIN.
LIKE IT NEVER HAPPENED.
YES, BUT YOU'RE NOT BLOODY BULLET-PROOF, ARE YA?
WHO KNOWS? I COULD BE.
WELL, WITH THIS, YOU WILL BE BULLETPROOF.
IT'S A SUIT THAT I'VE BEEN WORKING ON AS PART OF A JOINT U.S./CANADIAN MILITARY VENTURE. THE FIBERS ARE MADE WITH PROMETHIUM--A BRAND-NEW METALLIC COMPOUND FROM A LAB OUT IN NEW YORK. VERY EXCITING STUFF.
THEY WERE USING IT TO BUILD MILITARY VEHICLES, BUT WE'VE FOUND THAT IT HAS AN ARRAY OF USEFUL APPLICATIONS.
IT'S LIGHT ENOUGH THAT IT'S NOT GOING TO WEIGH YOU DOWN IN COMBAT. THE FABRIC IS SELF-HEALING AND, LIKE I SAID, BULLET-PROOF. PERFECT FOR SOLDIERS.
AND THEY'RE OKAY WITH YOU JUST HANDING THESE OUT?
NO. WE'RE STILL EXPERIMENTING WITH THE SUITS. PLENTY HAVE BEEN WRITTEN OFF AS NON-EFFECTIVE--THE PROMETHIUM IS NOT ALWAYS AS...STABLE AS WE MIGHT LIKE. IT WAS EASY TO WRITE THIS ONE OFF AS SUCH.
BUT DON'T WORRY, THIS ONE IS THE REAL DEAL. AND IT'D BE AN HONOR FOR ME TO LET YOU TEST IT OUT IN THE FIELD.
NOW, GO ON...

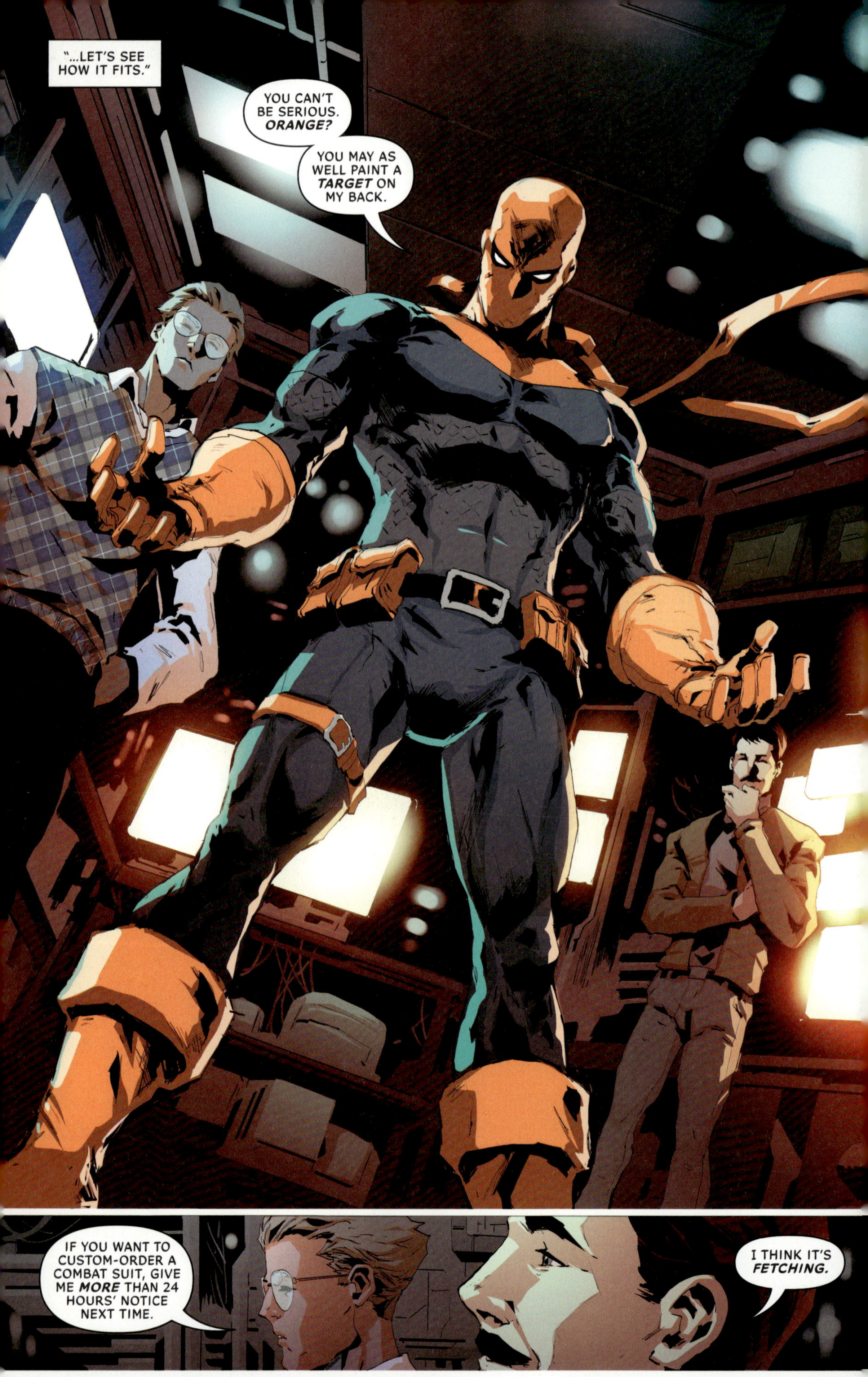
"...LET'S SEE HOW IT FITS."
YOU CAN'T BE SERIOUS. ORANGE?
YOU MAY AS WELL PAINT A TARGET ON MY BACK.
IF YOU WANT TO CUSTOM-ORDER A COMBAT SUIT, GIVE ME MORE THAN 24 HOURS' NOTICE NEXT TIME.
I THINK IT'S FETCHING.

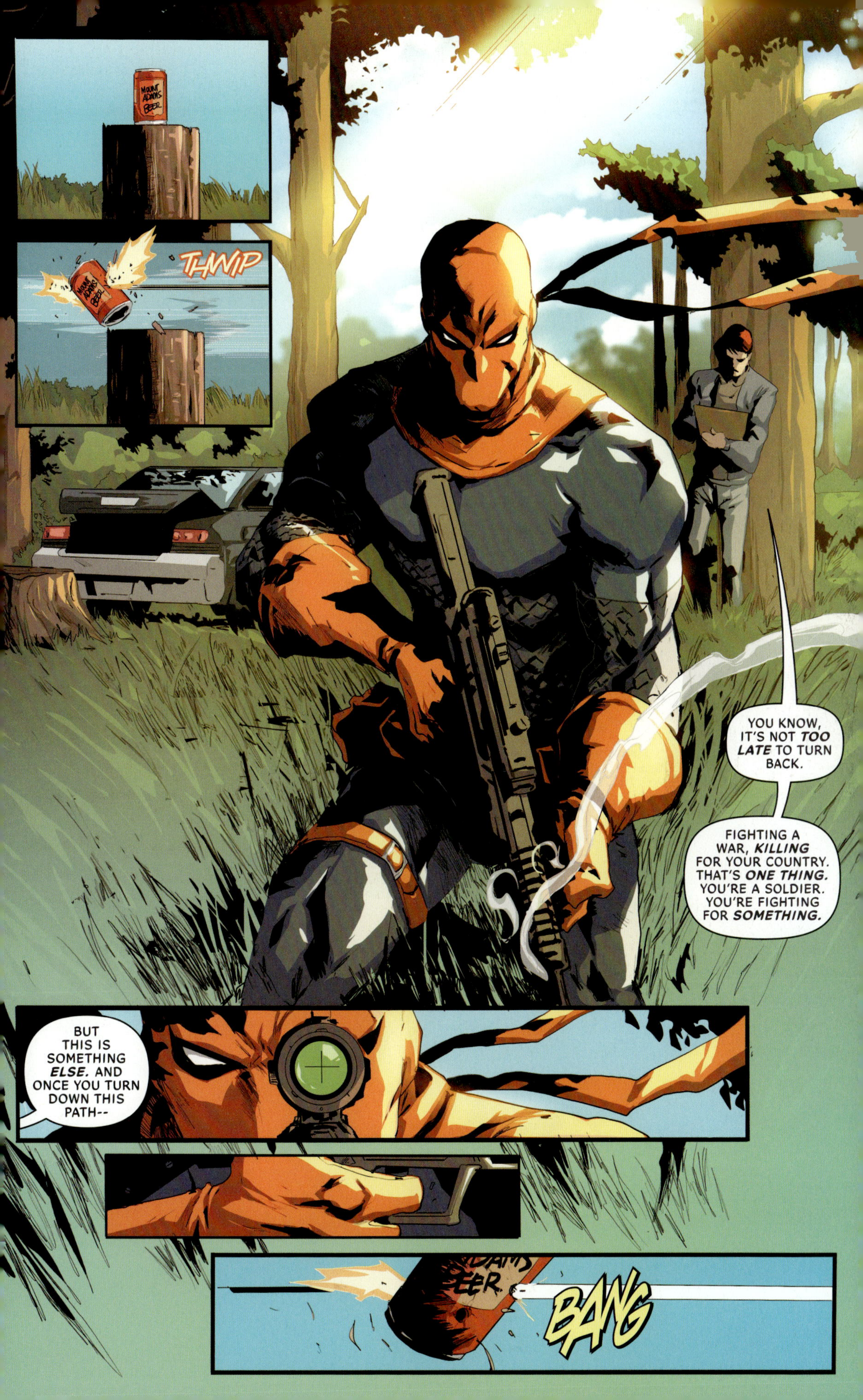
MOUNT ADAMS BEER
THWIP
MOUNT ADAMS BEER
YOU KNOW, IT'S NOT *TOO LATE* TO TURN BACK.
FIGHTING A WAR, *KILLING* FOR YOUR COUNTRY. THAT'S *ONE THING.* YOU'RE A SOLDIER. YOU'RE FIGHTING FOR *SOMETHING.*
BUT THIS IS SOMETHING *ELSE.* AND ONCE YOU TURN DOWN THIS PATH--
BANG

CAMPBELL EXPERIMENTED ON ME. HE LIED TO ME ABOUT WHAT IT WAS AND THAT LIE NEARLY KILLED ME.
ADELINE WOULD HAVE BEEN A WIDOW AND GRANT AN ORPHAN.
NEARLY. YOU SURVIVED. YOU STILL HAVE YOUR FAMILY. THEY STILL HAVE YOU.
47 OTHER SOLDIERS WEREN'T AS LUCKY. THEY NEVER GOT TO GO HOME TO THEIR FAMILIES.
NOW THAT SCUMBAG IS GOING TO NEGOTIATE HIMSELF A SWEETHEART DEAL AND NEVER HAVE TO SUFFER FOR WHAT HE DID.
YOU KNOW THAT IT'S GOING TO BE FEDERAL AGENTS PROTECTING HIM, RIGHT? SOME OF THEM EX-SOLDIERS.
YOU GOING TO FIND A WAY TO DO THIS WITHOUT HURTING THEM?
THEY KNOW WHAT THEY SIGNED UP FOR.
THEY'VE GOT A JOB TO DO...

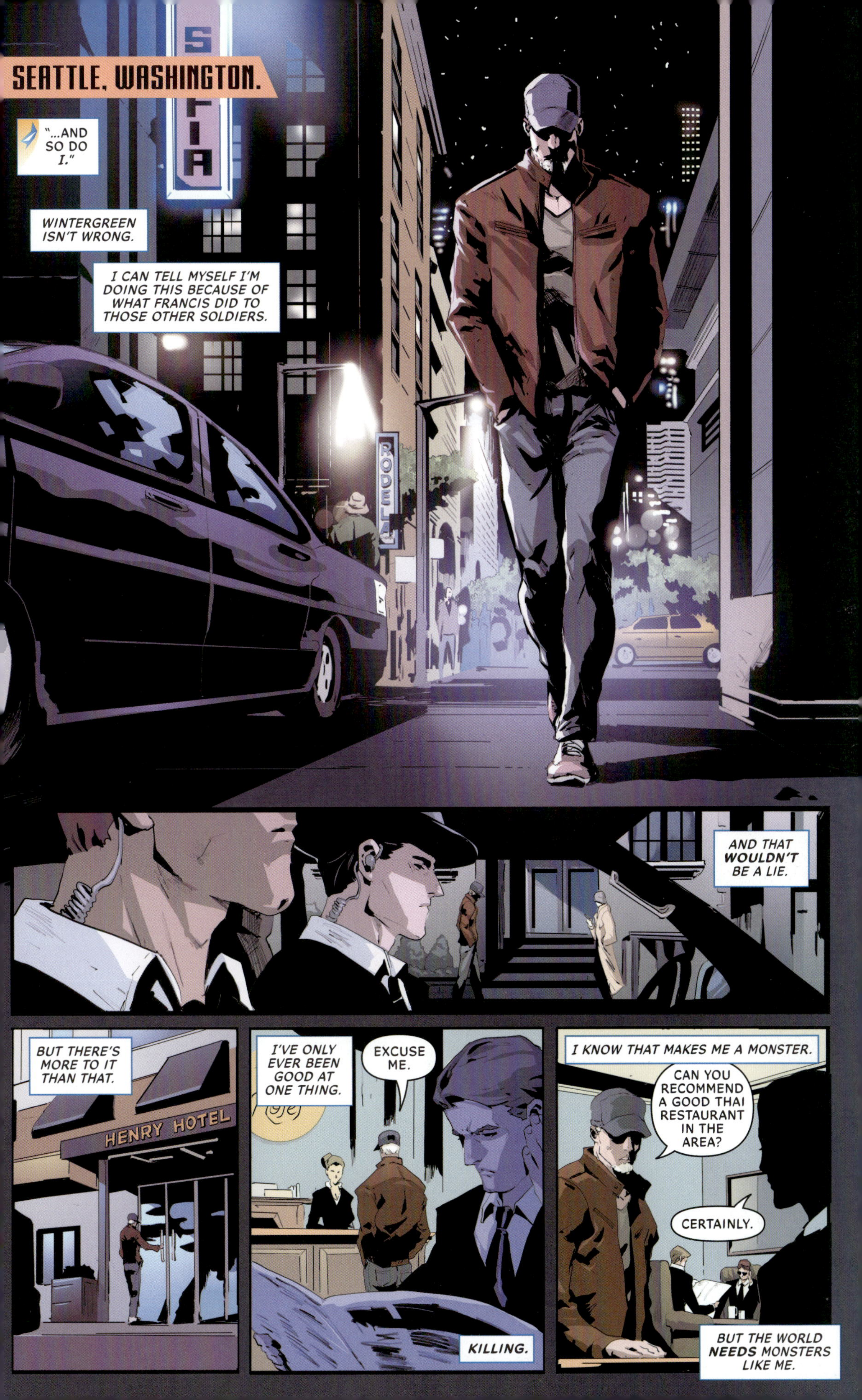
SEATTLE, WASHINGTON.
"...AND SO DO I."
WINTERGREEN ISN'T WRONG.
I CAN TELL MYSELF I'M DOING THIS BECAUSE OF WHAT FRANCIS DID TO THOSE OTHER SOLDIERS.
SOFIA
RODELA
AND THAT WOULDN'T BE A LIE.
BUT THERE'S MORE TO IT THAN THAT.
HENRY HOTEL
I'VE ONLY EVER BEEN GOOD AT ONE THING.
EXCUSE ME.
KILLING.
I KNOW THAT MAKES ME A MONSTER.
CAN YOU RECOMMEND A GOOD THAI RESTAURANT IN THE AREA?
CERTAINLY.
BUT THE WORLD NEEDS MONSTERS LIKE ME.

GROUND FLOOR PLAN
STREET
THEY'VE GOT EYES ALL OVER THE HOTEL.
GOING IN THE FRONT ISN'T AN OPTION.
AND IF THEY'VE GOT THIS MANY MEN OUT FRONT, THEN WE CAN ASSUME THAT THEY'VE GOT TWICE AS MANY INSIDE ON THE TARGET.
SO, HOW ARE YOU GOING TO DO THIS?
COULD ALWAYS POST UP NEARBY, SNIPE HIM. CLEAN AND EASY.
NO.
I WANT TO DO THIS CLOSE.

"I WANT HIM TO *KNOW* IT'S ME."
7th FLR.
DOORS ARE DONE.
CHARGES IN PLACE.
MAINTAINANCE
EXIT
OKAY. WE'RE GOOD.
TIME?
CHARGES ARE SET TO GO IN FIVE MINUTES AND...
EXIT
...37 SECONDS.
JUST ENOUGH TIME FOR ME TO GET INTO PLACE.
ARE YOU READY?

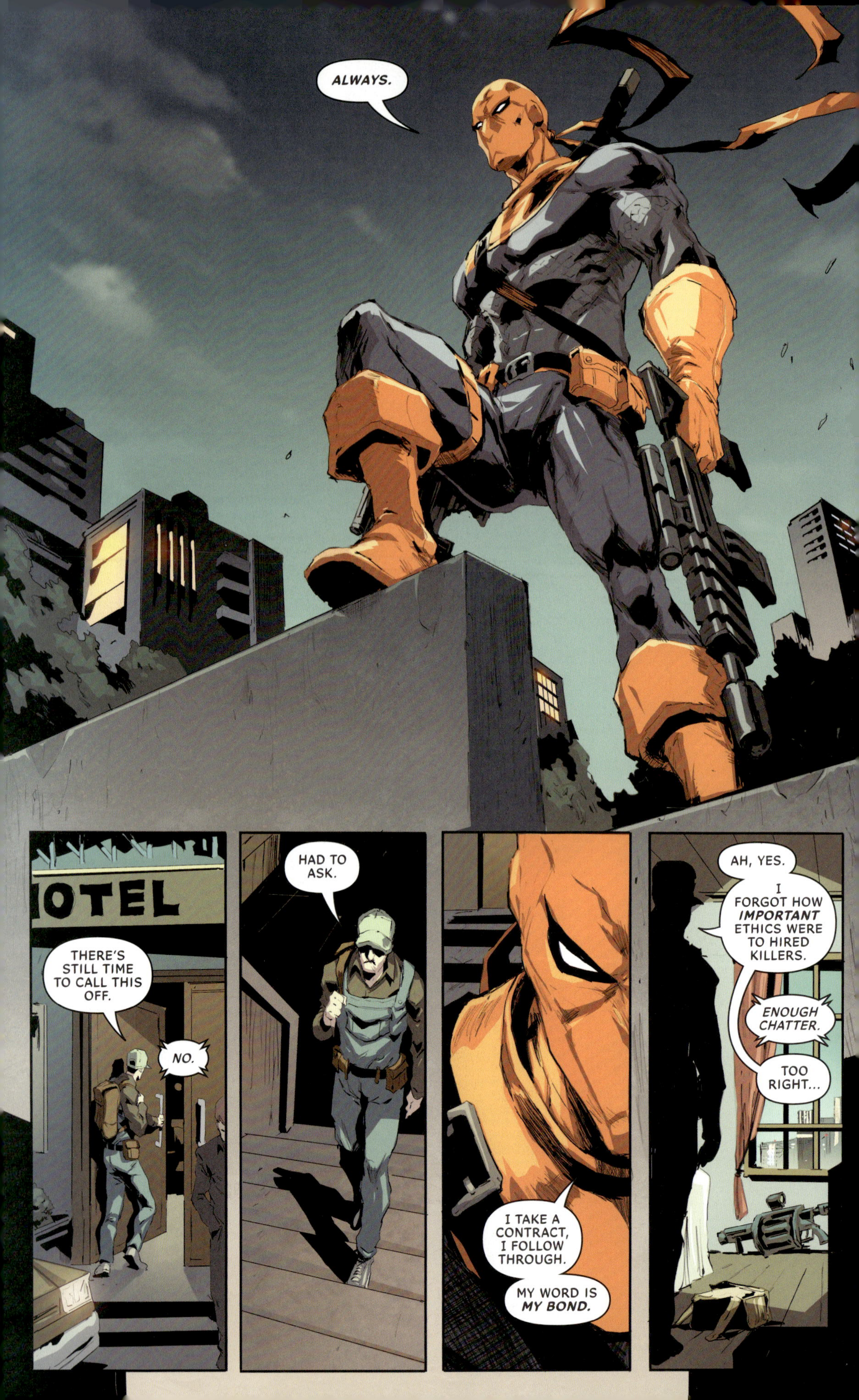
ALWAYS.
OTEL
THERE'S STILL TIME TO CALL THIS OFF.
NO.
HAD TO ASK.
I TAKE A CONTRACT, I FOLLOW THROUGH.
MY WORD IS *MY BOND.*
AH, YES.
I FORGOT HOW *IMPORTANT* ETHICS WERE TO HIRED KILLERS.
ENOUGH CHATTER.
TOO RIGHT...

"IT'S GO TIME."
00:01
WHOOM
THE HELL WAS THAT?!
Henry Hayes
GET ON THE DOORS! NO ONE IN OR OUT.
THIS IS AGENT NADLER.
POWER'S OUT. ELEVATORS WITH IT. DOORS FROM LOBBY HAVE BEEN LOCKED FROM INSIDE THE STAIRWELLS.
WE'RE STUCK ON THE GROUND FLOOR.

WHAT'S THE SITUATION UP THERE?
WE'RE SITTING IN THE DARK.
REST OF THE STREET IS STILL ON.
WH...WHAT'S HAPPENING?!
SEE IF THE HOTEL HAS A BACKUP GENERATOR. I WANT THAT POWER BACK ON STAT.
KEEP CAMPBELL AWAY FROM--
KRSSSH
PSSSSSSSSSSST
DAMMIT.
MOVE OUT! MOVE OUT!
ALL RIGHT, SLADE...

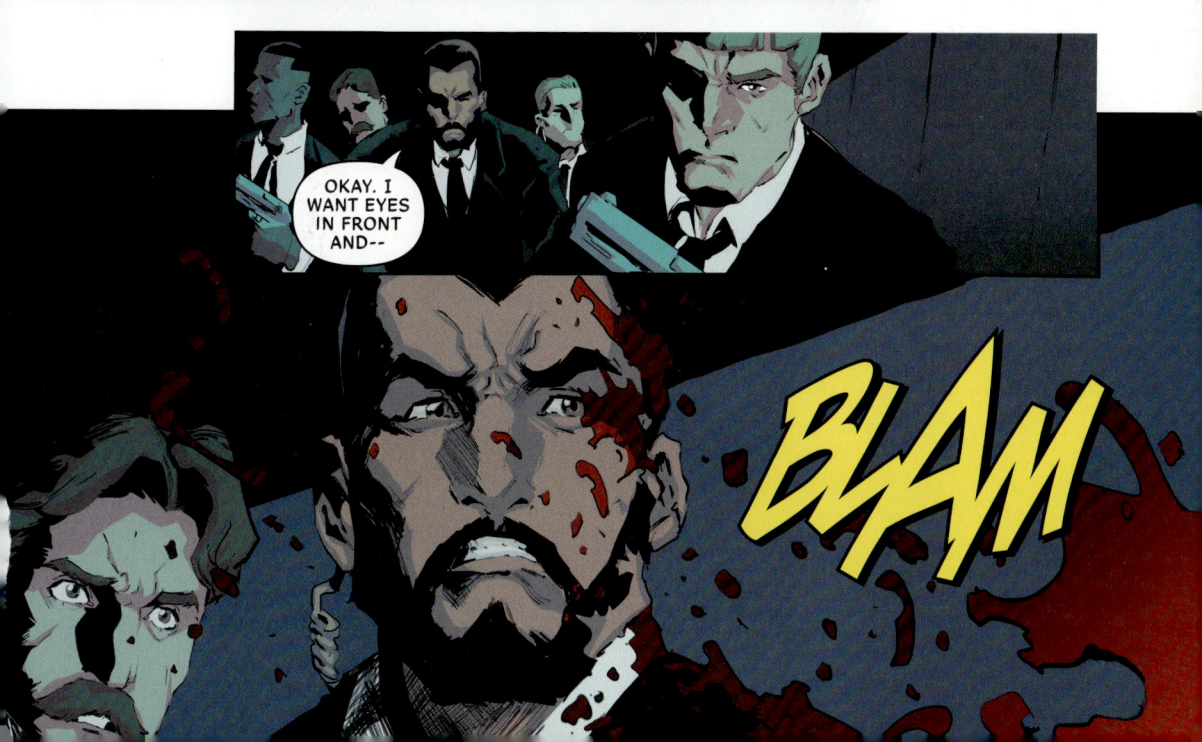

"...YOU'RE ON."

KEEP A TIGHT PERIMETER AROUND CAMPBELL.

WE ARE *NOT* LOSING HIM ON MY WATCH.

DAMMIT. *JAMMED!*

OVER HERE!

THIS ONE'S OPEN.

CLEAR.

OKAY. I WANT EYES IN FRONT AND--

BLAM

SNIPER!
MOVE! MOVE!
BLAM
BLAM
BLAMBLAM
BLAM
THIS IS AGENT JEDDRIE. WE ARE UNDER ATTACK IN THE WEST STAIRWELL, BETWEEN FLOORS SEVEN AND EIGHT.
TWO...
...THREE AGENTS DOWN.
NEED ASSISTANCE STAT!
BLAMBLAM

LOCKED!
8th FLR
KEEP MOVING!
WE NEED AN EXTRACTION ON THE ROOF.
BLAM
BLAM
BLAM
WHAT THE--
BOOOM
HEAD TO THE ROOF.

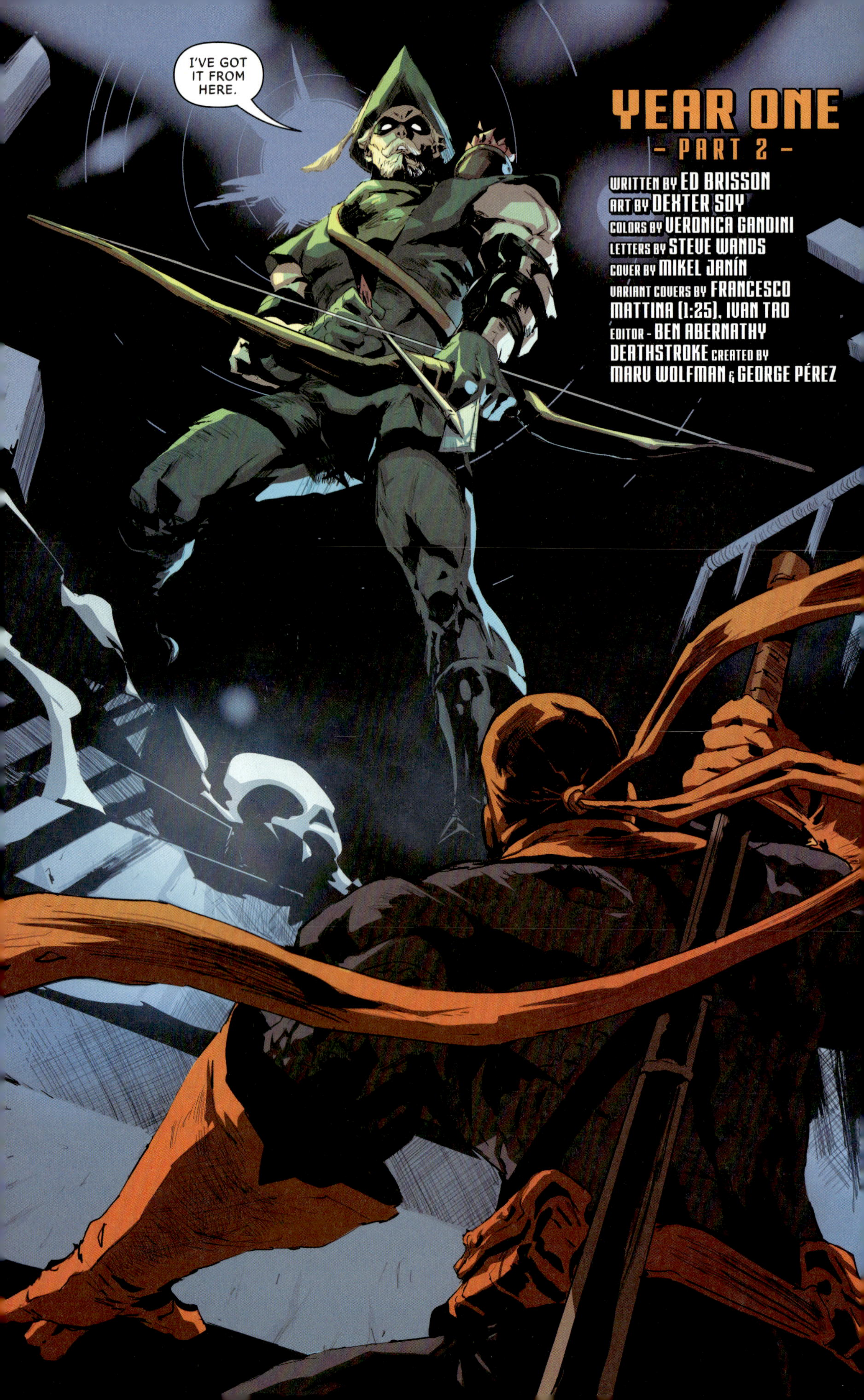
I'VE GOT IT FROM HERE.
YEAR ONE
- PART 2 -
WRITTEN BY ED BRISSON
ART BY DEXTER SOY
COLORS BY VERONICA GANDINI
LETTERS BY STEVE WANDS
COVER BY MIKEL JANÍN
VARIANT COVERS BY FRANCESCO MATTINA (1:25), IVAN TAO
EDITOR - BEN ABERNATHY
DEATHSTROKE CREATED BY MARV WOLFMAN & GEORGE PÉREZ

DEATHSTROKE INC. #12
cover art by MIKEL JANÍN

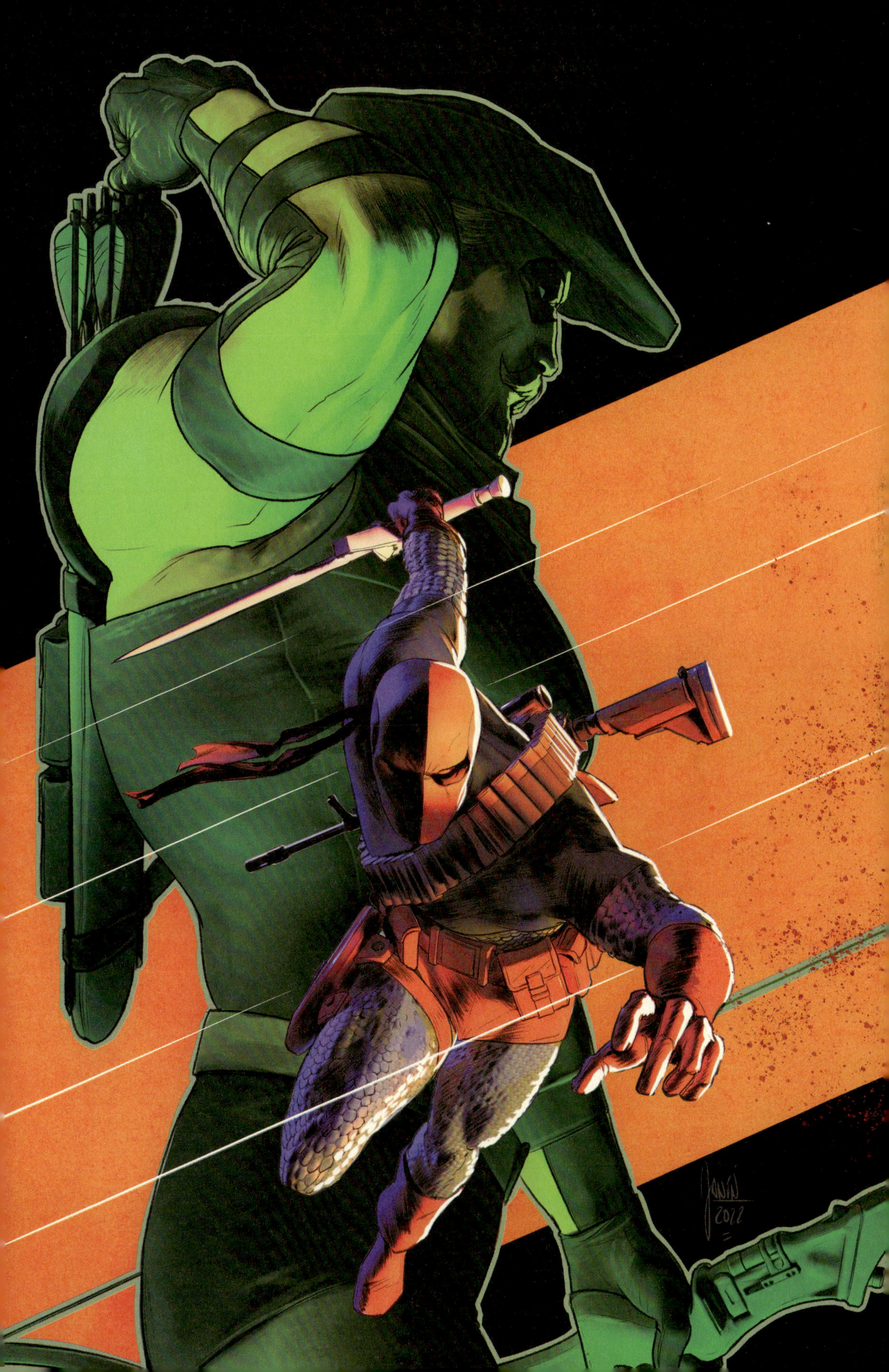

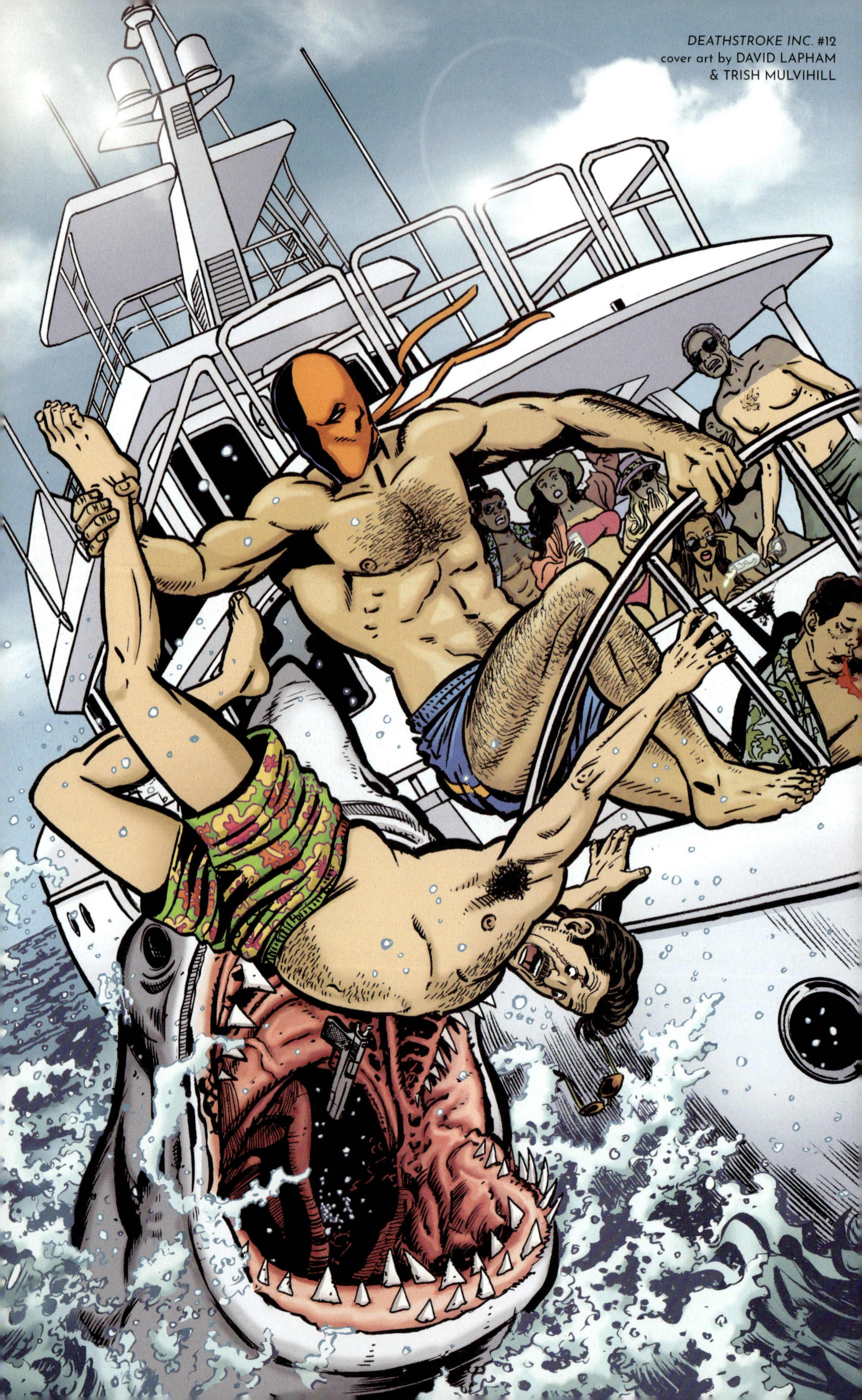

DEATHSTROKE INC. #12
cover art by DAVID LAPHAM
& TRISH MULVIHILL

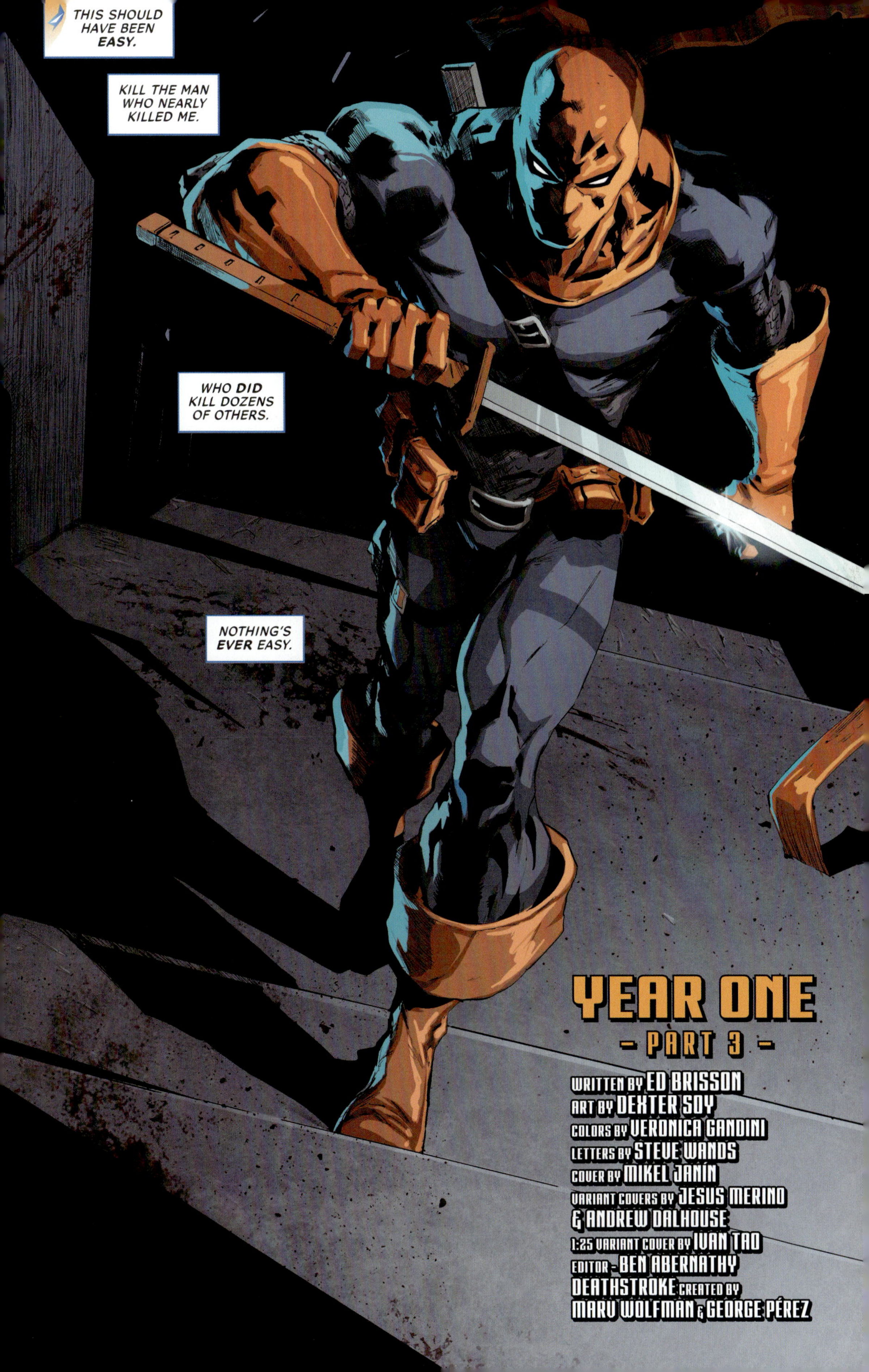
THIS SHOULD HAVE BEEN EASY.
KILL THE MAN WHO NEARLY KILLED ME.
WHO DID KILL DOZENS OF OTHERS.
NOTHING'S EVER EASY.
YEAR ONE
- PART 3 -
WRITTEN BY ED BRISSON
ART BY DEXTER SOY
COLORS BY VERONICA GANDINI
LETTERS BY STEVE WANDS
COVER BY MIKEL JANÍN
VARIANT COVERS BY JESUS MERINO & ANDREW DALHOUSE
1:25 VARIANT COVER BY IVAN TAO
EDITOR - BEN ABERNATHY
DEATHSTROKE CREATED BY MARV WOLFMAN & GEORGE PÉREZ

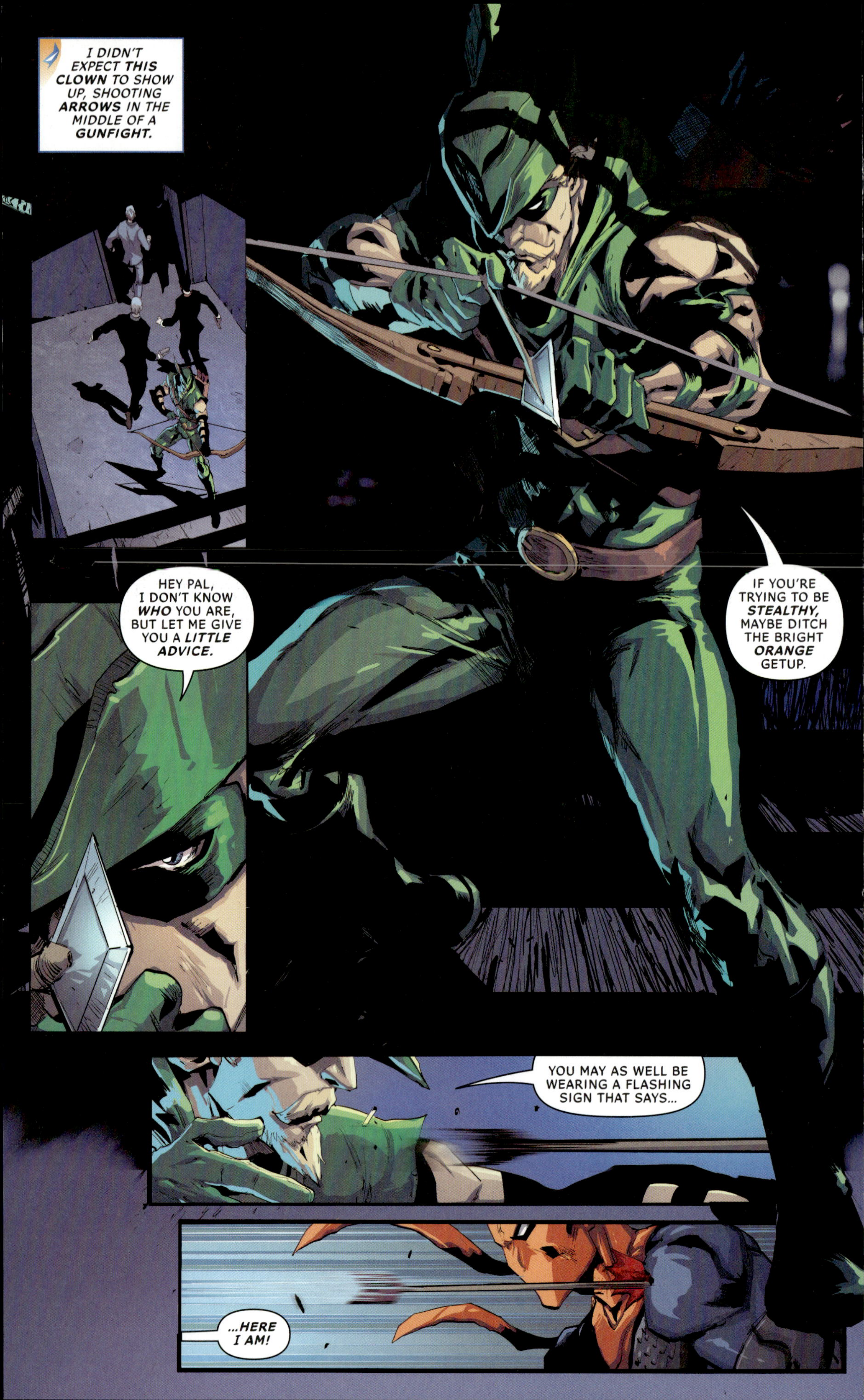
I DIDN'T EXPECT THIS CLOWN TO SHOW UP, SHOOTING ARROWS IN THE MIDDLE OF A GUNFIGHT.
HEY PAL, I DON'T KNOW WHO YOU ARE, BUT LET ME GIVE YOU A LITTLE ADVICE.
IF YOU'RE TRYING TO BE STEALTHY, MAYBE DITCH THE BRIGHT ORANGE GETUP.
YOU MAY AS WELL BE WEARING A FLASHING SIGN THAT SAYS...
...HERE I AM!

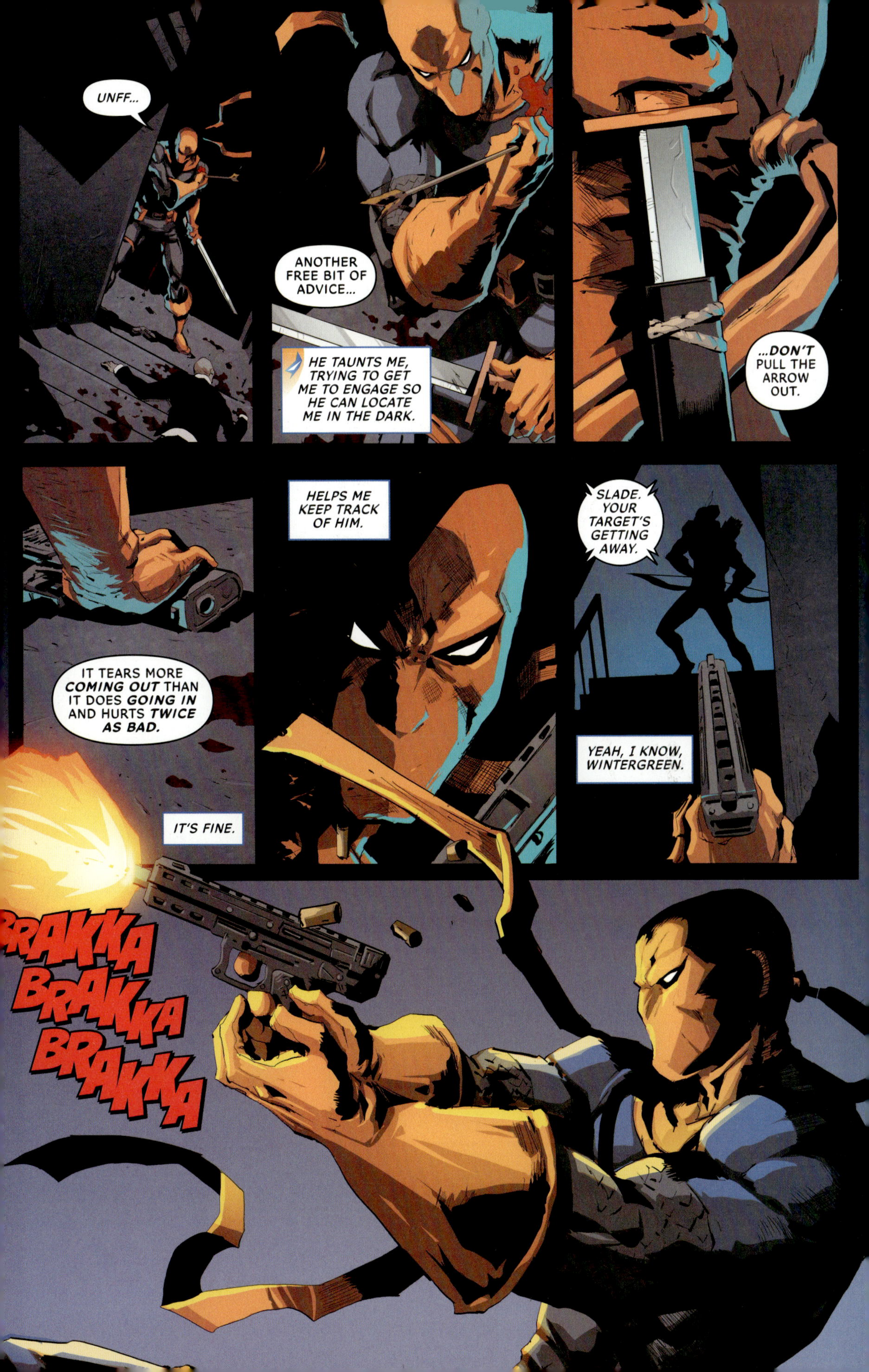
UNFF...
ANOTHER FREE BIT OF ADVICE...
HE TAUNTS ME, TRYING TO GET ME TO ENGAGE SO HE CAN LOCATE ME IN THE DARK.
...DON'T PULL THE ARROW OUT.
IT TEARS MORE COMING OUT THAN IT DOES GOING IN AND HURTS TWICE AS BAD.
IT'S FINE.
HELPS ME KEEP TRACK OF HIM.
SLADE. YOUR TARGET'S GETTING AWAY.
YEAH, I KNOW, WINTERGREEN.
BRAKKA BRAKKA BRAKKA

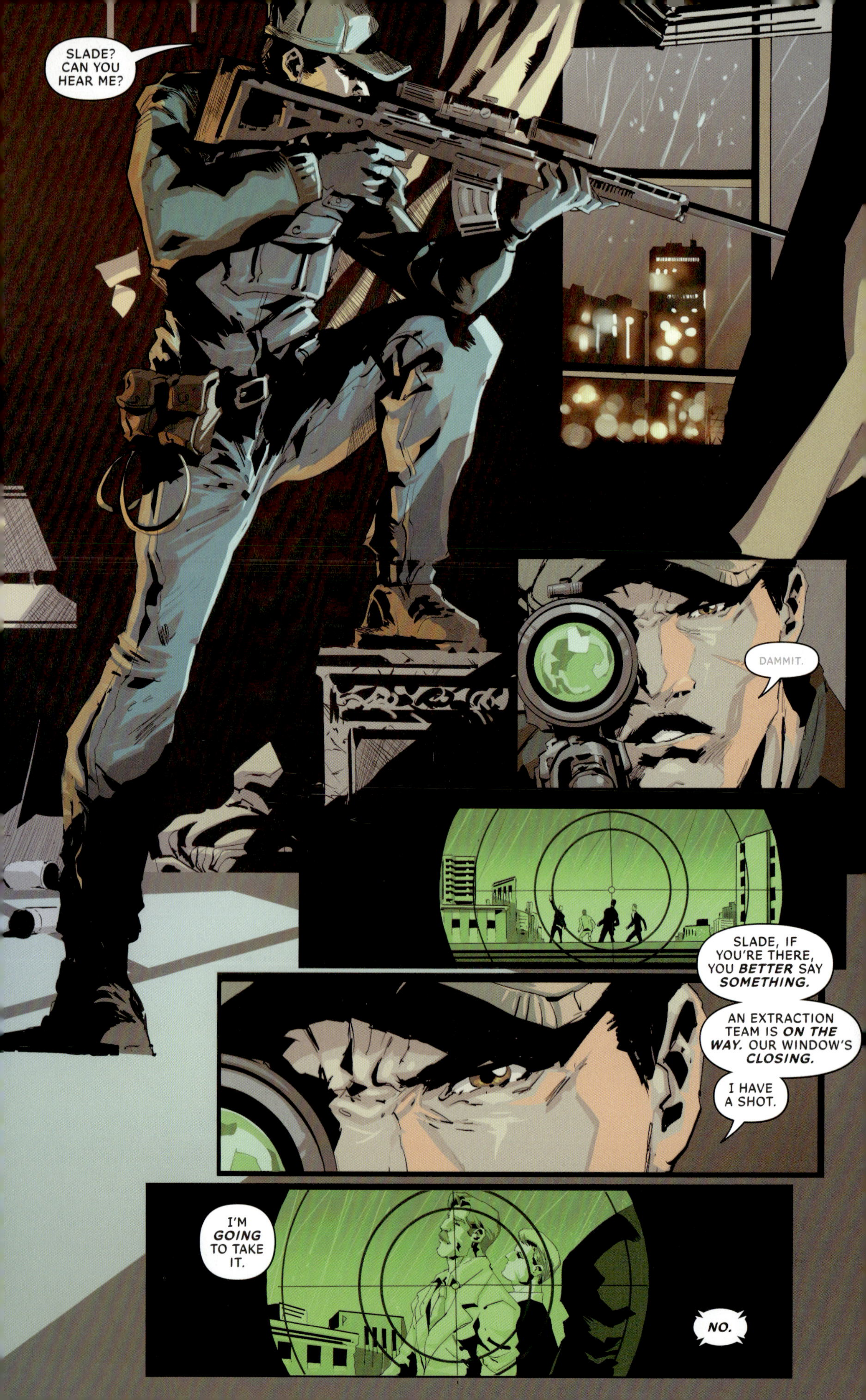
SLADE? CAN YOU HEAR ME?
DAMMIT.
SLADE, IF YOU'RE THERE, YOU **BETTER** SAY **SOMETHING.**
AN EXTRACTION TEAM IS **ON THE WAY.** OUR WINDOW'S **CLOSING.**
I HAVE A SHOT.
I'M **GOING** TO TAKE IT.
NO.

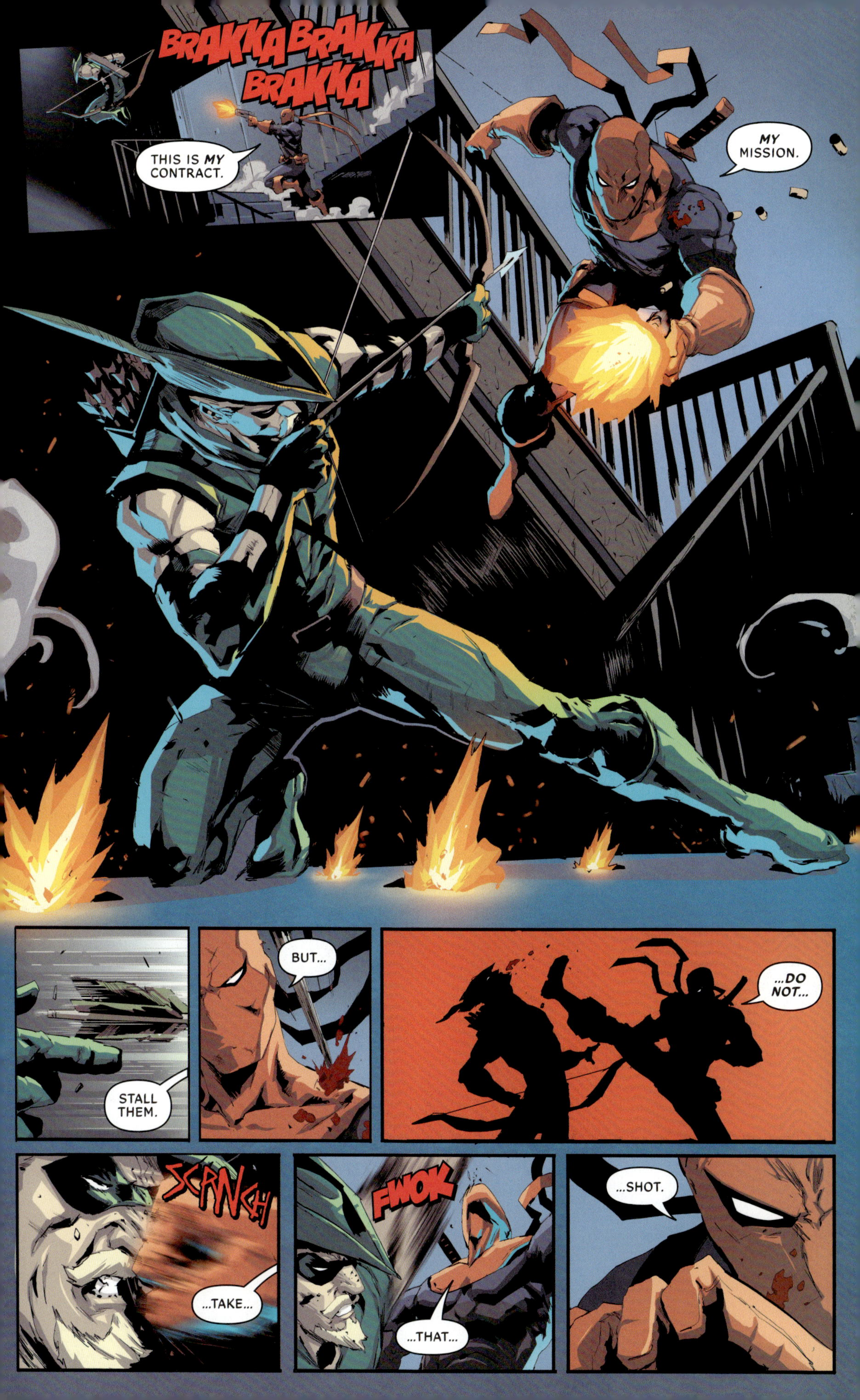

BRAKKA BRAKKA BRAKKA
THIS IS MY CONTRACT.
MY MISSION.
STALL THEM.
BUT...
...DO NOT...
SCRNCH
...TAKE...
FWOK
...THAT...
...SHOT.

I DON'T KNOW WHO YOU ARE, YOU ROBIN HOOD-LOOKING **SON OF A %!$@#...**
...BUT YOU'RE IN ***WAY*** OVER YOUR HEAD.
BOWS AND ARROWS? THIS ISN'T A REN FAIRE.
BLAM
I'M ***GREEN ARROW.***
AND THIS CITY IS UNDER MY PROTEC--
FWUMP
IF ***YOU'RE*** WHAT THIS CITY HAS FOR PROTECTION...
...THEN THIS CITY IS ***$#&!.***
BLAM
BLAM
BLAM

YOU SAID...YOU SAID I'D BE SAFE. THAT NO ONE WOULD KNOW WHERE I WAS. YOU SAID IT. YOU PROMISED IT. YOU--
I JUST LOST A LOT OF GOOD MEN TRYING TO KEEP YOU SAFE, CAMPBELL.
MEN WITH FAMILIES. WITH PEOPLE WHO LOVED THEM.
SO PUT A %$&# CORK IN IT WHILE WE GET YOUR SORRY ASS OUT OF--
BLAM
NO MORE RUNNING.
THIS IS WHERE YOU DIE, CAMPBELL.

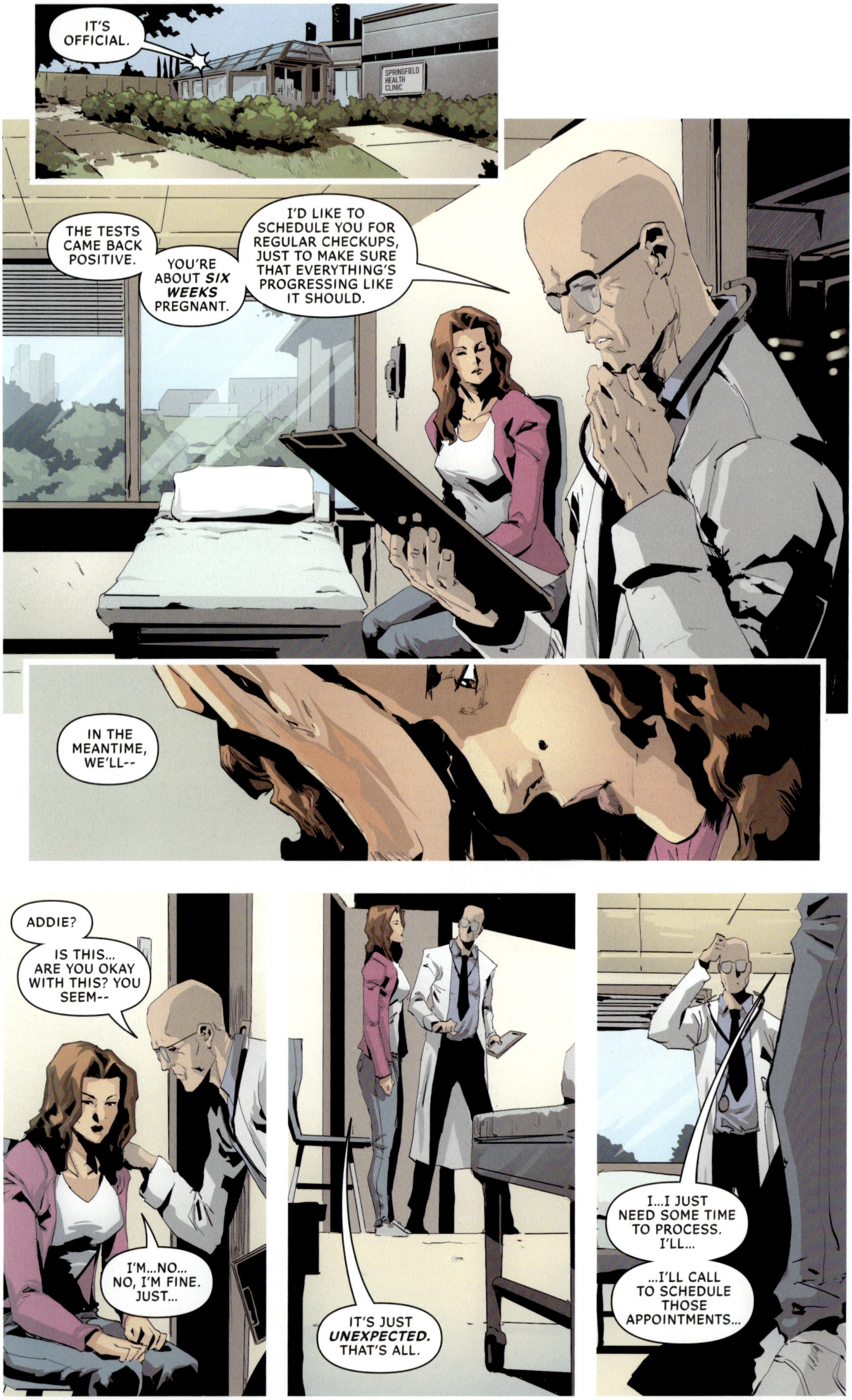
IT'S OFFICIAL.
SPRINGFIELD HEALTH CLINIC
THE TESTS CAME BACK POSITIVE.
YOU'RE ABOUT **SIX WEEKS** PREGNANT.
I'D LIKE TO SCHEDULE YOU FOR REGULAR CHECKUPS, JUST TO MAKE SURE THAT EVERYTHING'S PROGRESSING LIKE IT SHOULD.
IN THE MEANTIME, WE'LL--
ADDIE?
IS THIS... ARE YOU OKAY WITH THIS? YOU SEEM--
I'M...NO... NO, I'M FINE. JUST...
IT'S JUST **UNEXPECTED.** THAT'S ALL.
I...I JUST NEED SOME TIME TO PROCESS. I'LL...
...I'LL CALL TO SCHEDULE THOSE APPOINTMENTS...

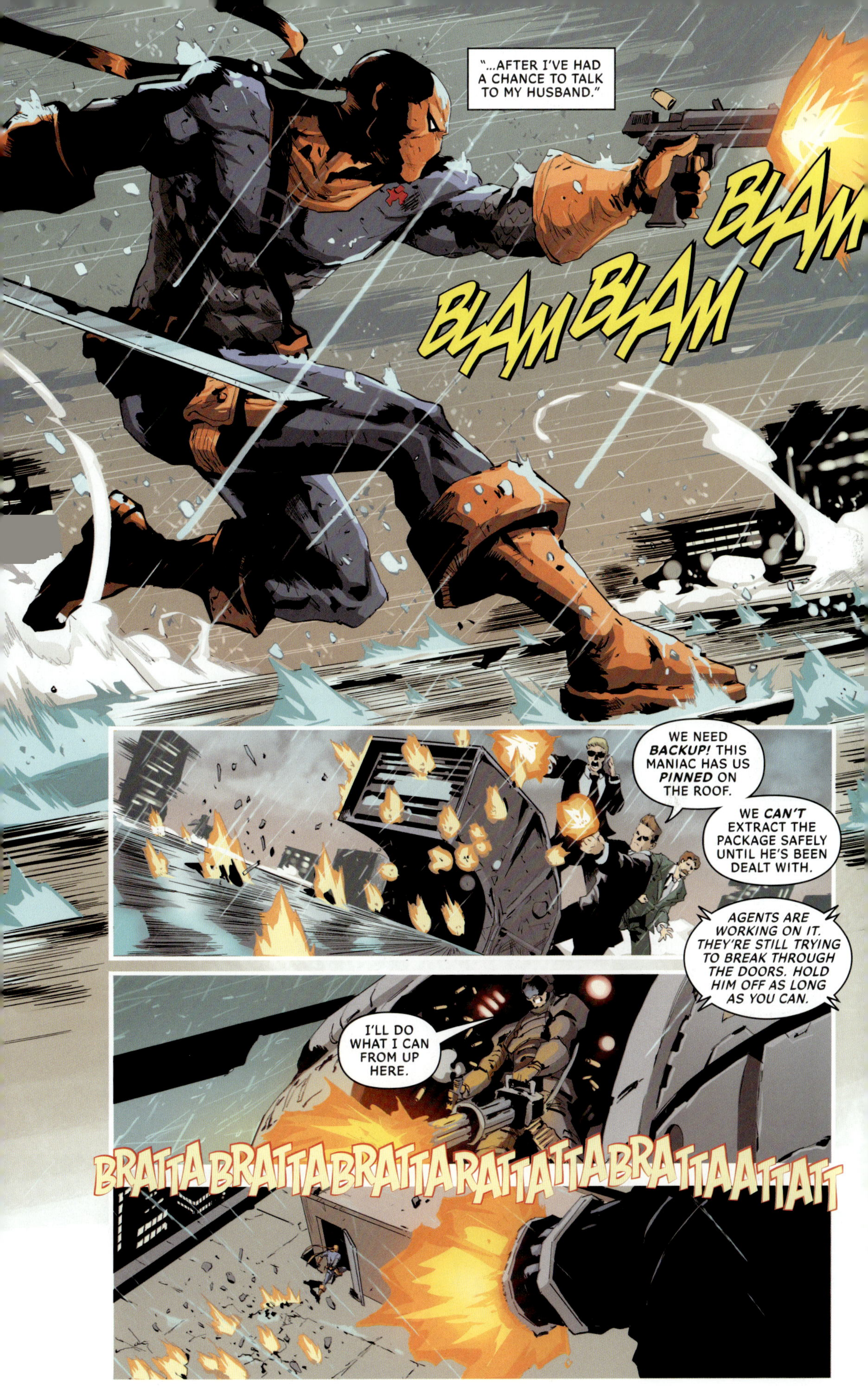
"...AFTER I'VE HAD A CHANCE TO TALK TO MY HUSBAND."
BLAM BLAM BLAM
WE NEED BACKUP! THIS MANIAC HAS US PINNED ON THE ROOF.
WE CAN'T EXTRACT THE PACKAGE SAFELY UNTIL HE'S BEEN DEALT WITH.
AGENTS ARE WORKING ON IT. THEY'RE STILL TRYING TO BREAK THROUGH THE DOORS. HOLD HIM OFF AS LONG AS YOU CAN.
I'LL DO WHAT I CAN FROM UP HERE.
BRATTABRATTABRATTARATTATTABRATTAATTATT

"WINTERGREEN..."

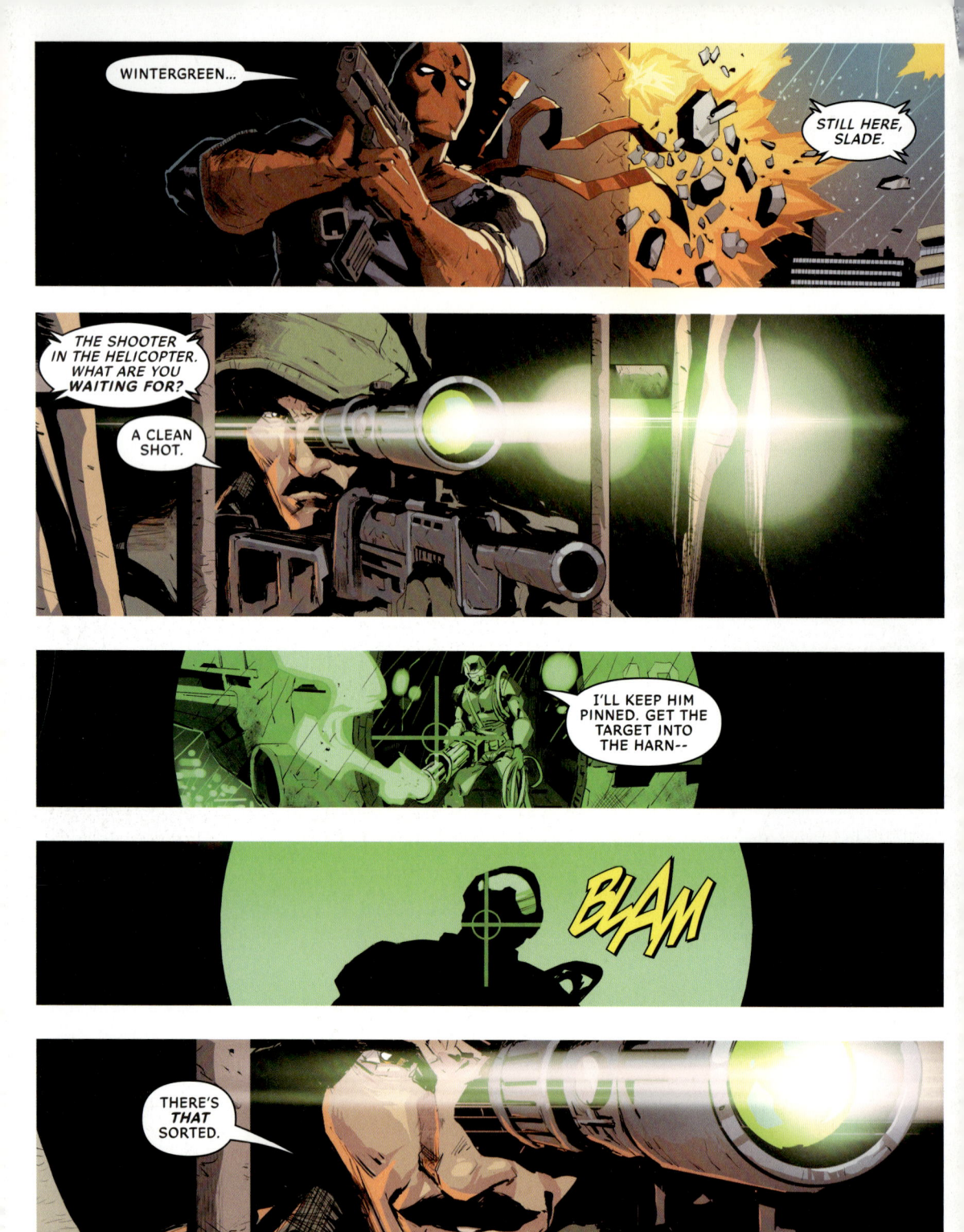

"STILL HERE, SLADE."

"THE SHOOTER IN THE HELICOPTER. WHAT ARE YOU WAITING FOR?"

"A CLEAN SHOT."

"I'LL KEEP HIM PINNED. GET THE TARGET INTO THE HARN--"

BLAM

"THERE'S *THAT* SORTED."

FWAK

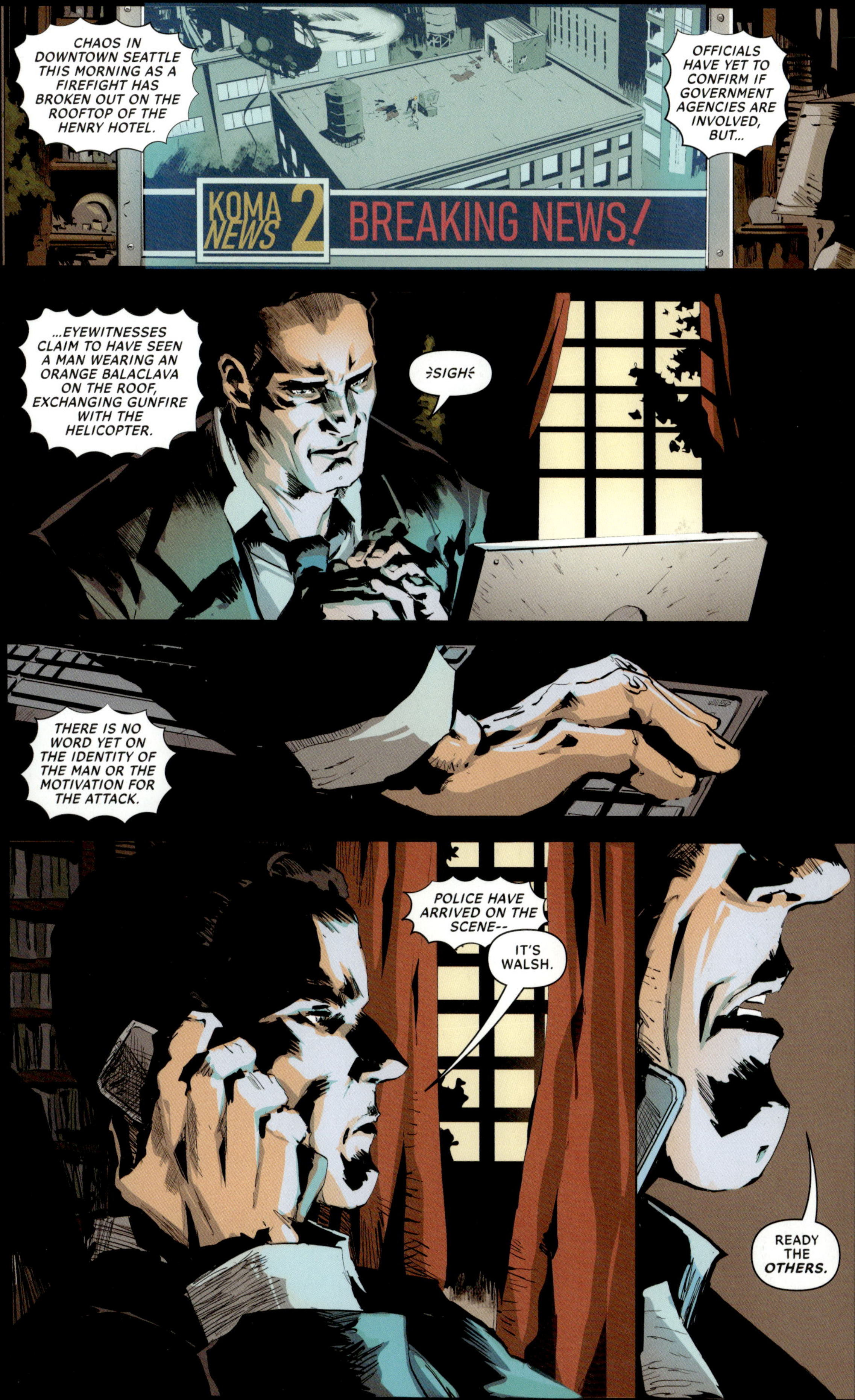
CHAOS IN DOWNTOWN SEATTLE THIS MORNING AS A FIREFIGHT HAS BROKEN OUT ON THE ROOFTOP OF THE HENRY HOTEL.
KOMA NEWS 2
BREAKING NEWS!
OFFICIALS HAVE YET TO CONFIRM IF GOVERNMENT AGENCIES ARE INVOLVED, BUT...
...EYEWITNESSES CLAIM TO HAVE SEEN A MAN WEARING AN ORANGE BALACLAVA ON THE ROOF, EXCHANGING GUNFIRE WITH THE HELICOPTER.
SIGH
THERE IS NO WORD YET ON THE IDENTITY OF THE MAN OR THE MOTIVATION FOR THE ATTACK.
POLICE HAVE ARRIVED ON THE SCENE--
IT'S WALSH.
READY THE OTHERS.

"SLADE HAS FAILED."
BLAM BLAM BLAM
HE'S GOING TO KILL ME. YOU HAVE TO GET ME OUT OF THIS THING!
SHUT UP, YOU WHINY LITTLE $#&@. I SWEAR TO GOD, I'LL KILL YOU MYSELF IF YOU DON'T.
YOU GET ONE CHANCE TO WALK AWAY FROM THIS.
STEP AWAY FROM DR. CAMPBELL AND--
FWUNK

HURRY, GET HIM OUT OF HERE WHILE I--
KRAKK
KRNNCH
YOU'VE GOT **STONES,** KID...I'LL GIVE YOU THAT. BUT **ENOUGH'S ENOUGH.**
LIKE I TOLD YOU.
KRAK
THIS CITY...
...IS UNDER...
...**MY** PROTECTION.

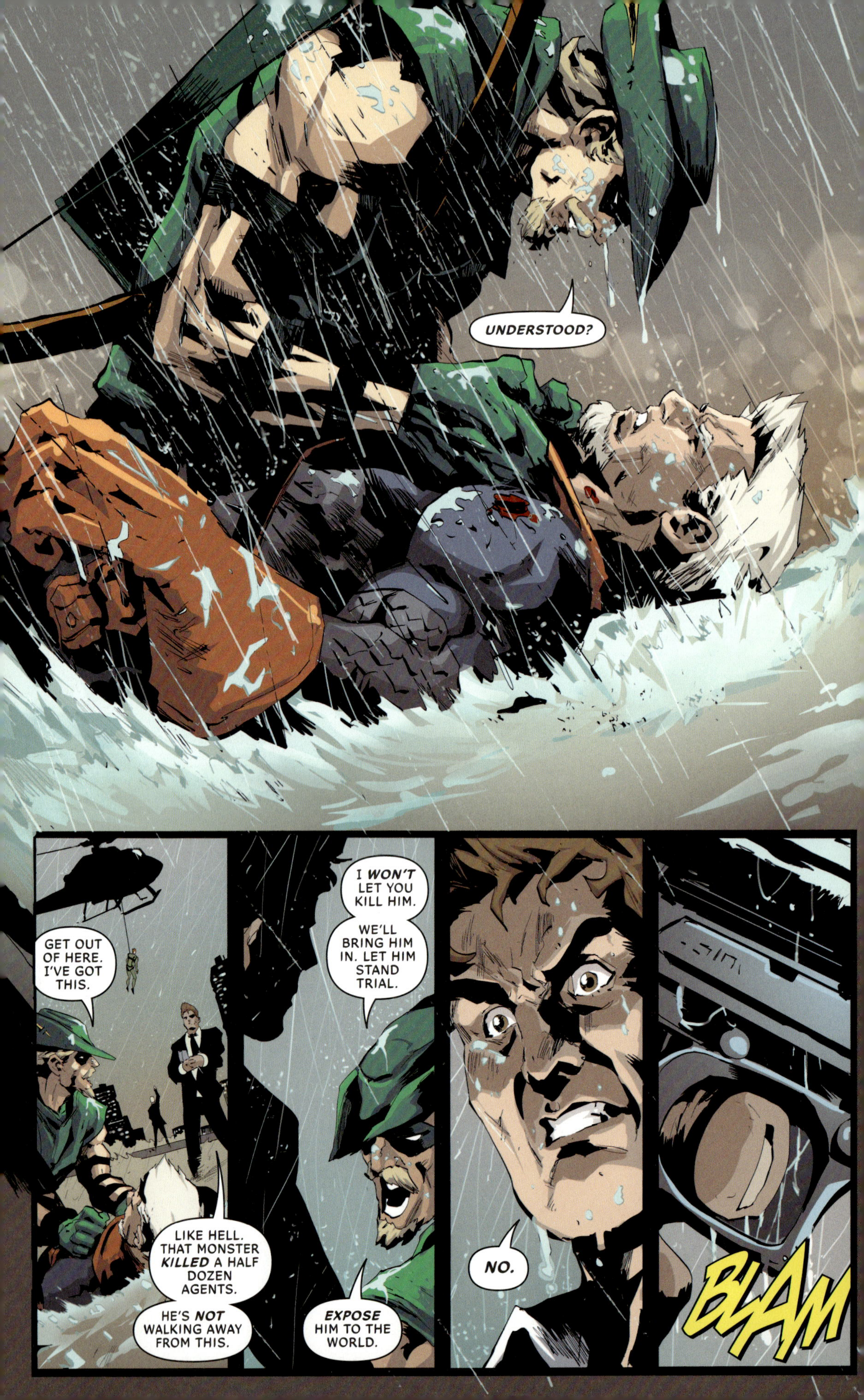
UNDERSTOOD?
GET OUT OF HERE. I'VE GOT THIS.
LIKE HELL. THAT MONSTER KILLED A HALF DOZEN AGENTS.
HE'S NOT WALKING AWAY FROM THIS.
I WON'T LET YOU KILL HIM.
WE'LL BRING HIM IN. LET HIM STAND TRIAL.
EXPOSE HIM TO THE WORLD.
NO.
BLAM

YOU'RE WELCOME, SLADE. THAT'S TWICE I'VE PULLED YOUR FAT FROM THE FIRE THIS MORNING.
IF YOU'RE KEEPING TRACK.
YOU'RE NOT ALONE.
THAT'S OKAY, YOU CAN BOTH STAND TRIAL.
WINTERGREEN, GET OUT OF THERE.
BUT--
NOW!
UNFFF...
MY KNEE IS TAKING IT'S SWEET TIME TO HEAL. CAN'T PUT ANY WEIGHT ON IT.
DON'T.
MOVE.
I'M DEAD IN THE WATER HERE.
ALL RIGHT.

HOTEL
Lenox
ENRY HOTEL
BZZT
BZZT
BZZT
ADDIE
BZZ--
IS HE WITH YOU?
NO "HOW ARE YOU, MY DEAR WINTERGREEN"?
ADDIE! TO WHAT DO I OWE THE PLEASURE?
WINTERGREEN. I'VE BEEN TRYING TO GET AHOLD OF SLADE.
IT'S *IMPORTANT.*
IT *ALWAYS* IS.
HE'S NOT WITH ME RIGHT NOW, NO. I'M AFRAID...

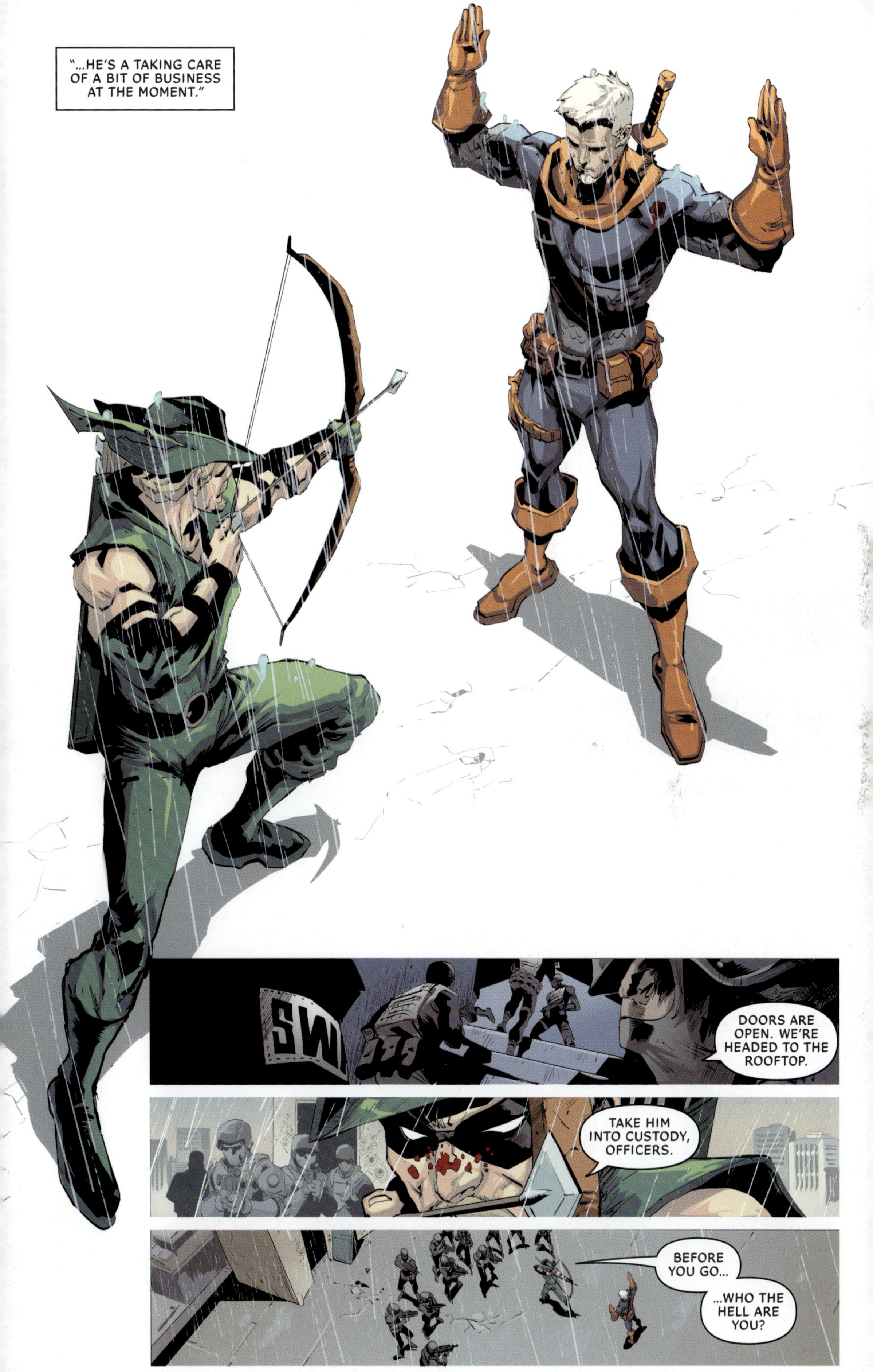
"...HE'S A TAKING CARE OF A BIT OF BUSINESS AT THE MOMENT."
DOORS ARE OPEN. WE'RE HEADED TO THE ROOFTOP.
TAKE HIM INTO CUSTODY, OFFICERS.
BEFORE YOU GO...
...WHO THE HELL ARE YOU?

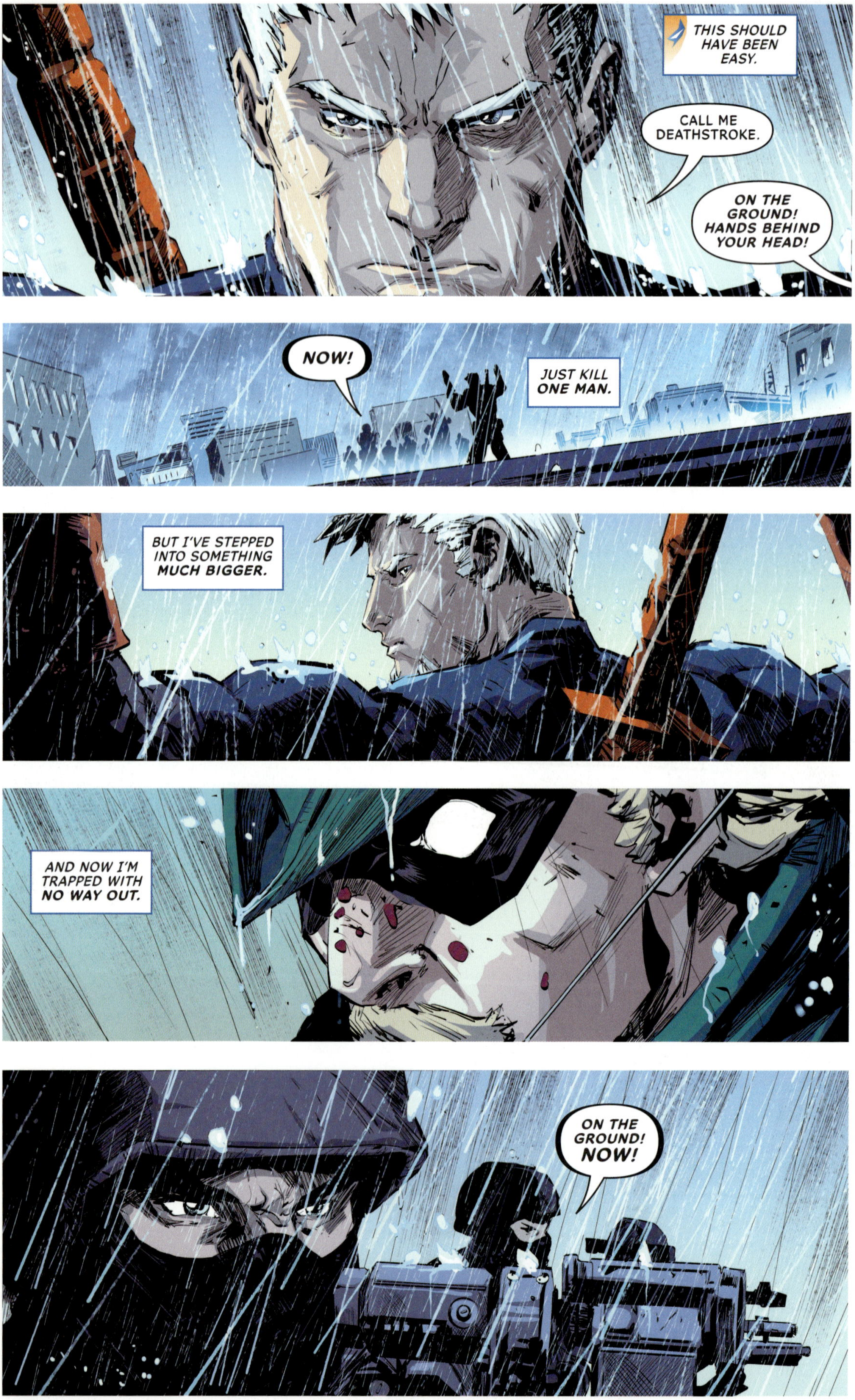
THIS SHOULD HAVE BEEN EASY.
CALL ME DEATHSTROKE.
ON THE GROUND! HANDS BEHIND YOUR HEAD!
NOW!
JUST KILL ONE MAN.
BUT I'VE STEPPED INTO SOMETHING MUCH BIGGER.
AND NOW I'M TRAPPED WITH NO WAY OUT.
ON THE GROUND! NOW!

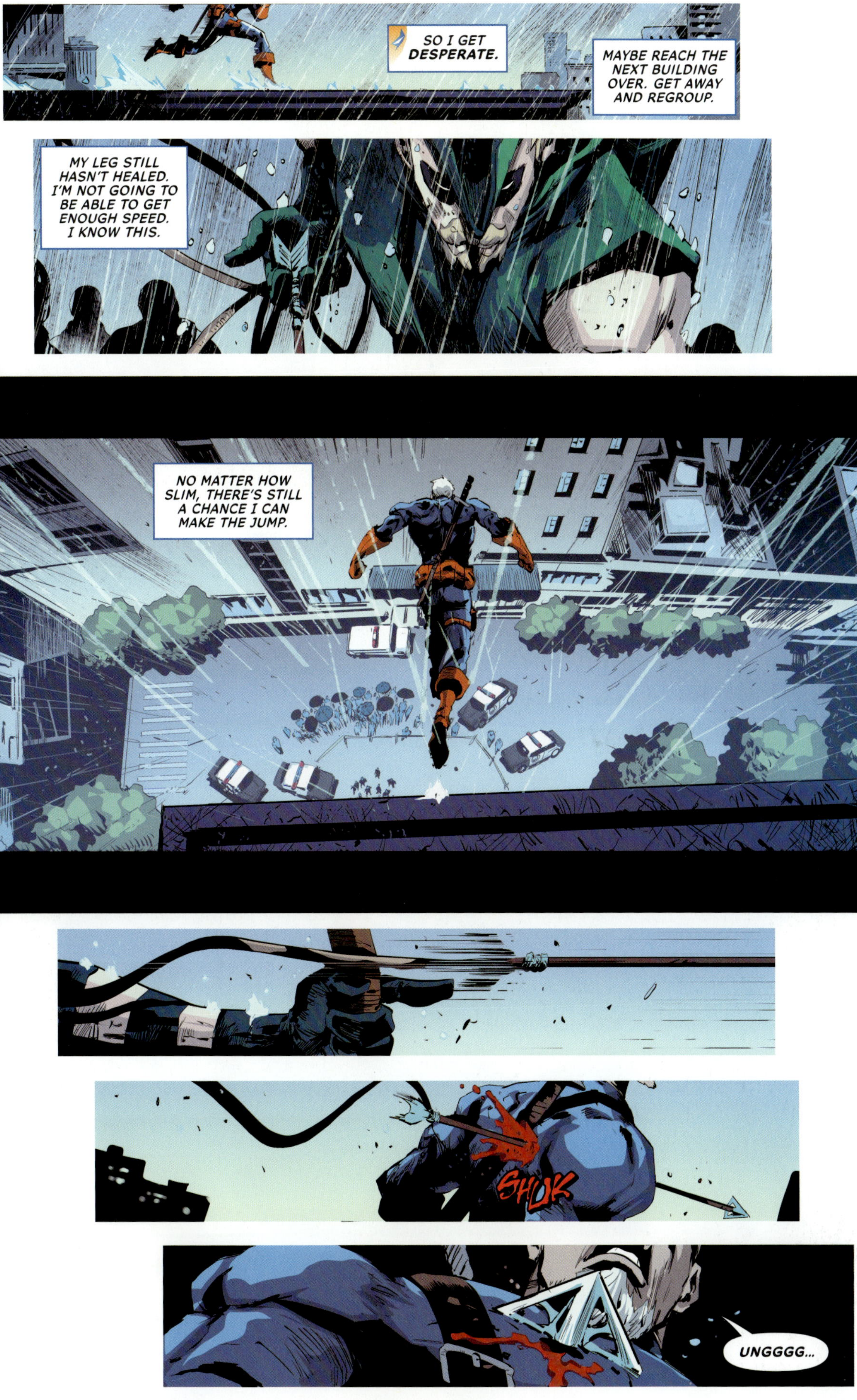
SO I GET **DESPERATE.**
MAYBE REACH THE NEXT BUILDING OVER. GET AWAY AND REGROUP.
MY LEG STILL HASN'T HEALED. I'M NOT GOING TO BE ABLE TO GET ENOUGH SPEED. I KNOW THIS.
NO MATTER HOW SLIM, THERE'S STILL A CHANCE I CAN MAKE THE JUMP.
SHUK
UNGGGG...

THIS KID'S PRECISE.

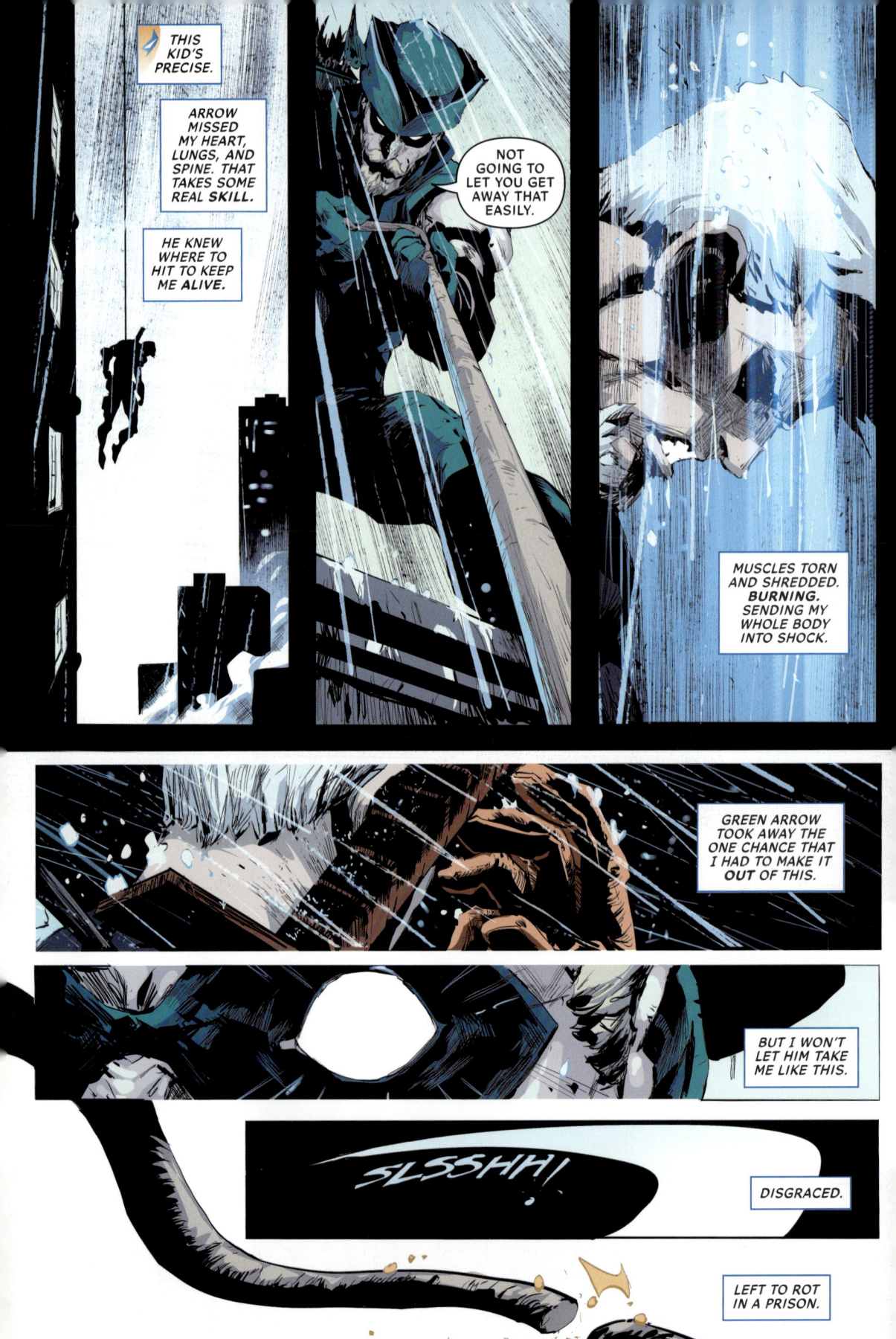

ARROW MISSED MY HEART, LUNGS, AND SPINE. THAT TAKES SOME REAL SKILL.

HE KNEW WHERE TO HIT TO KEEP ME ALIVE.

NOT GOING TO LET YOU GET AWAY THAT EASILY.

MUSCLES TORN AND SHREDDED. BURNING. SENDING MY WHOLE BODY INTO SHOCK.

GREEN ARROW TOOK AWAY THE ONE CHANCE THAT I HAD TO MAKE IT OUT OF THIS.

BUT I WON'T LET HIM TAKE ME LIKE THIS.

SLSSHH!

DISGRACED.

LEFT TO ROT IN A PRISON.

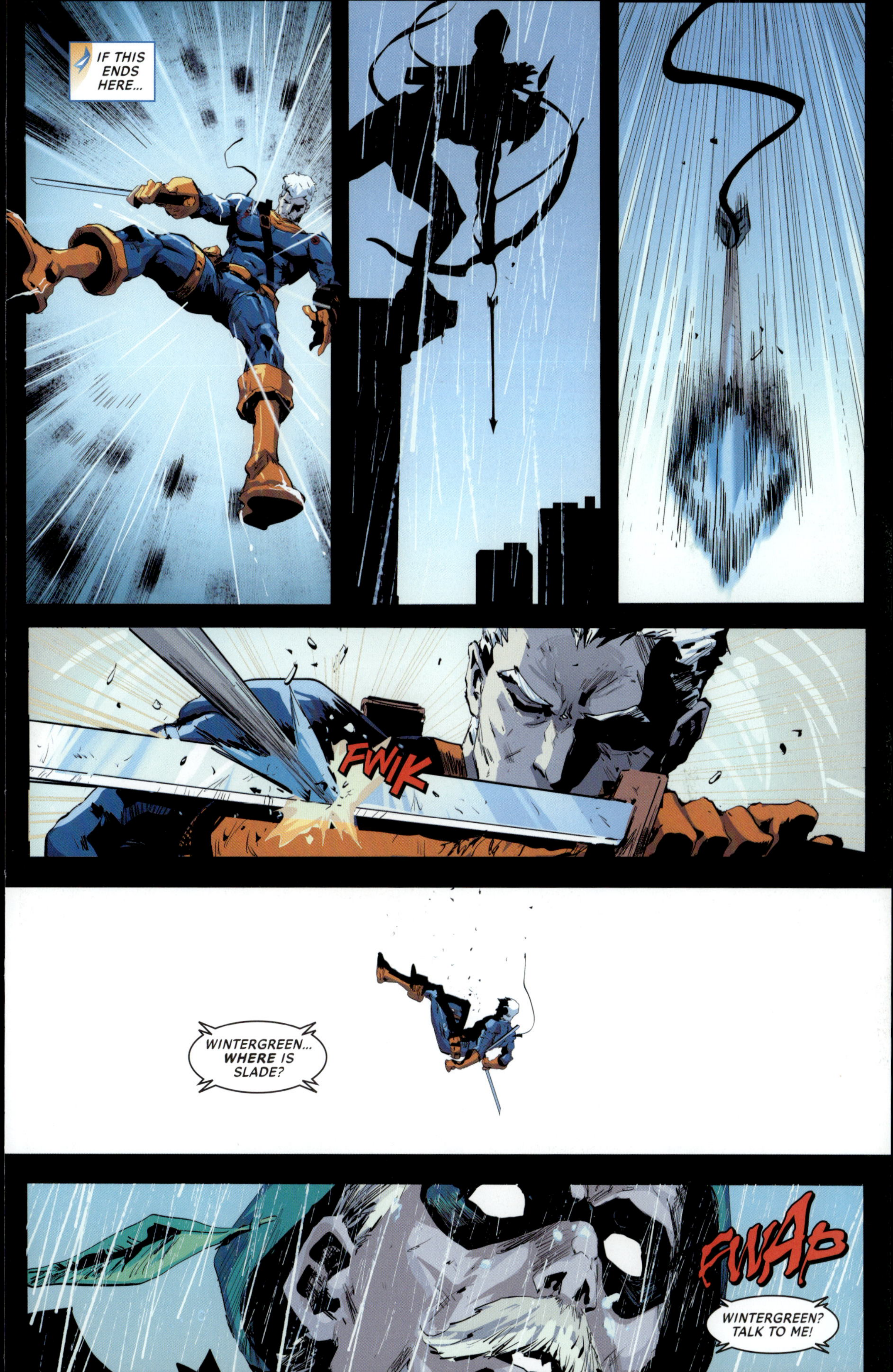
IF THIS ENDS HERE...
FWIK
WINTERGREEN... WHERE IS SLADE?
FWAP
WINTERGREEN? TALK TO ME!

...THEN IT ENDS ON MY TERMS.
I...I'M GOING TO HAVE TO CALL YOU BACK, ADDIE.

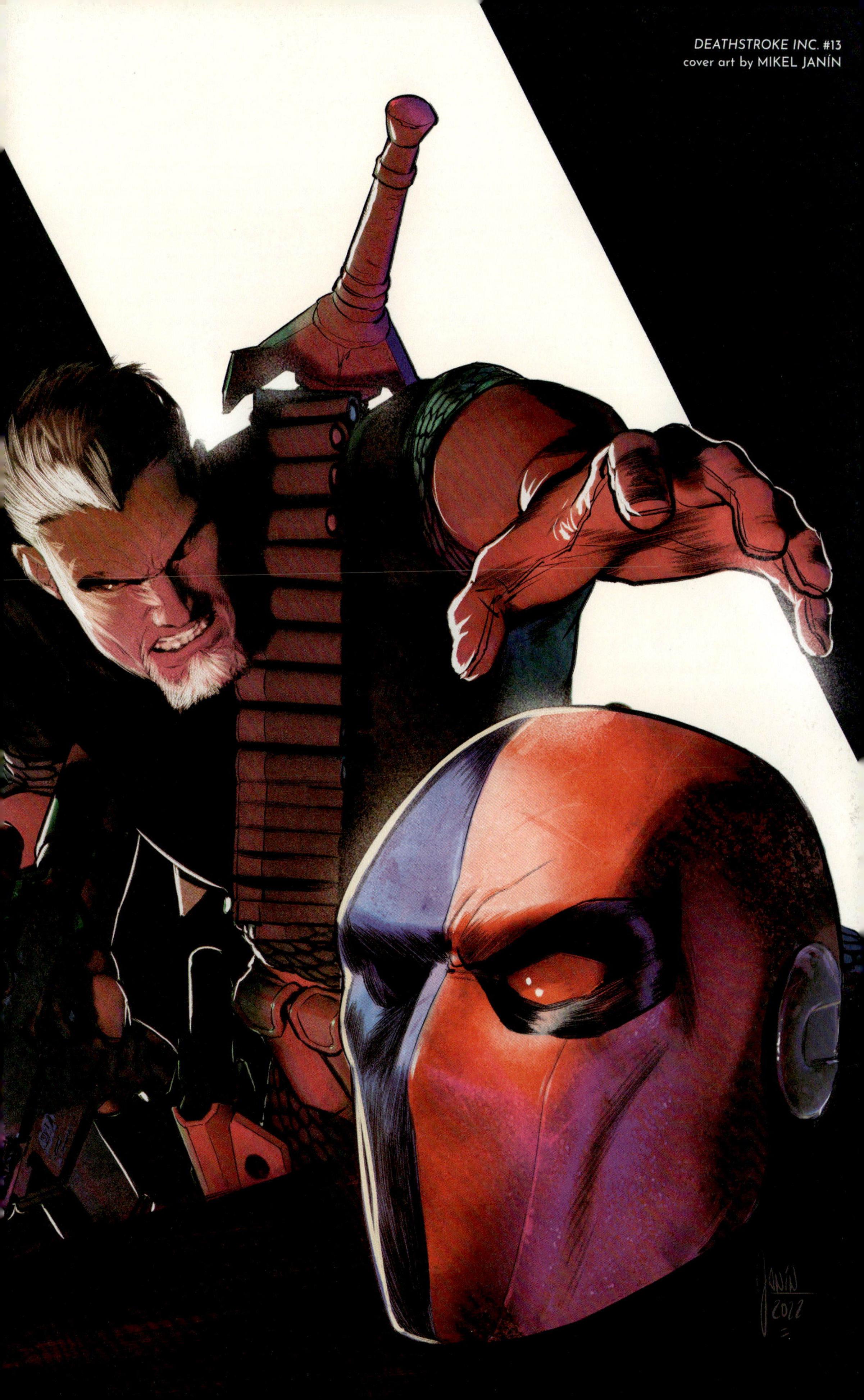

DEATHSTROKE INC. #13
cover art by MIKEL JANÍN

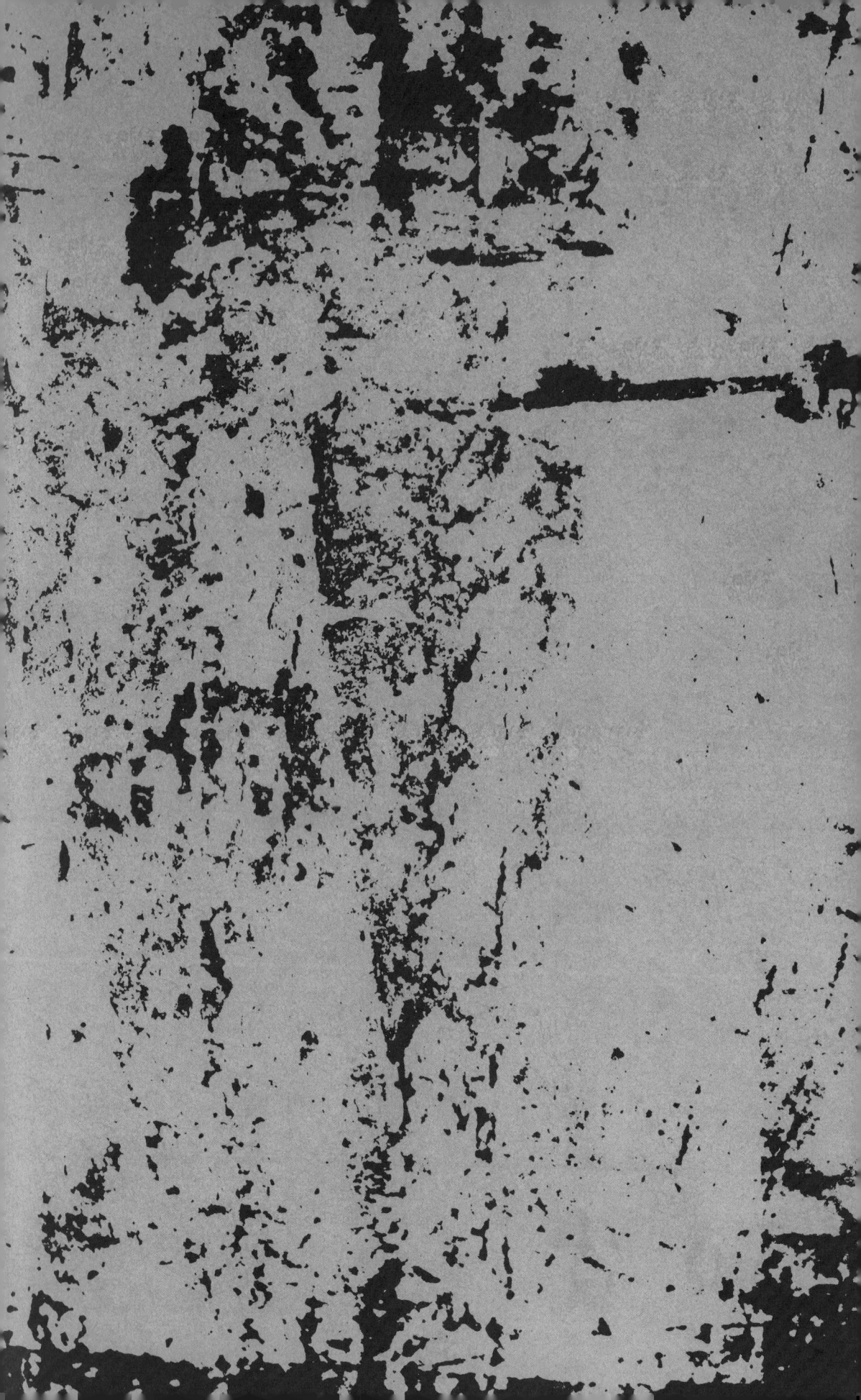

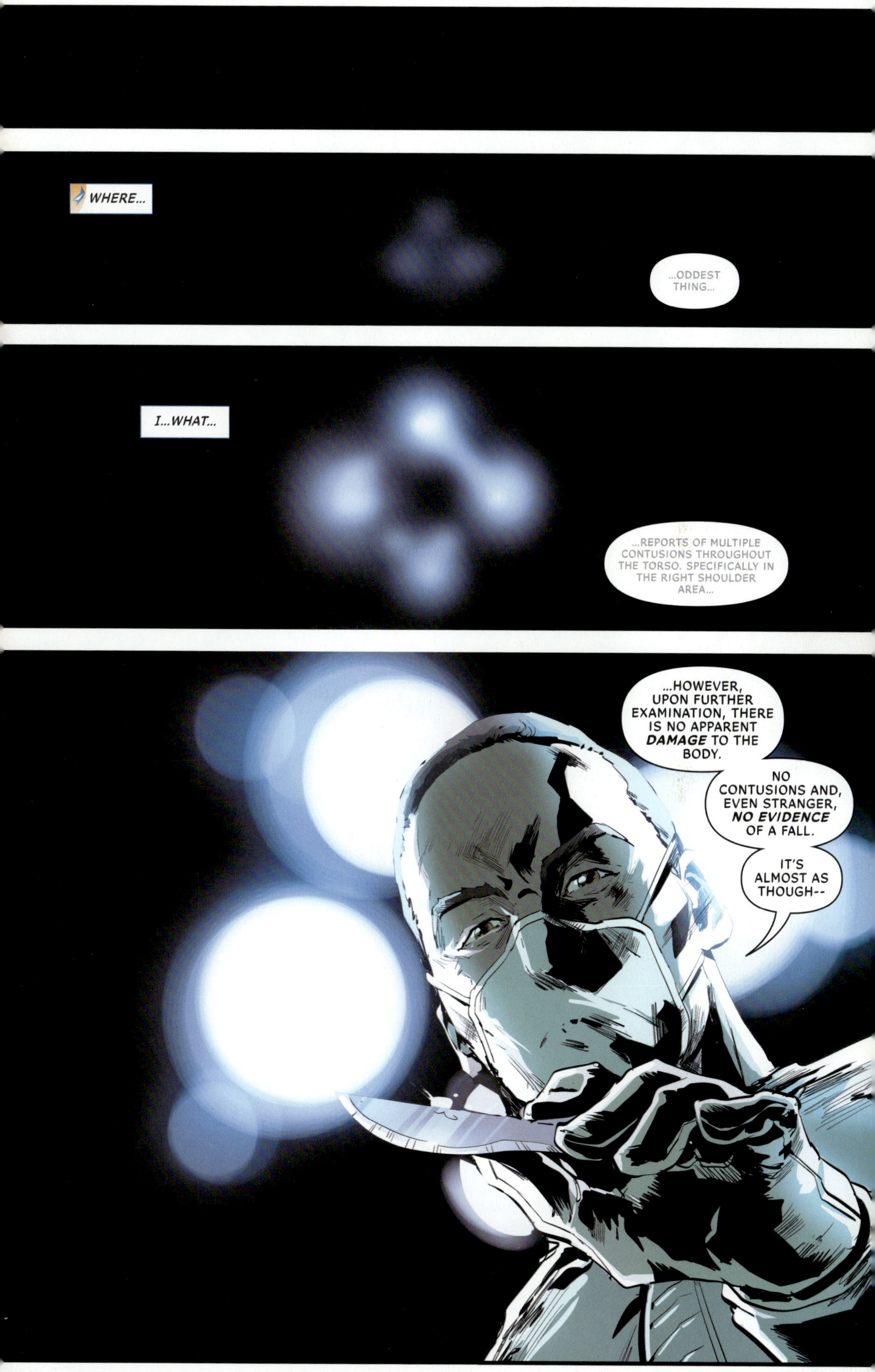
WHERE...
...ODDEST THING...
I...WHAT...
...REPORTS OF MULTIPLE CONTUSIONS THROUGHOUT THE TORSO. SPECIFICALLY IN THE RIGHT SHOULDER AREA...
...HOWEVER, UPON FURTHER EXAMINATION, THERE IS NO APPARENT DAMAGE TO THE BODY.
NO CONTUSIONS AND, EVEN STRANGER, NO EVIDENCE OF A FALL.
IT'S ALMOST AS THOUGH--

PUT THE BLADE DOWN.
AHHH! OH GOD. OH GOD. OH GOD.
WHERE AM I?
I...GOD, I THOUGHT YOU WERE DEAD. I SWEAR. WHEN THEY BROUGHT YOU HERE, I--
WHEN WHO BROUGHT ME HERE?
THE MEDICAL EXAMINER.
THERE WERE SO MANY BODIES.
MAYBE THEY...MAYBE THEY WERE IN A RUSH AND...
IF I HAD ANY QUESTION OF HOW FAR I CAN PUSH MY HEALING FACTOR...
...IT'S BEEN ANSWERED.

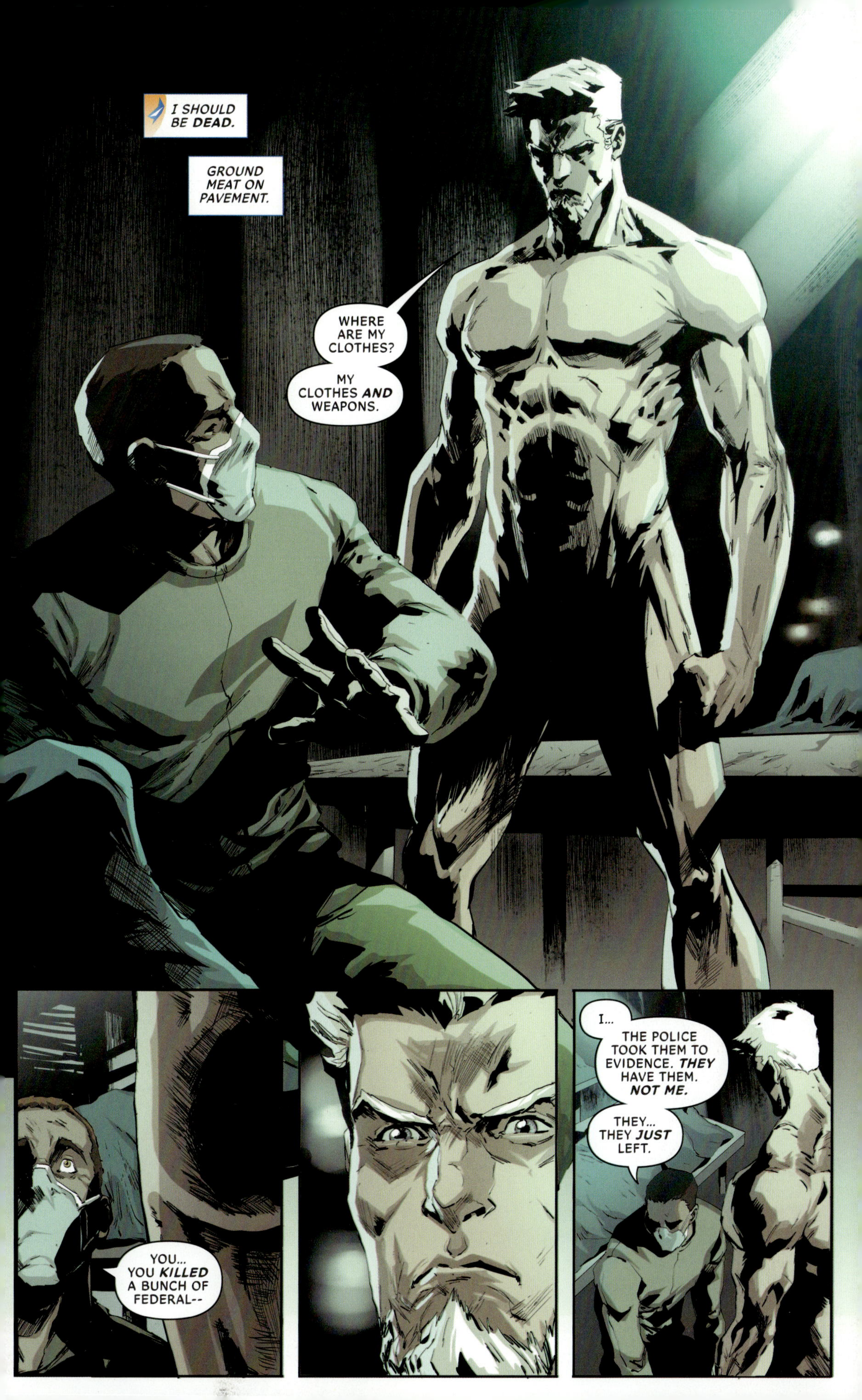
I SHOULD BE DEAD.
GROUND MEAT ON PAVEMENT.
WHERE ARE MY CLOTHES?
MY CLOTHES AND WEAPONS.
YOU... YOU KILLED A BUNCH OF FEDERAL--
I... THE POLICE TOOK THEM TO EVIDENCE. THEY HAVE THEM. NOT ME.
THEY... THEY JUST LEFT.

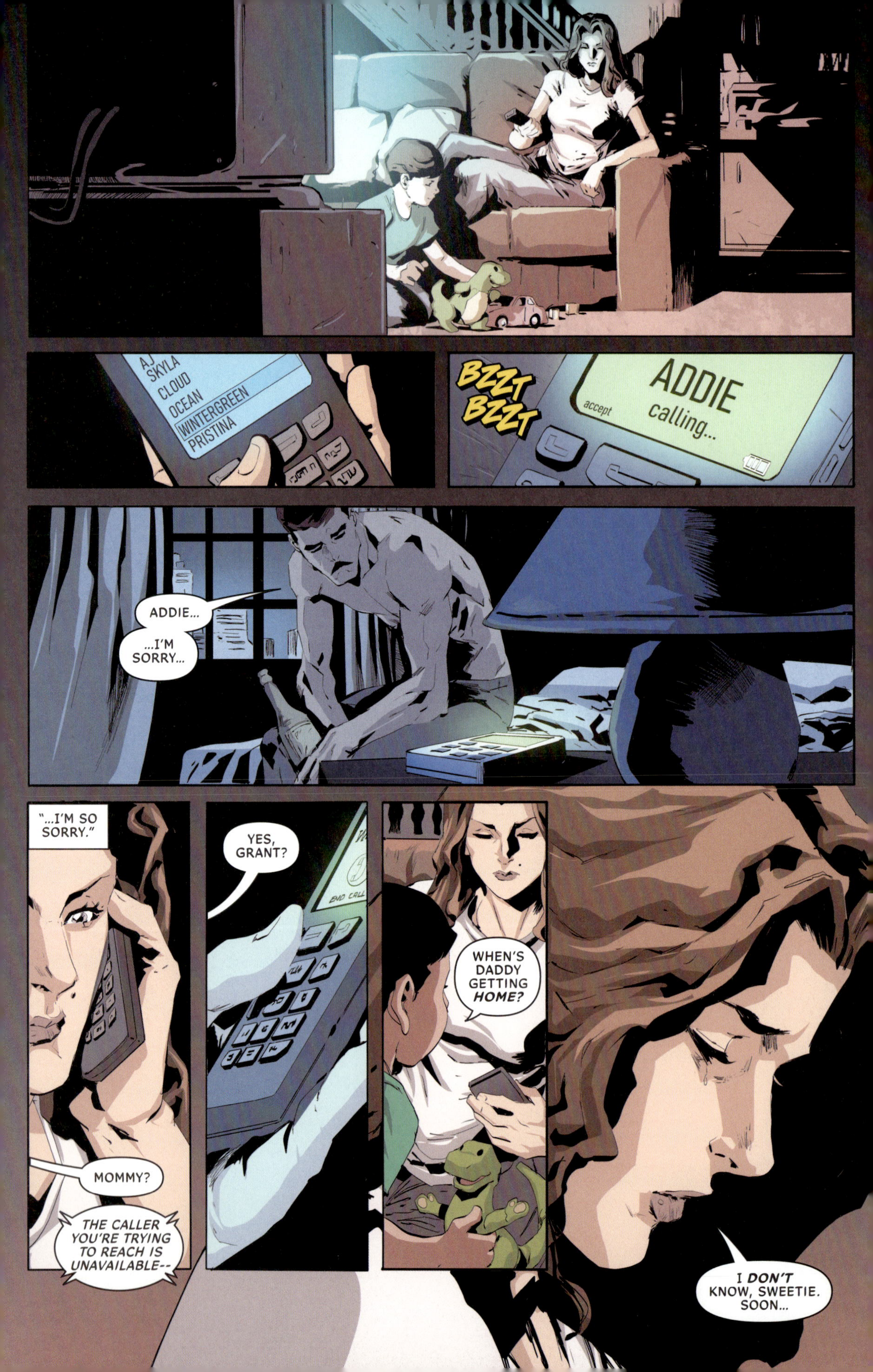
AJ
SKYLA
CLOUD
OCEAN
WINTERGREEN
PRISTINA
BZZT BZZT
ADDIE
calling...
accept
ADDIE...
...I'M SORRY...
"...I'M SO SORRY."
YES, GRANT?
END CALL
MOMMY?
THE CALLER YOU'RE TRYING TO REACH IS UNAVAILABLE--
WHEN'S DADDY GETTING *HOME?*
I *DON'T* KNOW, SWEETIE. SOON...

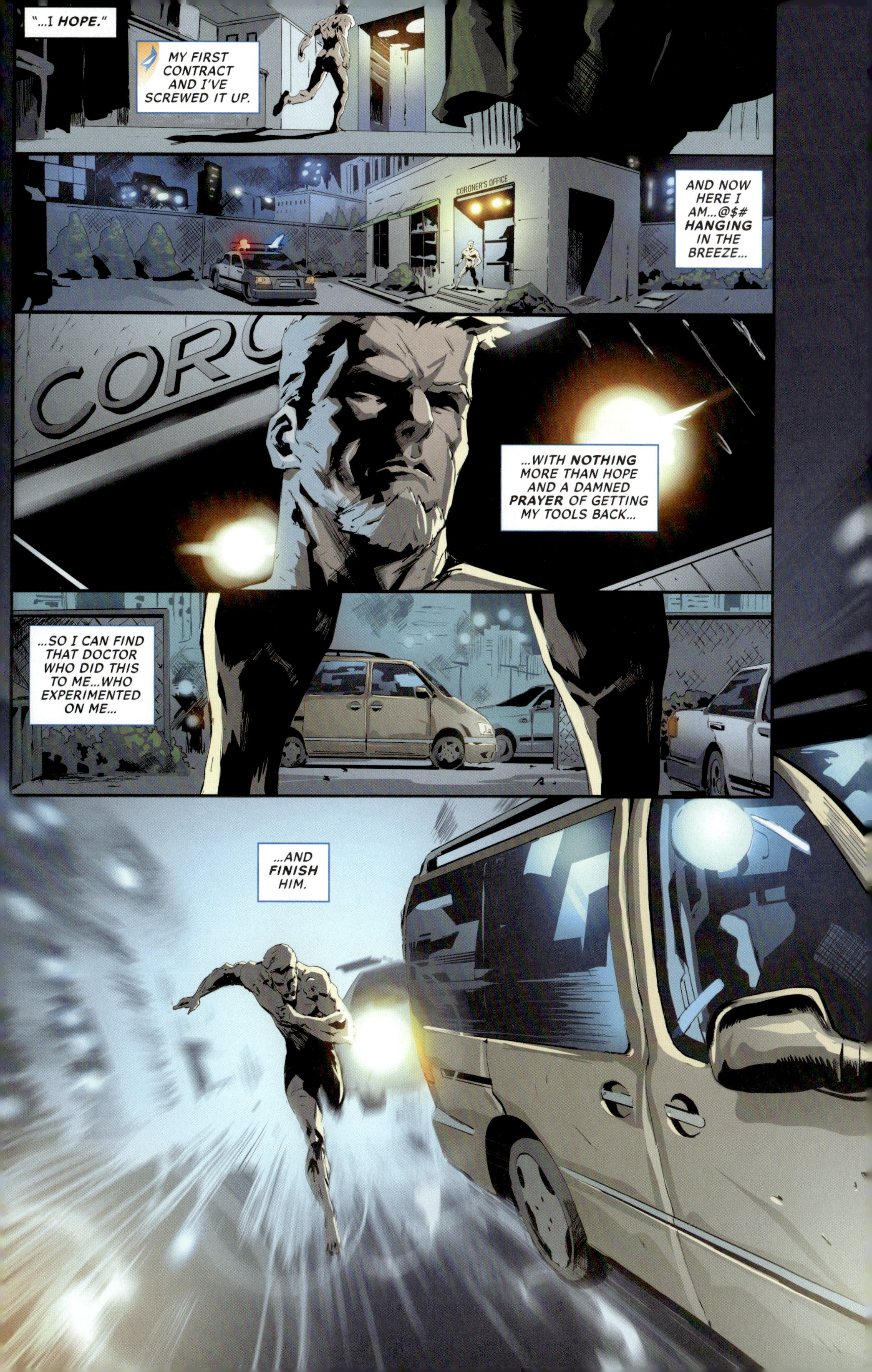
"...I HOPE."
MY FIRST CONTRACT AND I'VE SCREWED IT UP.
CORONER'S OFFICE
AND NOW HERE I AM...@$# HANGING IN THE BREEZE...
CORO
...WITH NOTHING MORE THAN HOPE AND A DAMNED PRAYER OF GETTING MY TOOLS BACK...
...SO I CAN FIND THAT DOCTOR WHO DID THIS TO ME...WHO EXPERIMENTED ON ME...
...AND FINISH HIM.

STOP!
I NEED YOUR CAR.
NO, I...OH GOD. PLEASE HELP!
POLICE! POLICE!
OUT.
NOW.
SKEEEEEEE

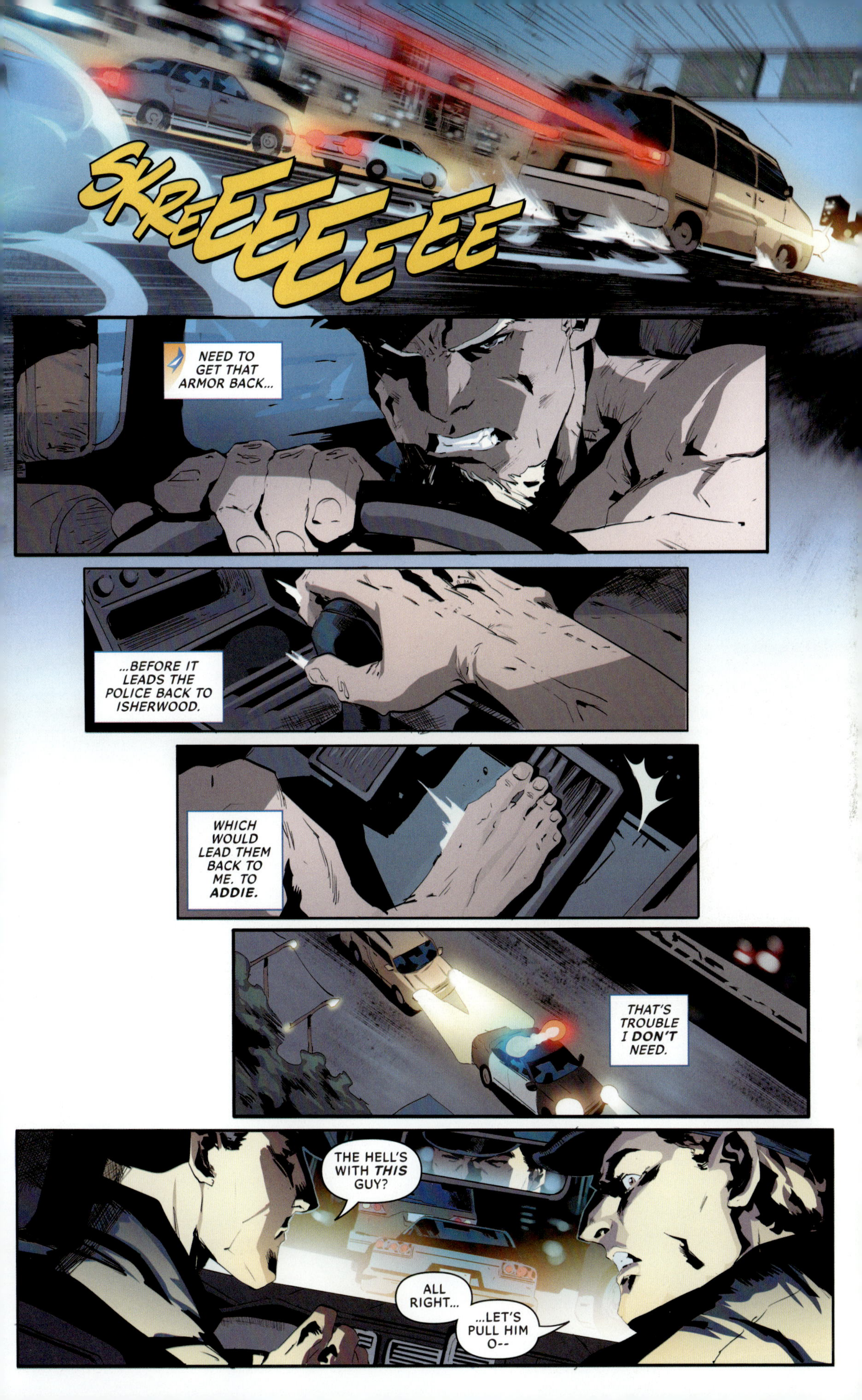
SKREEEEEEEEE
NEED TO GET THAT ARMOR BACK...
...BEFORE IT LEADS THE POLICE BACK TO ISHERWOOD.
WHICH WOULD LEAD THEM BACK TO ME. TO ADDIE.
THAT'S TROUBLE I DON'T NEED.
THE HELL'S WITH THIS GUY?
ALL RIGHT...
...LET'S PULL HIM O--

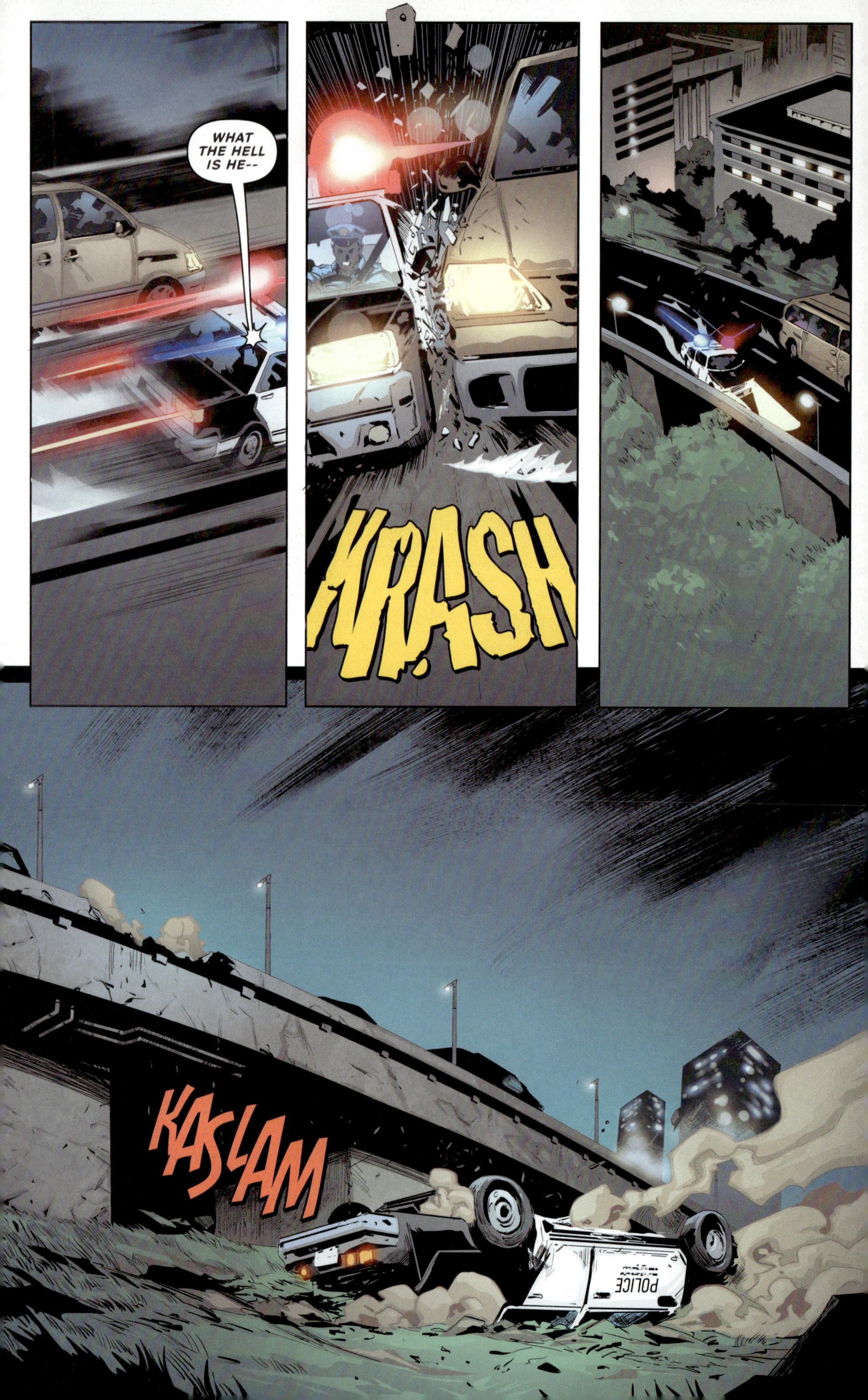
WHAT THE HELL IS HE--
KRASH
KASLAM
POLICE

PAT...YOU OKAY? PAT?
MY...GUH... I NEED AN AMBULANCE. I...GOD...
WE'VE GOT AN OFFICER-INVOLVED ACCIDENT ALONG THE I-5, JUST SOUTH OF THE--
PUT THE RADIO DOWN.
THE EVIDENCE YOU'RE TRANSPORTING. WHERE IS IT?
POLICE
%&*# YOU, PSYCHO.
YOU'VE GOT THREE SECONDS TO TELL ME WHERE THE EVIDENCE IS BEFORE I SET THIS CAR ON FIRE AND LEAVE THE TWO OF YOU TO BURN.
ONE.
TWO.
OKAY. OKAY.

CLIK
BEER
SHOW YOUR HANDS OR I'LL BLAST YOU RIGHT THROUGH THIS DOOR.
WHAT ARE YOU SITTING AROUND FOR, WINTERGREEN?
WE'VE STILL GOT WORK TO DO.

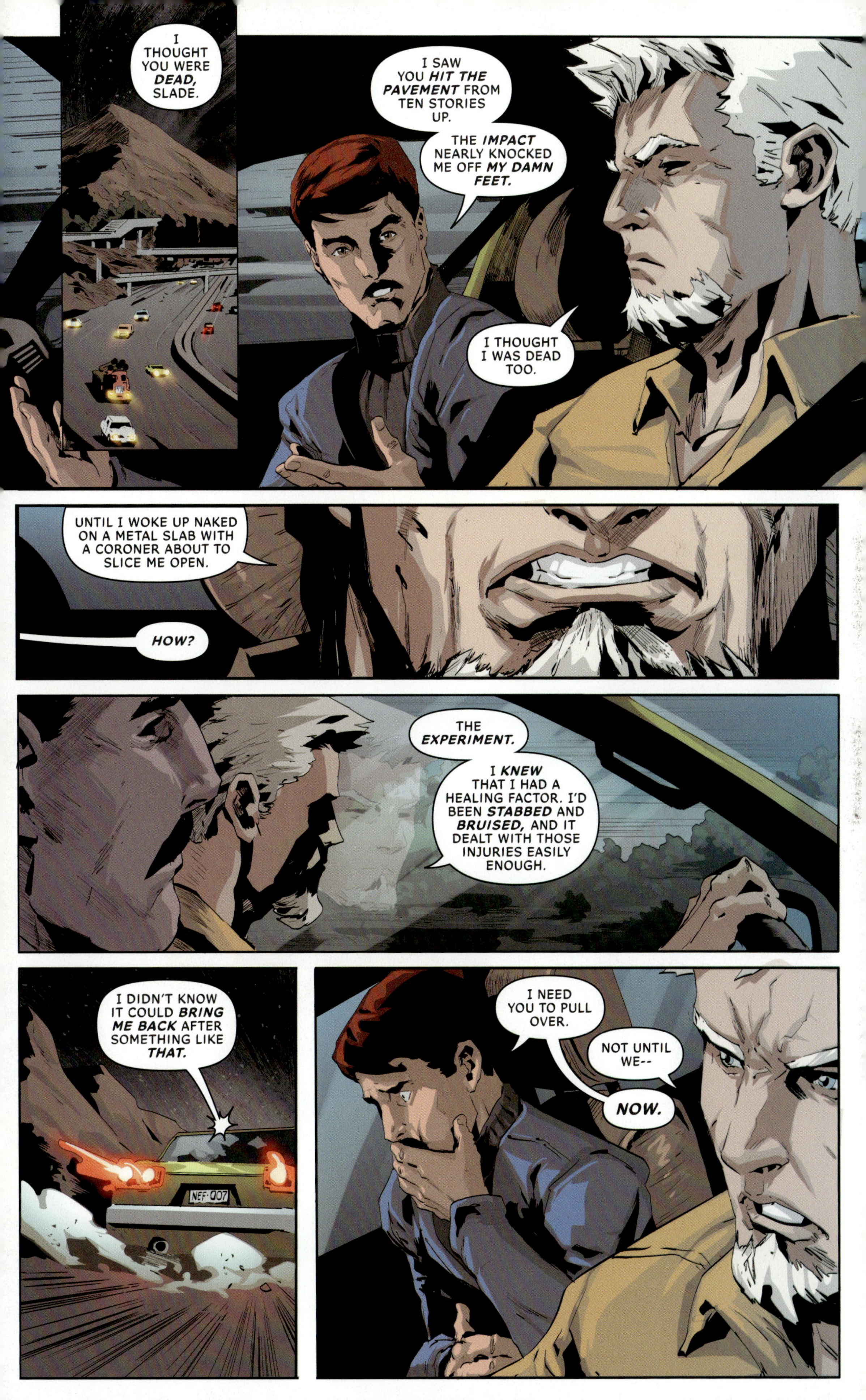
I THOUGHT YOU WERE DEAD, SLADE.
I SAW YOU HIT THE PAVEMENT FROM TEN STORIES UP.
THE IMPACT NEARLY KNOCKED ME OFF MY DAMN FEET.
I THOUGHT I WAS DEAD TOO.
UNTIL I WOKE UP NAKED ON A METAL SLAB WITH A CORONER ABOUT TO SLICE ME OPEN.
HOW?
THE EXPERIMENT.
I KNEW THAT I HAD A HEALING FACTOR. I'D BEEN STABBED AND BRUISED, AND IT DEALT WITH THOSE INJURIES EASILY ENOUGH.
I DIDN'T KNOW IT COULD BRING ME BACK AFTER SOMETHING LIKE THAT.
NEF-007
I NEED YOU TO PULL OVER.
NOT UNTIL WE--
NOW.

HRRRRRK...
WHAT MADE YOU THINK DOWNING A BOTTLE OF WHISKEY WHILE ON MISSION WAS A *GOOD IDEA?*
NEEDED TO BUILD UP THE *COURAGE* TO CALL ADDIE, TO TELL HER THAT YOU WOULDN'T BE COMING HOME.
OH GOD, ADDIE, SHE'S BEEN CALLING NONSTOP.
YOU NEED TO--
HRKRRRK...
SHE'LL HAVE TO *WAIT.*
FIRST, WE NEED TO FIGURE OUT WHERE THEY TOOK DR. CAMPBELL.
I *STILL* HAVE A CONTRACT TO FULFILL.
I *KNOW* WHERE HE IS.
BUT BEFORE WE DO ANYTHING, I NEED A COUPLE LITERS OF COFFEE TO SOBER UP.

Pares
DINER
REFILL YER COFFEE, BOYS?
THANK YOU, LOVE.
YOU HAVE NO IDEA HOW *BADLY* I NEEDED THIS.
LORD. THIS STUFF IS PURE *GUT ROT.*
THIS SLUDGE WOULD GIVE THAT HEALING FACTOR OF YOURS A REAL CHALLENGE, I BET.
THE TARGET? *WHERE* DID THEY TAKE HIM?
RIGHT. RIGHT.
THE CHOPPER WAS MILITARY. I COPPED ITS I.D. NUMBER AND CALLED IN A COUPLE *FAVORS.*
WAS ABLE TO TRACK IT TO A PRIVATE AIRFIELD IN SEATTLE. IT'S *STILL* SITTING THERE.
HOWEVER, SHORTLY AFTER, ANOTHER FLIGHT LEFT FROM THE *SAME* AIRFIELD, HEADED TOWARD A MILITARY BASE IN BEAR VALLEY, CALIFORNIA.
NOTHING IN OR OUT SINCE.
TENNER SAYS WE FIND OUR MAN AT THAT BASE.

SO, WHEN YOU THOUGHT I WAS DEAD...
...YOU WERE GOING TO WHAT? WALK IN THERE *YOURSELF?*
TAKE *CARE* OF HIM?
SOMETHING LIKE THAT.
GUH.
I DON'T KNOW *WHY* I EXPECTED IT TO TASTE *ANY* BETTER.
YOU AND I ARE *SUPPOSED* TO BE OFF ON A HUNTING TRIP.
WHEN I THOUGHT YOU'D DIED, I...WELL, I BEGAN TO FEEL THAT *I* WAS *RESPONSIBLE.*
AND THAT ADDIE AND GRANT WERE GOING TO BE LEFT WITH... *WHAT?*
ADDIE'S TOUGH. SHE CAN TAKE CARE OF *HERSELF.*
MAYBE SO.
BUT SHE COULD TAKE CARE OF HERSELF AND GRANT A HELL OF A LOT BETTER WITH THE *MILLION DOLLARS* THE CONTRACT PAYS OUT.

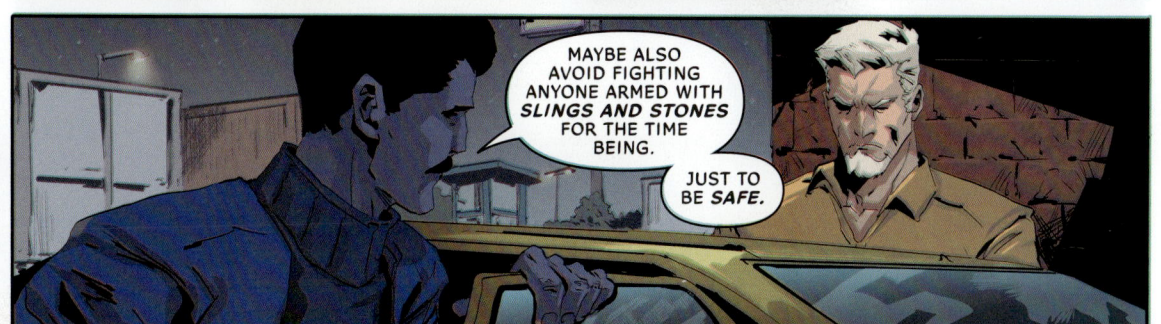

CAN'T BELIEVE YOU CHASED DOWN THE POLICE TO GET THE ARMOR BACK.

I STILL NEEDED IT.

AND I DIDN'T WANT THEM TO TRACE IT BACK TO ISHERWOOD.

NOT BEFORE I HAD THE CHANCE TO WRING HIS NECK.

WHY? WHAT DID ISHERWOOD DO TO DESERVE SUCH TREATMENT?

HE SAID IT WOULD BE BULLETPROOF, AND YEAH... HURTS LIKE HELL, BUT NOTHING GOT THROUGH.

BUT GREEN ARROW...HIS ARROWS SLASHED RIGHT THOUGH THE ARMOR LIKE IT WAS NOTHING.

I'M NOT THRILLED ABOUT THAT.

ARROWS AREN'T BULLETS.

I HAVE TO ASSUME THAT ISHERWOOD AND THE U.S. MILITARY DIDN'T CONSIDER THAT THE SUIT WOULD BE USED AGAINST WEAPONRY THAT'S BEEN OBSOLETE FOR TWO HUNDRED YEARS.

MAYBE ALSO AVOID FIGHTING ANYONE ARMED WITH SLINGS AND STONES FOR THE TIME BEING.

JUST TO BE SAFE.

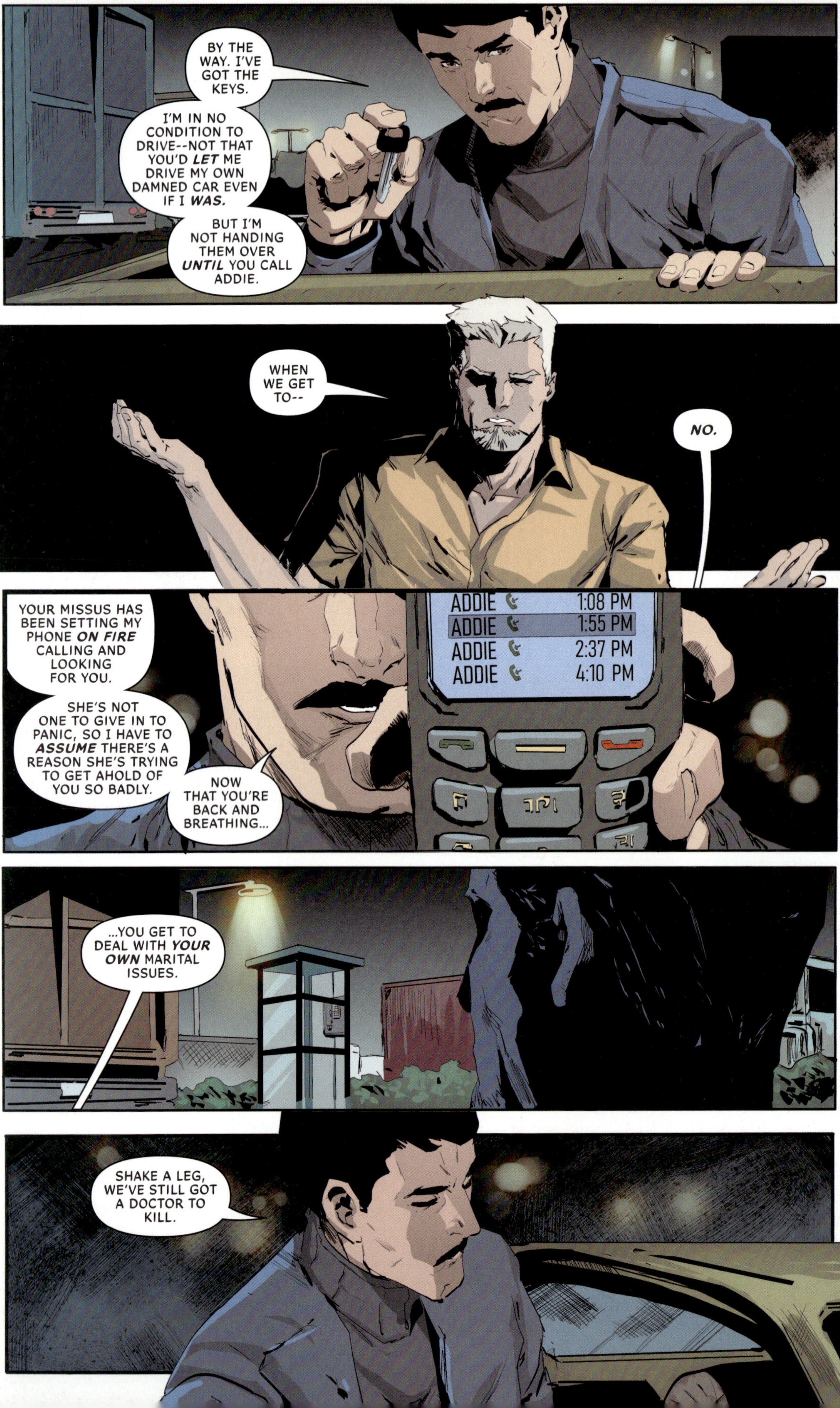
BY THE WAY. I'VE GOT THE KEYS.
I'M IN NO CONDITION TO DRIVE--NOT THAT YOU'D LET ME DRIVE MY OWN DAMNED CAR EVEN IF I WAS.
BUT I'M NOT HANDING THEM OVER UNTIL YOU CALL ADDIE.
WHEN WE GET TO--
NO.
YOUR MISSUS HAS BEEN SETTING MY PHONE ON FIRE CALLING AND LOOKING FOR YOU.
SHE'S NOT ONE TO GIVE IN TO PANIC, SO I HAVE TO ASSUME THERE'S A REASON SHE'S TRYING TO GET AHOLD OF YOU SO BADLY.
NOW THAT YOU'RE BACK AND BREATHING...
ADDIE 1:08 PM
ADDIE 1:55 PM
ADDIE 2:37 PM
ADDIE 4:10 PM
...YOU GET TO DEAL WITH YOUR OWN MARITAL ISSUES.
SHAKE A LEG, WE'VE STILL GOT A DOCTOR TO KILL.

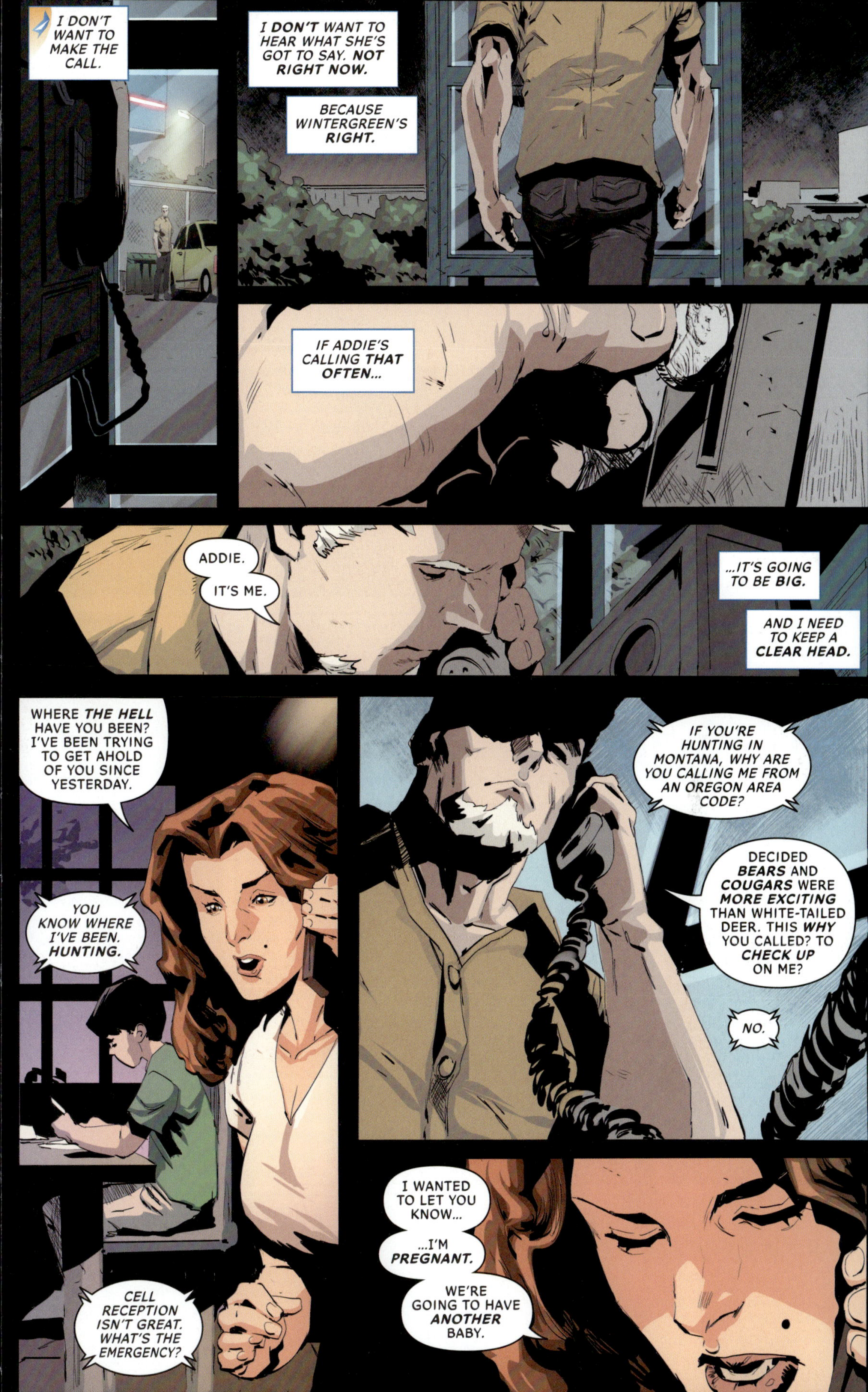
I DON'T WANT TO MAKE THE CALL.
I **DON'T** WANT TO HEAR WHAT SHE'S GOT TO SAY. **NOT RIGHT NOW.**
BECAUSE WINTERGREEN'S **RIGHT.**
IF ADDIE'S CALLING **THAT OFTEN...**
ADDIE.
IT'S ME.
...IT'S GOING TO BE **BIG.**
AND I NEED TO KEEP A **CLEAR HEAD.**
WHERE **THE HELL** HAVE YOU BEEN? I'VE BEEN TRYING TO GET AHOLD OF YOU SINCE YESTERDAY.
YOU KNOW WHERE I'VE BEEN. **HUNTING.**
IF YOU'RE HUNTING IN MONTANA, WHY ARE YOU CALLING ME FROM AN OREGON AREA CODE?
DECIDED **BEARS** AND **COUGARS** WERE **MORE EXCITING** THAN WHITE-TAILED DEER. THIS **WHY** YOU CALLED? TO **CHECK UP** ON ME?
NO.
CELL RECEPTION ISN'T GREAT. WHAT'S THE EMERGENCY?
I WANTED TO LET YOU KNOW...
...I'M **PREGNANT.**
WE'RE GOING TO HAVE **ANOTHER** BABY.

SLADE?
OKAY.
OKAY?
I TELL YOU WE'RE GOING TO HAVE ANOTHER KID AND YOUR RESPONSE IS "OKAY"?
WHAT THE HELL'S GOING ON?
LOOK, ADDIE...
...WINTERGREEN'S WAITING. I'VE GOT TO GO.
WE'LL TALK LATER.
KLIK
SMASH
EVERYTHING'S GOOD ON THE HOME FRONT, I SEE.
YEAH. GREAT.
LET'S GO.

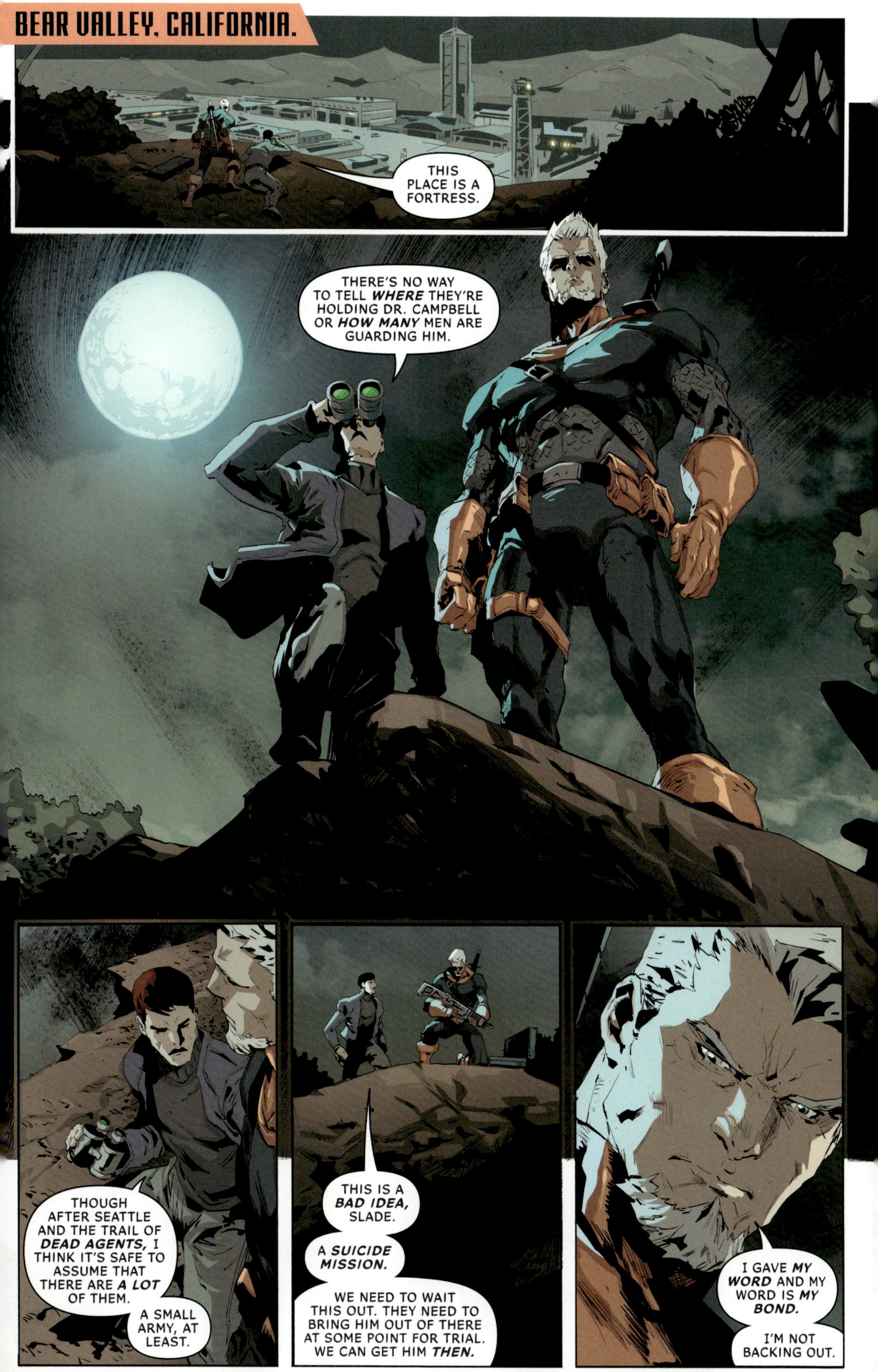
BEAR VALLEY, CALIFORNIA.
THIS PLACE IS A FORTRESS.
THERE'S NO WAY TO TELL *WHERE* THEY'RE HOLDING DR. CAMPBELL OR *HOW MANY* MEN ARE GUARDING HIM.
THOUGH AFTER SEATTLE AND THE TRAIL OF *DEAD AGENTS,* I THINK IT'S SAFE TO ASSUME THAT THERE ARE *A LOT* OF THEM.
A SMALL ARMY, AT LEAST.
THIS IS A *BAD IDEA,* SLADE.
A *SUICIDE MISSION.*
WE NEED TO WAIT THIS OUT. THEY NEED TO BRING HIM OUT OF THERE AT SOME POINT FOR TRIAL. WE CAN GET HIM *THEN.*
I GAVE *MY WORD* AND MY WORD IS *MY BOND.*
I'M NOT BACKING OUT.

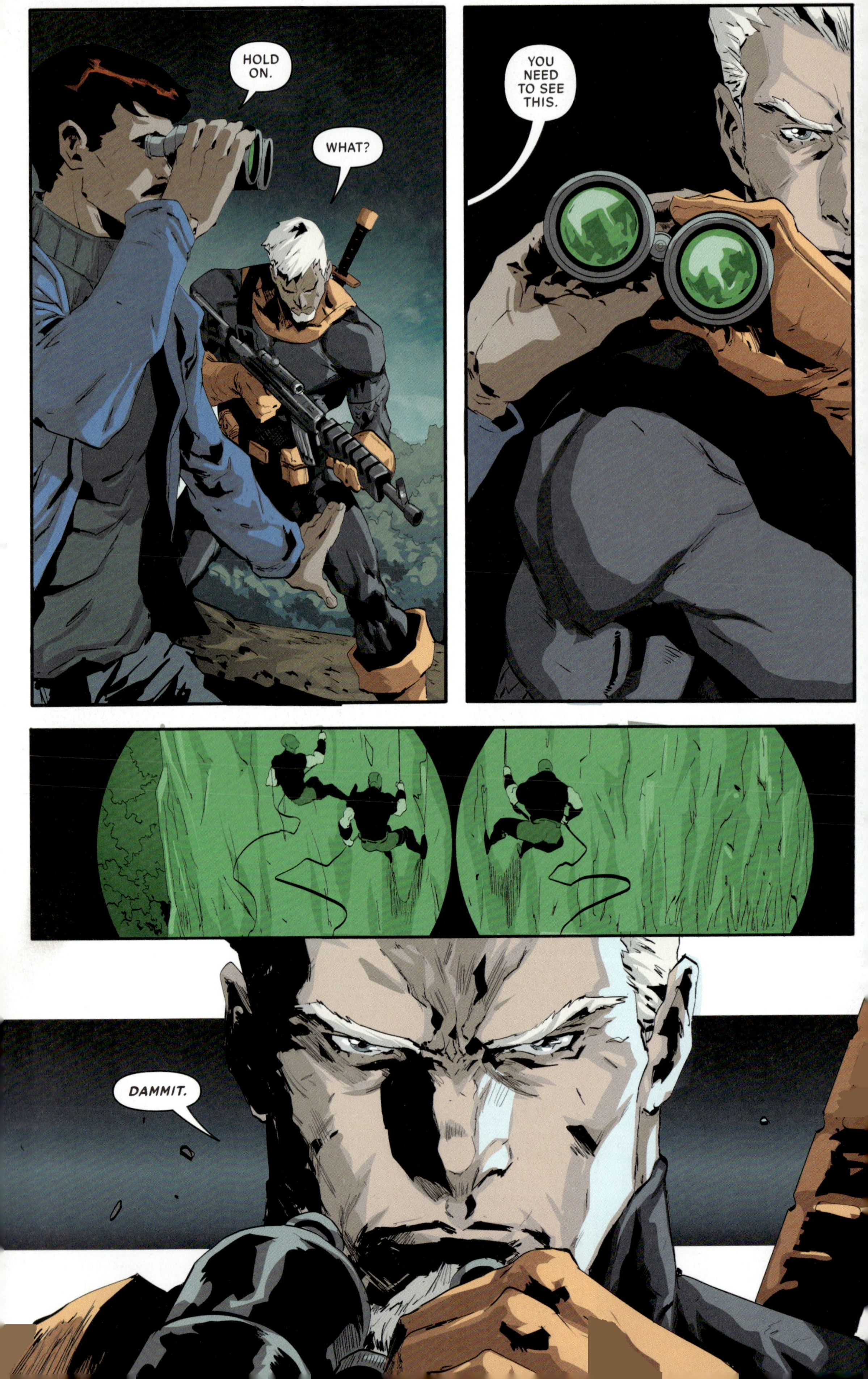
HOLD ON.
WHAT?
YOU NEED TO SEE THIS.
DAMMIT.

YOU RECOGNIZE THEM?
NO.
MY GUESS IS THEY'RE WALSH'S ***CONTINGENCY PLAN.***
AFTER THE ***$#!&@%*&*** IN SEATTLE, HE THINKS I'M DEAD AND WANTS TO MAKE SURE THAT SOMEONE TAKES DR. CAMPBELL OUT.
TO BE FAIR...
...I THOUGHT YOU WERE DEAD. SO DID GREEN ARROW AND THE SEATTLE CORONER.
YEAH, WELL...
...I'M ***NOT.***

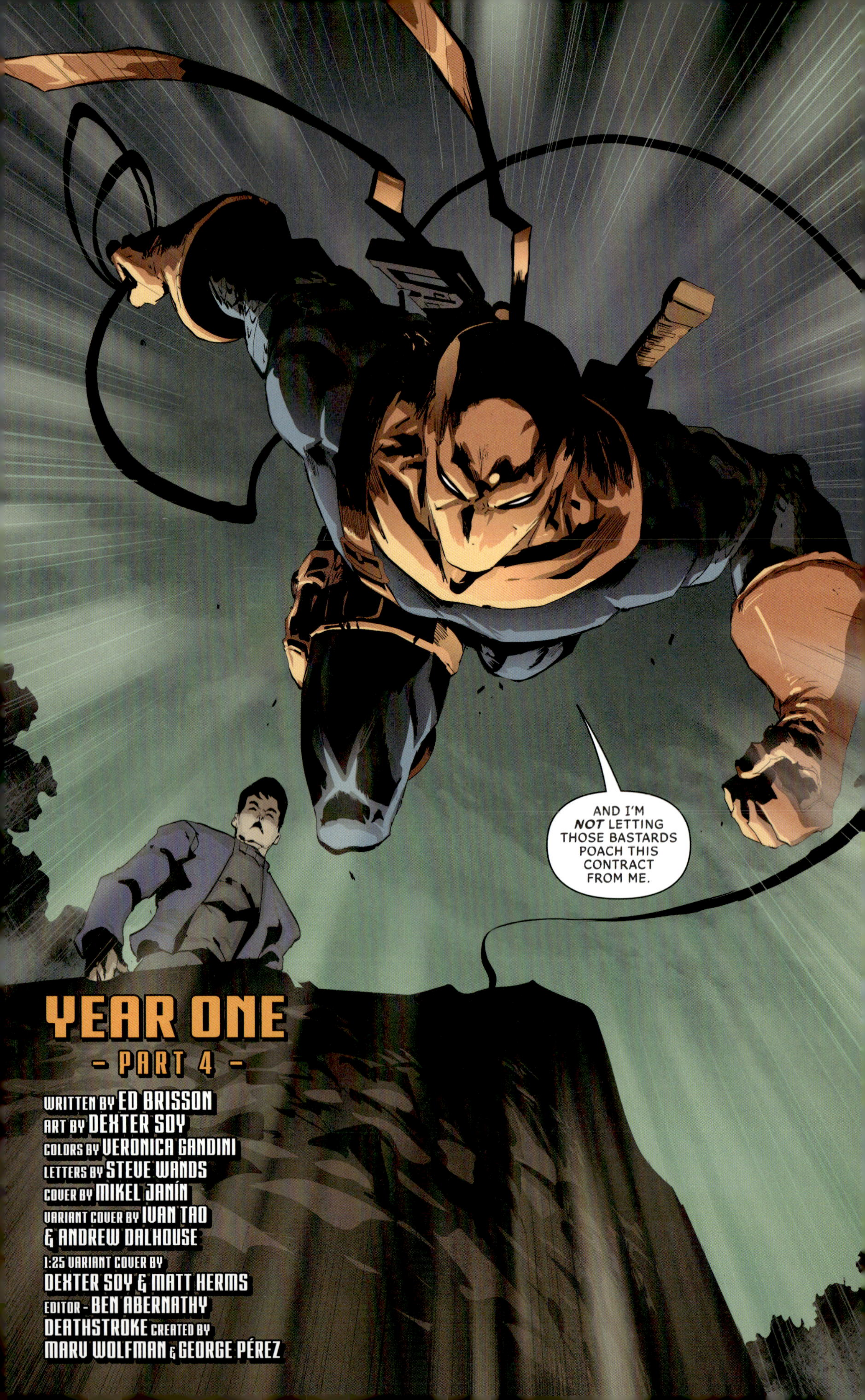
AND I'M *NOT* LETTING THOSE BASTARDS POACH THIS CONTRACT FROM ME.
YEAR ONE
- PART 4 -
WRITTEN BY ED BRISSON
ART BY DEXTER SOY
COLORS BY VERONICA GANDINI
LETTERS BY STEVE WANDS
COVER BY MIKEL JANÍN
VARIANT COVER BY IVAN TAO & ANDREW DALHOUSE
1:25 VARIANT COVER BY DEXTER SOY & MATT HERMS
EDITOR - BEN ABERNATHY
DEATHSTROKE CREATED BY MARV WOLFMAN & GEORGE PÉREZ

DEATHSTROKE INC. #14
cover art by MIKEL JANÍN

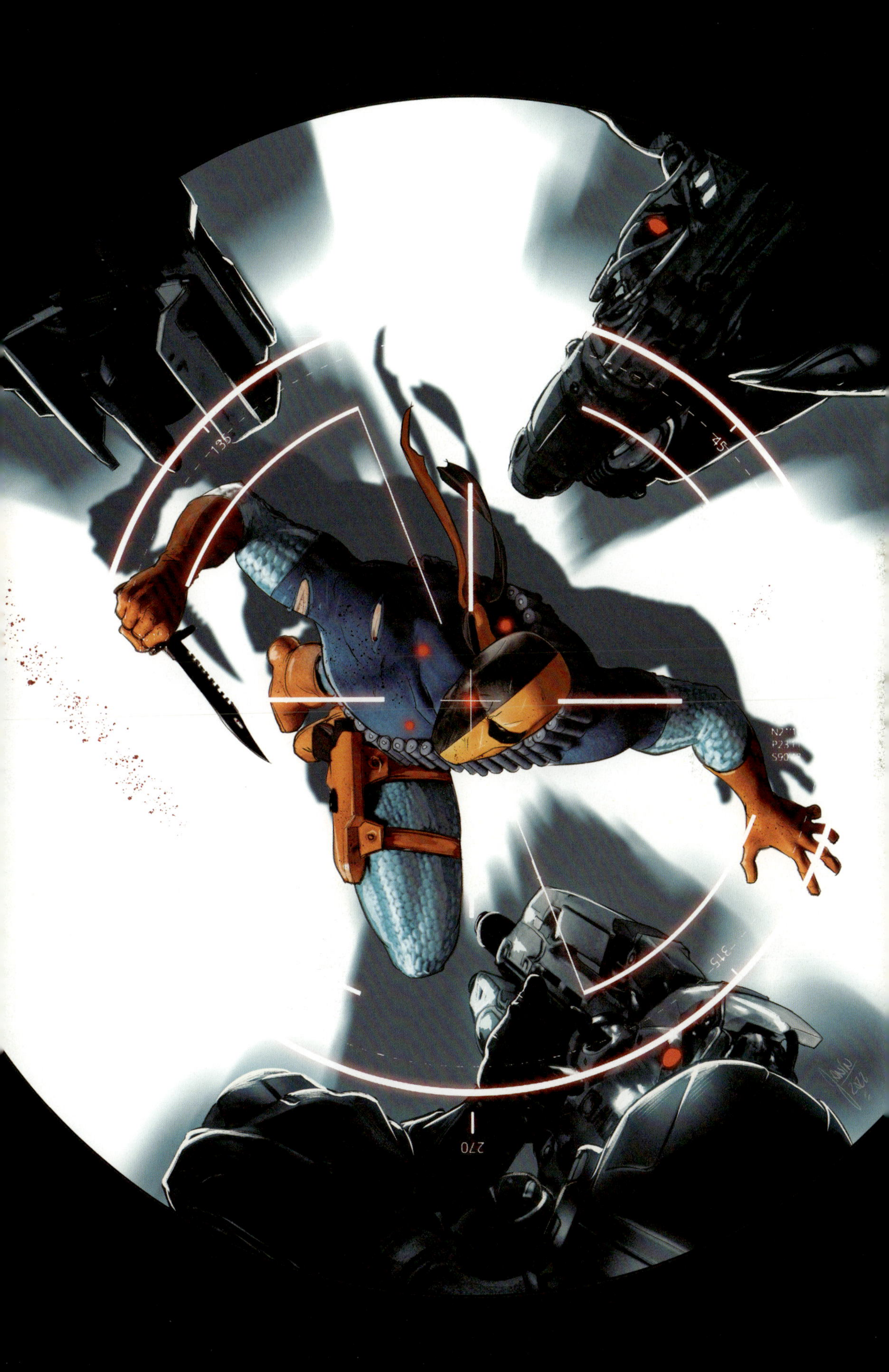

135
45
315
270

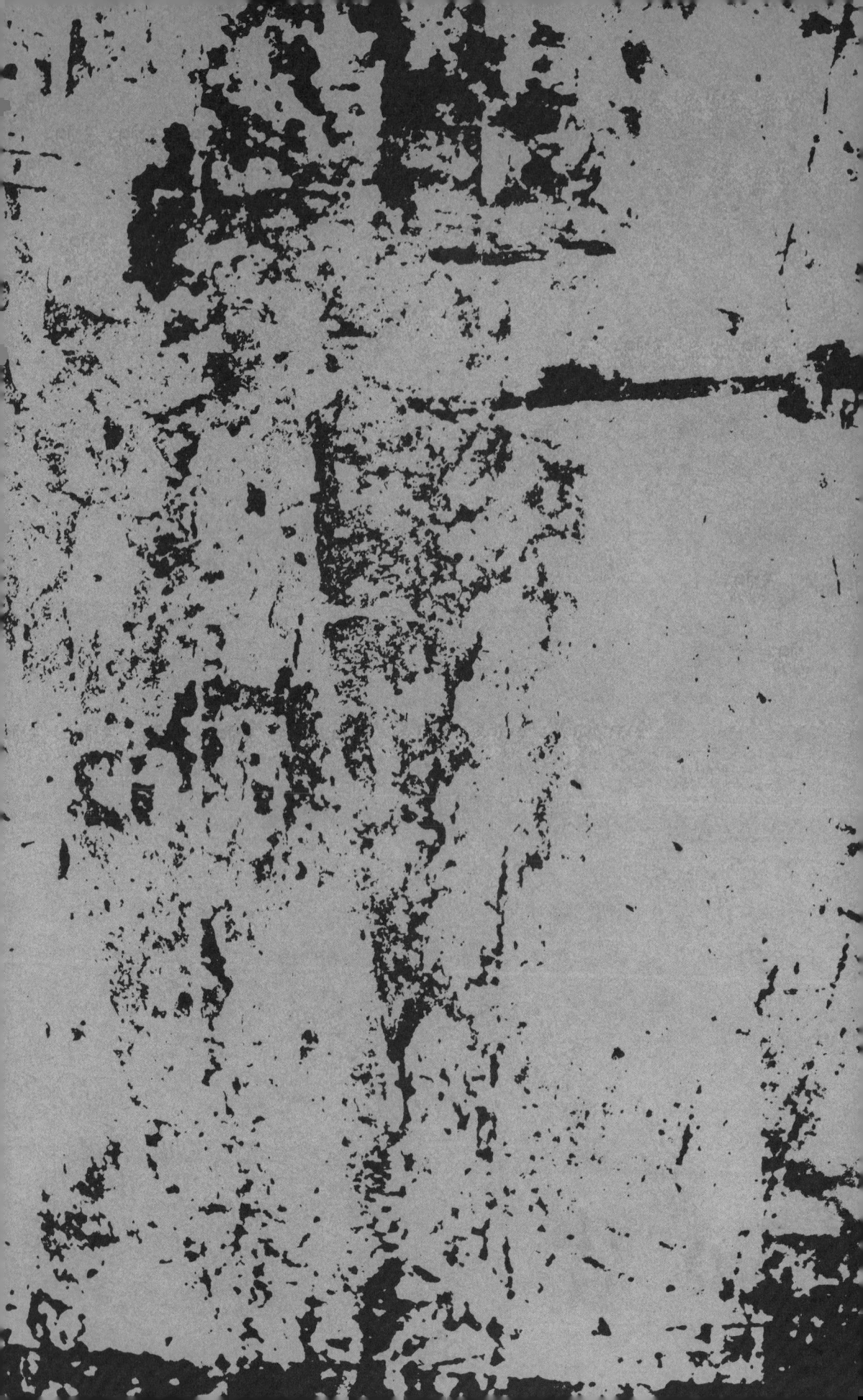

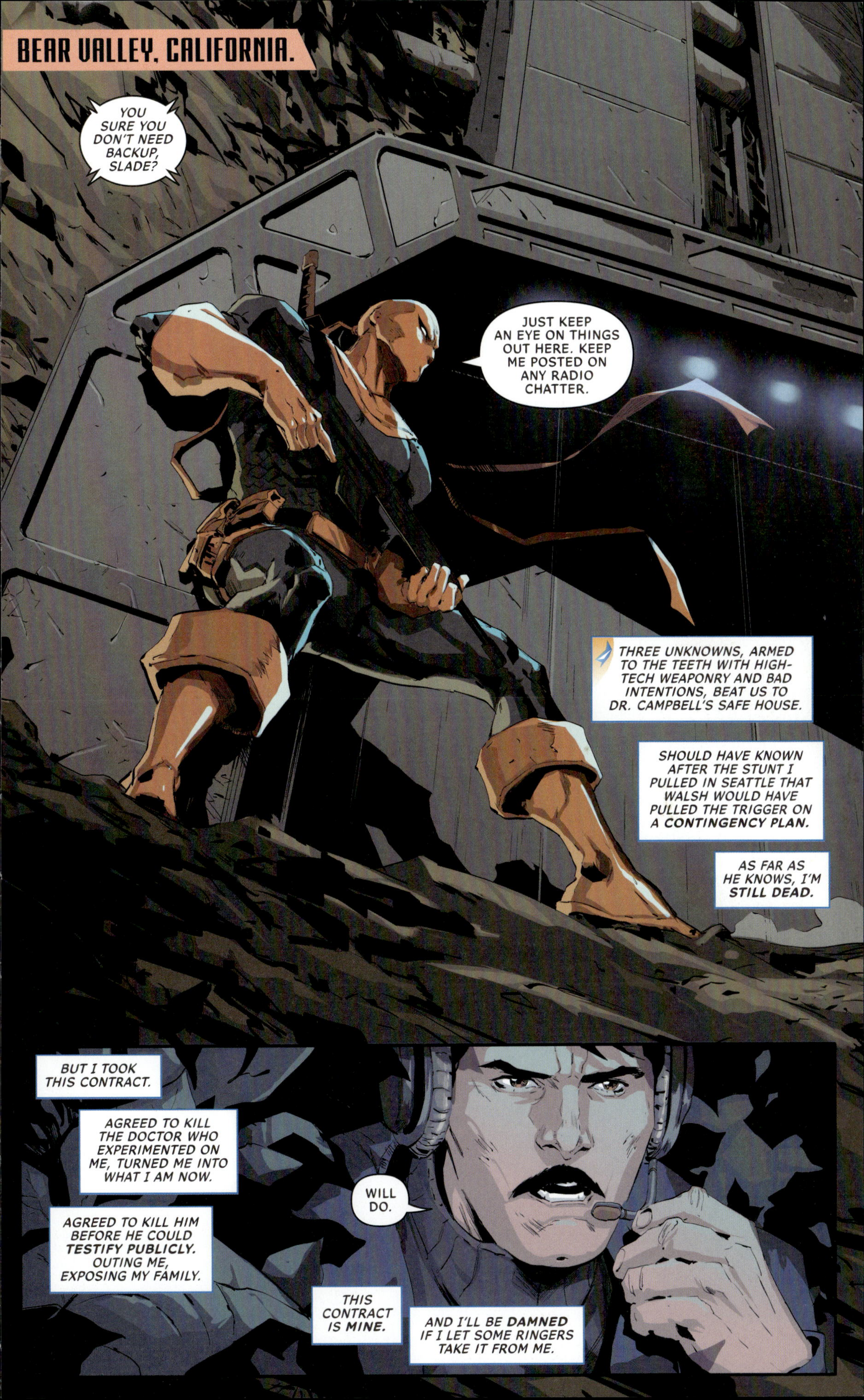
BEAR VALLEY, CALIFORNIA.
YOU SURE YOU DON'T NEED BACKUP, SLADE?
JUST KEEP AN EYE ON THINGS OUT HERE. KEEP ME POSTED ON ANY RADIO CHATTER.
THREE UNKNOWNS, ARMED TO THE TEETH WITH HIGH-TECH WEAPONRY AND BAD INTENTIONS, BEAT US TO DR. CAMPBELL'S SAFE HOUSE.
SHOULD HAVE KNOWN AFTER THE STUNT I PULLED IN SEATTLE THAT WALSH WOULD HAVE PULLED THE TRIGGER ON A CONTINGENCY PLAN.
AS FAR AS HE KNOWS, I'M STILL DEAD.
BUT I TOOK THIS CONTRACT.
AGREED TO KILL THE DOCTOR WHO EXPERIMENTED ON ME, TURNED ME INTO WHAT I AM NOW.
WILL DO.
AGREED TO KILL HIM BEFORE HE COULD TESTIFY PUBLICLY. OUTING ME, EXPOSING MY FAMILY.
THIS CONTRACT IS MINE.
AND I'LL BE DAMNED IF I LET SOME RINGERS TAKE IT FROM ME.

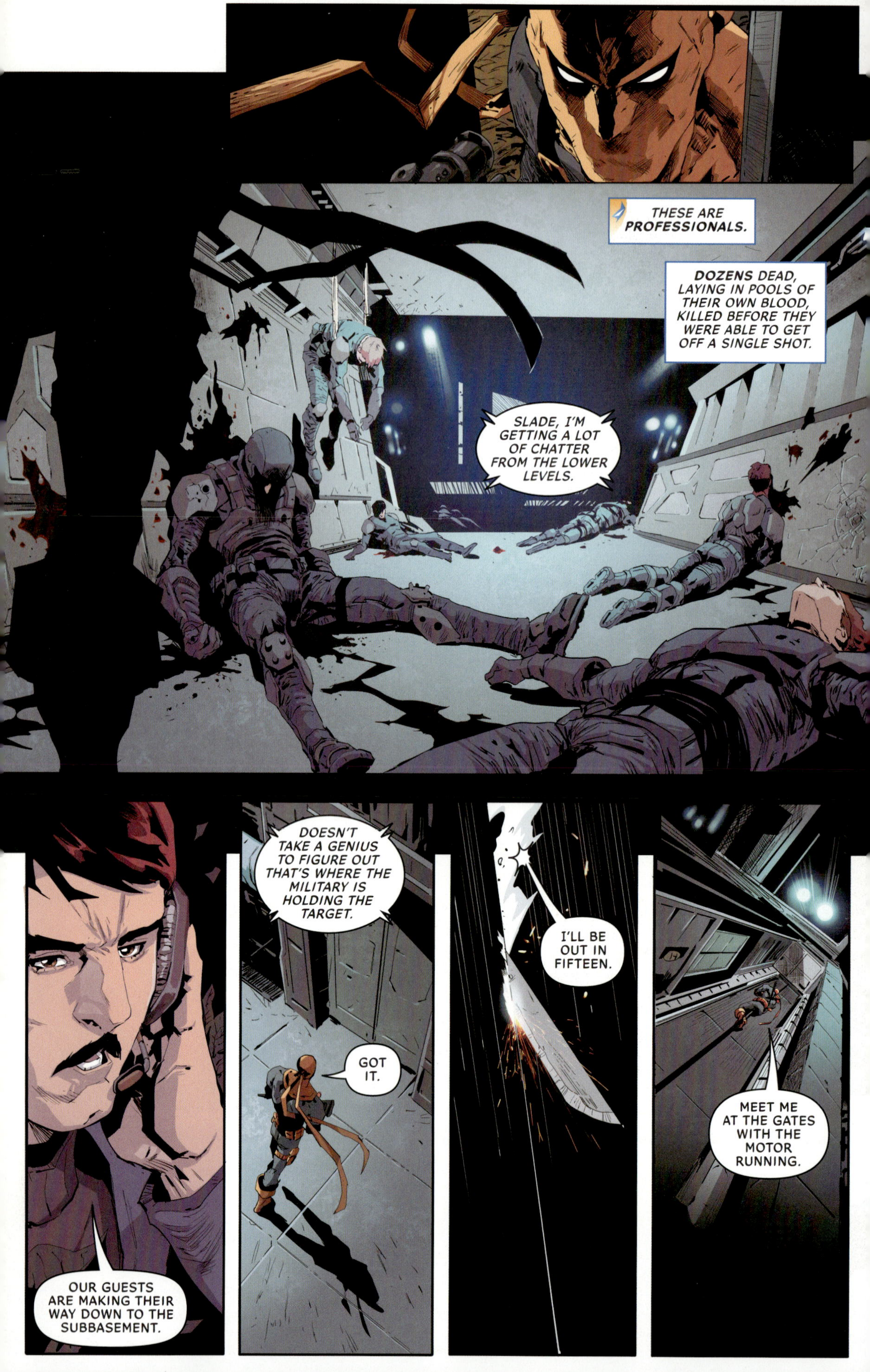

THESE ARE PROFESSIONALS.
DOZENS DEAD, LAYING IN POOLS OF THEIR OWN BLOOD, KILLED BEFORE THEY WERE ABLE TO GET OFF A SINGLE SHOT.
SLADE, I'M GETTING A LOT OF CHATTER FROM THE LOWER LEVELS.
OUR GUESTS ARE MAKING THEIR WAY DOWN TO THE SUBBASEMENT.
DOESN'T TAKE A GENIUS TO FIGURE OUT THAT'S WHERE THE MILITARY IS HOLDING THE TARGET.
GOT IT.
I'LL BE OUT IN FIFTEEN.
MEET ME AT THE GATES WITH THE MOTOR RUNNING.

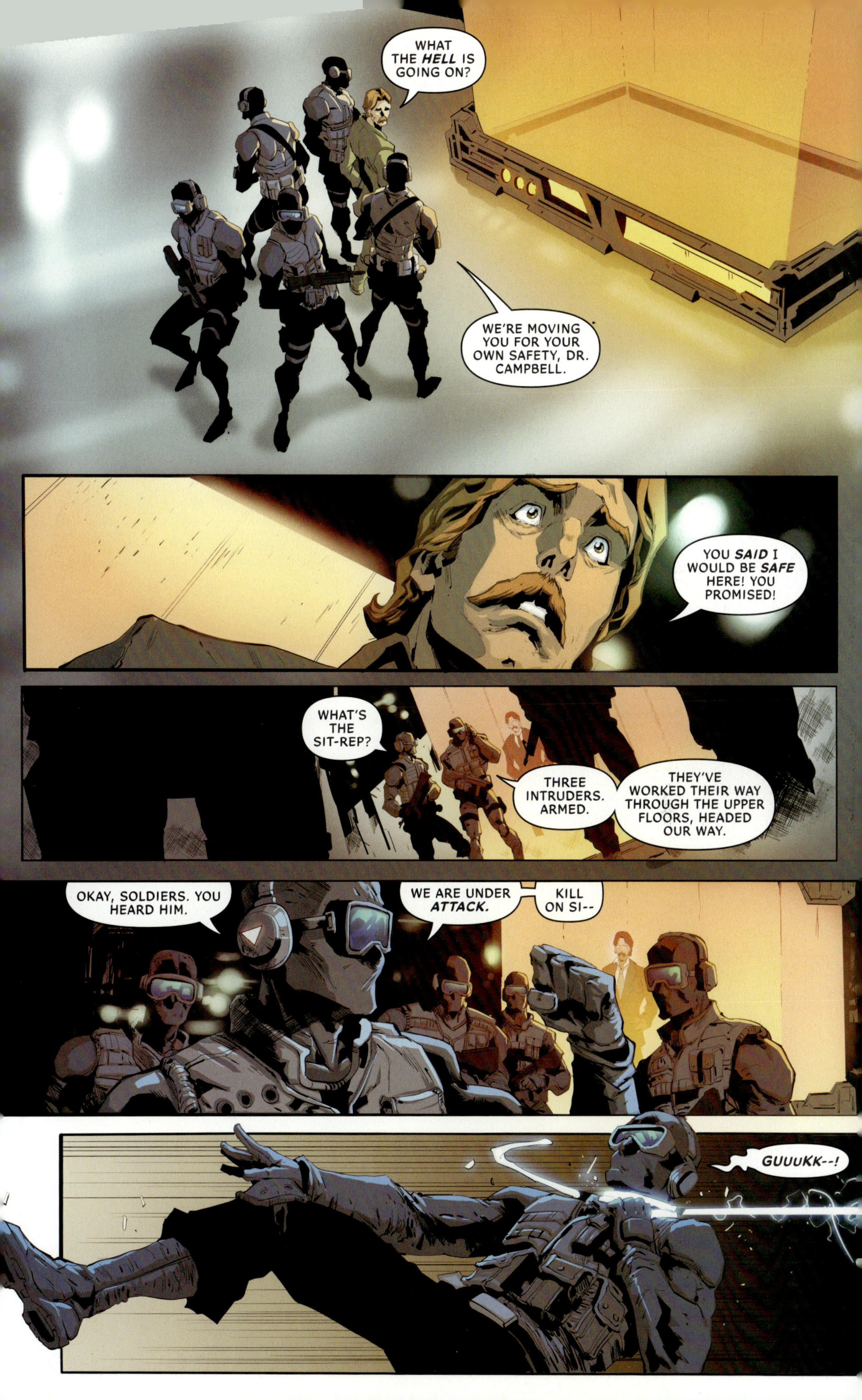
WHAT THE HELL IS GOING ON?
WE'RE MOVING YOU FOR YOUR OWN SAFETY, DR. CAMPBELL.
YOU SAID I WOULD BE SAFE HERE! YOU PROMISED!
WHAT'S THE SIT-REP?
THREE INTRUDERS. ARMED.
THEY'VE WORKED THEIR WAY THROUGH THE UPPER FLOORS, HEADED OUR WAY.
OKAY, SOLDIERS. YOU HEARD HIM.
WE ARE UNDER ATTACK.
KILL ON SI--
GUUUKK--!

GGUUUUGGNN...
SHUNK
WHOEVER'S OUT THERE, I PROMISE YOU, YOU ARE NOT GETTING INTO THIS ROOM.
DROP YOUR WEAPONS AND STEP INTO THE LIGHT WITH YOUR HANDS OVER YOUR HEADS. **NOW!**
NO...

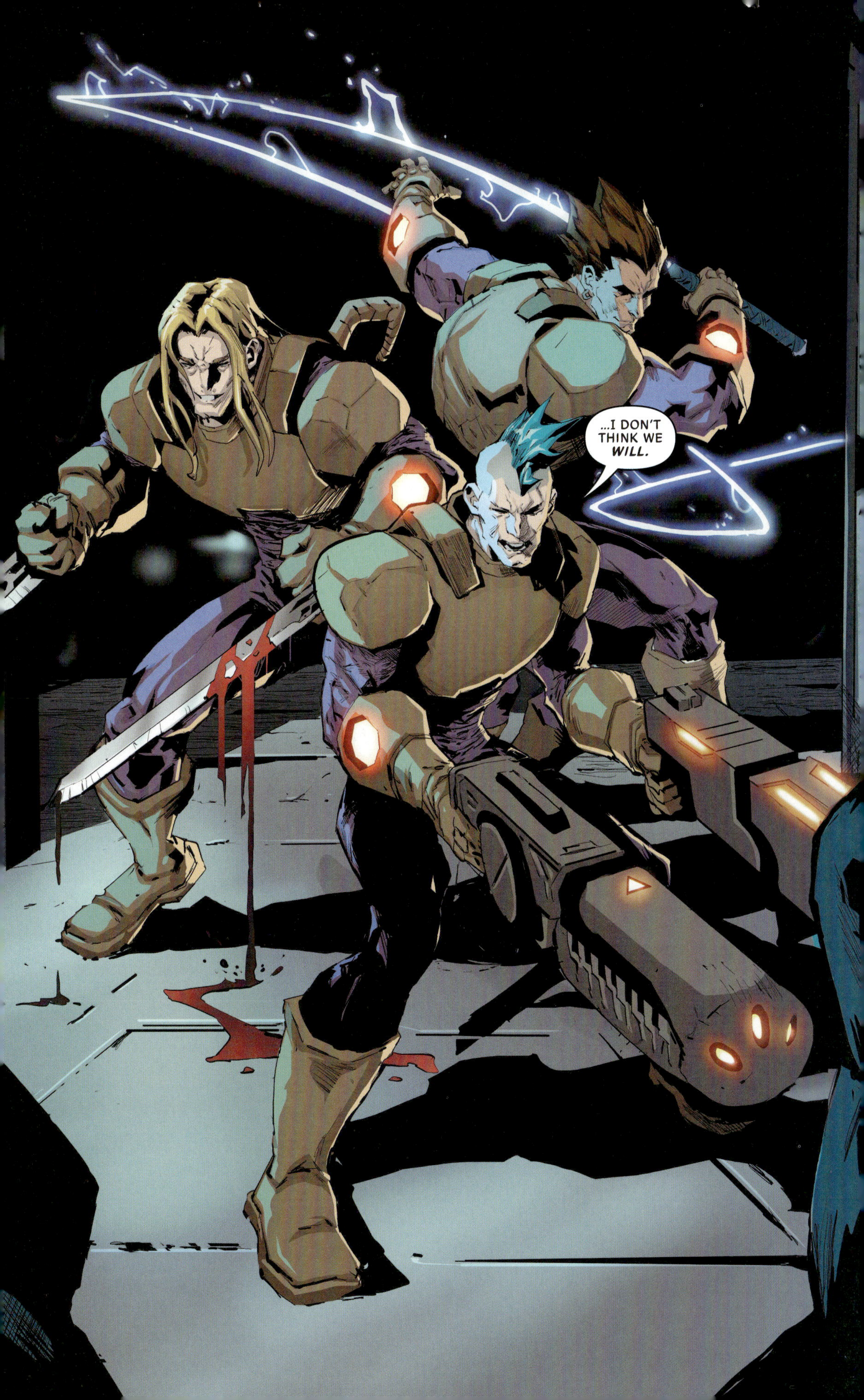
...I DON'T THINK WE WILL.

BOLSTER, GET THE TARGET.
ON IT.
NO, PLEASE. *YOU DON'T HAVE TO DO THIS!*
SORRY, DOC, THERE'S A MILLION-DOLLAR PAYOUT THAT SAYS OTHERWISE.
BUT DON'T YOU WORRY NONE. WE *AIN'T* SADISTS. WE'LL MAKE IT NICE AND QUICK FOR YOU.
OH GOD... NO...
BRAKKA
BRAKKA

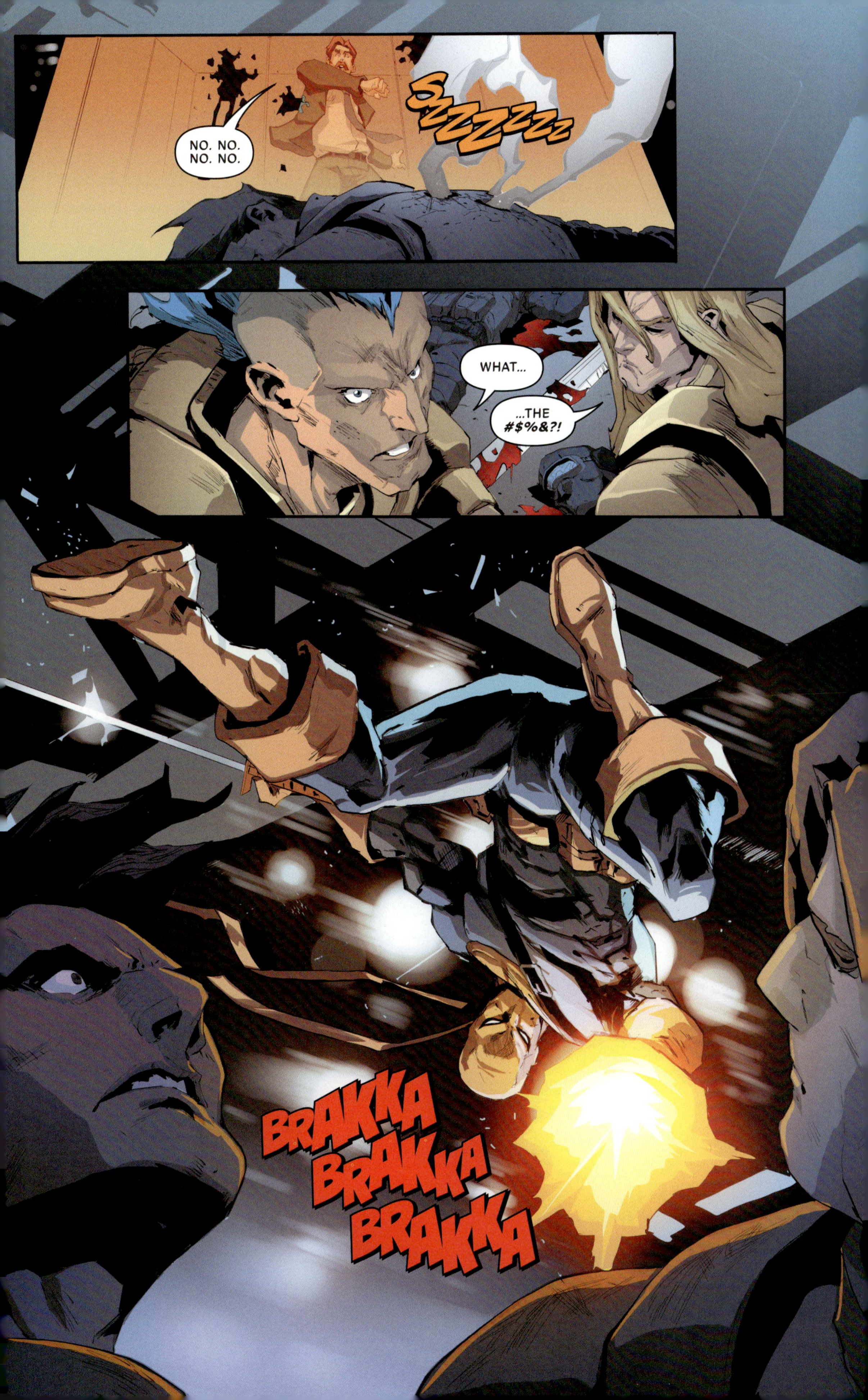
NO. NO.
NO. NO.
SZZZZZZ
WHAT...
...THE #$%&?!
BRAKKA
BRAKKA
BRAKKA

SHIIK
KACHUNK
FASTER THAN I ANTICIPATED.
GUESS I'M NOT THE ONLY AUGMENTED SOLDIER WALSH HAS IN HIS ROLODEX.
SAW WHAT YOU DID IN SEATTLE.
SHUNK
HOW YOU GOT YOUR ASS HANDED TO YOU BY GREEN ARROW.
THOUGHT HE'D KILLED YOU. YOU GET IN OVER YOUR HEAD AND HAVE TO PLAY POSSUM?
STUPID.

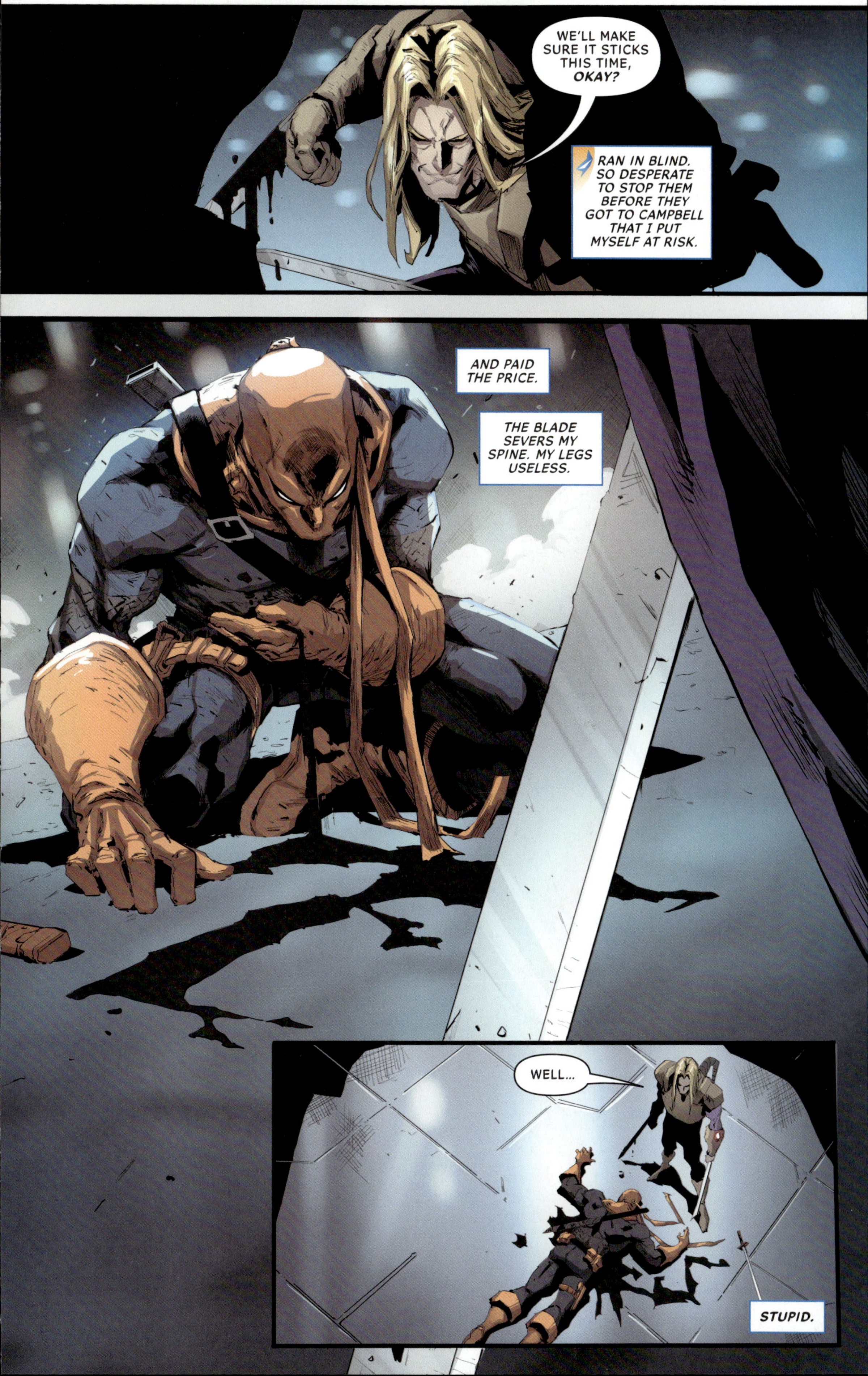
WE'LL MAKE SURE IT STICKS THIS TIME, OKAY?
RAN IN BLIND. SO DESPERATE TO STOP THEM BEFORE THEY GOT TO CAMPBELL THAT I PUT MYSELF AT RISK.
AND PAID THE PRICE.
THE BLADE SEVERS MY SPINE. MY LEGS USELESS.
WELL...
STUPID.

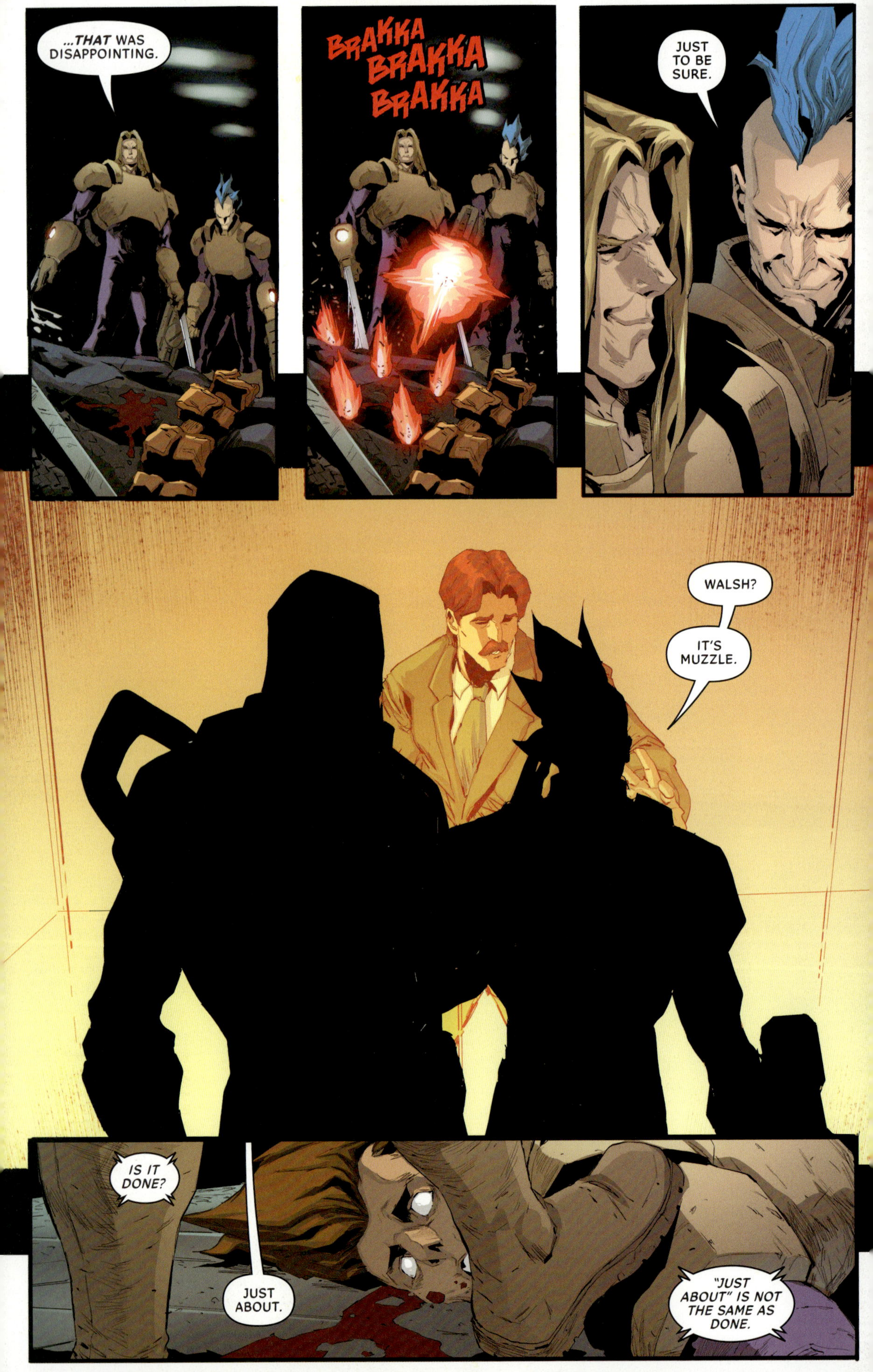
...THAT WAS DISAPPOINTING.
BRAKKA BRAKKA BRAKKA
JUST TO BE SURE.
WALSH?
IT'S MUZZLE.
IS IT DONE?
JUST ABOUT.
"JUST ABOUT" IS NOT THE SAME AS DONE.

YEAH, WELL, WE RAN INTO A BIT OF A *PROBLEM* WITH YOUR BOY FROM SEATTLE.
SNUCK UP ON US. KILLED BOLSTER.
A MILLION SPLIT TWO WAYS IS SURELY BETTER THAN A MILLION SPLIT THREE WAYS.
*TRUE. BUT BOLSTER WAS ONE OF **US.***
CASUALTIES ARE ALWAYS A POSSIBILITY.
TELL HIM WE WANT A RAISE. TWO MILLION.
ARE YOU *CERTAIN* THAT YOU WERE ATTACKED BY THE *SAME* MAN FROM SEATTLE?
DID YOU CONFIRM HIS IDENTITY?
I DON'T KNOW TOO MANY IDIOTS RUNNING AROUND WITH A ***FLAMING-ORANGE MASK.***
*I WANT TO **SEE** HIS FACE.*
SEND ME A VISUAL CONFIRMATION.
ALL RIGHT. ALL RIGHT. DON'T GET YOUR PANTIES IN A KNOT. IT'S NOT LIKE HE'S GOING ANY--
$#!&...

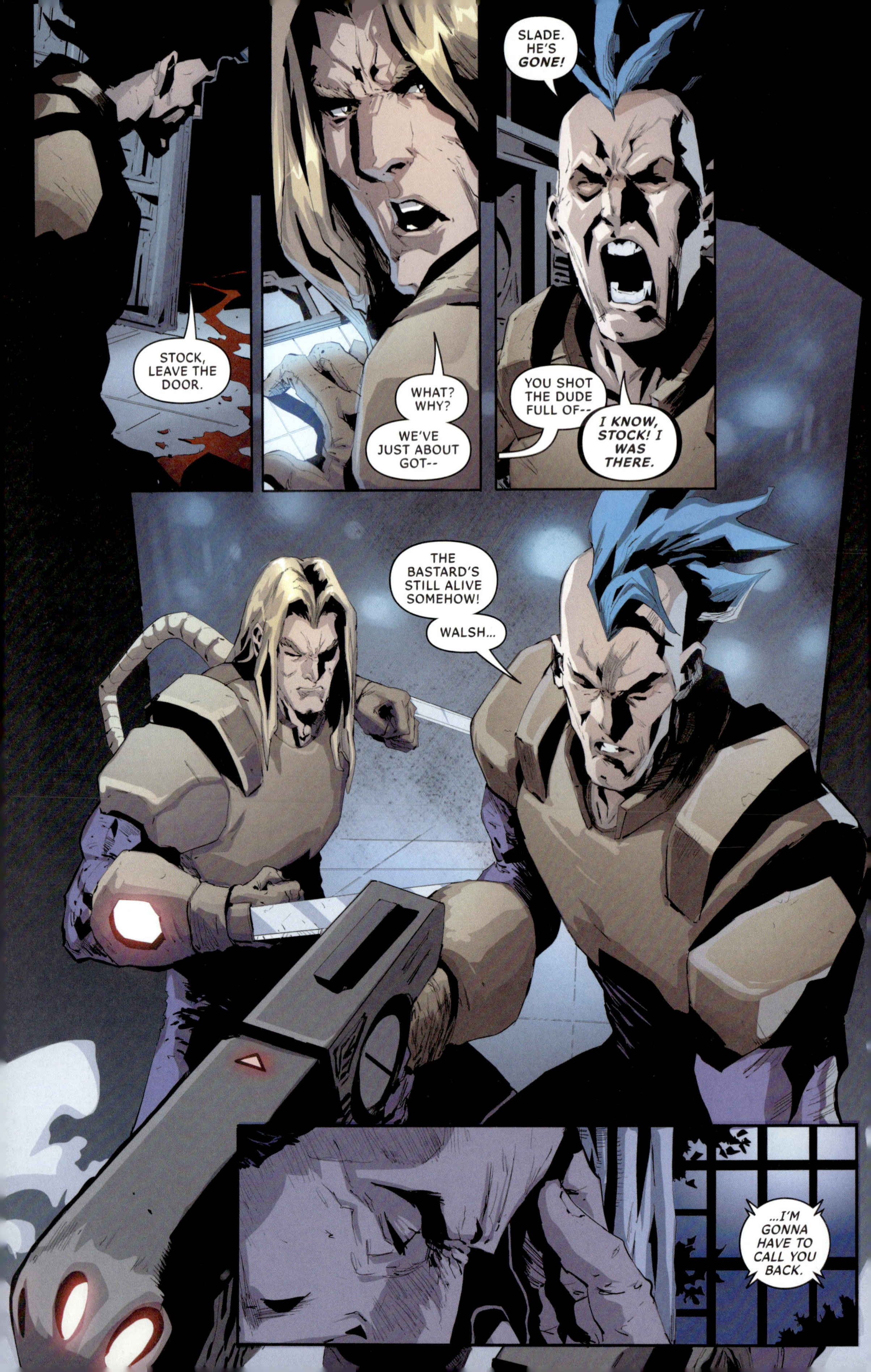
STOCK, LEAVE THE DOOR.
WHAT? WHY?
WE'VE JUST ABOUT GOT--
SLADE. HE'S GONE!
YOU SHOT THE DUDE FULL OF--
I KNOW, STOCK! I WAS THERE.
THE BASTARD'S STILL ALIVE SOMEHOW!
WALSH...
...I'M GONNA HAVE TO CALL YOU BACK.

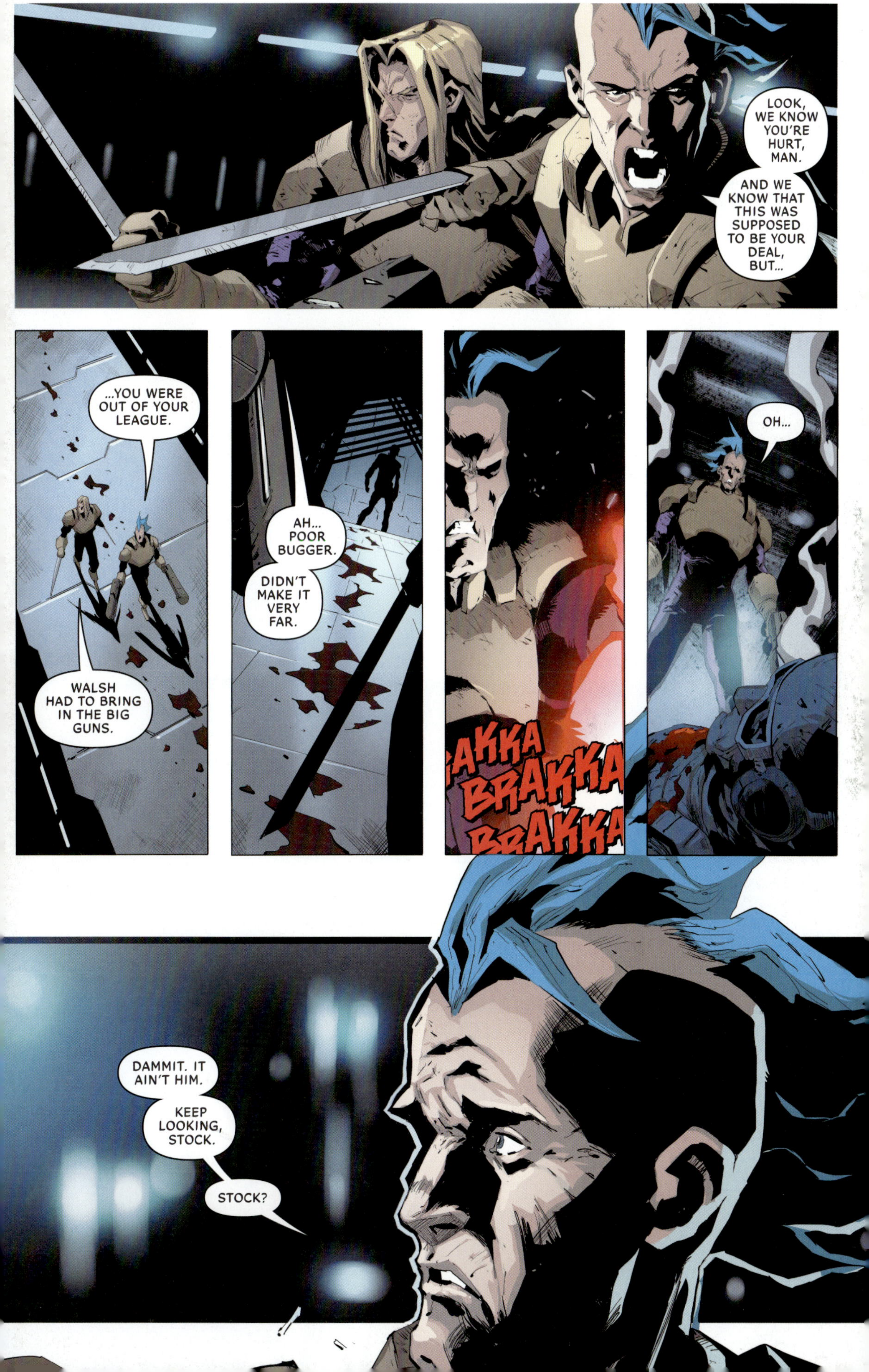
LOOK, WE KNOW YOU'RE HURT, MAN.
AND WE KNOW THAT THIS WAS SUPPOSED TO BE YOUR DEAL, BUT...
...YOU WERE OUT OF YOUR LEAGUE.
WALSH HAD TO BRING IN THE BIG GUNS.
AH... POOR BUGGER.
DIDN'T MAKE IT VERY FAR.
BRAKKA BRAKKA BRAKKA
OH...
DAMMIT. IT AIN'T HIM.
KEEP LOOKING, STOCK.
STOCK?

YOUR PARTNER IS RIGHT, THIS WAS SUPPOSED TO BE MY DEAL.
BUT HE'S WRONG ABOUT ME BEING OUT OF MY LEAGUE.
YOU'RE *GOOD.*
I'M *BETTER.*
THWUMP
YOU CAN TALK #$@& ALL YOU WANT, MAN.
BUT WORDS WITHOUT ACTION DON'T MEAN--
SHIK

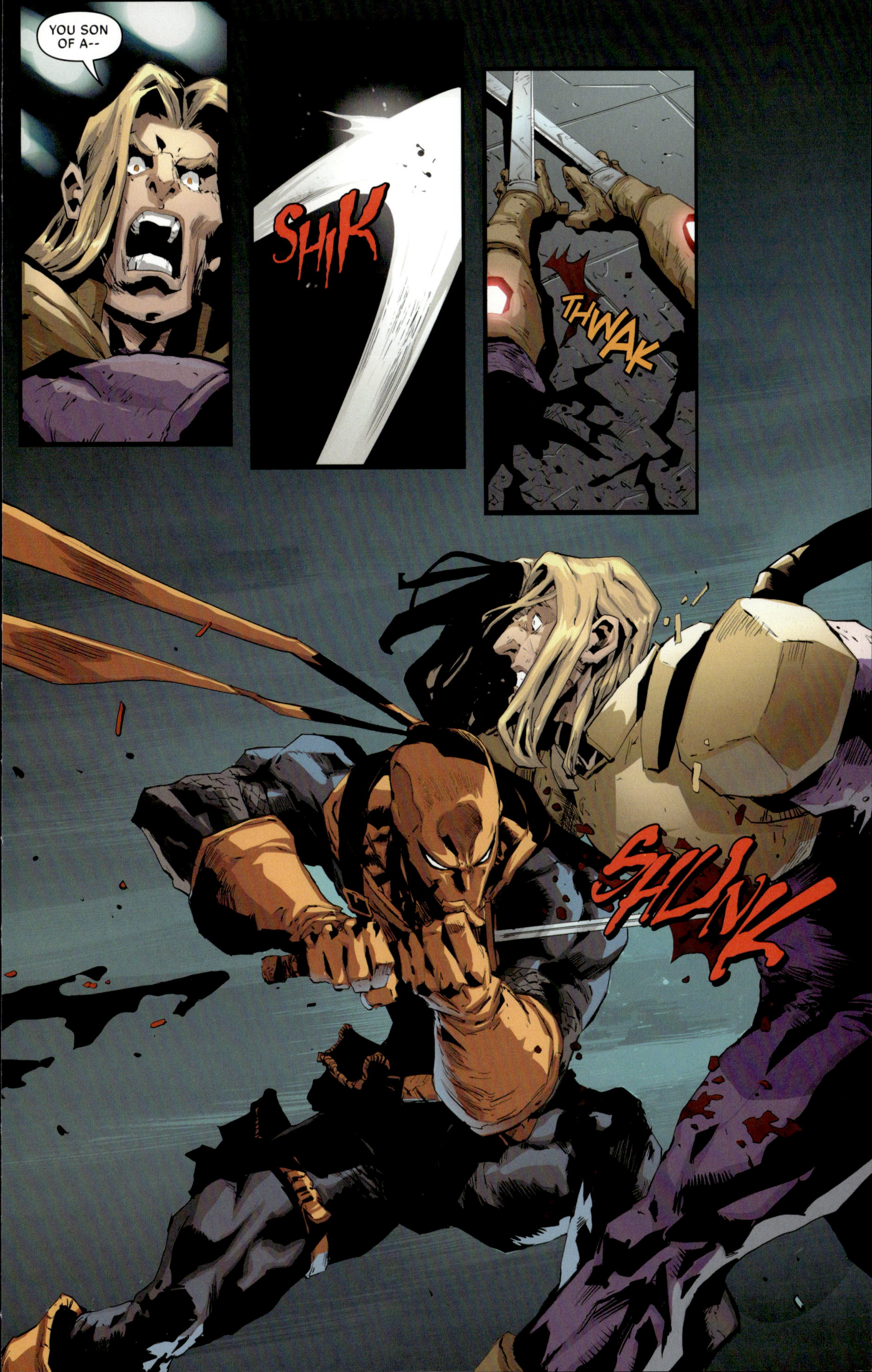
YOU SON OF A--
SHIK
THWAK
SHUNK

STOCK?
ANSWER ME!
STOCK!
I'M GOING TO KILL THAT @%#$ FOR WHAT HE DID TO YOU.
I SWEAR IT, MAN. I SWEAR I'LL--
YOU TALK A PRETTY BIG GAME, KID.
BUT YOU'RE *SLOPPY AS HELL* LETTING *EMOTIONS* GET IN THE WAY LIKE THAT.

BRAKKA BRAKKA
%#&$ YOU! YOU WERE DEAD. I SAW IT!
BLAM BLAM BLAM
UNFF...
OUTFIT'S BULLETPROOF.
YOU MIGHT WANT TO LOOK INTO IT.
BANG

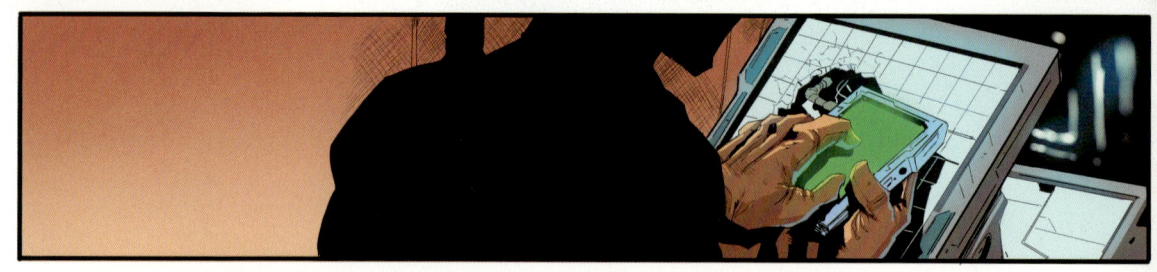

PLEASE! PLEASE DON'T KILL ME!

TELL WALSH I WON'T TESTIFY. I SWEAR.

I'LL VANISH. I'LL JUST...I'LL DISAPPEAR FOREVER.

I'M NOT DOING THIS FOR WALSH.

YOU EXPERIMENTED ON ME.

NEARLY KILLED ME.

NEARLY LEFT MY WIFE A WIDOW, MY SON AN ORPHAN.

YOU LIED TO ME ABOUT WHAT I WAS SIGNING UP FOR.

LIED TO 47 OTHERS SOLDIERS.

KILLED THEM. LEFT THEIR WIVES AND HUSBANDS WIDOWS, THEIR CHILDREN ORPHANS.

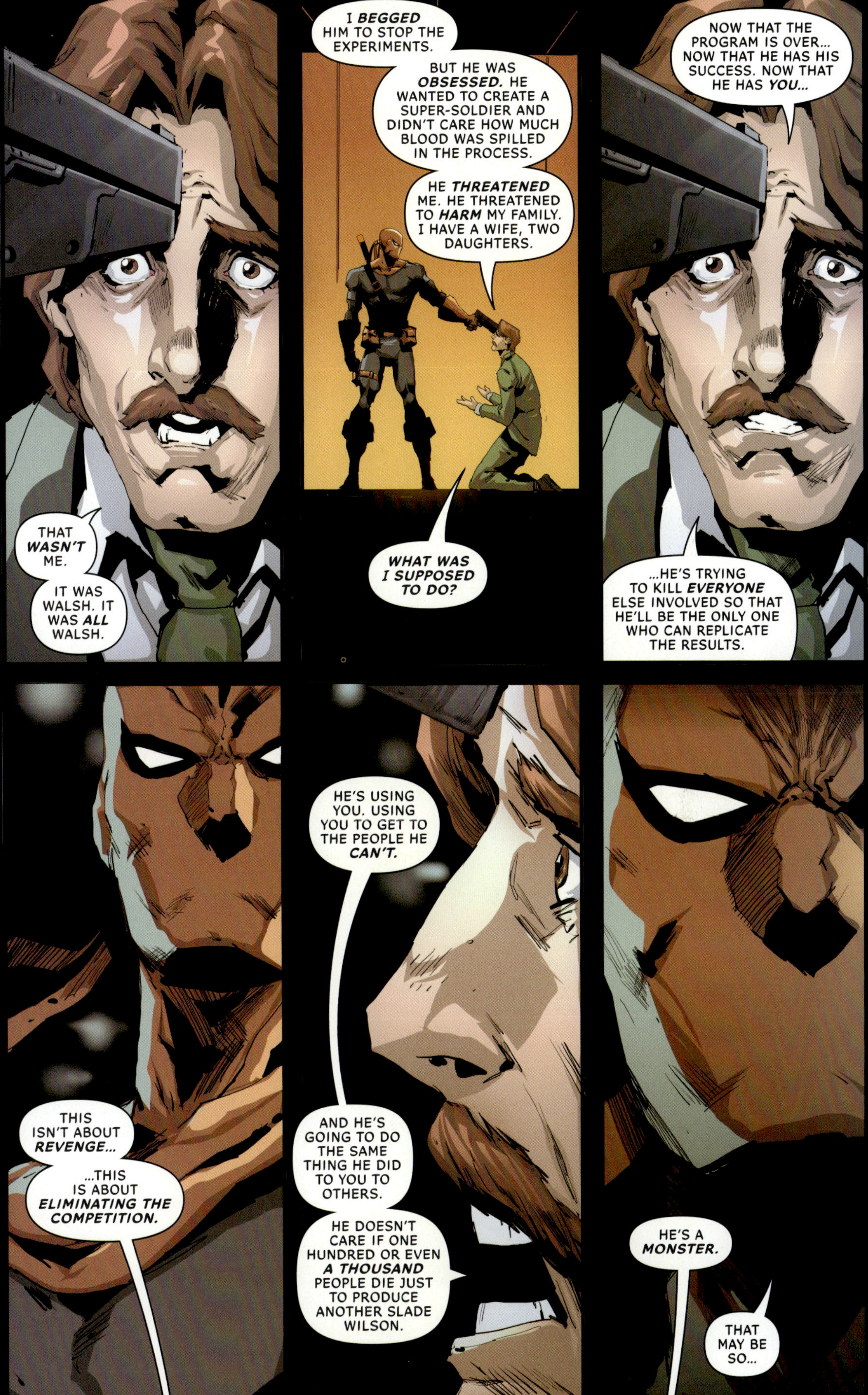

THAT WASN'T ME.
IT WAS WALSH. IT WAS ALL WALSH.
I BEGGED HIM TO STOP THE EXPERIMENTS.
BUT HE WAS OBSESSED. HE WANTED TO CREATE A SUPER-SOLDIER AND DIDN'T CARE HOW MUCH BLOOD WAS SPILLED IN THE PROCESS.
HE THREATENED ME. HE THREATENED TO HARM MY FAMILY. I HAVE A WIFE, TWO DAUGHTERS.
WHAT WAS I SUPPOSED TO DO?
NOW THAT THE PROGRAM IS OVER... NOW THAT HE HAS HIS SUCCESS. NOW THAT HE HAS YOU...
...HE'S TRYING TO KILL EVERYONE ELSE INVOLVED SO THAT HE'LL BE THE ONLY ONE WHO CAN REPLICATE THE RESULTS.
THIS ISN'T ABOUT REVENGE...
...THIS IS ABOUT ELIMINATING THE COMPETITION.
HE'S USING YOU. USING YOU TO GET TO THE PEOPLE HE CAN'T.
AND HE'S GOING TO DO THE SAME THING HE DID TO YOU TO OTHERS.
HE DOESN'T CARE IF ONE HUNDRED OR EVEN A THOUSAND PEOPLE DIE JUST TO PRODUCE ANOTHER SLADE WILSON.
HE'S A MONSTER.
THAT MAY BE SO...

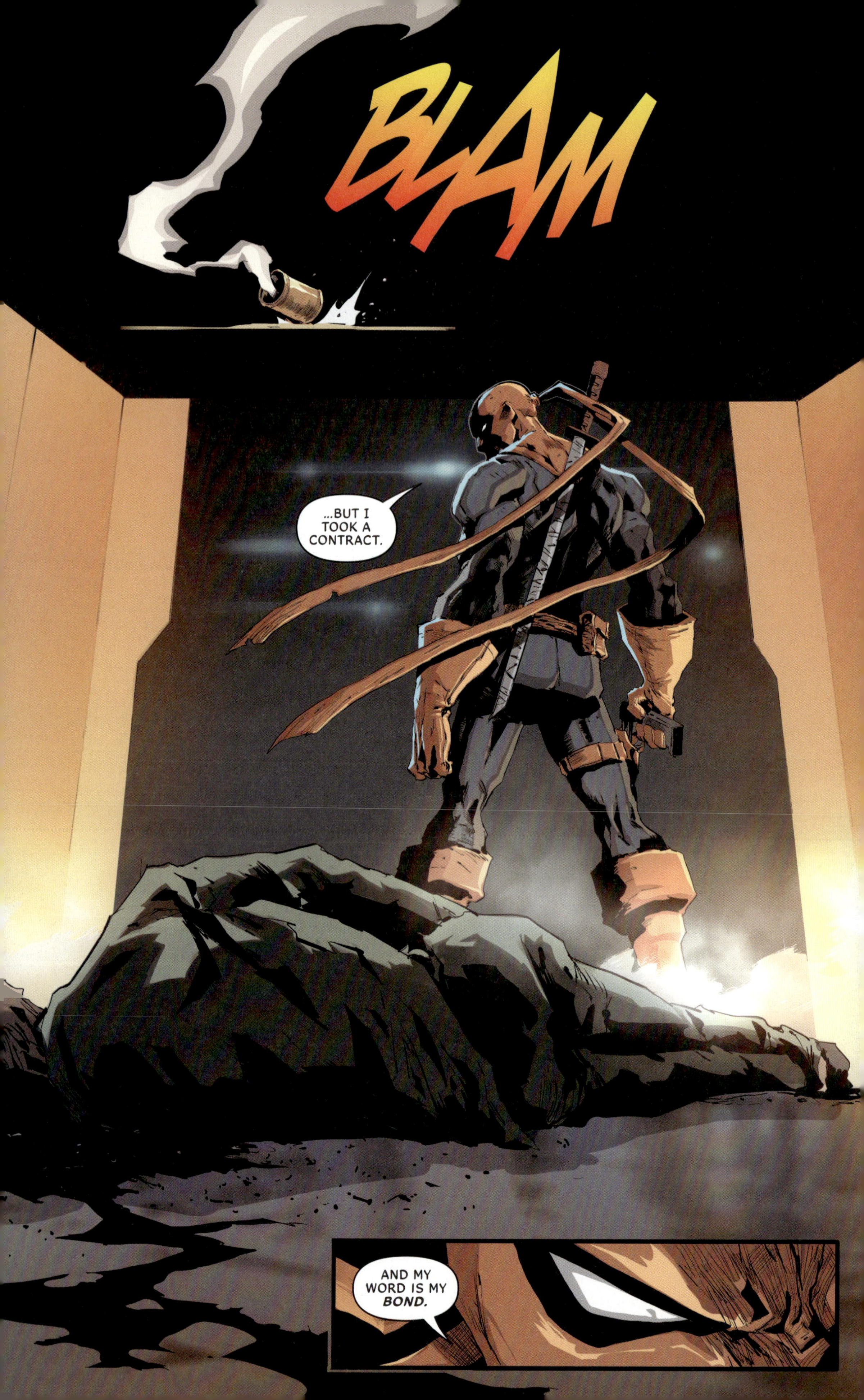
BLAM
...BUT I TOOK A CONTRACT.
AND MY WORD IS MY *BOND.*

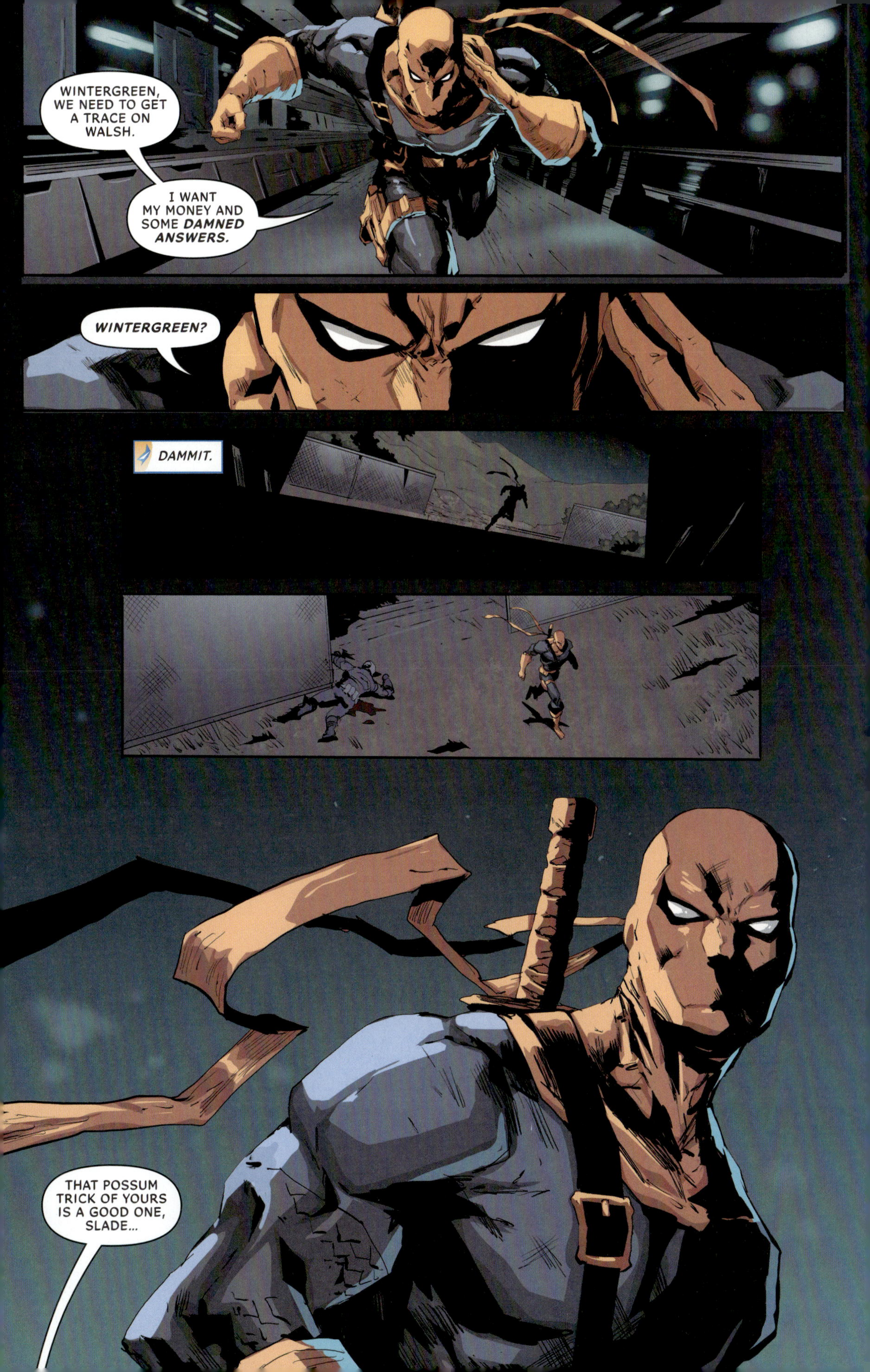
WINTERGREEN, WE NEED TO GET A TRACE ON WALSH.
I WANT MY MONEY AND SOME *DAMNED ANSWERS.*
WINTERGREEN?
DAMMIT.
THAT POSSUM TRICK OF YOURS IS A GOOD ONE, SLADE...

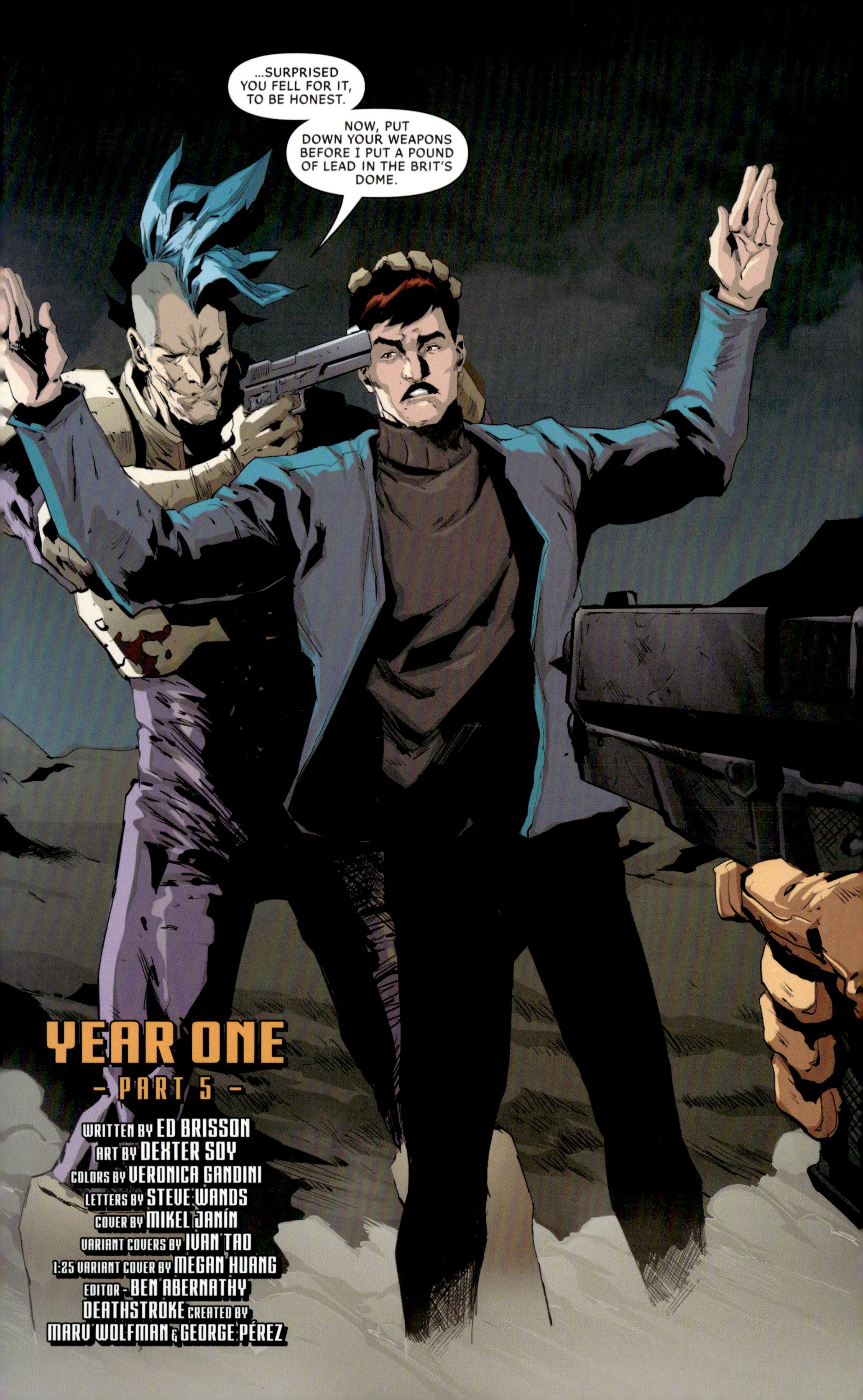

...SURPRISED YOU FELL FOR IT, TO BE HONEST.
NOW, PUT DOWN YOUR WEAPONS BEFORE I PUT A POUND OF LEAD IN THE BRIT'S DOME.
YEAR ONE
- PART 5 -
WRITTEN BY ED BRISSON
ART BY DEXTER SOY
COLORS BY VERONICA GANDINI
LETTERS BY STEVE WANDS
COVER BY MIKEL JANÍN
VARIANT COVERS BY IVAN TAO
1:25 VARIANT COVER BY MEGAN HUANG
EDITOR - BEN ABERNATHY
DEATHSTROKE CREATED BY
MARV WOLFMAN & GEORGE PÉREZ

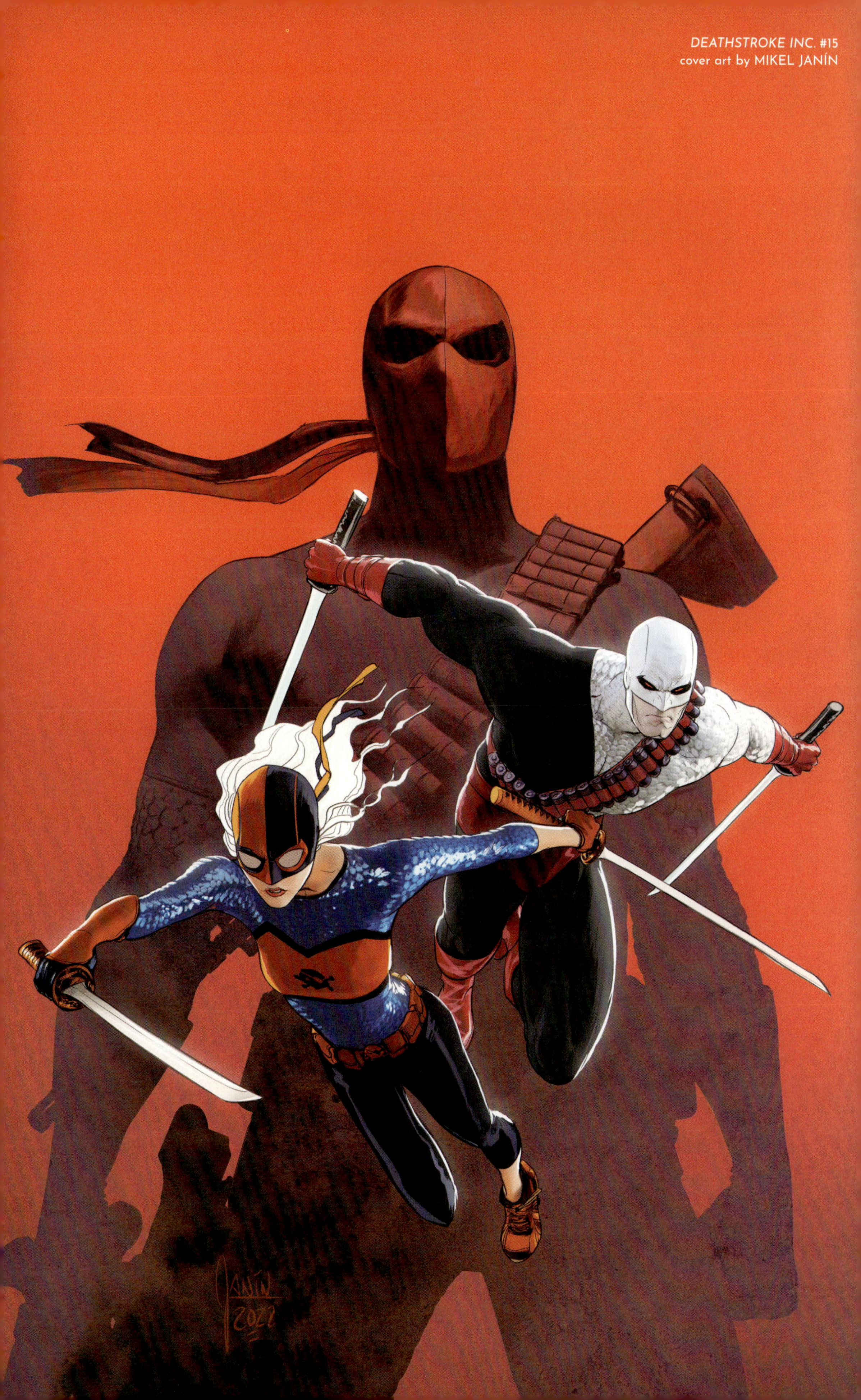

DEATHSTROKE INC. #15
cover art by MIKEL JANÍN

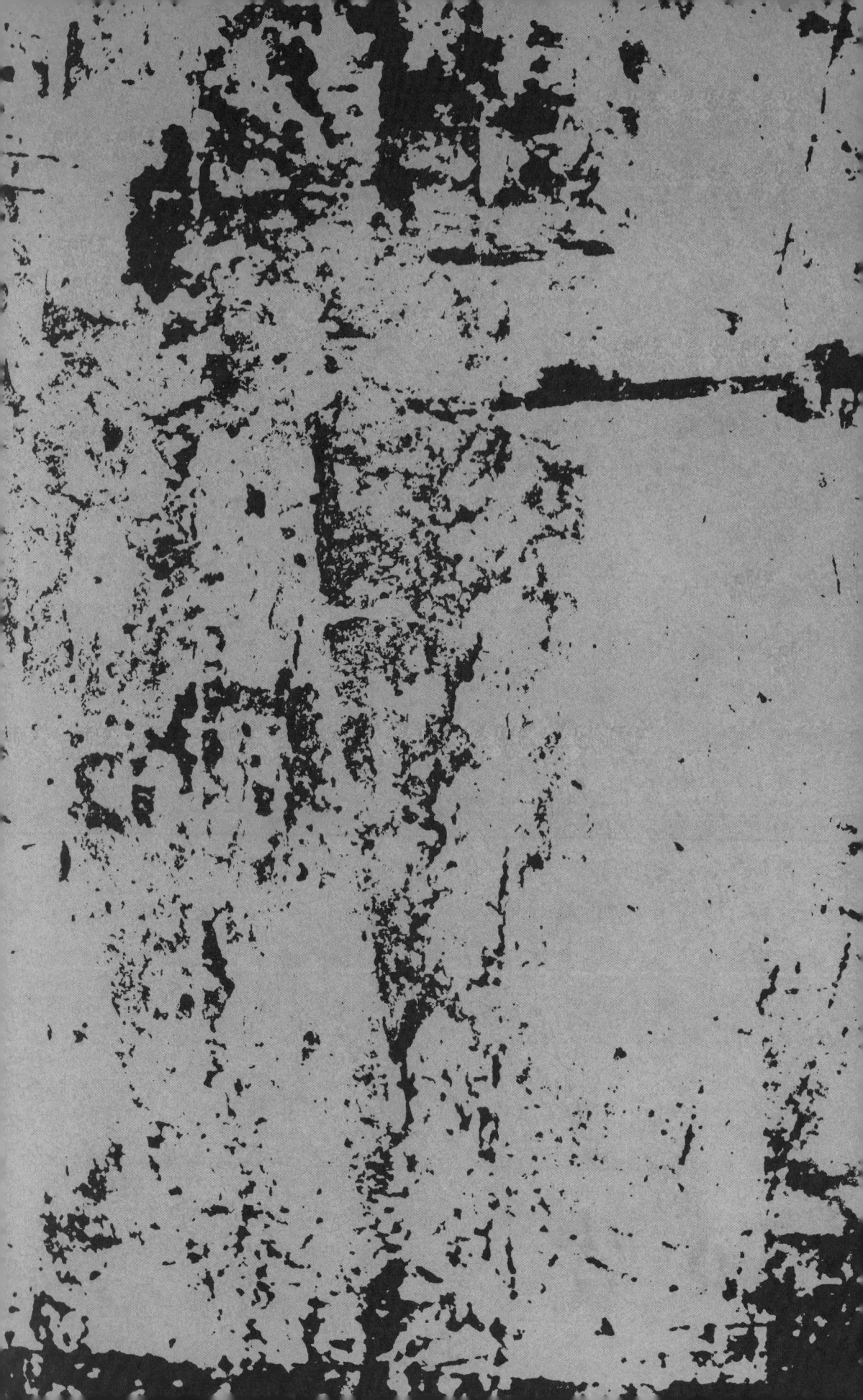

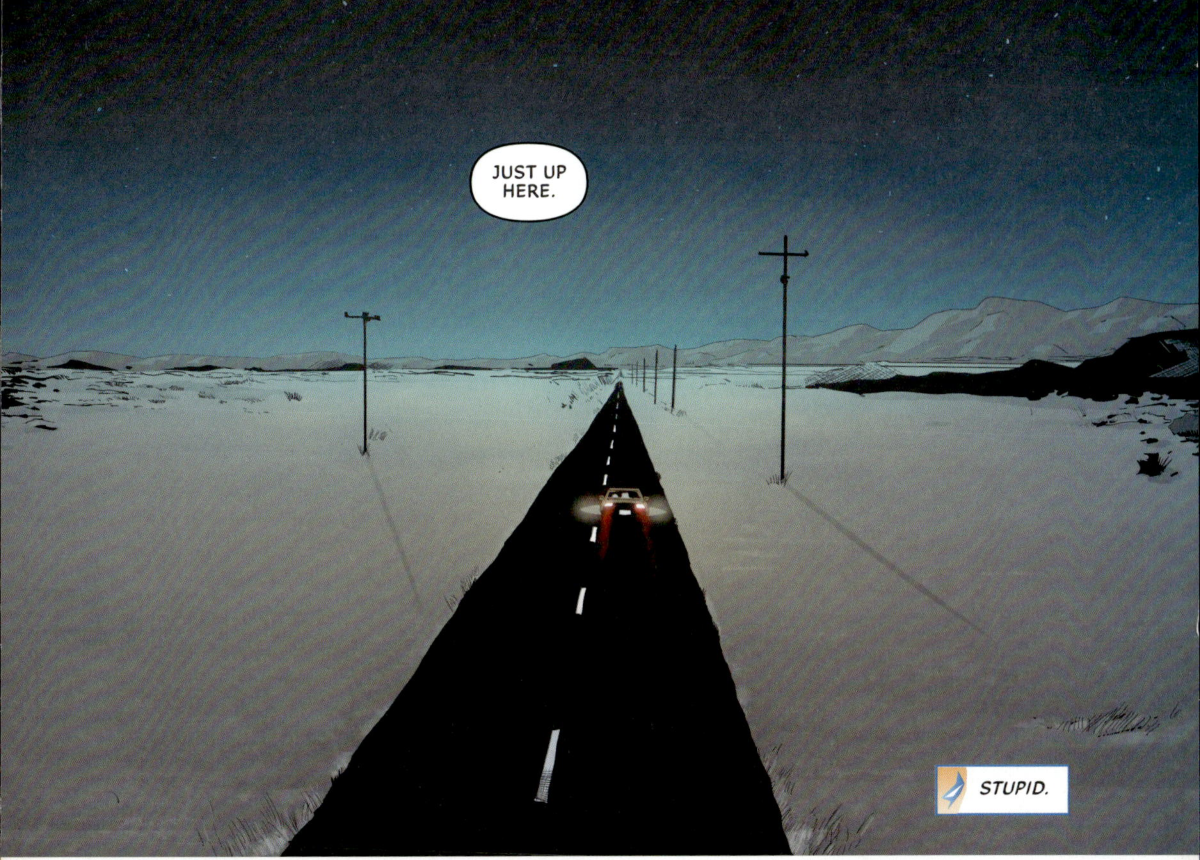
JUST UP HERE.
STUPID.

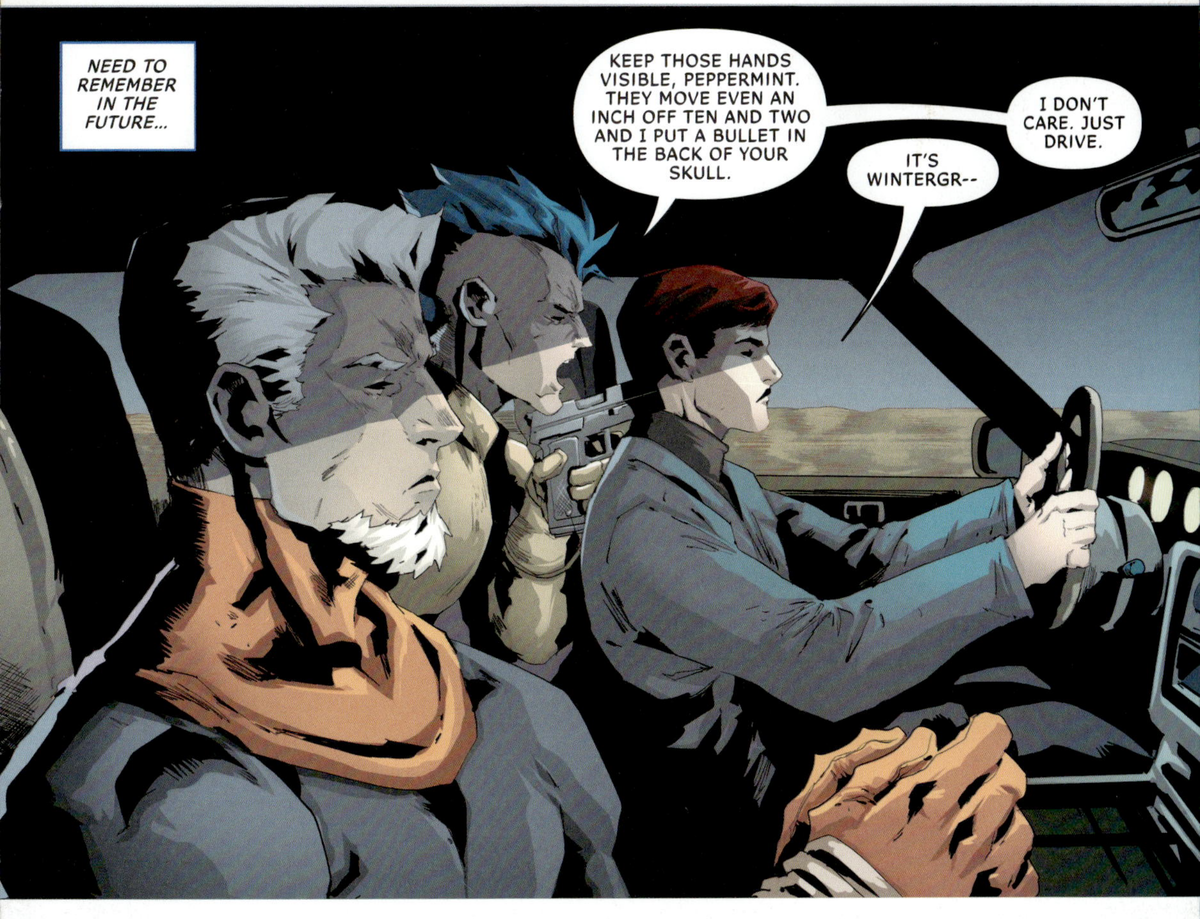
NEED TO REMEMBER IN THE FUTURE...
KEEP THOSE HANDS VISIBLE, PEPPERMINT. THEY MOVE EVEN AN INCH OFF TEN AND TWO AND I PUT A BULLET IN THE BACK OF YOUR SKULL.
I DON'T CARE. JUST DRIVE.
IT'S WINTERGR--

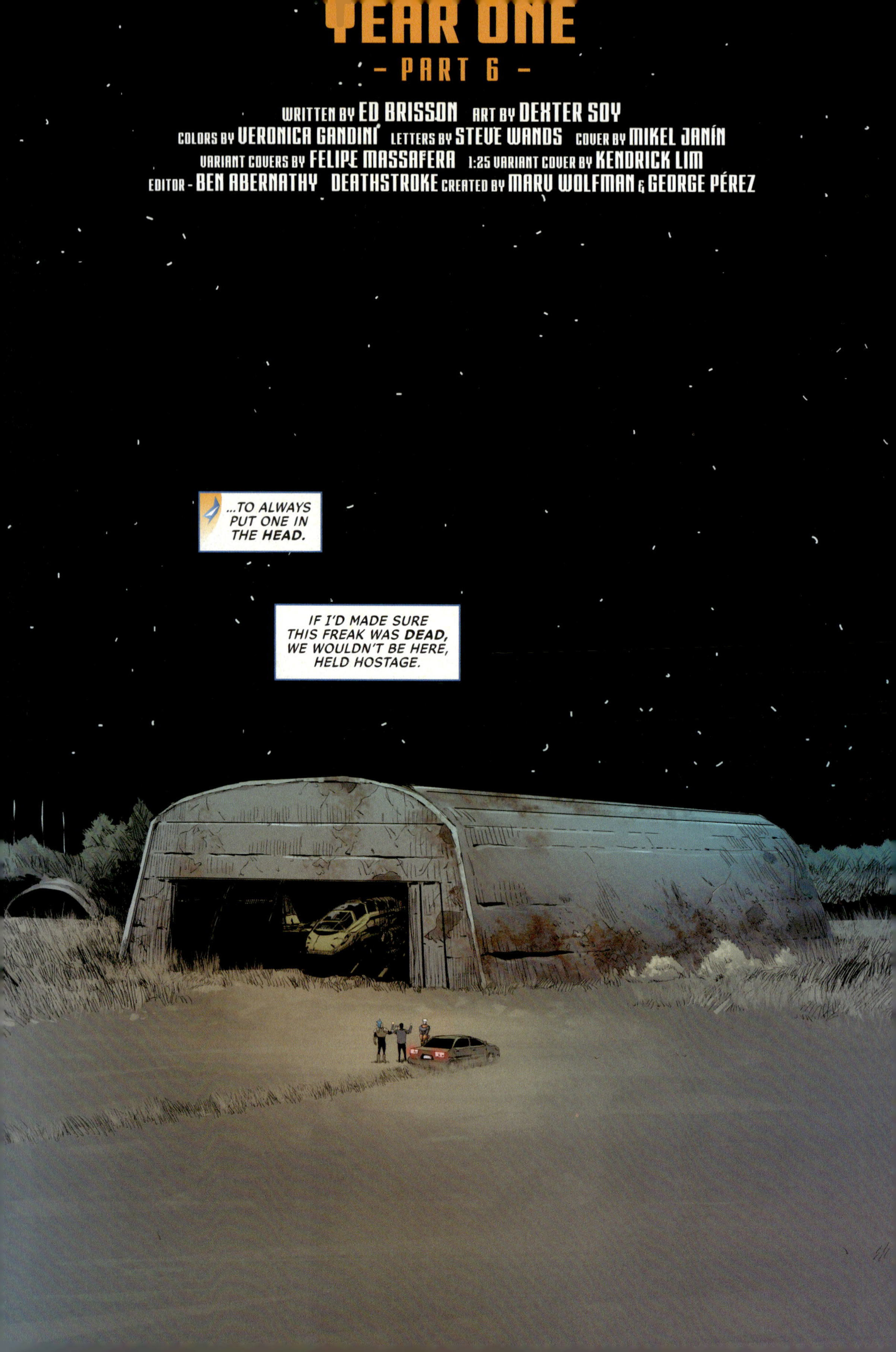
YEAR ONE
- PART 6 -
WRITTEN BY ED BRISSON ART BY DEXTER SOY
COLORS BY VERONICA GANDINI LETTERS BY STEVE WANDS COVER BY MIKEL JANÍN
VARIANT COVERS BY FELIPE MASSAFERA 1:25 VARIANT COVER BY KENDRICK LIM
EDITOR - BEN ABERNATHY DEATHSTROKE CREATED BY MARV WOLFMAN & GEORGE PÉREZ
...TO ALWAYS PUT ONE IN THE HEAD.
IF I'D MADE SURE THIS FREAK WAS DEAD, WE WOULDN'T BE HERE, HELD HOSTAGE.

PRETTY SWEET RIDE, AIN'T SHE?
WALSH KNOWS HOW TO SPOIL HIS FAVORITES.
IF IT WAS UP TO ME, I'D TAKE YOU TWO UP AS HIGH AS THIS BAD BOY WILL GO AND DROP YOU.
BUT WALSH WANTS A WORD.
AFTER HE HAS HIS WORD THOUGH...
...I'M GOING TO MAKE YOU SUFFER, SLADE.
I'M GOING TO TAKE YOU APART BIT BY BIT. FLAY OFF YOUR SKIN, PULL OUT YOUR FINGERNAILS, PULL YOUR TEETH OUT ONE BY ONE.
THEN LET THAT HEALING FACTOR OF YOURS KICK IN AND DO IT ALL OVER AGAIN.
YOU'RE GOING TO BEG ME TO END IT, SLADE.
BOLSTER AND STOCK WERE MY CREW.
AND YOU CAN'T KILL MY CREW AND THINK YOU CAN WALK AWAY.

IT JUST OCCURRED TO ME...
...WALSH DON'T NEED THE BRIT.
AND NOW THAT I GOT YOU TIED UP ALL NICE LIKE, I GUESS I DON'T MUCH NEED HIM ANYMORE EITHER.
SHOULDN'T YOU BE PILOTING THE SHIP?
YOU SEEN THIS THING? HIGH-TECH AS $#%@. AUTOPILOT AND ALL THAT. ALL I'M DOIN' UP THERE IS TWIDDLIN' MY THUMBS.
MUZZLE, YOU DO ANYTHING TO WINTERGREEN AND I SWEAR TO GOD I'LL BREAK THESE CHAINS AND GUT YOU.
SURE, SURE.

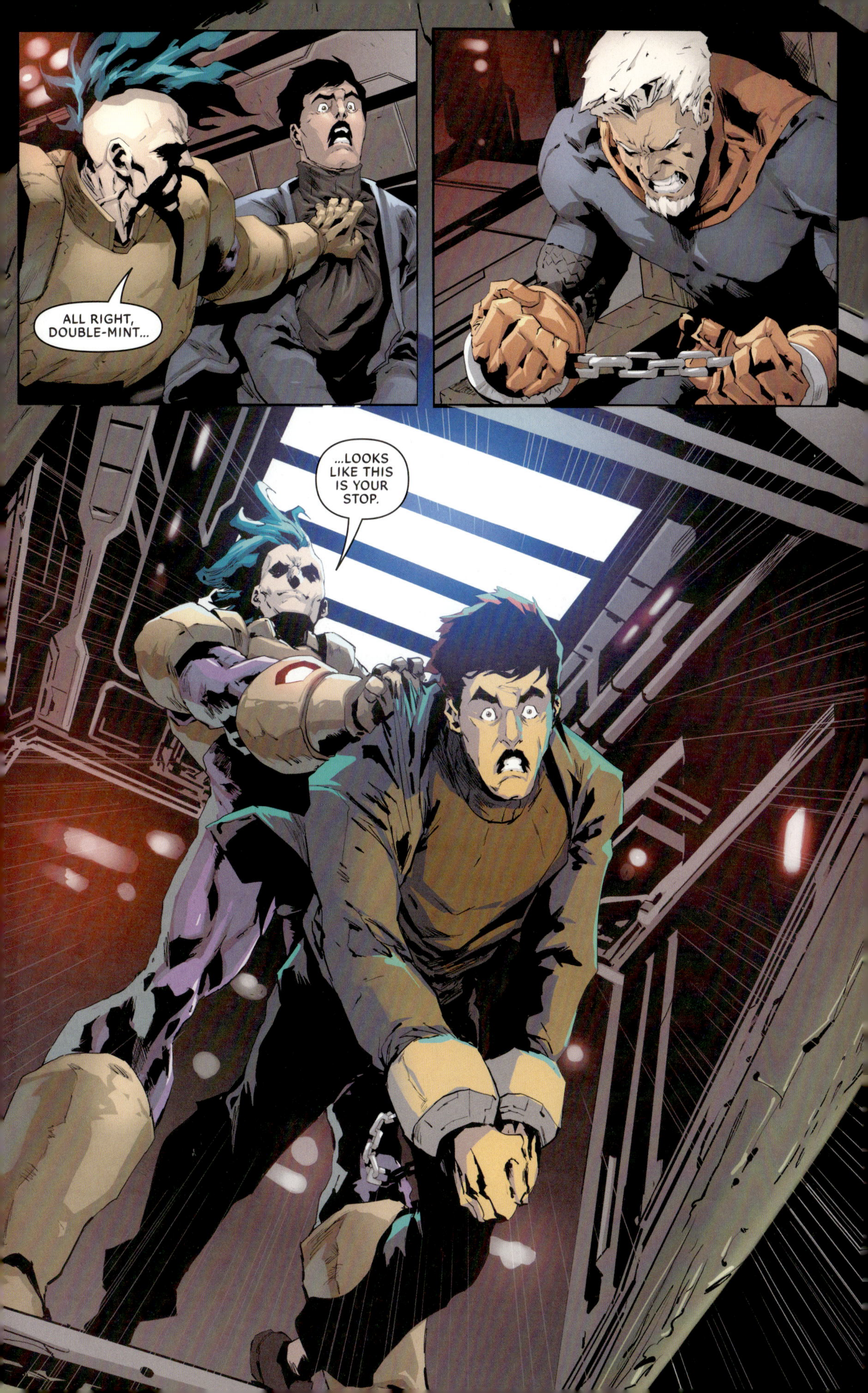
ALL RIGHT, DOUBLE-MINT...
...LOOKS LIKE THIS IS YOUR STOP.

ANYTHING YOU WANT TO SAY TO YOUR FRIEND BEFORE HE GOES *BYE-BYE?*
MAYBE YOU WANT TO APOLOGIZE FOR *KILLING* MY FRIENDS...
...AND PUTTING HIM IN THIS PREDICAMENT IN THE *FIRST PLACE?*
NO?
AH WELL.
GUESS SOME PEOPLE JUST CAN'T ADMIT WHEN THEY'VE *$@%& UP.*
LATER, WINTERGREEN.

GUKKk--!
WINTERGREEN, YOU OKAY?
I'M DANGLING AT ABOUT 30,000 FEET...
...FROM A JET THAT'S MOVING 900 KLICKS AN HOUR, BUT OTHER THAN THAT...
...JUST PEACHY.
GKKKKK...
FWACK
UNFF.
THAT'S IT.
I DON'T GIVE A $#&@ THAT WALSH WANTS YOU ALIVE.
HE'S JUST GONNA HAVE TO DEAL WITH THE DISAPPOINT--

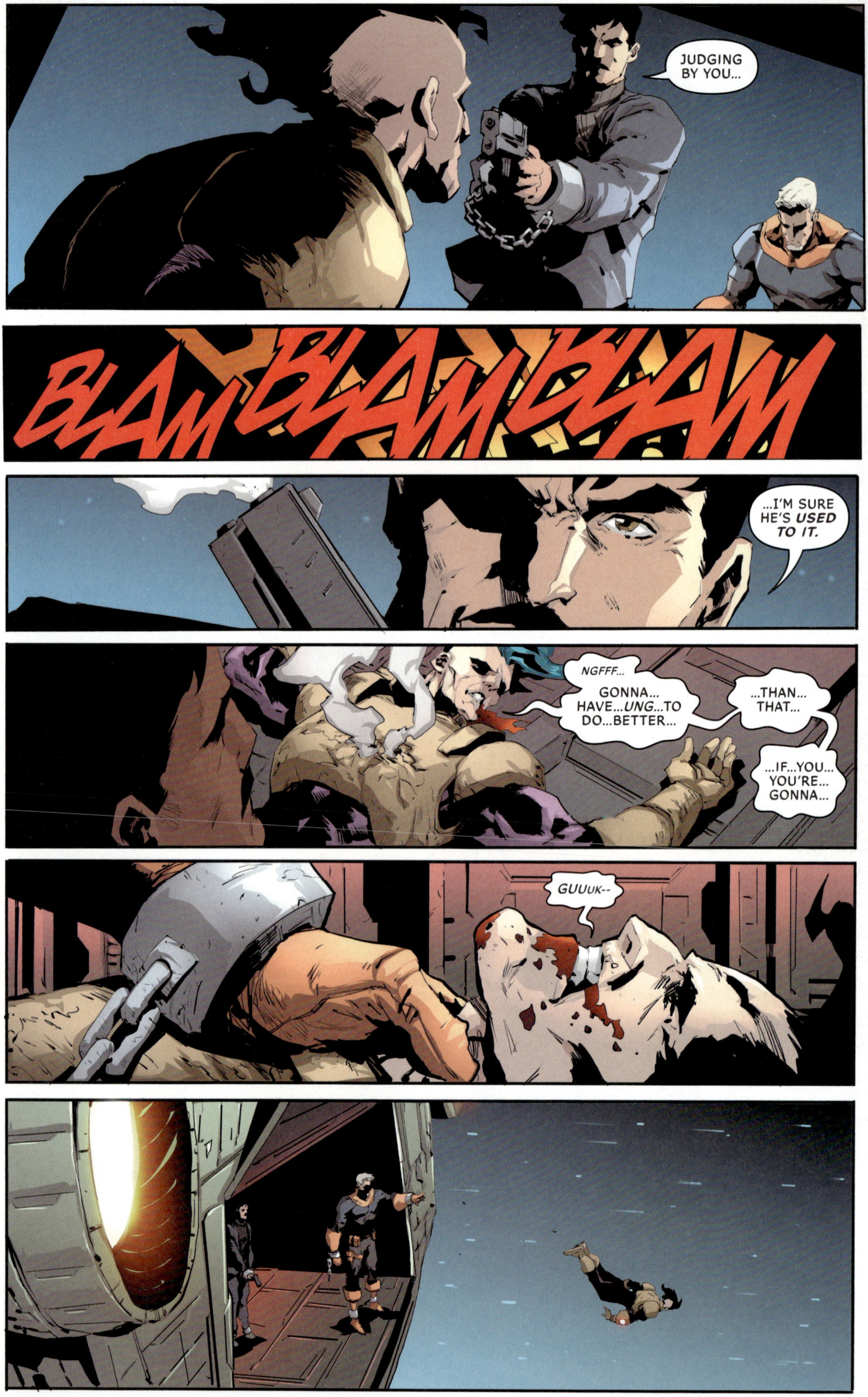
JUDGING BY YOU...
BLAM BLAM BLAM
...I'M SURE HE'S *USED TO IT.*
NGFFF...
GONNA... HAVE...*UNG*...TO DO...BETTER...
...THAN... THAT...
...IF...YOU... YOU'RE... GONNA...
GUUUK--

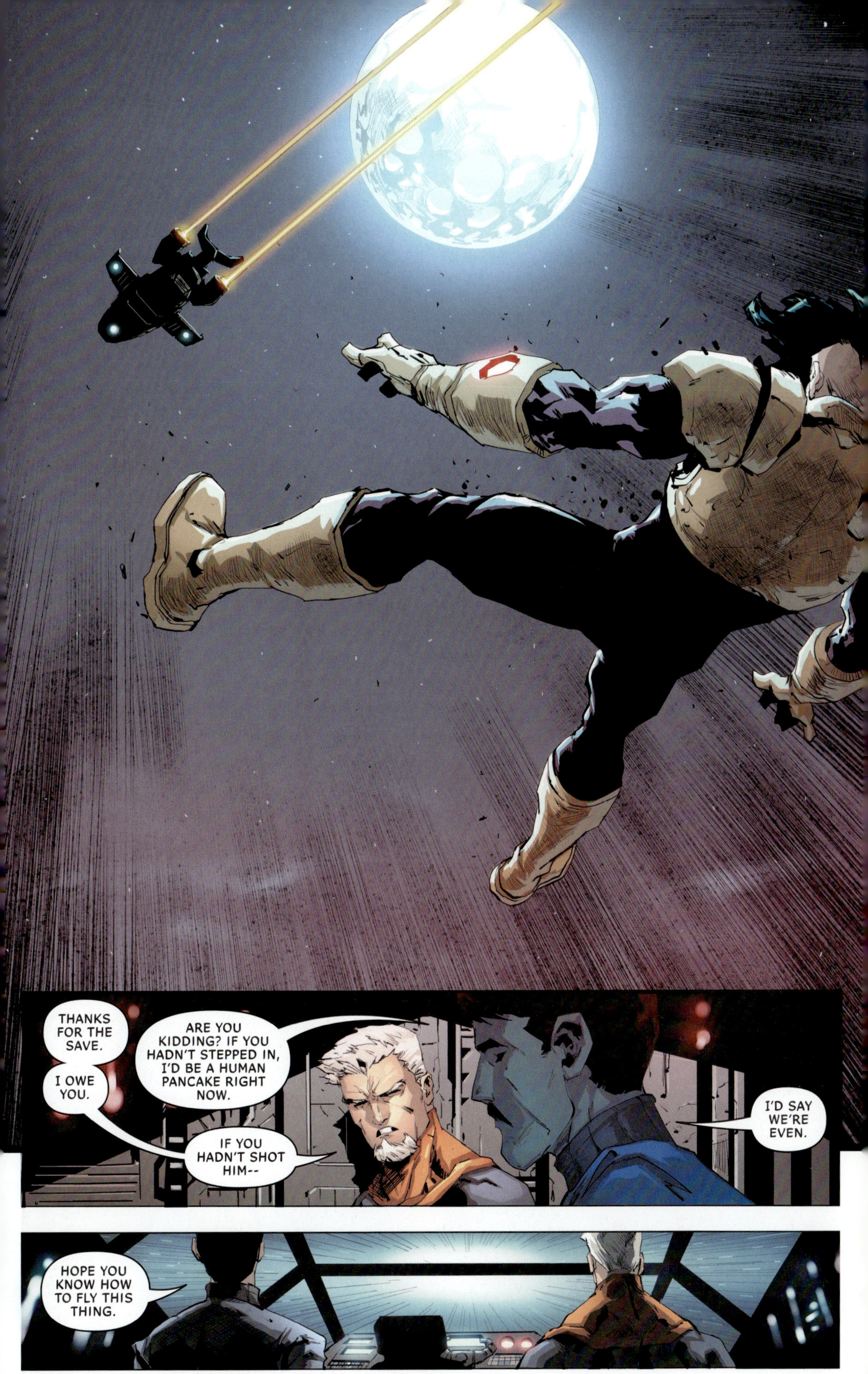
THANKS FOR THE SAVE.
I OWE YOU.
ARE YOU KIDDING? IF YOU HADN'T STEPPED IN, I'D BE A HUMAN PANCAKE RIGHT NOW.
IF YOU HADN'T SHOT HIM--
I'D SAY WE'RE EVEN.
HOPE YOU KNOW HOW TO FLY THIS THING.

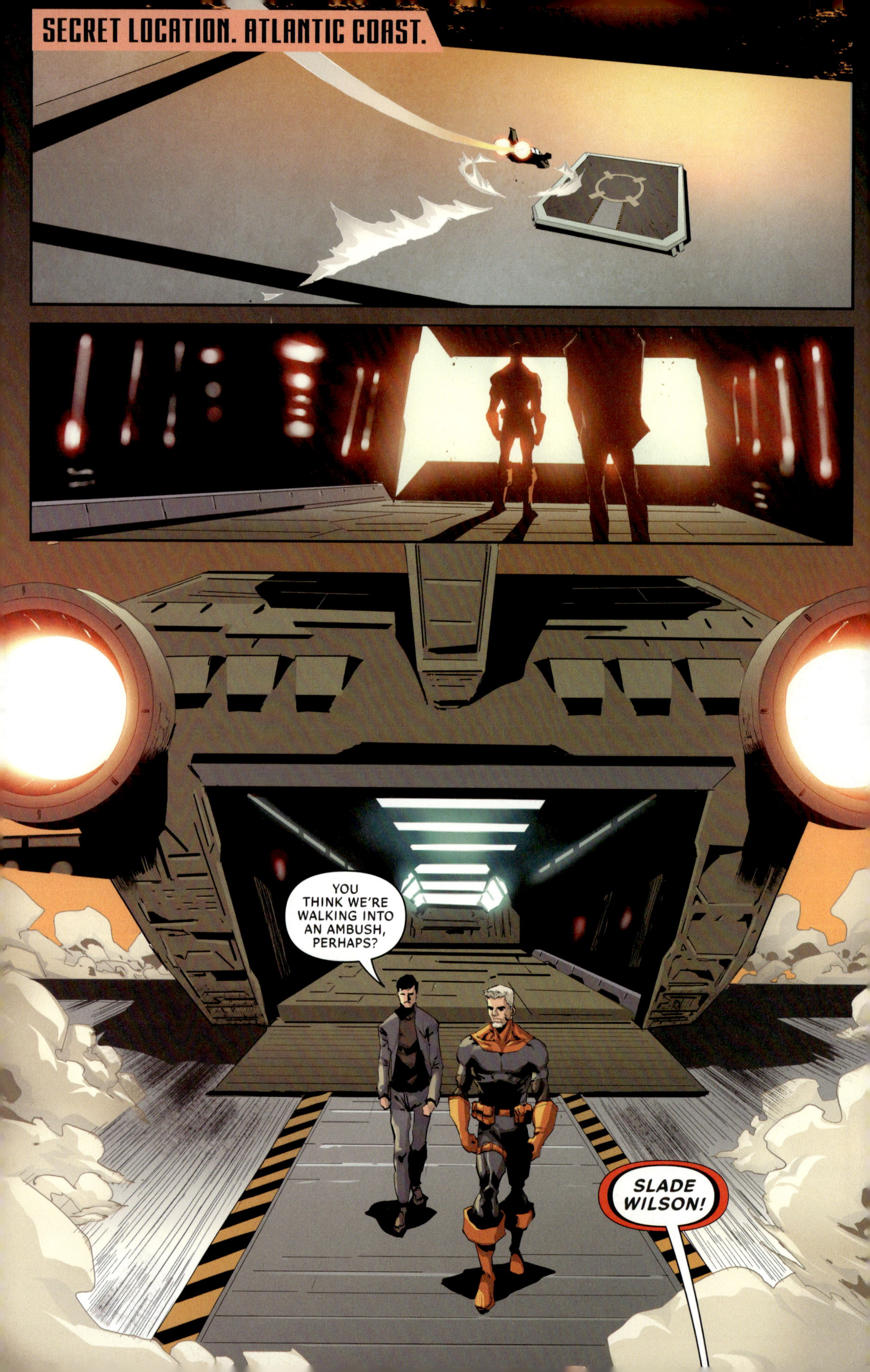
SECRET LOCATION. ATLANTIC COAST.
YOU THINK WE'RE WALKING INTO AN AMBUSH, PERHAPS?
SLADE WILSON!

THAT WAS *QUITE THE SHOW.*
THOUGHT THAT YOU'D DIED BACK IN SEATTLE.
I DON'T SEE MUZZLE?
LAST I HEARD FROM HIM, HE SAID YOU'D KILLED BOLSTER AND STOCK, BUT HE'D MANAGED TO TAKE YOU PRISONER.
WE DROPPED MUZZLE OFF SOMEWHERE OVER UTAH.
THOSE WERE MY *BEST MEN.*
DO YOU KNOW HOW MUCH *MONEY,* HOW MANY *HOURS,* WE'D INVESTED IN THEM?
I DON'T CARE.
THE CONTRACT WAS MINE. YOU SHOULDN'T HAVE SENT ANYONE ELSE AFTER IT.
AND IF *THOSE* WERE YOUR BEST MEN...
...YOU NEED TO DO *BETTER.*

NOW...
...I BELIEVE YOU OWE ME A MILLION DOLLARS FOR SERVICES RENDERED.
OF COURSE. RIGHT TO BUSINESS.
I HOPE THAT *CASH* IS OKAY?
WE'RE BORROWING THE JET *AS WELL.* YOU CAN SEND ONE OF YOUR MEN TO PICK IT UP WHEN WE'RE DONE WITH IT.
YOU'RE NOT GOING TO COUNT IT?
NO.
IF IT'S SHORT, I KNOW WHERE TO FIND YOU.
PRAY IT'S NOT SHORT.

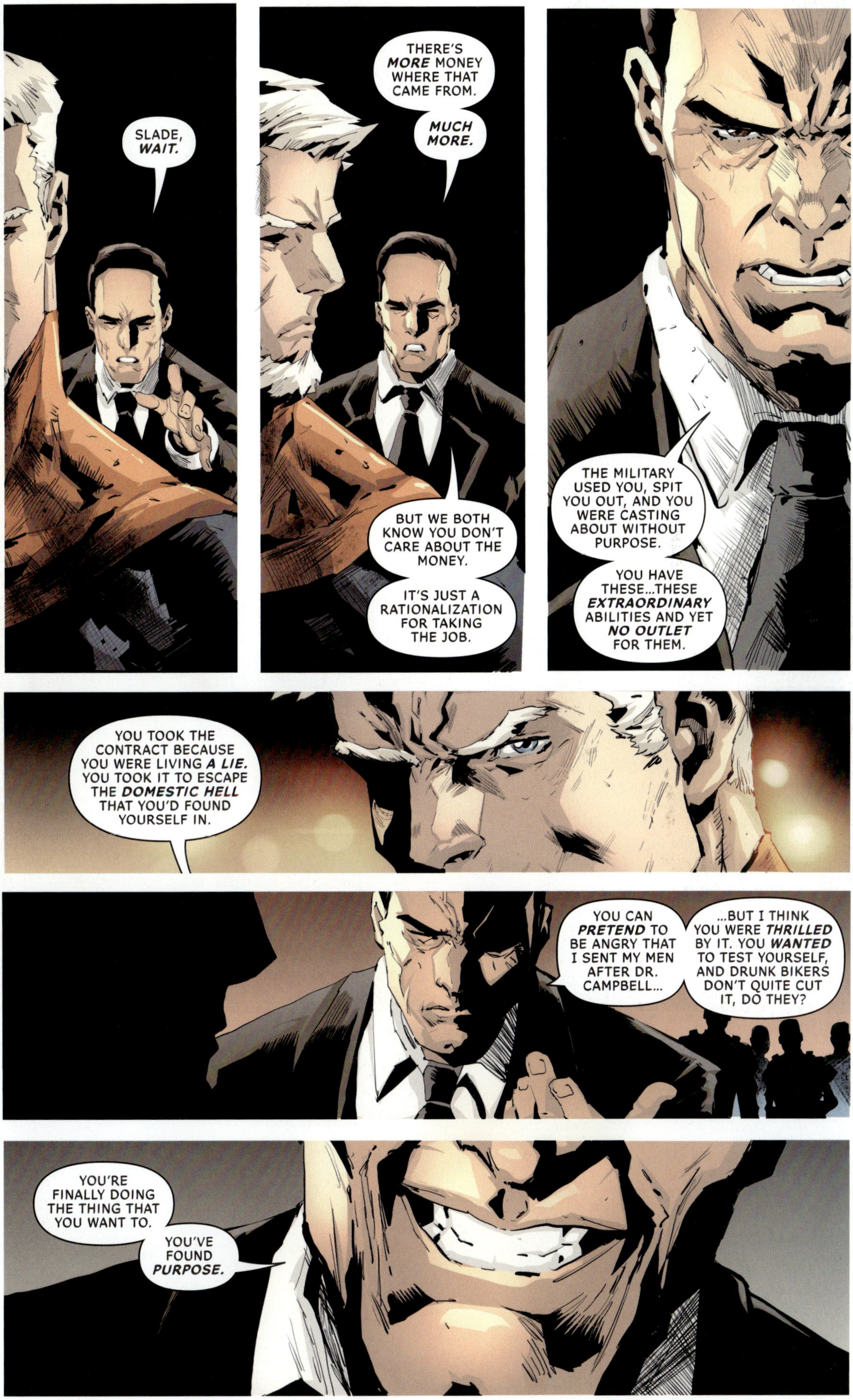

SLADE, *WAIT.*
THERE'S *MORE* MONEY WHERE THAT CAME FROM.
MUCH MORE.
BUT WE BOTH KNOW YOU DON'T CARE ABOUT THE MONEY.
IT'S JUST A RATIONALIZATION FOR TAKING THE JOB.
THE MILITARY USED YOU, SPIT YOU OUT, AND YOU WERE CASTING ABOUT WITHOUT PURPOSE.
YOU HAVE THESE...THESE *EXTRAORDINARY* ABILITIES AND YET *NO OUTLET* FOR THEM.
YOU TOOK THE CONTRACT BECAUSE YOU WERE LIVING *A LIE.* YOU TOOK IT TO ESCAPE THE *DOMESTIC HELL* THAT YOU'D FOUND YOURSELF IN.
YOU CAN *PRETEND* TO BE ANGRY THAT I SENT MY MEN AFTER DR. CAMPBELL...
...BUT I THINK YOU WERE *THRILLED* BY IT. YOU *WANTED* TO TEST YOURSELF, AND DRUNK BIKERS DON'T QUITE CUT IT, DO THEY?
YOU'RE FINALLY DOING THE THING THAT YOU WANT TO.
YOU'VE FOUND *PURPOSE.*

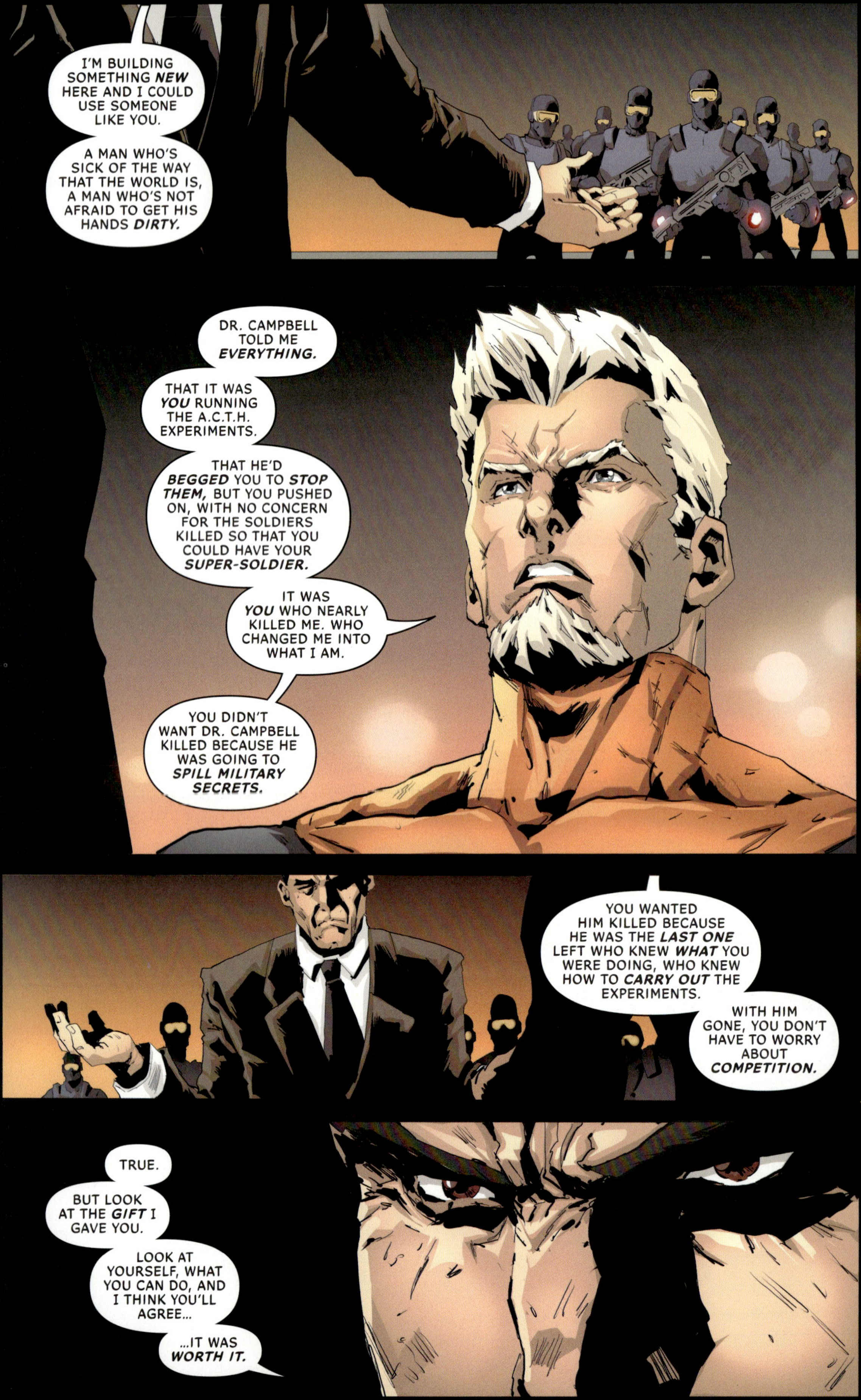

I'M BUILDING SOMETHING NEW HERE AND I COULD USE SOMEONE LIKE YOU.
A MAN WHO'S SICK OF THE WAY THAT THE WORLD IS, A MAN WHO'S NOT AFRAID TO GET HIS HANDS DIRTY.
DR. CAMPBELL TOLD ME EVERYTHING.
THAT IT WAS YOU RUNNING THE A.C.T.H. EXPERIMENTS.
THAT HE'D BEGGED YOU TO STOP THEM, BUT YOU PUSHED ON, WITH NO CONCERN FOR THE SOLDIERS KILLED SO THAT YOU COULD HAVE YOUR SUPER-SOLDIER.
IT WAS YOU WHO NEARLY KILLED ME. WHO CHANGED ME INTO WHAT I AM.
YOU DIDN'T WANT DR. CAMPBELL KILLED BECAUSE HE WAS GOING TO SPILL MILITARY SECRETS.
YOU WANTED HIM KILLED BECAUSE HE WAS THE LAST ONE LEFT WHO KNEW WHAT YOU WERE DOING, WHO KNEW HOW TO CARRY OUT THE EXPERIMENTS.
WITH HIM GONE, YOU DON'T HAVE TO WORRY ABOUT COMPETITION.
TRUE.
BUT LOOK AT THE GIFT I GAVE YOU.
LOOK AT YOURSELF, WHAT YOU CAN DO, AND I THINK YOU'LL AGREE...
...IT WAS WORTH IT.

I TOOK THE CONTRACT. I GAVE MY WORD.
AND MY WORD IS MY BOND.
BUT I'M NOT INTERESTED IN JOINING YOUR LITTLE CLUB.
I'M A *FREE AGENT.*
YOU WANT TO HIRE ME, YOU KNOW WHERE TO FIND ME.
SOMEONE WANTS TO HIRE ME TO COME AFTER YOU...
...WELL.
YOU HAD TO DO IT, DIDN'T YOU?
BAIT THE MAN WHILE HE'S GOT AN ARMED MILITIA ITCHING TO BLOW OUR BRAINS OUT.
I WASN'T BAITING HIM...
"...I WAS TELLING HIM HOW IT IS."

ADDIE, GRANT. I'M HOME.
DADDY! I'VE MISSED YOU.
WHERE'S YOUR MOM?
I'M HERE.
YOU SON OF A @$#%.
SMACK
IT'S GOOD TO SEE YOU TOO, ADDIE.
WINTERGREEN, IF YOU DON'T MIND.
ON IT.
GRANT, WHY DON'T YOU AND I GO PLAY CATCH OUTSIDE WHILE MOMMY AND DADDY TALK?

I DON'T SEE ANY DEER MEAT OR BEAR HIDES.
IF YOU'RE GOING TO LIE TO ME ABOUT *WHERE* YOU'RE GOING, YOU'RE GOING TO NEED TO BE *BETTER* ABOUT IT.
ADDIE, I--
I'M NOT DONE.
I KNOW THAT DOING THIS...THIS SUBURBAN HUSBAND-AND-WIFE TWO-CAR-GARAGE LIFE...
I KNOW IT'S *TORTURE* FOR YOU.
IT'S KILLING *ME TOO.* YOU'RE NOT THE ONLY ONE WHO GAVE UP SOMETHING FOR ALL OF THIS.
I THOUGHT THAT THIS WAS WHAT I WANTED, WHAT *WE* WANTED.
MAYBE I WAS *WRONG.*
BUT IT'S TOO LATE TO GO BACK. YOU'VE GOT ONE SON OUT THERE WHO THINKS THE SUN RISES AND SHINES ON YOUR ASS...
...AND *ANOTHER* ON THE WAY.
IT'S YOUR JOB TO BE HERE FOR THEM WHEN THEY NEED YOU.
WE'RE ALREADY IN THIS. IT'S TIME TO MAN THE %$&@ UP.

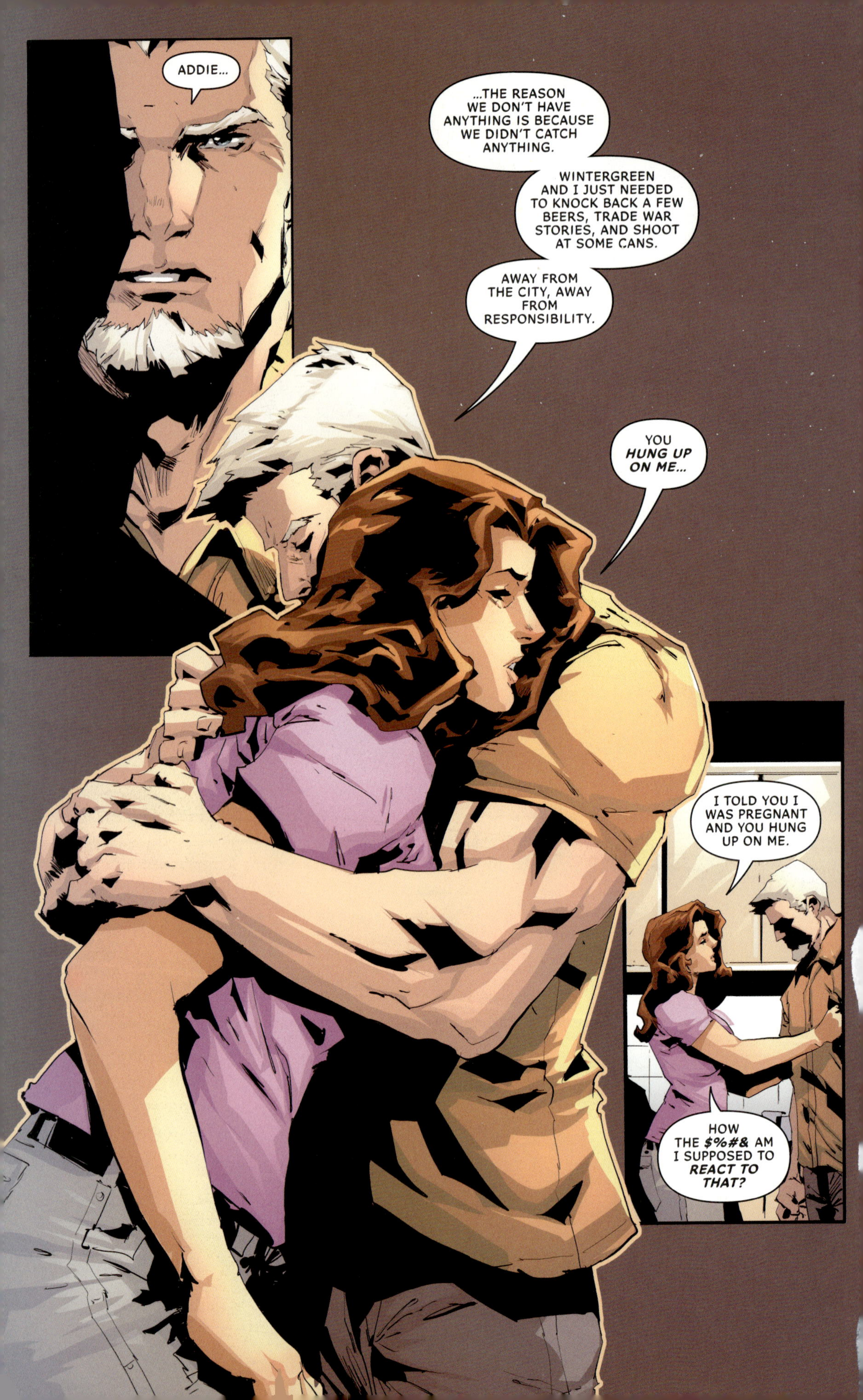

ADDIE...
...THE REASON WE DON'T HAVE ANYTHING IS BECAUSE WE DIDN'T CATCH ANYTHING.
WINTERGREEN AND I JUST NEEDED TO KNOCK BACK A FEW BEERS, TRADE WAR STORIES, AND SHOOT AT SOME CANS.
AWAY FROM THE CITY, AWAY FROM RESPONSIBILITY.
YOU *HUNG UP ON ME...*
I TOLD YOU I WAS PREGNANT AND YOU HUNG UP ON ME.
HOW THE *$%#&* AM I SUPPOSED TO *REACT TO THAT?*

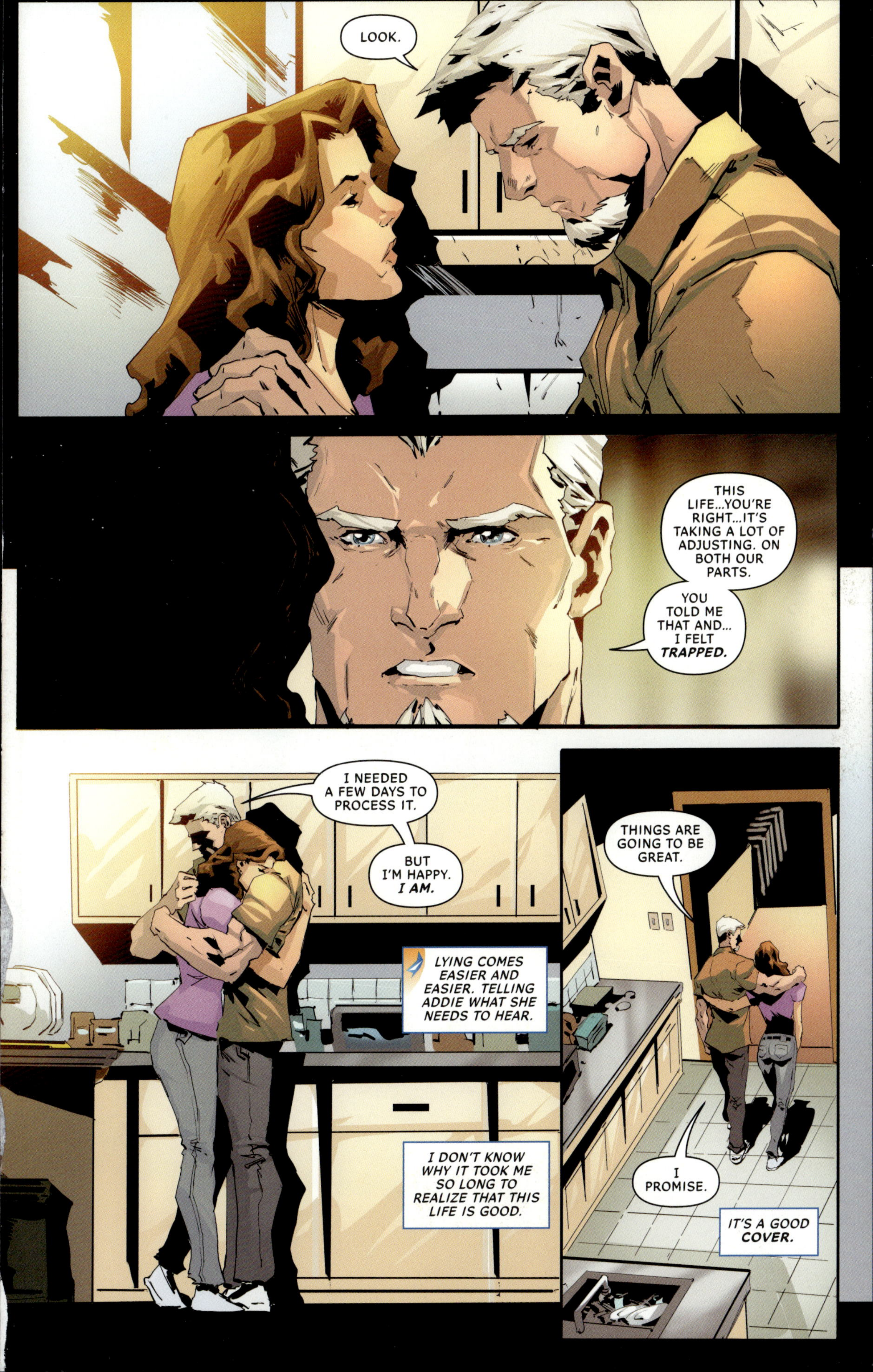
LOOK.
THIS LIFE...YOU'RE RIGHT...IT'S TAKING A LOT OF ADJUSTING. ON BOTH OUR PARTS.
YOU TOLD ME THAT AND... I FELT *TRAPPED.*
I NEEDED A FEW DAYS TO PROCESS IT.
BUT I'M HAPPY. *I AM.*
LYING COMES EASIER AND EASIER. TELLING ADDIE WHAT SHE NEEDS TO HEAR.
I DON'T KNOW WHY IT TOOK ME SO LONG TO REALIZE THAT THIS LIFE IS GOOD.
THINGS ARE GOING TO BE GREAT.
I PROMISE.
IT'S A GOOD *COVER.*

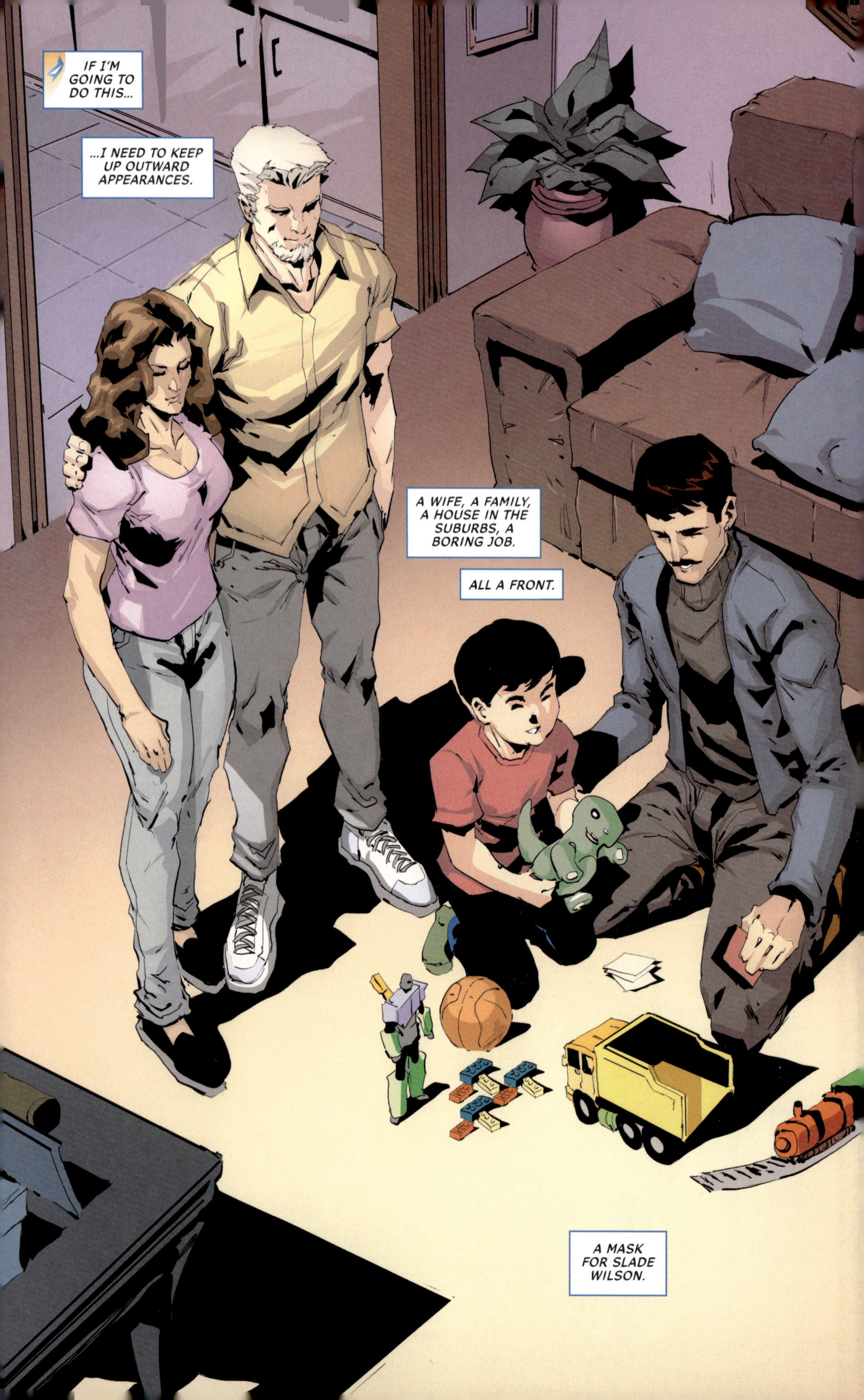
IF I'M GOING TO DO THIS...
...I NEED TO KEEP UP OUTWARD APPEARANCES.
A WIFE, A FAMILY, A HOUSE IN THE SUBURBS, A BORING JOB.
ALL A FRONT.
A MASK FOR SLADE WILSON.

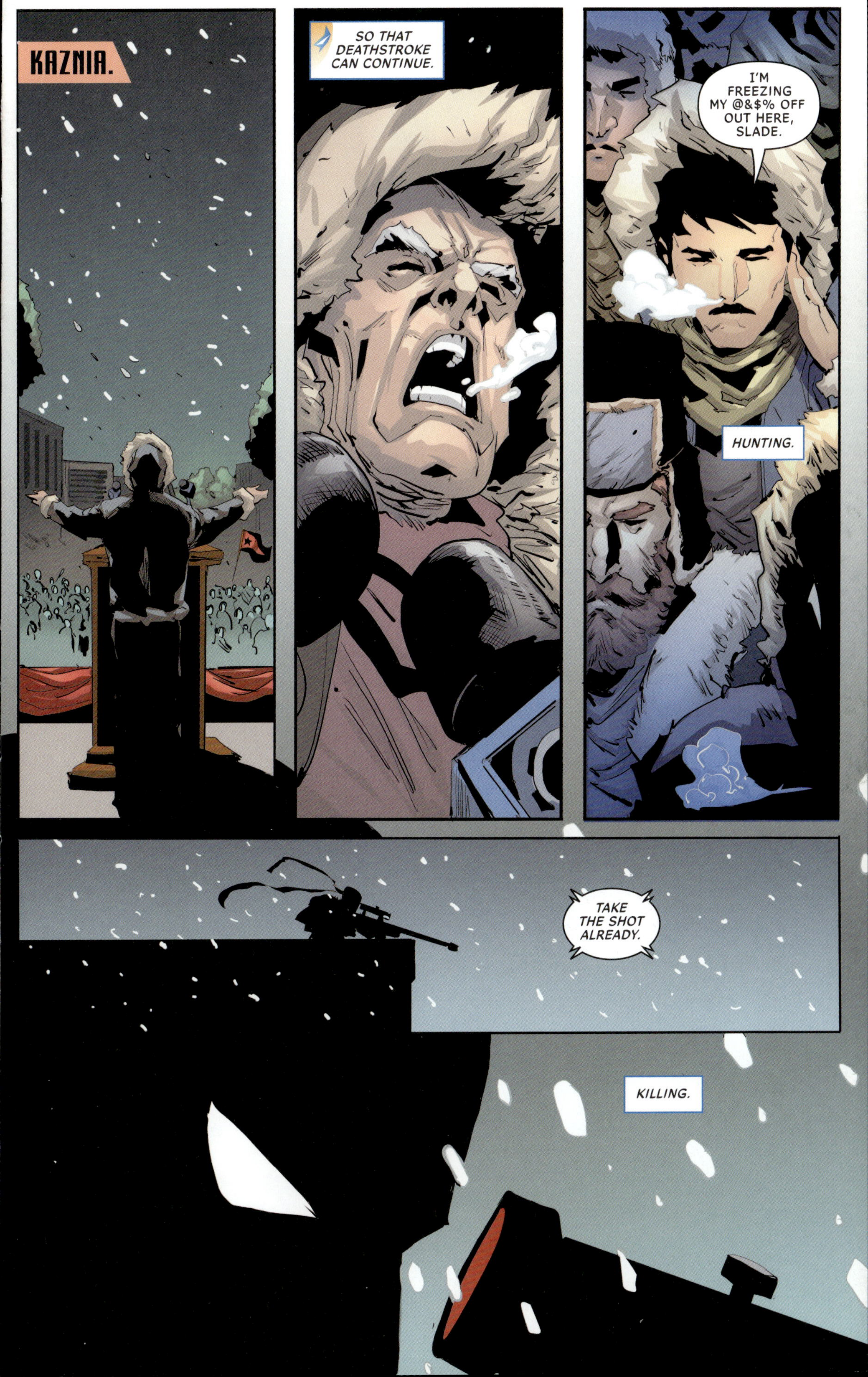
KAZNIA.
SO THAT DEATHSTROKE CAN CONTINUE.
I'M FREEZING MY @&$% OFF OUT HERE, SLADE.
HUNTING.
TAKE THE SHOT ALREADY.
KILLING.

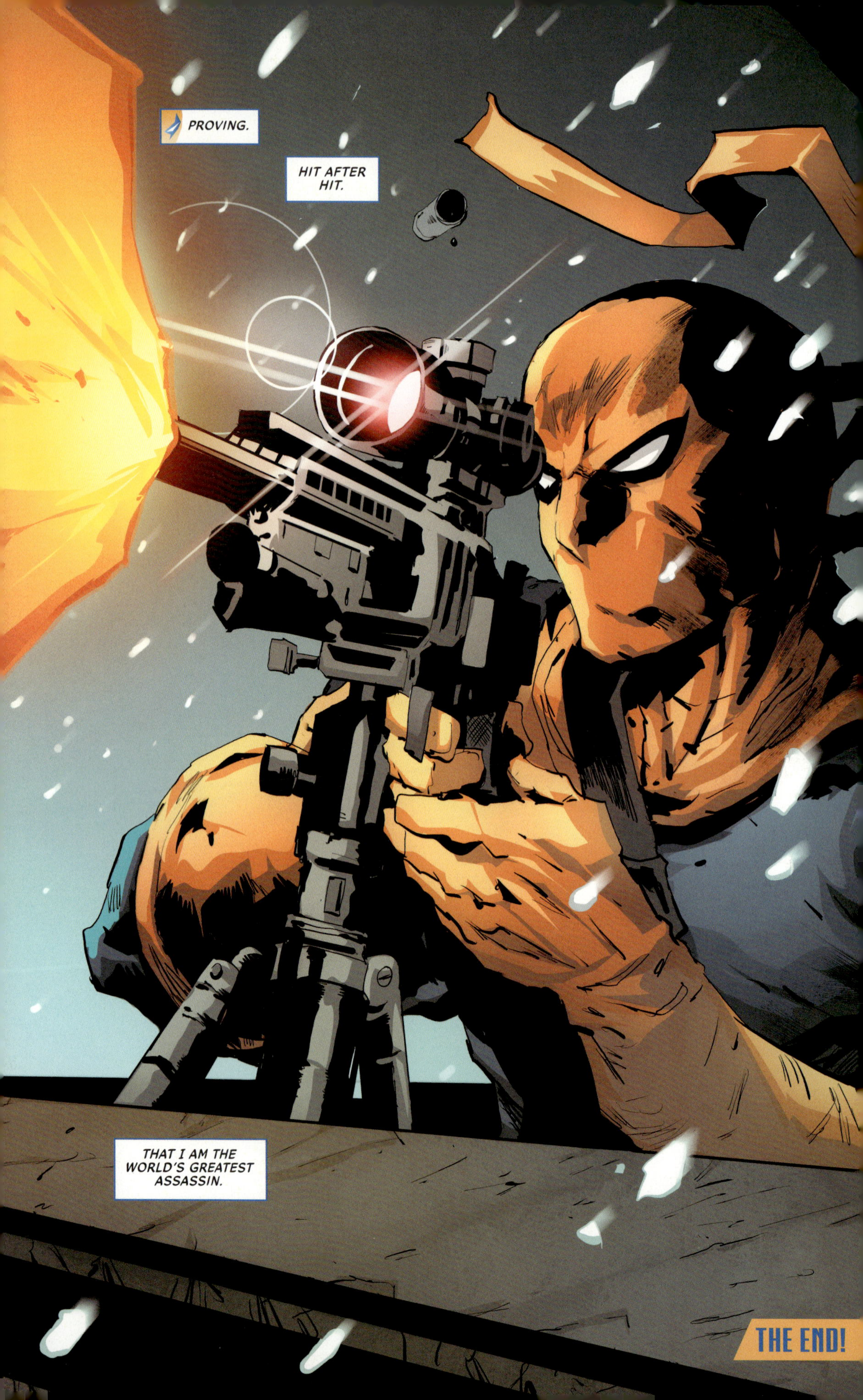
PROVING.
HIT AFTER HIT.
THAT I AM THE WORLD'S GREATEST ASSASSIN.
THE END!

ART & DESIGN GALLERY

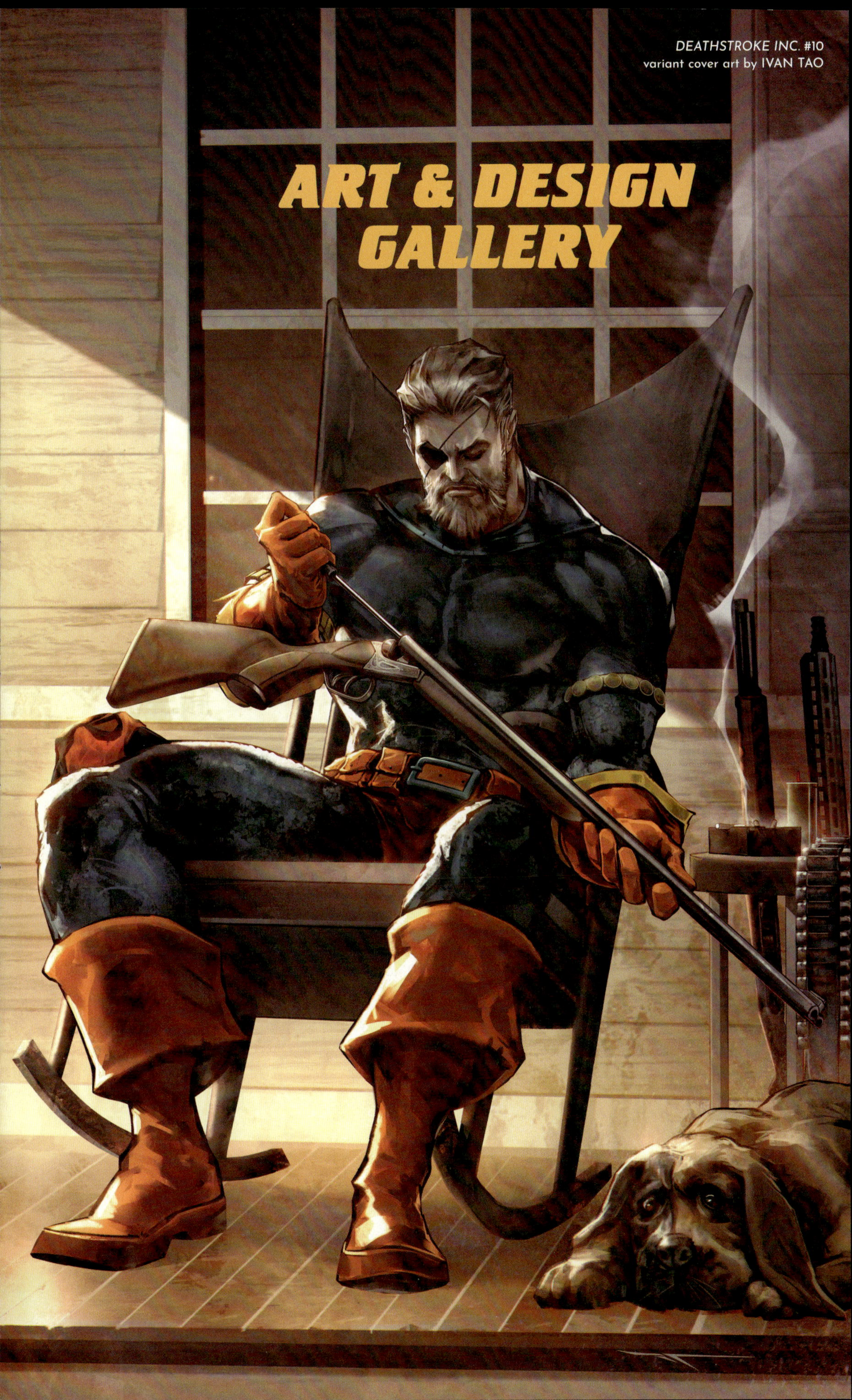

DEATHSTROKE INC. #10
variant cover art by IVAN TAO

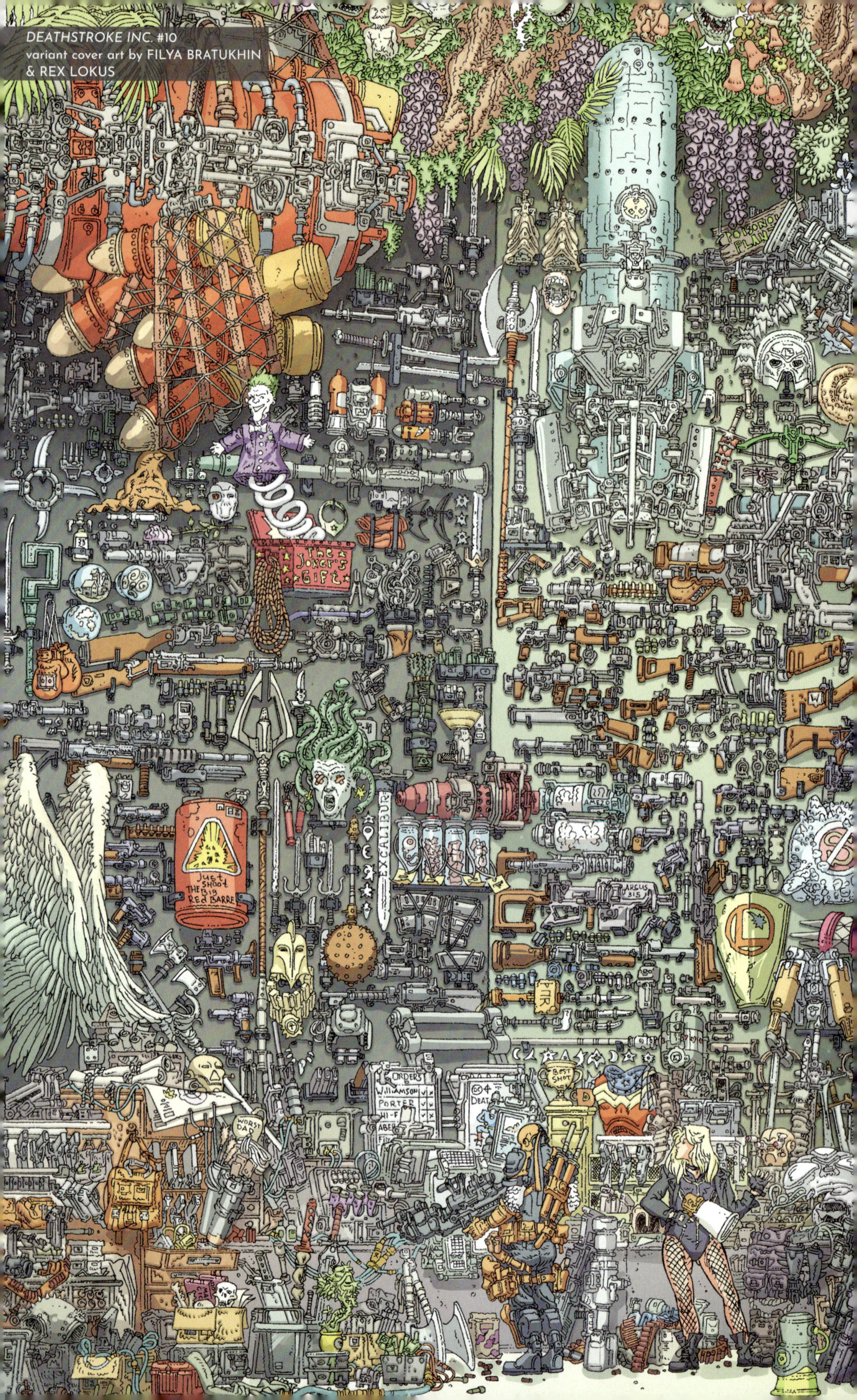
The Joker's Gift
EXCALIBUR
ORDERS
Williamson
Porter
DEATHSTROKE INC. #10
variant cover art by FILYA BRATUKHIN
& REX LOKUS

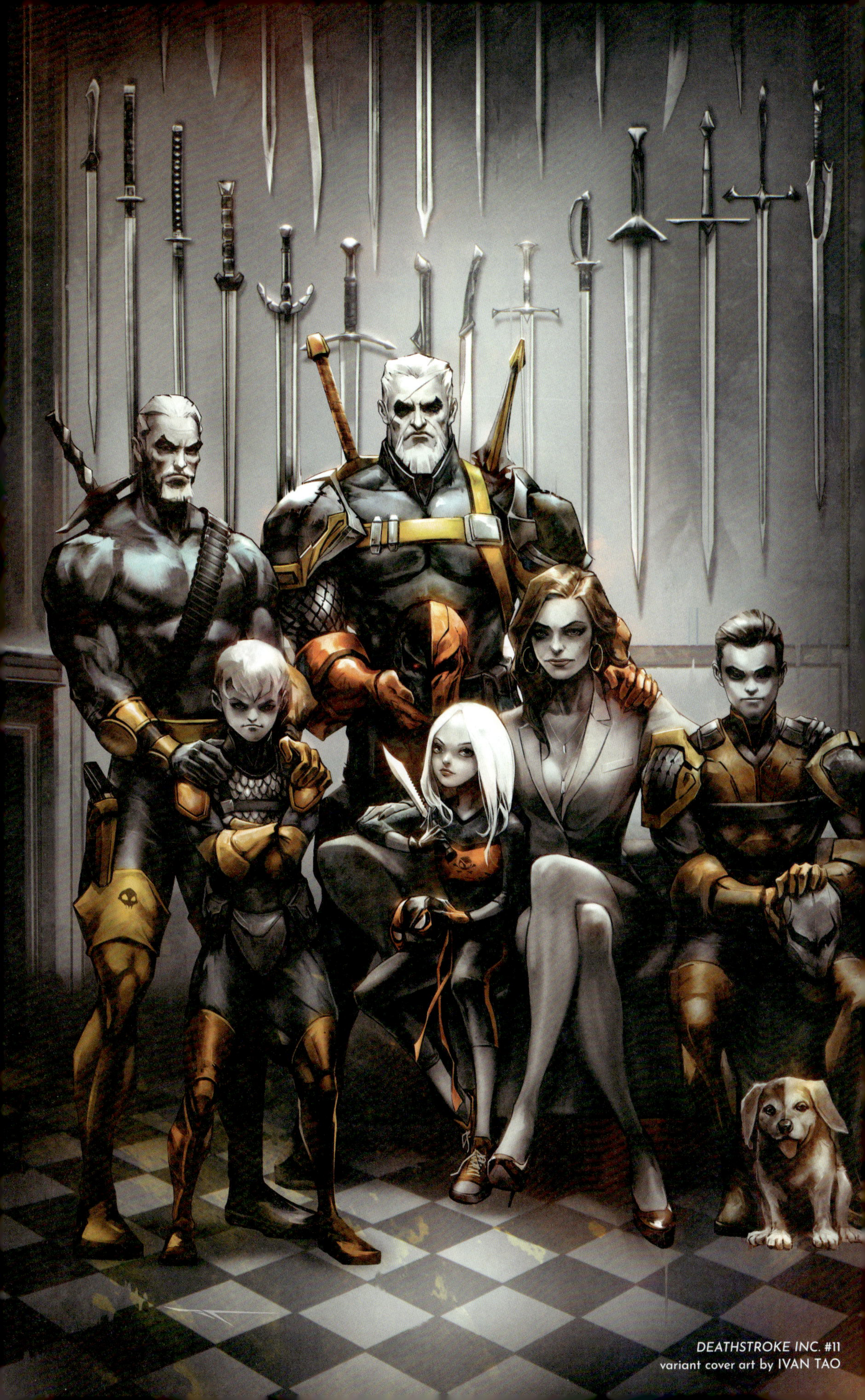

DEATHSTROKE INC. #11
variant cover art by IVAN TAO

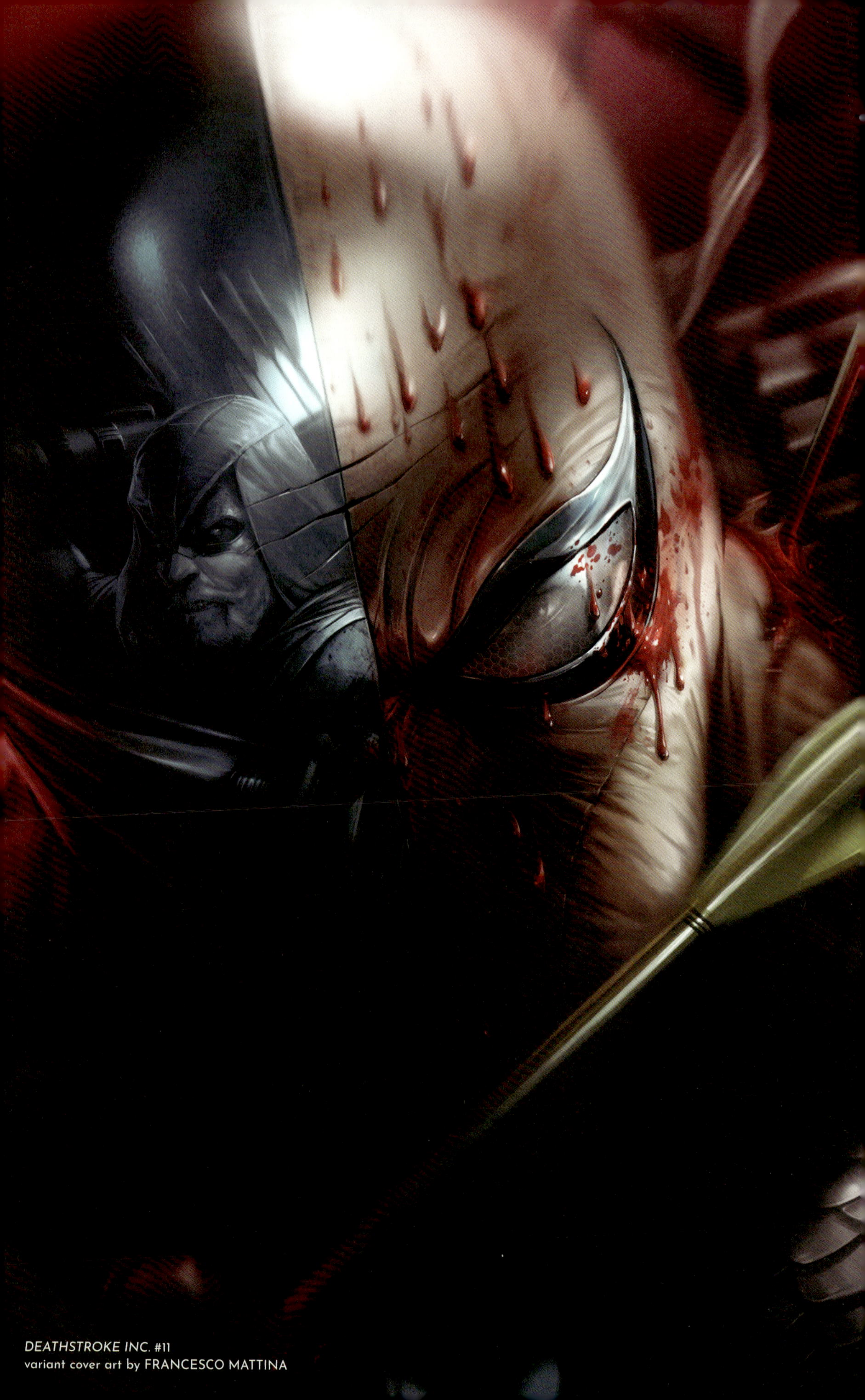

DEATHSTROKE INC. #11
variant cover art by FRANCESCO MATTINA

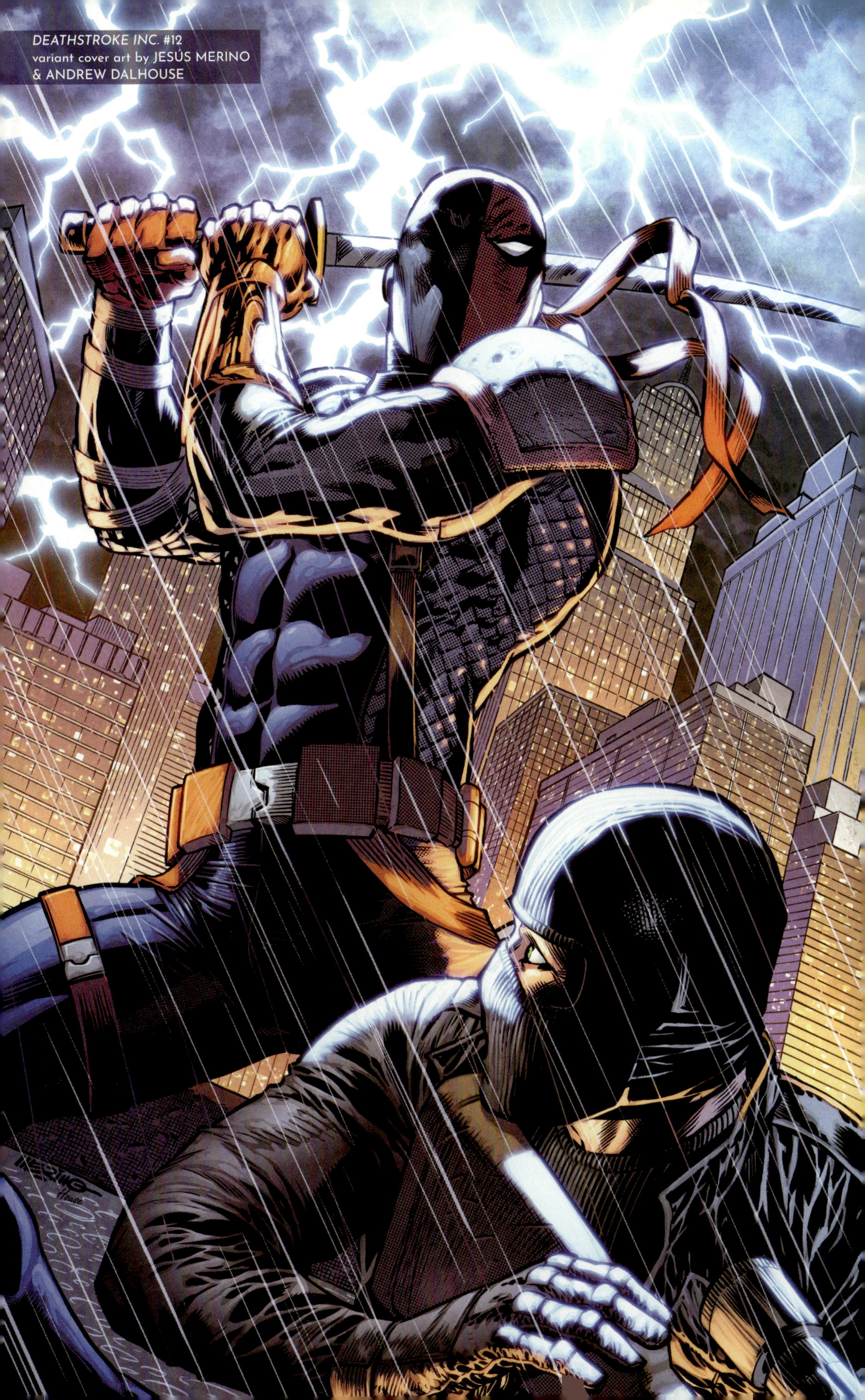

DEATHSTROKE INC. #12
variant cover art by JESÚS MERINO
& ANDREW DALHOUSE

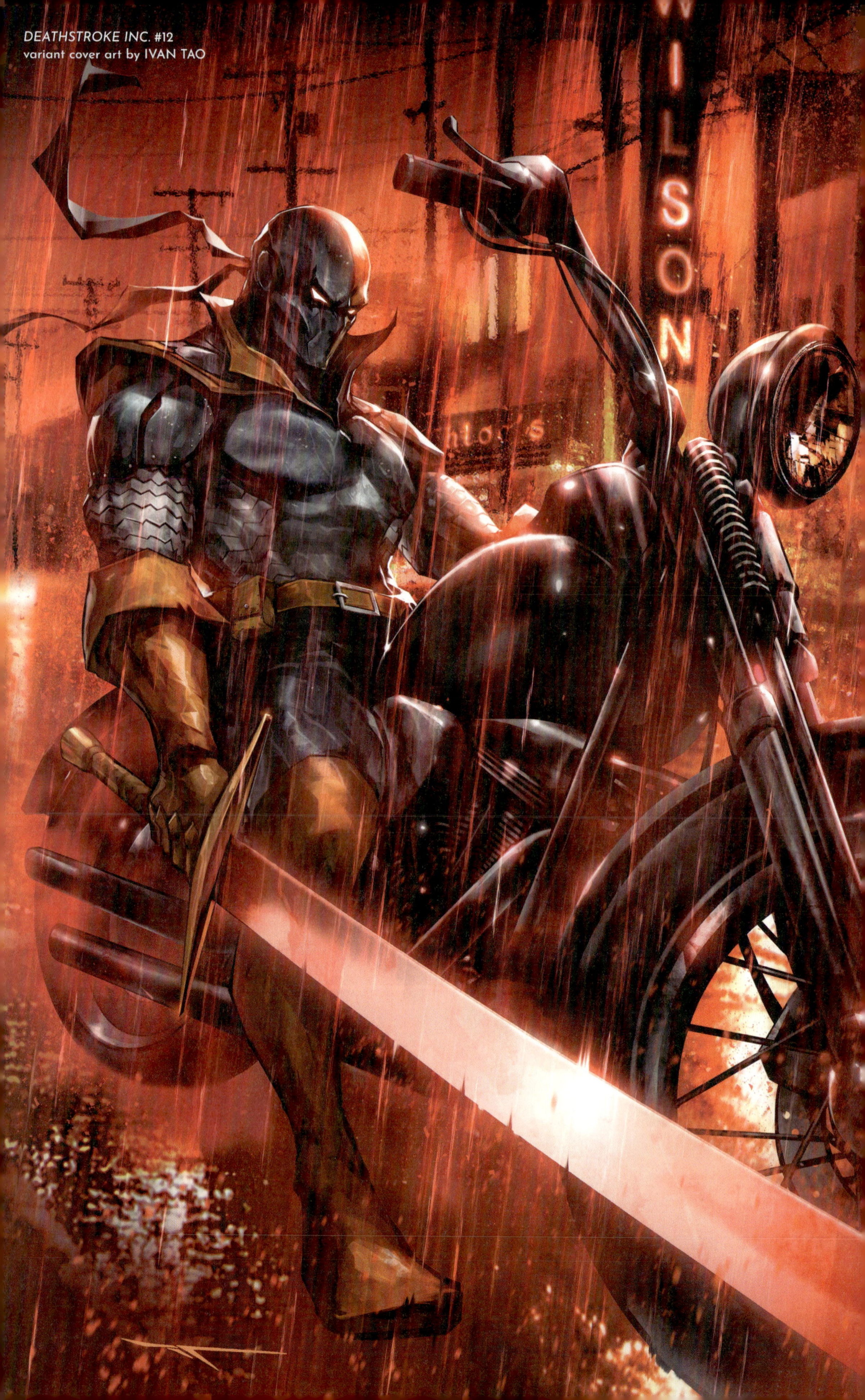
WILSON

DEATHSTROKE INC. #12
variant cover art by IVAN TAO

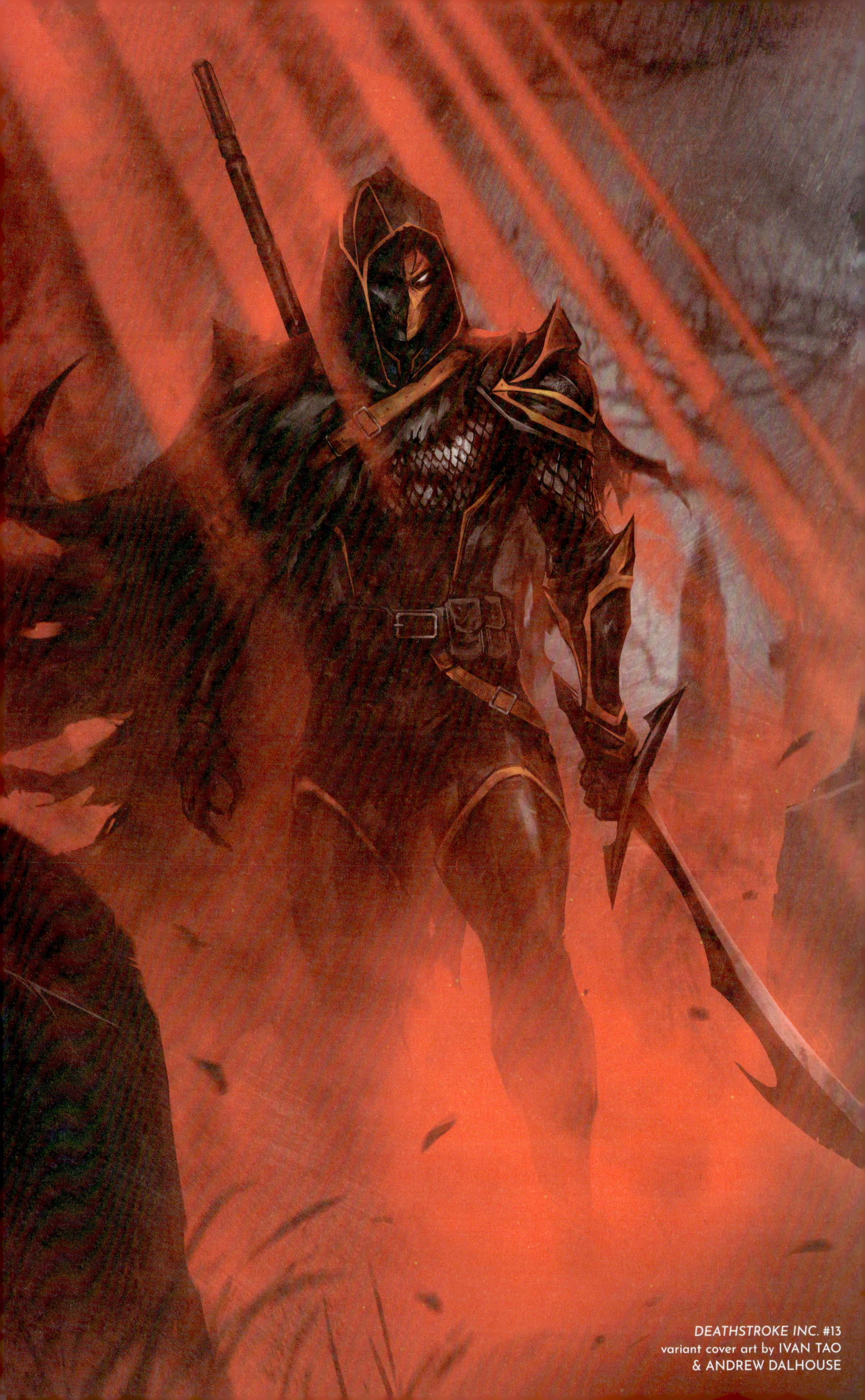

DEATHSTROKE INC. #13
variant cover art by IVAN TAO
& ANDREW DALHOUSE

DEATHSTROKE INC. #13
variant cover art by DEXTER SOY
& MATT HERMS

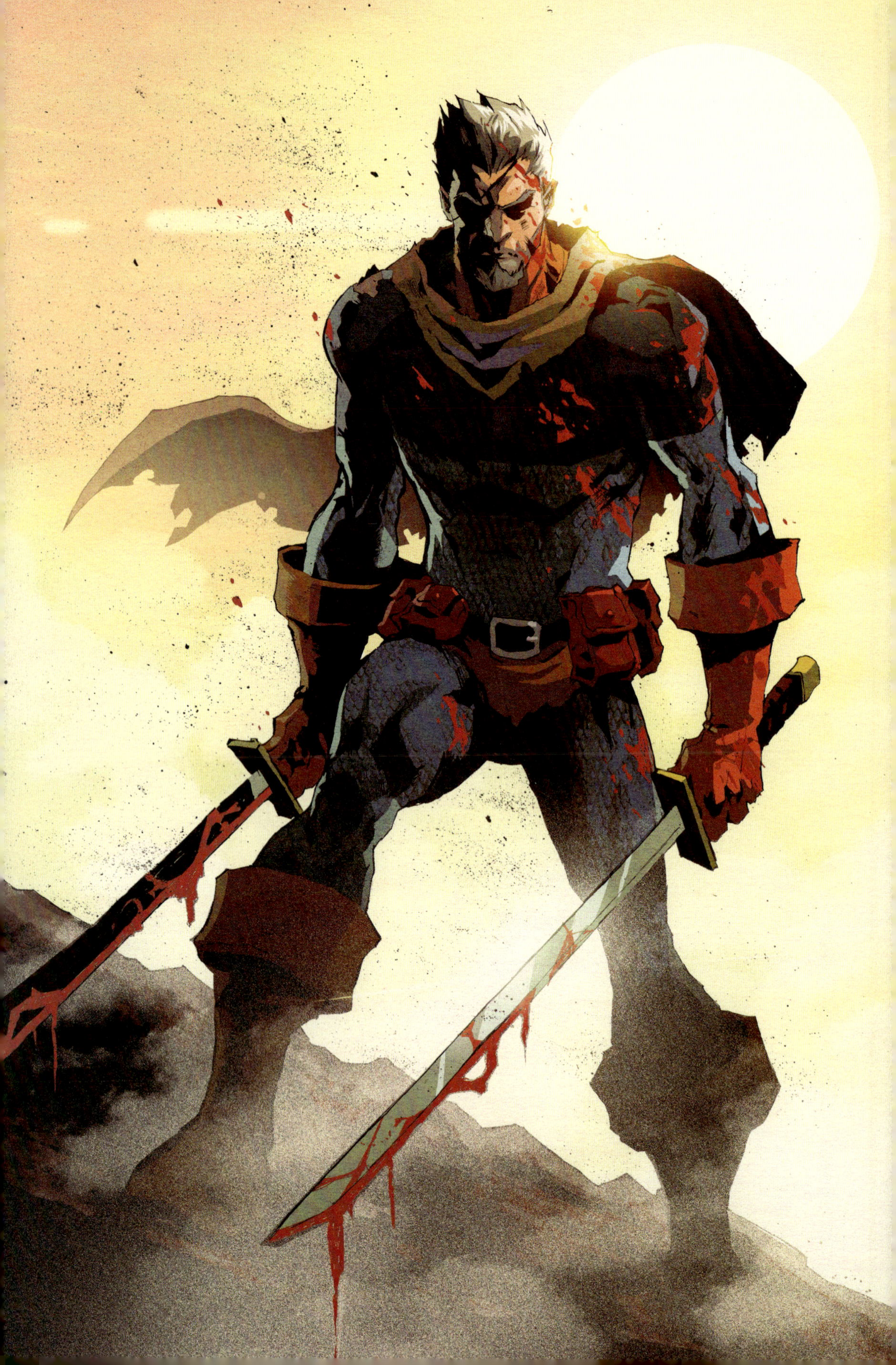

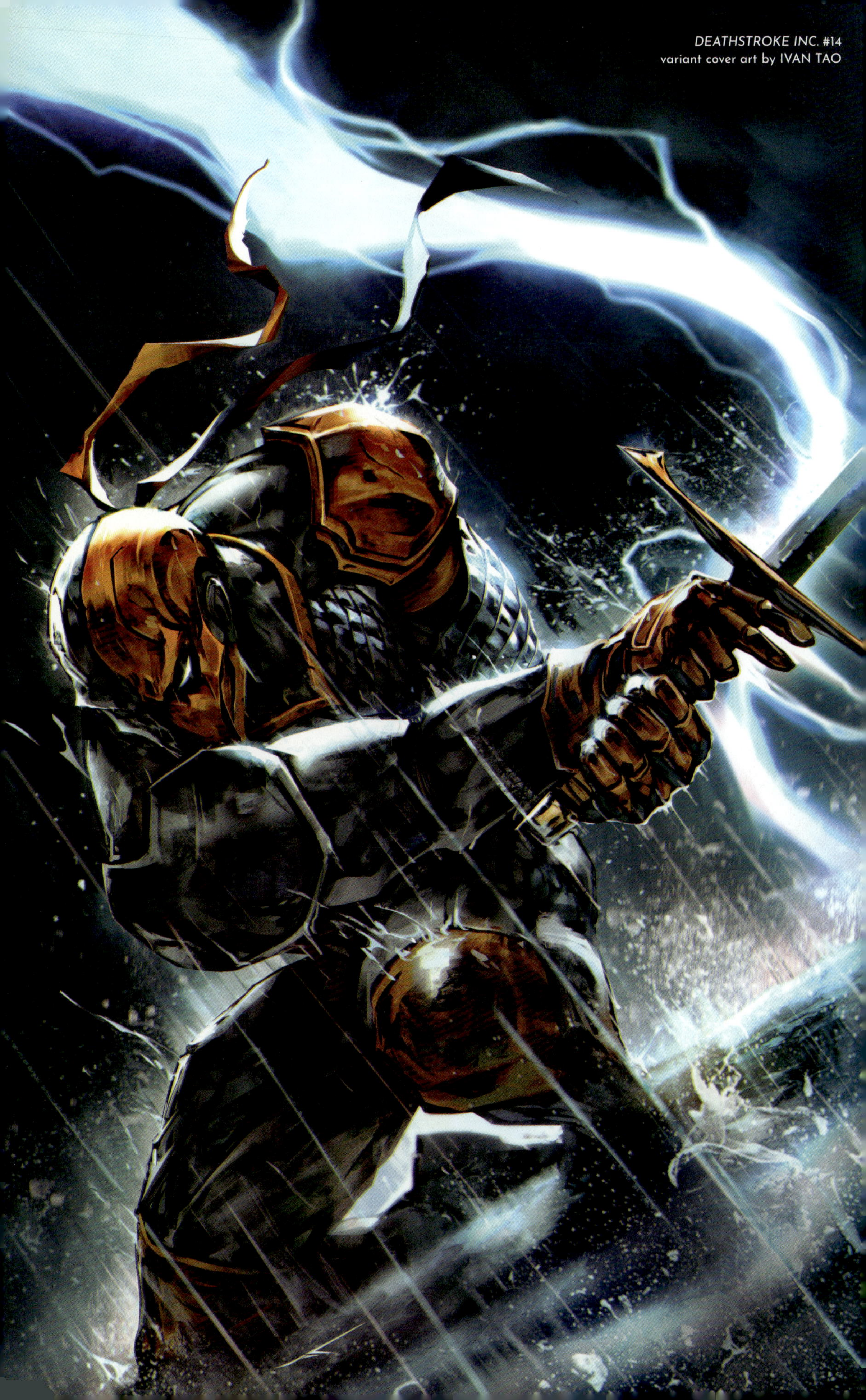

DEATHSTROKE INC. #14
variant cover art by IVAN TAO

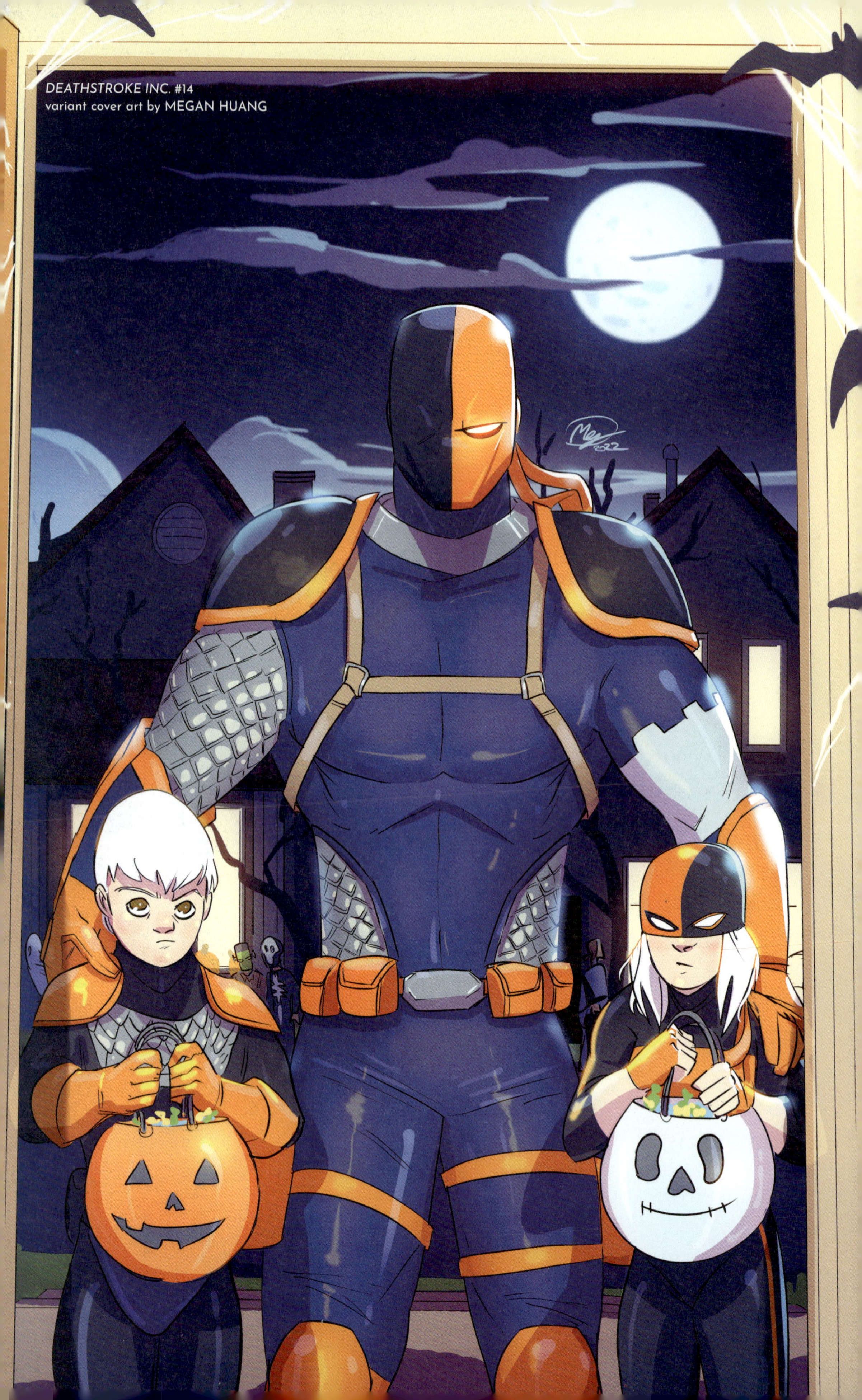

DEATHSTROKE INC. #14
variant cover art by MEGAN HUANG

DEATHSTROKE INC. #15
variant cover art by FELIPE MASSAFERA

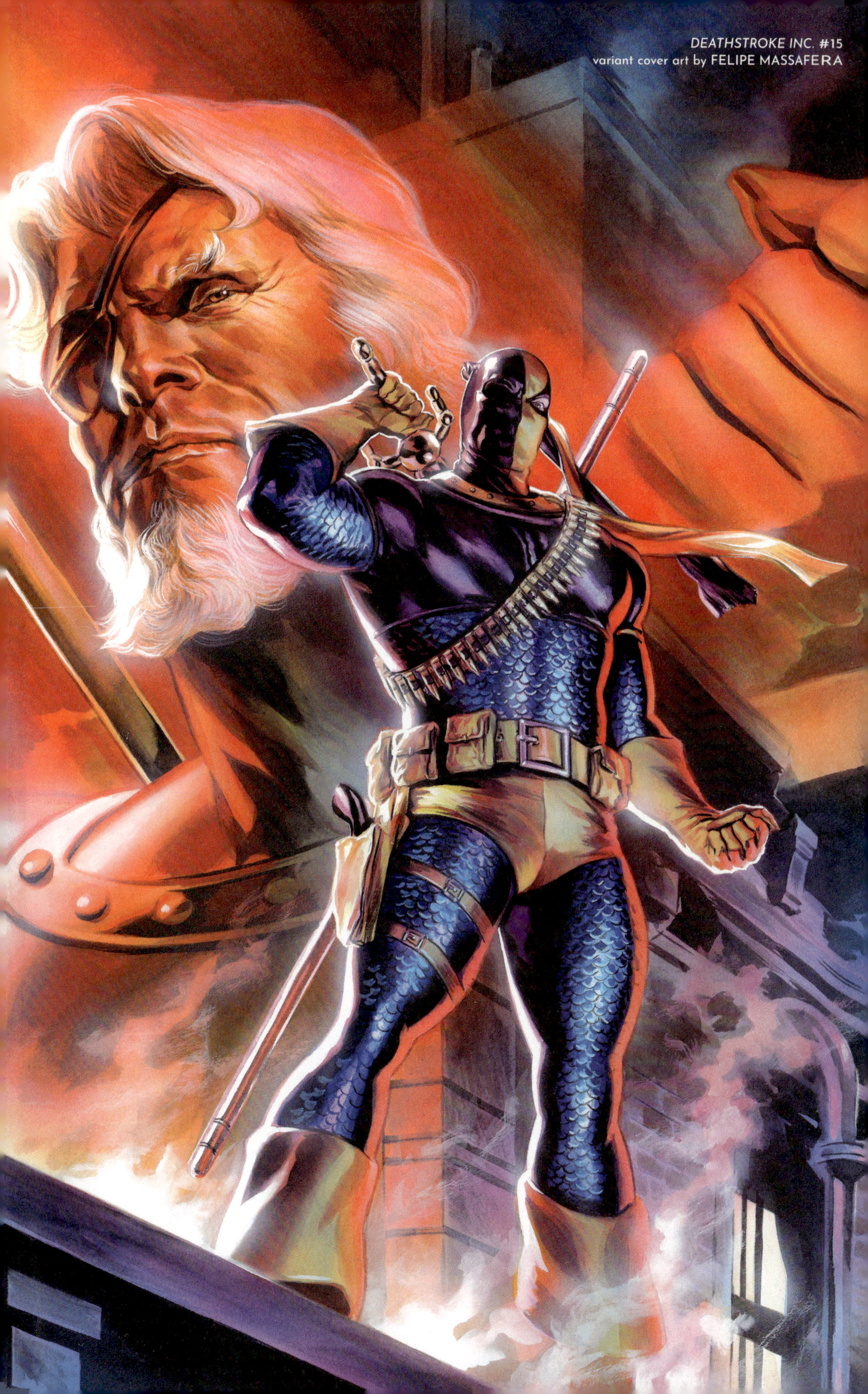